The Lady
of
Steinbrekka

Kristi Strong

The Lady of Steinbrekka

ISBN-13: 978-0615677392

ISBN-10: 0615677398

The Lady of Steinbrekka is the result of a dream. It is the culmination of both my life-long dream to publish a novel, and the type of dream that comes to a person during sleep. It would still be a thought in the wind if not for some very important people.

My parents, who have always encouraged me to write, and to follow my dreams. Without their constant support this book would have never been possible.

My husband, who will do anything for our family and has shown me what love and loyalty truly mean.

Many thanks also must go to friend and fellow author, Kristina Circelli. Without her constant wisdom, encouragement, and excitement I would have never dreamed of other people reading the words that flow from my fingers.

Chapter One

Virginia, U.S.A.

No sunlight penetrated this far into the depths of the dank, musty dungeon. There was no light to shine upon the skulls, bones, pieces of stone and broken jars that made this lair their home. Mason jars filled with ancient dirt and pebbles held down folders that had been left next to the door, the corners of their yellowed and curled corners lifting gently in the breeze. Rats and mice scurried about the floor and shelves, casually searching for their next meal or their next home amid the boxes of shining glass shards and disintegrating pieces of parchment.

A light flickered off a piece of glass, and a small brown shadow went scurrying into a strategically created hole as giant footsteps pounded through the room. Multitudes of small eyes blinked at the bright sunlight flowing through the open door like molten lava as the dust particles flew into the air, causing it to shimmer and become alive with movement.

Rhea breathed a muffled curse as she walked deeper into the depths and her flashlight sputtered out its weak, unsteady, yellow beam. Her fingers traced along the wall for the light switch, leaving a wavering trail in the centuries old dust that had settled on the wall. She knew the darkness was necessary for the protection of her precious collection, the combined efforts of decades of blood, sweat and tears, but still cursed it as her hand scraped painfully over something sharp left carelessly on the shelf.

Finally she found the prize she sought and flicked the plastic switch upward. Eyes rolled to the ceiling in annoyance as the bare light bulb above her head flickered ominously, then steadied to create a weak circle of light directly below the bulb.

Next time, she decided, *I'm bringing my camp lantern.* Never mind that her coworkers would mock her endlessly for being wary of the dark; they were not the ones who had to spend seven hours of their day in a damp, dark, dusty basement where the imagination is left to run rampant and every sound is a signal of potential danger. Well, if you considered a hungry rodent or occasional raccoon as a danger.

The woman found the box she was looking for, a flimsy paper ream box with a small hole chewed out of the corner.

"Not you too! Oh poor KS7384 Upper Valley, is nothing safe down here?" Rhea used her house key to slice through the tape intended to protect the boxes from rodent invasions. She lifted the thin cardboard top, not even bothering to stifle her small shriek as a mouse family went scurrying out of the hole.

At least these mice had the decency not to land on my feet or jump onto my shoulder, she thought. One would assume that six months of evicting little mouse squatters from their unfortunate choice of homes would desensitize a person, but that was not the case. It was not that Rhea minded the small furry creatures, after all, she used to have pet rats when she was in high school, she just did not appreciate being snuck up on by them or having them destroy priceless artifacts. Besides, if it were not for these resourceful little creatures she could be out in the field right now working on a newly discovered ancient hunting site, instead of spending the third year of her fellowship trying to save all of the old boxes and artifacts from time's destruction. For the last seven years her life revolved around archaeology, about discovery and the careful excavation of the past. She spent her days carefully removing soil from an area one careful centimeter at a time and straining her eyes to label artifacts with numbers so small people thought it must have been created by a specialized machine. Her body reflected her craft. Rhea was lean but muscular, with wide hips her friends had deemed "child bearing" and strong legs accustomed to walking miles upon miles of rugged terrain.

The empty box was gingerly lifted off the shelf and placed on a nearby table for closer inspection. *Thank you for small favors*, she thought in the darkness, *at least this one is all lithics, rocks that held no allure to the teeth of small rodents*. Her boxes from last week all contained the archaeologists' field journals, and she spent days trying to put the pages back together so that she could enter them into the digital database they had begun at the lab. Rhea carefully pulled all of the artifact bags out of the shredded cardboard that made up the rodent's nest and held them to the meager light of the bulb above. A quartzite arrowhead slid out of a mouse-created hole in the bag and fell onto her shoe.

Another sigh escaped her, as they had for the thousands of times she had to write out a new artifact bag and, once again, record the identification tags for the items. The permanent marker almost seemed to take itself out of her pocket and write on the bag without needing any prompting from her mind.

At least this was her last day in the dark lair before her break. For the first time in her nineteen years of attending school Rhea was forcing herself to take off spring break week. She was not planning on going anywhere, or doing anything particularly fun, but at twenty-five years old she was ready for a week of doing absolutely nothing. Her roommates were all going to Florida for the week, her parents were busy moving into their new house across the country, and she was going to see just how long a person could sit in a bubble bath before they shriveled up like a prune.

That first night was not going to be all fun and games though. Every night for the last four years on March fifteenth she would light a candle on her porch and sit staring into the inky blackness of the sky until sleep claimed her, or pink and purple clouds summoned the morning. Two years ago her best friend went missing, and part of her heart told her that as long as she kept watching one day he would come back to her world, that he could not really be gone forever.

They had spent the night studying for an exam for their American Mythology and Superstitions course. There was always one teacher who had an exam the day after the break. After two hours of wine, popcorn, and passionate discussion about the disappearance of the people who traveled through the Bermuda Triangle, it was going on midnight and time for normal graduate students with work in the morning to collapse into sleep.

It was also the night that Matt decided to see if their four-year friendship could move into a romantic realm. They had perfected the ease of a romantic friendship. The hugs, the cheek kisses, never really thinking about what their flirting meant and assuming it was harmless fun. They were the emergency dates and the savior at parties. Matt had pretended to be her boyfriend more times than she could count when some sleazy frat brother would try to hit on her. They could talk openly and honestly with each other, knowing that even if the words hurt they would be considered and were meant to be helpful. To take that step above friendship would mean casting all of their history as friends into a cloud of confusion and turmoil.

Both had been in relationships before, both had helped each other through the good and the bad times of new flings and break-ups. She took the brunt of his anger for six long months when she told him his current girlfriend was cheating but he was not willing to believe, and he held her while she cried when her last boyfriend chose video games over spending time with her. Who do you turn to if your best friend is your boyfriend? Where is safety when you cannot talk about the little insignificant things that make a relationship a challenge and have them tell you to stop being a brat? Besides, he was graduating from the program that summer and going out into the world to see if he could put his political science degree to good use. Pursuing anything other than a friendship at that point would just be foolish.

That night they both showed to be the fools. As they walked to the door Matt took her hand and kissed it tenderly. She laughed, thinking that he needed a girlfriend if he was going to get all sappy before he left the safe little nest that is college life. Then he kissed her goodnight, and suddenly there was nothing in the world more

4

important than him. For the first time she noticed the smell of his cologne and his shampoo, how his shoulders felt firm and strong under her hands. He whispered, "Some things are just meant to be," and smiled as he walked down the sidewalk towards his apartment.

Rhea wiped her teary eyes and looked at a nearby mouse perched on a box, appearing to watch her work.

"They came around two A.M. little mouse, not even two hours later. His books and wallet were found on the sidewalk in the center of a bloodstain and he was nowhere to be found."

The police had questioned her for hours since she was the last person to see him, and Matt was labeled a missing person, suspected to be the victim of foul play but never confirmed. There were no hints, no clues, not even an idea of where he would have been taken. He was loved by everyone and had no enemies. The wallet was untouched, with the exception of its placement on the pavement, so authorities ruled out a robbery and no crime had happened like that in years. No bushes had been disturbed, no footprints left, it was as if the blood magically appeared and he disappeared at the same time. After a few months the police moved on, and everyone was told to accept just not knowing what happened. They had a candlelight vigil every day for a week after his disappearance, then everyone but Rhea gave up hope and went back to their regularly scheduled lives.

The airlock on the new storage bin popped loudly and echoed throughout the room, snapping Rhea out of her thoughts. She looked down at the aisle filled with threatened cardboard boxes and looked down at her turquoise and silver watch, a present from her great grandmother. *Alright*, she told herself, *one more box and then it's time for me to go relax.* She checked her list of inventory and groaned, "Of course the last box of the day is by the creepy mirror."

The creepy mirror was a legend among the grad students who were required to spend time in the dungeon of Shelton Hall. At ten feet by six feet the mirror was large enough to convince even the skeptics of the department that shadows were moving in the already ominous basement. Spiders made their cobweb traps over the glass corners, adding their ethereal forms to the mirrors reflections. It was rumored that the mirror, and others like it, covered the door to the tunnels that once ran under the school. A vast network had been created to help teachers and students avoid less than ideal weather in the 1920s, but had been closed for quite some time after cases of rape, abuse, and death had been reported in their halls. Students had tried to move it, to open it, many times in the past with no success, and anyone found in the tunnels starting in other buildings were threatened with expulsion.

Rhea hurried past the sinister piece of glass while she focused her vision at her feet and refused to make eye contact with her own reflection. It certainly did not help that every few months people would sneak into the basement to place plastic skeletons, masks, and robes in strategic positions that could only be seen by looking into the mirror's reflection.

Ten measured steps past the mirror and the woman was once again groping along the back of the shelves to find a light switch in the dimmest section of basement. Her fingers brushed against it and she pushed up, only to find the switch very firmly stuck in the off position.

"Well isn't that wonderful, just fabulous, ugh. Give me a break." She looked around for something to pry the switch up. "All of the junk we have down here and nothing to make a light switch work. Ah, here we go!" Her fingers closed around a ruler left on the shelf. She jumped as the door to the basement slammed shut with a thunderous boom that echoed through the space. The ruler fell from her fingers and she placed a hand over her frantically racing heart.

"Hello?" she called out, "Dr. Simeon, is that you? I'll be out in ten minutes."

Rhea looked down at her list again. One box stood between her and a glorious week with no classes, no papers to grade, no work, and no un-worked boxes hanging over her head. She bent over to pick up the dropped ruler as a crash and the sound of objects shifting caused her stomach to leap into her throat. "It's just the animals having some fun, stop over thinking this, you big scaredy cat," she told herself and willed her heart to beat in its regular cadence.

After a couple quick stabs with the ruler she realized the light switch was definitely stuck, and as she aimed her flashlight's weak beam at the wall, she could clearly see a layer of superglue holding the switch in the off position. She cursed softly, made a note of it, then jumped as yet another crash sounded through the basement.

The sound of light steps and shifting feet convinced the woman that she was done for the day. "Unfinished work, be damned," she whispered to herself, "I'm done with this creepy place for the next week!" She reminded herself that a person could hear everything going on above while in the basement and it was just students and professors moving around above her head.

Ten quick steps and she entered the main aisle, heading for the sunlight coming through the front door that was still slightly cracked open. Rhea slowed as she saw a pile of books lying in the middle of the aisle that were not there on her way in.

"Okay," she called out, "this isn't funny anymore. You won. I'm freaked out. You can feel good about yourself now!"

Something solid slid into the back of Rhea's heel and she screamed as she spun around. "You little-!" She laughed nervously as a baby raccoon rapidly backed away from her flashlight beam. "It's been a baby raccoon giving me mild heart attacks." Rhea chuckled again and took in a shaky breath. "I really need to lay off the sci-fi books, little raccoon. They start making you imagine things that aren't real."

She looked up into the reflection of the mirror. *I look like such a mess,* she thought. Her ponytail had pieces of hair pulled out here and there from her habit of putting her pencil through the elastic band, her cheeks were smudged with dust and her red shirt was grey with the dirt from the boxes. She frowned at her pants, skin sticking through in places where the jean fabric had worn thin with use and thought she should probably buy a new pair over spring break. Then she looked at the mirror again, and her heart skipped a beat as her mind put together the forms of three men standing behind her.

She spun around and hit the first man with a well-placed knee to the groin, then bolted down the side aisle. *This is not happening, this is not happening,* she thought as she raced through the narrow aisle, not daring to glance behind her. If she could just make it to the edge of the room she could duck into a corner, could become invisible in a stack of old shovels and equipment. She found a break between shelves and dove into the space, quickly wedging herself between the shelf and the wall. Dust particles danced in front of her face as she tried desperately to keep her breathing shallow and silent. Cobwebs tickled at her neck and small crickets danced around her feet while she stood there shaking with fright. A stack of mildewed newspapers on the shelf in front of her seemed to mock her, the traitorous papers lifting ever so slightly in rhythm with her breath. *If I just stay here, just stay quiet, they will go away,* she told herself. The seconds ticked by like hours and silence fell over the gloom, a silence so profound she thought anyone could hear her heart beat from a mile away.

Suddenly the newspapers in front of her flew at her face, and, as Rhea threw up her hands in defense, she saw a man smile. "Hello, little mouse." Rhea bolted out of her hole, too frightened to know if she was heading away from the door or towards safety. Direction did not matter; all that mattered was getting away from the person who pursued her. The un-swept floors threatened to betray her as her sneaker soles slid on the years of sand and dirt. She turned the corner as the second man stepped into the aisle, then tripped over a box as she quickly backed up.

"What do you want? I have money, take it, it's yours."

The man gave a hollow laugh that echoed off the walls of the basement. Rhea grabbed an old volume off the shelf and threw it at him, using the precious seconds of confusion to force her feet to move and run down the next aisle. She could see the main aisle, could see freedom streaming through the door and took a precious second to inhale for a scream of help. A large hand clamped across her mouth, an arm lifted her from the ground and took that precious freedom away.

"It is not worth it to struggle, little one. You have no chance of winning."

Rhea caught a finger between her teeth and bit down hard, wildly kicking her feet out to try to contact any body part of her assailant. She growled, "It's always worth trying," and then cried out in pain as he grabbed her by the back of her neck like a kitten. He forced her on her knees into a stillness born of agony as the second man approached.

"I thought she was going to be an easy one, eh, so much for a painless job."

The man holding her laughed, "I suspect it will be well worth it, my brother. They do not come this feisty all the time!" His grip hardened on her neck as he dragged her onto her feet. "Now, are you going to come quietly girl, or will you be taking the hard way out?"

Rhea spat at him and tried to twist out of his grip. She felt a quick, hard blow to her head and the world began to move like slow molasses around her. She fought a quick wave of nausea and tried to coerce her feet to move, to will the stars to stop creating a tunnel in front of her face. She saw the mirror in front of her slide to the side, and felt herself being forced into the space it once occupied. She momentarily thought, *that's crazy, the mirror doesn't do that*, as the darkness consumed her.

Chapter Two

The Court

A wave of nausea forced her back into consciousness and twisted her stomach with its iron grip as she continued her journey through the elevator. Rhea carefully cracked open an eye and found herself sprawled across a glass floor, with nothing but stars and blackness below her. She grabbed the railing above her head, gasping for air, and convinced her legs to get under her, to straighten up. The situation was far from ideal. She was trapped in a strange glass elevator-like box with three guards, one of which who obviously had no problem using force to get his way.

This entire situation can't be real, she thought. *Did they drug me when I was out?* There was no other logical explanation for this elevator, or the fact that the guards were dressed like a science fiction war movie. They had on pants and a shirt that seemed like liquid leather on their skin, and a shirt on their broad chests that looked like a renaissance fair met a bulletproof vest supplier. Masks of leather covered their faces, only revealing their eyes and giving her captors an animalistic look. Either they had not noticed she was awake, or they decided she was not enough of a threat to care, because none were looking her way. The two larger men were standing in front of her. Spines straight, feet placed at hip width with hands loosely clasped behind their back. They looked like Marines waiting to spring into action. The smaller of the men stood a few feet away from her in the corner, with his eyes closed and looking equally uncomfortable by their swift decent into the inky space below.

Rhea gave a small moan as the elevator dropped faster and put her hands out to the sides of the transparent walls. It was very disconcerting to feel yourself fall but not be able to see anything on the horizon to gauge the distance.

One of the large guards in front of her turned slightly and chuckled. "Ah, our little woman has decided to wake up again. You look quite ill, little one, not liking your journey into our world?"

Rhea just glared at him and took in a few deep breaths to push her rising stomach back down where it belonged.

The second large man looked at a small light display on the side of the room. "It appears we will be dropping soon." He turned to Rhea and grinned, his mask giving her the distinct impression that he was a wolf about to consume her as his dinner meal. "You might want to come over here and hold onto me, feisty kitten; you will not like the feel of this at all."

"Not likely." Rhea turned away. Then the floor began to feel less than solid, like a step in a balloon room from her childhood. Rhea stared down as the clear glass below her began to ripple and sparkle. She felt something solid touch her side and turned towards it, grabbing anything her hands could find. The feel of a metal buckle under her fingers caused Rhea to look up, straight into the green eyes of the third guard. She had grabbed onto him in her desperation and, with no outward emotion, he wrapped a strong arm around her waist as the floor fully dissolved, and, unbelievably, they were floating in thin air.

A fast drop, a quick thud of impact and Rhea could feel her feet touch solid ground once again. She shoved away from the guard quickly, her heel catching the edge of the door as she spilled backwards out of the elevator. The two men bent over and picked her up by each arm, moving her down a gray hallway with no windows, no doors, and no other way out.

After what seemed like ages a door appeared at the end of the long hallway, emitting a bright blue light and sounds of people. A glimmer of hope began to surface in Rhea's heart. Maybe someone here would take pity on her; surely someone here would have a way for her to call home, to contact someone, anyone, to help her.

The guards holding her stopped suddenly, and the third guard stepped ahead, leading the party into the lit room. The four entered and Rhea blinked in amazement. *This can't be real*, she thought, *this has to be a dream, some drug-induced hallucination, or stress-induced nightmare maybe, but this cannot be real.*

Walls of grey stone rose to meet vaulted arches high above her head. Wooden beams created a rooftop with an occasional splinter dropping down to the floor below. The air was so cold it raised the hair on her arms and created puffy clouds with her shallow breaths.

The people were like none she had seen before. Hair the color of ashy charcoal and eyes as black as obsidian orbs were placed into jaundiced, gaunt faces. There was no look of curiosity as they glanced her way, no look of pity or fear. It was as if the people could not have cared less about her presence or that of the imposing guards. They continued about their business, watering dying house plants in the corners, scrubbing the veined marble floors until their reflections shone back at them, and wiping dusty windows that displayed a bleak darkness on the other side of the pane.

All movement stopped as the green-eyed guard stepped in front of two large, oaken doors and removed his leather mask. Close-cropped hair, the color of an old penny, fell over his darkened skin. If he had been in Rhea's world he would have been suspected of Egyptian or Persian heritage by his facial features. If he were not a man who had kidnapped her, Rhea would have called him handsome and certainly would have flirted with him in a bar setting. Here, he was an anomaly, a person who did not look like others in the realm, whose green eyes set him apart from the obsidian stares around him. He pushed open the doors and led the party into a room as opposite as night to day.

Plush rugs cushioned the foot falls of patrons leisurely drifting in social conduct throughout the room. Vivid reds, greens and bright whites reflected off the gleaming white walls and flowed up into the elaborate ball gowns of the women. All eyes moved towards the party as they silently made their way towards another, smaller door at the far end of the room. Rhea could hear the whispers behind the hands of the women as she was forced past the small groups and the calculating looks in the eyes of the men. They followed her path through the room, blue-eyed women and men. Every one of them as blonde as the Swiss supermodels her ex-boyfriend used to lust after. She held her chin higher and glared back in their direction. She would find a way out of here; that was the only possible outcome of this bizarre day.

The guard stepped into the final room ahead of them, and Rhea winced as her arms were forced behind her back and iron manacles were placed onto her wrists. She looked up at the leather masked face in amazement and disbelief. "What do you think I'm going to do? Jump onto a magic unicorn and fly out of this place?"

A low rumble of angry voices came through the open door and the guards exchanged concerned glances at one another. That did not sound like the praise they must have been expecting to receive for their troubles. The third guard stalked out the door, snapped at the guards that King wanted to speak with them, then took Rhea's elbow and guided her down the hallway.

"You could take off these cuffs you know." Rhea spared a glance at the man. "It's not like I can go anywhere at this point. I obviously have no clue where I am or how to get home." She tripped over the edge of a blue rug and bounced off of the guard's broad shoulder. *Get him talking,* she thought. *Distract him, do something before it is too late.* "You could always take me back. I promise I wouldn't tell anyone about this. You could just say that I escaped and no one would know."

Eyes shifted her way and then forward again. "Watch your step," he told her as a hand on her elbow guided her up a step under the archway and down a short flight of stairs.

They walked in silence then, Rhea and the guard, down a labyrinth of hallways and corridors. There were no other people to be seen on their short journey. Rhea could hear muffled footsteps around her, ghostly sounds of people in various rooms and above her head. From the sound around her the floor above was filled with motion and people. She did not anticipate these people would be any help to her, whether they were the gray somber workers or the extravagant patrons in the last room.

The hallway opened up to a receiving room, modest in size and with a small stone bench along one wall. A tall figure stood in the shadows of one corner, cloaked in dark ambiguity and silent as death. It was the energy radiating off the figure that made Rhea halt her step, caused the intake of breath. In a normal situation it would have been called charisma, presence, maybe an aura. In this situation it set the woman's heart to pounding and brought moisture to her palms.

The man bowed low, and beside him Rhea found herself following his actions, uninstructed.

"Dear Washitza," he straightened as the figure extended one hand from the robes and bid him to move, "I have come, at the bidding of the King, with this woman for your care."

A feminine voice came from the shadowed robe. "And are you alone guard? In this darkness one cannot tell which eyes you would wear."

The man chuckled as he replied, "Risalka, you know I always wear the same green eyes when it counts."

Slender hands pulled the deep violet hood off the woman's head. Rhea thought the woman was stunning and felt her breath catch in her chest at the power from those eyes. Black hair that shone in the lamplight from the wall covered a face exquisite in every detail. A slender neck faded delicately into the cowl around her shoulders and the air in the room seemed to ripple as the tall woman stepped towards her visitors. "One can never be too safe, De Nespa. This is the first hunt you have volunteered for after all."

"I think that would be best discussed at a later time than this." The man frowned and glanced at Rhea. "She is yours now. Do what you wish." He gave Rhea's shoulders a firm push that sent her stumbling towards the shadows.

"Ah, youth. So impetuous, so lost at times." Dark eyes shifted from the man to the woman standing in front of her. "So, you are the one they have brought for me. What color are my eyes, child?"

Rhea gathered her courage and looked up into her eyes. At first she found herself getting pulled into the dark black orbs that seemed to have no end and caused her stomach to knot and twist upon itself. She gathered her courage and looked deeper. The eyes shifted then, blackness giving away to eyes the color of autumn leaves, with bright green specks dotting areas around the dark pupils.

"Ah then, you might have potential, little one. I can see my own eyes in yours, but we must change that for just a little while." The woman opened a door and swept Rhea into a sunlit room.

Another woman walked over. "Shackles, mother? Really? Is this how we are going to do things now?"

The tall woman sighed. "Yes well, we must maintain the image and all of that. Here, hand me that key." The manacles fell to the floor silently, cushioned by inches of soft fabric. "My name is Risalka. I am the Washitza for this household, the head of help if you will. This is my daughter, Lianna."

Lianna assessed Rhea from the side of a large piece of furniture. "We need to find something more suitable for you to wear. This should do." She emerged from the wardrobe with an emerald green gown, complete with a bodice that sparkled with hundreds of small crystals.

The older of the women herded Rhea into an adjoining room with a porcelain tub. "Let us get you all cleaned up then. You will feel much better."

Rhea stared at the tub filling with water. "I'll feel much better after a bath? You really think that a bath will make the fact that I've been kidnapped all better? You people are insane."

Woodland eyes locked onto Rhea's. "Yes, we are all a bit crazy here. It is the best way to survive after all. Now listen, there is no going home for you. There is no escape, there is no running away. The sooner you realize this the easier your life will become. From now on this is your home and you will behave accordingly. Right now, that means you are going to strip down, get in this tub and wash yourself. I will even step into the next room so you have some privacy but will be back in one turning of the quarter hour glass." She set down a pile of thick towels and a tray of cleaning products and left the room.

"Rule number one for self defense, listen to your attacker and assess the situation." Rhea stared at the tub. "Situation...I'm not getting out of here anytime soon so I will play their game." *For now,* she silently added. The bath was quick and efficient; the last thing the woman wanted was for her captors to walk in on her in such a vulnerable state. Small glass bottles helped her to identify the hair supplies and a bar of soap in a delicate swan design did not seem to be diminished by her use.

The woman called Risalka walked back in as Rhea wrapped herself in one of the thick gray towels. "I have brought in some underclothes for you along with the dress. I will turn around until you need assistance."

Rhea took the clothing offered and stepped into the green gown gingerly. Her arms slid into the long, fitted sleeves as if it had been made for her body, the curves of the bodice boning caused the silk to fall in perfect curves over her hips, then draped down to kiss the stone floor. She cleared her throat and Risalka turned around to help secure the delicate buttons along the back of the dress.

The younger lady walked in. "Now for the hair. I can take over from here, Mother. I know tonight will be busy for you."

Rhea sat down on a cushioned stool in front of the mirror and watched Risalka leave the room. Lianna picked up a fine tooth comb and began to work out the tangles created during the struggle. "The confusion usually only lasts a few weeks at best, then you will not even remember how your life used to be."

"I don't want to forget about my old life. My old life is my only life, staying here is not even an option. I don't know what game is being played but I will have nothing to do with it. Soon people will know I'm missing and come searching for me."

Kind eyes met hers as Lianna gently twisted her hair into a simple design. "But how many people will ever find you here? People cannot come to this place without invitation, Rhea, just as people cannot get out after they are here."

The woman's eyes welled up in tears. "I cannot accept that," Rhea said. "I will not accept that."

"That is all fine and good; you say what you need to keep yourself going." Lianna patted her on the shoulder. "Now come on, I will show you to your room."

~ * ~ * ~

The room was much more than Rhea could have expected given her initial treatment. Wide and airy, the scent of unseen flowers filled the space and sunlight poured through the one small window. The large bed was covered in soft, finely woven sheets and a plump silk comforter filled with down rested atop the mattress. A small cloth chair sat as a companion to a small, round table in front of a modestly sized fire hearth. Rugs covered the floor and provided protection against the chill of the stone below. A wardrobe held the space of one corner and a series of stacked trunks stood against a free wall. Candles were placed on a small table to the side of the headboard and Rhea found a box of small matches in the bedside drawer. No sound penetrated the walls of the room; none of the footfalls or shifts of movement that could be heard so readily in the corridors made their way to the woman's ears. Any move, any sound that was made inside the room seemed to echo against the walls, filling the woman's head with sound.

Lianna had shown Rhea to her new room, and then left as a guard took up his post outside the heavy oak door. That had been some time ago, long before the sun had set, and still no one came for Rhea. No one came to offer food or water and the woman was left to her own devices.

For the first hour curiosity and the instinctive need to investigate her current environment led Rhea on a search of her immediate surroundings. She found matches used to light the candles but there was no wood for the fireplace. The window provided light for some time, but now the room was slowly being cast into the dim glow of the single candle.

The wardrobe revealed a full set of gowns and shifts that seemed to be Rhea's size. Most of the dresses were dark shades of brown, muted beiges, and a few exquisitely decorated gowns of pure white. An exploration into the trunks revealed several dresses of various green hues, perfectly hand stitched and without any sign of previous wear. A second chest revealed several cloaks made of finely spun wool in deep crimsons, violets and azure. On the fireplace mantle was a book entitled <u>Proper Protocol of Court</u> with several dog-eared pages, yellow and crisp with age.

As the room faded to a single glow, Rhea slowly began to realize the situation. She had been kidnapped and taken to some bizarre world where no one was going to help her. She had no way of getting the basic necessities and no knowledge of the outside landscape. If she was going to get anywhere, she thought, it would be by keeping them off guard and earning their trust.

Male voices began to leak under the space at the bottom of the door. At first Rhea thought she was imagining them, already wanting proof that someone else existed in this world, but even after she shook her head the voices could be heard. She very carefully tiptoed over to the door and pressed her ear against the wood.

"So how long do you suppose this one is going to last?"

"Longer than the others at least." Rhea recognized the voice of the green-eyed guard, the one who handed her to the women. "She gave Eitri and Brokkan a good fight before they were able to get her through the mirror."

The second voice laughed, deep bass echoing off the stone corridor. "Good girl. Will they be giving her food or water in the morning?"

Silence then, and a low sigh. "We can only hope they will extend small mercies. How did she look when they brought her up here?"

"Honestly, man? She is beautiful and radiates passion in a way I have not seen in some time. "

A harsh laugh followed. "Only the best for the Prince, you know that. Provided she survives long enough to see him and does not have all the passion extinguished like everyone else"

The voices quieted and Rhea heard footsteps going away from the door. *Only the best for the prince? What on earth could that have meant?* She honestly was not sure she wanted to know. Rhea looked at the large bed and decided it would be safer to curl up on the chair by the empty hearth. She did not expect sleep to come easily, but the last thing she wanted was to sleep deeply and miss any sounds of intrusion into her prison.

Chapter Three

The Court

Rhea let herself drift in a half-asleep state, convinced she was back in her apartment dozing on the lounge chair. Her breath caught as she heard the sound of a door open and boot heels thudded across the marble floor. She screwed her eyes tightly shut, refusing to acknowledge reality by staying in the safety of darkness.

"I know you are awake, girl." The deep male voice from the door boomed through the bedroom. "Here is food and drink. Take it now, it might be all you get for the day."

Rhea held herself very still, scarcely daring to breathe. *This is not real, this is not real. This is a dream. I ate something bad or drank something too strong and it's a dream. When I open my eyes I will be in my house and write a crazy story about a bad dream.* The woman cracked open an eye as the large wooden door slammed shut and the sound of a bolt sliding sealed her off from outside sounds.

"Well then, I guess the crazy dream continues." Rhea stood up slowly, muscles cramped after spending the night curled up in a chair not meant for sleeping. She wandered over to a basin of water on a table and cautiously dipped a finger into the liquid, warm water. A soap and soft hand towel were also located nearby, along with some eye shadow applicators and a jar of, what appeared to be, lip stain. Rhea quickly splashed water on her face and toweled it dry. To the left of the basin was a finely made comb, which the woman picked up and ran through the tangles of her long hair.

"Alright, let's inspect this food," she said quietly to herself, talking for the sake of hearing a sound. A crystal goblet occupied one corner of the breakfast tray, filled with a dark chocolate-colored liquid. A small bowl seemed to contain cut fruit of some sort, similar to a grapefruit or other citrus fruit, and beside it sat a plate with a type of oatmeal and hash mixture. One bite of the oatmeal proved uneventful, but on the second bite of fruit Rhea's throat began to feel itchy, like the beginnings of a cold. She pushed the fruit to the side. The first bite of the potato hash mixture brought a threatening pounding to her temples and Rhea quickly pushed the food aside.

"Rule Number … something of wilderness survival, if the food gives you a headache, stop eating it." The liquid in the goblet beckoned her, but Rhea did not dare touch it to her lips after the results of the food testing. There was a small flush toilet in the side room and she quickly poured the liquid and remaining food down the drain. "Better to go without than to be poisoned or drugged," she told herself as she curled her body into the chair once again.

The guard came in a few hours later to remove the tray and cast an assessing eye over Rhea's face. She just glared back at him, every ounce of her being willing him to go away. After a quick inspection of the room he left, and the bolt slid shut once again.

The shadows had fallen towards evening before the woman was jolted out of her nap by a shadow sliding across her face. Her eyes popped open and she looked around the room frantically, and then allowed her heart to settle as she realized there was no one in the room and the shadow had come through the window. Hunger had started to set in now, accompanied by the dryness in her tongue to remind her that she had not had food or water in over a day. Rhea looked at the bowl that had been put out for washing. *Well,* she reasoned, *it's reasonably clean and probably not poisoned.* She walked over and cupped her hand into the now cool water, then brought it to her mouth and took a tentative sip. It was not high-quality water, and had a slightly soapy taste, but it cooled her thirst and did not appear to have anything added to it.

Her stomach growled again and Rhea poked her abdomen. "Shut up in there," she chastised herself. "You've gone without before and you'll be fine." All she needed was a distraction, something to keep her mind off of the hunger pains and her current predicament.

I'm trained to people watch and observe, so let's observe and see what I can learn. The woman dragged one of the sturdy chests over to below the window and climbed up. The window was small and had iron bars across the outside. The glass was hazy but she was able to wipe away decades of dust to get a clear picture of outside.

Her room was high in a castle, opposite to two tall towers that soared above the castle walls. Everything was made of stone with the exception of the roofs, which seemed to be either wooden planking or thatch depending on the structure. A long, low building was seen if she pressed her nose to the glass and looked left, and a series of what appeared to be horse stables was to her right. A courtyard sprawled in front of her view large enough to fit half of a football field, and led to a wide iron gate surrounded by stone walls. Beyond the stone walls was a town. Layers upon layers of houses which seemed to revolve around larger mansions as far as the eye could see, all encircled by a protective layer of more stone walls. What lie beyond those walls Rhea could not see, only the lowering glow of the sun as it tucked its way down into the horizon.

The courtyard was a hub of activity filled with men and women from a variety of social standings. Common workers were clothed in grey outfits with no fancy embellishments, while patrons of the realm could be seen in gaudy blue, yellow, orange and crimson garments. It did not seem that the rich paid the poor for their goods, instead they just pointed what they wanted from the variety of stands and a simply dressed person behind them picked up the item and placed it into the basket they carried. She assumed that these people were a slight bit higher than the vendors in status but well below that of the colorful men and women.

It seemed that only specialty items were sold in the courtyard. Rhea could not see what she considered staples of life, things like bread, plain clothing, or tools. Instead the stands were filled with the bright colors of exotic fruits, brightly colored tapestries, beaded clothing, and displays of shimmering crystal jewels. A small boy could be observed standing just behind one table filled with beautiful shawls that had been woven so finely that the intricate designs could be seen from Rhea's tower. Jeweled fringes brushed against the stone courtyard as one woman, and then another threw the shawl over her shoulder then dropped it back onto the table in a disorderly heap of fabric

The stable area seemed to be much quieter. Few people or horses seemed to be moving to and from the stable area, but the many shadows passing by the windows gave the impression of a busy hive of workers within the wooden walls. The few people who went inside the doors appeared to be of the servant caste, with their drab uniforms and downcast eyes, while an occasional well-dressed man waited impatiently for a horse to be brought out to him.

Rhea watched curiously as a servant's head shot up in response to a question from a patron, and then gestured angrily towards the barn. An argument then appeared to play out; though the woman could not hear any sounds in her prison the body language was quite clear that both parties were very unhappy. The servant continued to point his finger at the stable in aggravation, finally making a gesture that implied to Rhea the conversation was over and the servant had made a decision.

The servant made two steps towards the stable before two leather clad guards were upon him, forcing him to his knees and demanding what appeared to be an explanation. The servant gave one, his lips moving but eyes still downcast. Finally they let him up with a cuff to the back of his head and a boot to the knee, laughing as the servant walked back into the bar with a defeated limp.

Several tense minutes later the servant emerged from the barn leading the most beautiful horse that Rhea had ever seen. The woman had been an avid rider in her teenage years and could recognize a horse with grace and power the moment she saw one. This horse had all of that and more. A beautifully proportioned head led to a perfectly curved neck, down to a muscular yet delicate body supported by long, lean legs. The black coat was so pure it appeared to shimmer in blue waves as she danced in place, pulling at the reins that were held by the servant. A long black mane, dappled with grey, had been meticulously groomed and flowed down past the horse's shoulders, and the tail was the fullest Rhea had seen. The most shocking feature of the horse however were the eyes. One was a deep brown, so vast that a person seemed to get sucked into the horse's soul by glancing into the orb. The horse flung her head up and Rhea could see the other was a brilliant aqua color, reflecting the people and buildings surrounding the horse.

A heavy leather saddle was placed on the horse's back, with a high pommel and stirrups so large the rider's entire legs would be encased by the thick leather. Gold trim lined the edge of the leather and caused the saddle to gleam in the light, leading nearby patrons and workers to shield their eyes or turn away. The horse was led, by the force of five men, over to the nearby platform that would serve as a mounting block, yet the man who had demanded this particular mount walked away with the guards.

Seconds later all activity stopped. Vendors quickly moved behind their tables and positioned themselves so as not to be seen, standing behind thick support poles or ducking under the table surface and crouching below. Patrons all moved quickly to the side of the courtyard, pushing together and casting their eyes upon the stone. Even the animals of the courtyard seemed to still themselves, to cease their chirp, bark, or bay, and hold perfectly still.

Then the air itself held its breath as a man walked out into the courtyard, surrounded by four servants mounted on pure white geldings. The man stepped up onto the mounting block and swung onto the horse, finding the stirrups while the horse squealed loudly in anger and danced on the stone. The man was beautiful in a cold way, the features of his face and his body so clean cut they appeared to be carved of stone. White blonde hair closely cut to cover a pale face, and blue eyes so striking they seemed to pierce through any person who dared look his way. An ivory vest was exquisitely sewn with gold thread and amber buttons that shone like the sun on his chest. Boots the color of purified milk encased his feet and his calves, and closely fitted white leather pants were finished with a gold belt.

The man gave a shout, and the entire mounted party galloped towards the gateway, the black mare spinning and snorting the entire way. The white geldings surrounded her and her rider, pushing her out of the gate as the rider laughed and applied his spurs.

"That would be the High Prince."

Rhea jumped at the soft voice behind her and spun around to see the young woman from the other day, Lianna, behind her. "I didn't hear you come in."

"Most people do not. You would be wise not to become so focused that you do not hear a bolt sliding open, or a door closing."

Lianna held out her hand for assistance as Rhea stepped down from her perch. "You have not been eating what has been provided and I was asked to bring you extra sustenance."

The woman was carrying a tray with a goblet of the chocolate-colored liquid, a hunk of risen bread, and a bowl of soup. Rhea eyed the entire tray suspiciously. "I'm not hungry, thank you."

Lianna gave a harsh laugh as Rhea's stomach betrayed her lie. "It is better to drink this than soapy water, and you cannot survive for very long without food." She set the tray down on the table and gestured for Rhea to sit at the adjacent chair.

"The human body can go for quite some time without food. Besides, it's better than being poi-" Rhea clamped her mouth shut, angry at herself for speaking so candidly with this stranger.

"Ah, you are as smart as we thought then. I prepared this food myself, in the servant's kitchen, so no harm will come from its consumption. Eat and drink, you will have a busy time ahead of you in the upcoming days and strength will be required." She gestured towards the food once more, and then silently walked out of the room.

The food looked exactly the same as yesterday, but when Rhea cautiously put it to her tongue there were no negative reactions. She tentatively took a spoonful of the warm, liquid soup. The broth was quite weak, but there was no resulting headache, no itchiness of the throat or feeling of immediate nausea. A sip of the chocolate liquid in the cup found the same results. The liquid tasted like a hazelnut chocolate blend, and was smooth on the tongue and easy on the throat. The bread was slightly dry and fairly tasteless, but worked sufficiently to soak up the last of the soup broth and fill the woman's empty stomach.

Waning light through the window beckoned, but Rhea felt sleepy satisfaction after the meal, and opted to sit in the chair and thumb through the book on protocol. "I guess it's better to know the enemy than not."

"Chapter 1: Hierarchy Of The Court"

The King is the highest ruler of the realm of Kaldalangra and not to be questioned. His word is law and unchallenged. The King is to never be engaged without applying for an audience and receiving approval from the Kontorist. Failure to contact the Kontorist before an audience with the King will result in one hundred lashes. A Patron is required to make his body prostrate upon view of the King and remain in this position until dismissed by His Highness.

The High Prince is the heir to the throne and second most powerful man in the realm. If a subject wishes an audience with the High Prince he must apply and receive approval from the Kontorist. The only exception is given to the woman approved as Forena to the High Prince. No patron of the realm is to cast eyes upon the High Prince unless directed to do so, and no servant of the realm is to be seen by the High Prince unless he or she is in direct service. Failure of a Patron to avert his eyes in the presence of the Prince will result in temporary imprisonment, and failure of a Servant to obey the law will result in immediate death. A patron is required to show submission upon view of the High Prince if he is indoors. When outside of the palace walls a Patron is only required to avert his eyes and show reverence in a manner deemed appropriate by the DamaTalous.

The DamaTalous are the members of the royal family. They are not to be approached at any time and all eyes must be averted in their presence. Patrons are not required to make themselves prostrate but are to provide the DamaTalous with absolute respect. Any observed lack of respect will be met swiftly with punishment by the Vagthund. The DamaTalous are to submit to the King upon entrance but are allowed free movement once released by the King.

The Vagthund is the first in charge after the King and High Prince. In the event the King and High Prince are incapacitated the Vagthund is considered head of the realm and his word is law. All Patrons are to avert their eyes when in the presence of the Vagthund and servants are to make themselves prostrate. Punishment for a Patron for not averting their eyes is twenty lashes. Punishment for servants for not prostrating is death.

The Kontorist is the authority of all human movement within the realm. A subject is required to contact the Kontorist in the event of immigration, birth of a child, or death of a subject.   Failure to contact the Kontorist in the event of immigration, birth, or death will result in immediate expulsion from the realm

Rhea put down the book and rubbed her eyes. The first section of the book was well over two-hundred pages and covered every nuance of society within the realm. Who was in charge of who, the proper way to apply for an audience, the punishments, how to greet a person of equal realm, everything one needed to know was in this book. She thumbed through the first chapter and read through the section devoted to Patrons of the court until darkness overtook the room and sleep claimed her, still seated in the chair by the cold fire.

Chapter Four

The Court

Hours turned into days as Rhea sat by the stone hearth. No living soul had entered her room since Lianna had left four days earlier, although the guard did place a cup of liquid by the door every morning. The wash water was left unchanged and the woman began to rely on rationing out the mystery drink in order to keep her wits about her. Extreme thirst does strange things to a person, and the wash water was diminished within the first twenty-four hours of her isolation.

The book of protocol was the only company Rhea received. An occasional murmur from the guard could be heard if she put her ear to the thick door, but it was generally so silent Rhea could hear her own breathing, ragged and raspy due to her throat, inflamed from lack of water.

Rhea read through the section on the distinguishing castes within the patrons, guards, and servants. Every person had their own place in society, recorded in great detail and with seemingly no movement between each caste. Rules were set for who could get married, who could get divorced, and who could walk freely within the realm. There were vague references to people outside of the castle walls but most seemed to just mention the people as "others" and not give any true identity. There were guides for how each caste was to stand, sit, eat, drink, or act while in public. Then all of these guides had secondary guides for how each caste was to do the same actions in the presence of higher ranking castes.

The amount of societal information made Rhea's head spin, and she wondered how anyone could possibly keep all of this information straight and make it through their lives unscathed. She did briefly entertain the morbid thought that maybe they could not keep it straight and were constantly punished. It would certainly account for the lack of movement she saw when the High Prince stepped outside the castle walls. It seemed the correct action to take in the presence of the royalty was not to look at them, not to move, and certainly not to speak at any time.

The noise of the bolt sliding in the door caused Rhea to jump. Dehydration made her skin feel like it was crawling over her muscles, drawn tight as dried leather across her bones. A guard the size of a giant walked into the room carrying a tray of food and a large glass of water. He set it down carefully on the small table next to the chair and gave Rhea a hard look. His deep voice softly told her, "Eat this now, and eat this carefully. If you cooperate over the next few days you will be allowed to return to the castle and eat again. If you chose to resist the path chosen for you, these items will be withheld until you change your mind or die. The choice is yours." The door clicked softly as he left the room and slid home the bolt.

Rhea willed herself to sit perfectly still in her chair as she felt her body demanding access to the items on the tray. *I must eat slowly,* she thought, *or my body will reject it and it will do me no good.* She carefully forced herself to take one long swallow from the cup of water, then three bites of food from the tray. Five minutes later she allowed another sip, and another few bites, and five minutes after that a few more. It took well over three hours until Rhea was finished with the meal and her body still protested the large amount of food that was now pushing against the edges of her stomach.

She dragged her leaden feet over to the window and stepped up to look outside. The sun was already beginning to set, and the ghostly image of the full moon could be seen high above the trees. The stable was a flurry of frantic movement with horses being moved, groomed, and saddled. Three gray-cloaked figures stood just outside the stable and appeared to be having a conversation in their small group. Judging from the sizes Rhea guessed the taller of the three were guards of some sort, with the smaller, slighter figure being a woman. A few minutes later the giant joined them, towering over the woman and several inches higher than the two men. They had a brief conference that ended when the giant and another one of the men made their way back to the castle, glancing up in her direction as they approached the entrance.

Time had no bearing in Rhea's world by now, and it seemed like mere seconds had passed when her door swung open and the two cloaked men walked into the room. She was wrapped up in a crimson-hued wool cloak, and then briskly ushered out of the room and down into the courtyard, every step agony on her weakened muscles and still dehydrated body.

The group arrived at the stable and Rhea looked around at the hard, cold, black eyes of the cloaked group. Gray horses were pulled out of the stable and led to a small bench where one of the guards and the lady smoothly swung into the saddles. Finally, a third horse was led out of the stable and Rhea was roughly picked up by the giant and placed on the mare's back. The cloaked woman took the lead rope of the animal and Rhea twisted her fingers into the horse's rough mane in an attempt to keep her weakened body upright. The two guards behind her mounted and the party walked out of the castle walls into the night.

As the horses began to canter through the rough terrain, Rhea's sense of direction vanished into the night. She was surrounded by rocky hills, piles of precariously stacked stones and trees so dead they appeared as obelisks in the night. Gravel and pebbles shifted under the horse's feet, causing the woman's leg muscles to scream in agony as she struggled to stay upright on the gentle mare. The moonlight bounced off of the landscape, creating a strange world of shadows and light as the five horses wound through canyons, under overhangs blocking all light, and through dried up river beds.

All movement suddenly stopped and Rhea forced her head upright to look in front of her. They were on an expanse of land covered with a slate floor as far as the eye could see. Uneven ground led to a large butte far to Rhea's right, with a large pool of glassy, still water resting in the shadow of the cliff. Small shadows skittered across the rocky crevices in various shades of black and gray, with slightly larger versions of the shadow creatures slowly approaching the water's edge to drink.

The dark woman gently encouraged her horse forward, followed by one of the guards, Rhea, and the final two guards. The small shadows danced around the horses' feet and Rhea could see her mounts eyes rolling back in terror as tiny teeth and claws could be seen on the shadows. As they approached the pool several of the larger shadows lifted their heads and stared at the humans, bright red eyes reflecting the moonlight as small drops of water dripped off of their exposed fangs. The party approached the rocky overhang and all movement of the creatures stopped, and seemingly as one they swung their red and white eyes toward the woman in the crimson cloak.

The shorter guard dismounted, small creatures scattering at his feet and hissing their displeasure at his intrusion into their world. With three carefully executed movements he was on top of a ledge outcrop overlooking the pool. Rhea's horse was led over to the ledge and she felt herself being lifted off the horse and onto the rocks above. The second woman was lifted as well and led the way up a small stone path to a higher point of the butte. Here the ground shone white as the moonlight reflected off the stone surfaces, smooth as blown glass and with the same reflective properties as a mirror. The figures dropped their cloaks, and Rhea blinked in confusion as she stared into the faces of Risalka and the man called de Nespa. Their eyes shone black as night, and Rhea felt a sense of dread fill her soul as Risalka began to talk.

"Tonight you will take the final step into becoming a person of Kaldalangra. You will remain on this rock until you allow the moonlight to overtake you, or until death claims your body and devours your soul. Embrace the darkness and the stone and let it become one with your heart, and let the light fill your body until there is no room for darkness." The woman bowed her head and stood still as the guards began to drop down off the ledge and gather the horses waiting below. She then lifted her face and turned to the guard's location. Satisfied they were well below and could not hear the women, Risalka turned back to Rhea, her eyes shifting back to a concerned emerald hue as she regarded the woman.

"I know you are strong, my dear. I know that, weakened as you are, you will fight the moonlight and the world around you as long as you can. You must give in and you must allow yourself to be taken if you want to survive. Only three people have survived the moonlight ceremony and they were not primed as you are, for failure." She ran a hand over Rhea's hair, caressed the long locks and gently pulled them out of the crimson cloak. "Tonight you must allow the transformation to complete. You must survive, only that. We will deal with the rest later."

Rhea watched as Risalka slowly walked down the rocky path to ledge, fear knotting her stomach into a dense ball as she heard the horse accept her slight weight and the riders began to walk away from the bright light and small shadows. A sharp gust of wind blew her hair across her face and for a moment Rhea thought the light color was merely a trick of the light caused by the moon. Second inspection proved that the light showed true, her previously auburn hair had somehow faded into a strawberry blonde, and seemed to be lightening before her very eyes.

She took a deep breath and sat down carefully on the rocky edge, gazing over the desolate landscape. The pool once again teemed with black shadowed life, red eyes reflecting in the surface of the pool as many creatures stopped to quench their thirst. Rhea held perfectly still as red and white eyes turned upward to look her way, her light hair and brightly colored cloak a beacon in the inky night, drawing all attention towards her. She slowly backed away from the edge and sat in the center of the moon's bright reflection against the stone. After some time Rhea closed her eyes against the light and slept, praying that the small creatures below did not have the ability to climb her new isolated home.

Rhea awoke as her arms were set with an itching so intense it felt like her skin was on fire. Rhea opened her eyes and looked down, alarmed to see rock the color of sand and glistening with the same glassy surface as the night before. She quickly got to her feet, arms red and inflamed from the heat reflecting off of the ground surface. The sun beat down upon her head, quickly raising water that she could not afford to lose from her skin and causing her already dry throat to swell as additional moisture was wicked away. Rhea glanced over the edge of the precipice and saw no shadows moving below, no creatures waiting with their glowing eyes. She slowly made her way down the path to the rocky ledge, staring in assessment at the twelve foot drop between her and the water.

Fear of the long drop kept her on that ledge throughout the daylight hours, though her throat could barely swallow the little saliva her mouth had produced; the small amount of liquid felt thick, like she was swallowing a cotton ball. Heat poured through the stones and Rhea spent the morning removing her cloak and loosening her dress to get rid of excess cloth, and then putting it back on to escape the searing air waves and sunlight that came from the stone around her. All the while the water stared at her, mocked her as she sat on the ledge. It called to her, encouraged her to drop off the ledge, even when she had no way of getting back up again and she would be left at the mercy of the small monsters.

No breeze cooled the air for her small ledge or the surrounding landscape. By noon any source of moisture outside of the pool had dried up, leaving small sand piles and dried tracks of the small black animals. By the time the sun began to set, the surface around the pool started to peel and split, rock and sand so dry the overheated clay began to bake and crack.

Sunset came, and with the darkness came the animals as they slowly writhed out towards the small basin of black water. They were vile beasts, shadows with teeth and fangs that hissed and squabbled with any creature nearby. A multitude of altercations broke out as they jostled for position near the water hole and many of the smaller creatures engaged in combat with no visible provocation, sinking fangs into the neck of nearby shadows. Many came to the rocks below the ledge and tried to climb the steep face, causing Rhea to retreat high onto the unprotected summit of the rocks.

The temperature plummeted on the rocks and Rhea's muscles were immediately seized by the cold shock. Her breath puffed white into the still air as she drew her thick cloak around her shoulders and head, and then tucked her hands into the long sleeves of her dress. She sat down quickly and curled herself into as tight of a ball as she could manage, drawing the heat from the core of her body in an attempt to spread it to her fingers and toes as her back clenched tightly with muscle spasms.

A sudden whistle of noise caused her to look up into the bleak darkness. The full moon was being orbited by long, thin strands of light. Brilliant cobalt, crimson, and emerald hues streaked around the moon in an orderly dance of speed and grace. Larger, slower strands of white and yellow lights circled the colors and formed a border around the beautiful dance of light in the sky. Rhea stared at the moon and the lights, entranced, and she no longer felt the cold frost that had settled on her eyelashes and stiffened her cloak with ice. The lights ceased at dawn, at which point Rhea blinked and shook her head, as she realized she had not slept all night and struggled to flex her frozen fingers in the cloak.

Within one hour of the sun being visible in the sky the temperature once again rose to an unbearable swelter, forcing Rhea into her ledge retreat. Her lungs felt on fire, angry at the rapid temperature changes and having been subjected to extreme cold, then blazing heats within such a short amount of time. The woman sat tucked in the ledge and stared at the inviting pool that once again seemed to mock her desire for a cool drink. Never in her life did she think she would have so badly wanted just one sip of water, one sip of a liquid she had taken for granted all of her previous life.

She stared down at the twelve foot drop once more. She felt confident she could handle the long drop down if she just lowered herself onto her stomach, dangled off the edge and dropped. The problem would arise in the return back up onto the ledge at sunset when the creatures returned. Rhea peered to the side of her ledge and saw a few shadows, promising but not clear in their formation from her spot. Her fingers found a solid handhold on the wall and she leaned to the side of the ledge, her hopes lifting when she found what seemed to be a crumbly rocky ladder leading down the edge. She carefully edged her way over the rungs created of banded sandstone, and inch by careful inch descended onto the floor below.

The water was slightly warm, but tasted clean and eased the sharp and constant burn within her throat. She removed her boots and splashed some water on her feet as she sat in the cool sand next to the pool. Her cupped hands lifted the water and let it splash over her hair, wet her heavy dress and bring her body temperature down before taking another long drink of water. Rhea leaned over the pool to splash water onto her lobster-red, sunburned skin, but stopped short at her reflection.

Hazel eyes that once shone brightly now were beginning to dull to an empty brown color. Her hair had lightened another shade of blonde, the red hues being replaced by white and giving her hair the color of dull straw. Rhea dashed at the water with her hand, turning her reflection into an abstract design of ripples of a female image. When the water settled they were still there, the dead dark eyes and light hair. *Somehow this place is changing how I look*, she bleakly thought, *along with exhausting my mind.*

"My name is Rhea Aralia. I am twenty-five years old. I am a student of archaeology and will spend the rest of my life not complaining about having to catalogue dusty artifacts instead of working in the field. I have a black belt in Tae Kwon Do, ride horses, and love animals. I have a strong belief in the spirits around me and that the universe takes care of Her people. My name is Rhea Aralia. I am twenty-five years old…"

Rhea continued her chant until the sun began to set, then put on her leather boots and made her way back to her rocky ladder. With the exception of an occasional slip as her toe caught the heavy dress she wore she was able to easily pull herself back onto the ledge and make her way onto the relative safety of the high platform. The small creatures came out with the moonlight, cautious and wary around the place where the woman had been sitting throughout the daylight hours. The size of the creatures seemed to be somehow connected to the levels of moonlight and the lateness of the hour, with the larger beings only coming to water as the night grew deeper.

The full moon appeared to have moved into its waning phase, just slightly off from being a perfect circle in the night. Rhea stared up at the shining orb with its surrounding light show for quite some time before a persistent breeze began to blow her hair across her eyes, breaking the connection. She blinked and shook her head in confusion, then wrapped her cloak more snuggly around her shoulders as she realized her exposed skin had become covered in small goose bumps brought on by the night, though not quite as frigid as the one before.

She curled up against a solitary rock on the surface of the butte with the intention to sleep. The cloak kept out the worst of the cold as long as the woman remained positioned as a tightly curled ball, and by now her body was so beyond protest of discomfort that she no longer felt the rocky surface below her or frigid air around her body. The stone below her began to reflect the bright lights that circled the moon, but the woman refused to look up, aware of how badly her body needed sleep. Rhea closed her eyes and began to doze just as the wind picked up, whipping her cloak off of her head and filling her ears with its oppressive hum.

"I'm trying to sleep here," Rhea croaked out to the darkness. The wind seemed to pick up in reply, gusting against her with new determination and howling like a banshee across the rocky surfaces. Rhea covered her ears with her hands as the world around her was suddenly filled with mournful sound, high whines like the air being letting out of a balloon filled her ears one moment, lower tones like air passing over a bottle opening the next. Her hands could not keep out the sounds of the rushing, howling wind, the skittering noises of the creatures below and the occasional scream as some flying creature passed overheard. The woman's whole body began to shudder uncontrollably at the onslaught of sound upon her ears and she wrapped her cloak around her entire body in an attempt to dim the furious noise.

The wind died down at the first ray of sunlight and Rhea cautiously pulled the cloak off her head. Sleep had not come the night before and every small sound made the pounding that had developed in her head beat across the back of her eyes. She made her way over to the ledge and down the small stone ladder with muscles that shook from lack of nourishment and exhaustion. Dry, chapped lips gulped at the still, cool water as Rhea allowed her body to simply lie in the wet sand at the edge of the pool. Straw-colored hair floated at the water's edge, danced gently on the surface as the water rippled in response to the woman's breathing, to the occasional disturbance of her hand breaking the surface to sprinkle the liquid over her already over-heated body.

Her eyes were even darker when Rhea stared at her reflection in the pool on this day. They were a black matte, with no reflection of light, no indication of the intelligence locked away in the mind. They were already the view of survival, of grim determination just to take the next breath, to live one more hour, then another, then another. A dull ache filled her chest as the view reminded her of one of her mother's common sayings. "I can always tell if you are sick by the lack of light in your eyes." She closed her eyes and let an exhausted sleep take her as she once again stretched in the cool sand, fingers and hair resting in the life giving water.

She awoke after several hours as the hot wind howled and wailed and the sun slid down into the rocky landscape. This night Rhea got no further than her rocky ledge before curling up in her cloak to try to muffle some of the pounding noise. After many hours Rhea became aware of a different noise, softer than the wailing of the wind, which seemed to be coming deep from the mountain. The woman cautiously removed the hood of her cloak from her head and turned towards the back of her rocky ledge. A black darkness now took the place of solid rock, and before stepping into the dark tunnel, Rhea paused to wonder if she was hallucinating from lack of nourishment.

The tunnel was long, with slick, wet walls formed as cool water gently seeped down the side of the stone. Just enough moonlight glowed off of the damp walls to light the way for the woman to walk slowly over the uneven stone floor. Soft wailing and keening flowed along the walls towards her ears and Rhea followed the sound, step by long step, until she saw fire light reflecting from a large cavernous room under the mountain.

Rhea flipped the cloak over her now bright blonde hair and cautiously moved towards the room. Three women stood around a small blue fire, hands linked in comfortable companionship and lips parted to create the keening noise Rhea had heard from her rocky ledge. Their eyes were closed, thick black lashes set against faces with skin so pale it was almost white. Long, ivory hair fell to the waist and all three women wore long, thin, gowns of gauzy alabaster fabric to cover their pale bodies.

Suddenly the woman directly facing Rhea abruptly stopped her song as her eyelids snapped open to reveal crystal blue eyes that seemed to pierce through the air towards Rhea. The other two women fell silent, as well, and then turned to see what had disrupted their sister's song.

Rhea stepped forward, convinced now that this was a starvation-induced nightmare. "Hello. My name is Rhea. Who are you?"

The woman stepped forward and in a voice that tinkled like crystals said, "We are the Aos Si. We keep watch over Steinbrekka and the creatures it keeps."

"Steinbrekka, is that the name of this place? Why am I here?"

"This is indeed Steinbrekka. Once a beautiful place, now it is a wasteland carved from stone. You have most likely been sent here to die, for that is the only reason why people tread this earth. How is it that you have not yet faded into the nothing?"

Rhea inched closer to the warmth of the fire. "Sheer stubbornness, I suppose. I guess I have a few more days until my body starts consuming itself from lack of nourishment."

The second, slightly shorter woman stepped aside to allow Rhea closer to the heat of the fire. "Yet you have survived for quite some time without water. How can that be? All of the others died within days of no water."

"Well, I – I drank from the pond, down below, during the day when those shadow creatures were not at the water pool. There is a stone ladder of sorts on the wall that I am able to climb down and up again."

The third woman hissed in displeasure, then silenced at a stern look from the first woman. "You drank from the pool?"

"Yes ma'am. I'm sorry if I wasn't supposed to do so. It's not like anyone is giving me instructions here. I'm just trying to figure out things as I go and stay alive until I can go home."

The second woman chuckled softly, the sound bore resemblance to a cat purr. "No, I suppose they did not. Most people do not get instructions for how to die."

The third woman spat into the fire. "She should not be here. She should not have taken water from the pool!"

"Yes, yes, but she did and is here now. Come child, sit by the fire and warm your soul for a moment as we sing."

Rhea sat by the fire, legs curled up and her chin tucked on her knee, for quite some time. The women continued their singing, the melody changing now to a soothing, healing song. Tears fell down Rhea's face as the enormity of the events of the past days; weeks even, finally made their way through her altered state. Not only had she been kidnapped into a strange world with kings and a prince, but someone out there was actively trying to kill her by starving her and leaving her out in this soul-starved world.

After far too short of a time the women gently helped her up and led her back to the cave entrance. The first woman kissed Rhea on each of her closed eyelids. "My name is Sorella. I will keep you in my heart."

Rhea was immediately assaulted by the sounds of the wind, of the creatures skittering below, of her own heart that beat heavily and strained against her ribcage. Her hair whipped around her face even in the shelter of the rocky ledge and small pieces of stone flew into her body, barely buffered by the heavy woolen cloak around her shoulders. She cautiously stepped onto the path leading towards the top of the hill and was blown back into the rocks by the force of an invisible hand.

Several failed attempts at leaving the rocky ledge finally convinced Rhea that she would get no further that night. She curled up against the stone wall where the tunnel was just moments before and covered herself with her cloak. Head tucked between her knees, Rhea fell into a restless sleep with her back pressed against the cold rocks.

She awoke a few hours later to the sound of absolute silence and incredible warmth surrounding her once frozen body. Rhea looked up at the sky, amazed at the clarity of the stars in the black sky above her head. She was certain that there had not been any stars since she came to this place, yet there they were above her head, sparkling like small diamonds scattered on a velvet cloth. The moon was high and round in the sky but no longer blinding; instead it seemed to cast off a glow like a small heat lamp in the night. The swirling colors of the past nights had settled into bright, stationary star patterns beautiful in design and soothing to view. Something beside her moved, and Rhea froze after turning her head to the side.

One very large green eyeball was staring straight at her. As it slowly blinked shut, Rhea looked in fear and wonder at the head of soft white fur the size of a small suitcase, which was then connected to a body of tawny brown fur as soft as individual strands of silk. Rhea's head was resting on a large furry paw the size of a throw pillow and a long fluffy tail was curled around her body, providing the warmth she had so desperately needed. The animal yawned, revealing rows of white canines set in a mouth large enough to pull in Rhea's head like a person eating a grape.

The woman held herself perfectly still as the animal sniffed her face, then gently moved away from her, jumped off the ledge and disappeared into the night. *I'm dead*, she thought. *That's the only explanation there is for what just happened. I kicked the bucket and am in some sort of screwed up heaven where there are giant white lions with fluffy squirrel tails that curl up with you in rock crevices to keep away the wind which is trying to drive you mad.*

She sat up in the rocky shelter and realized how desperately thirsty she felt. The small creatures were still down around the water hole, yet tonight there was something different about them, something more real. Tonight she could see rich mahogany-colored fur on their bodies instead of just shadows, and could hear small snuffling noises along with the skittering of their claws. Instead of looking feral and vicious the animals appeared to be playing with one another, grooming, or curled up on the floor below in what seemed like companionship.

Rhea took a step towards her stone ladder. Maybe she could just sneak down there and get a sip of water, just a small one, to tide her over until morning. Maybe the creatures would not notice her in their current state of mind.

"I would not do that if I were you." The soft, halting accent made Rhea stop in her tracks. "You may be seeing them more clearly now, but your presence will not be welcome until you see yourself more clearly. Come with me to the top, I have what you seek." Rhea slowly turned to see an ancient woman standing serenely by the path to the higher ground. She beckoned to Rhea, a gentle smile on her face, then turned and silently glided up the rocky slope with a slow grace that Rhea attributed to a lifetime of walking over uneven ground. Rhea scrambled up the slope behind her and her feet stumbled over the loose stones. "Who are you? Why are you here? Where did you come from? Am I dead?"

"Ah, so many questions." The woman reached the top and sat in the center of the moonlight, gathering her wiry limbs into a comfortable position on the hard ground. The light of the moon seemed to be absorbed into her hair and clothing, casting the woman's body into various hues of gray shadow. Silver hair was pulled into the ashy colored hooded cloak loosely draped over the woman's head. Clear yellow eyes fixed on Rhea as hands with skin so thin it was nearly transparent patted the ground next to her. "Come sit, child."

Rhea cautiously sat down next to the old woman, mentally exhausted from all that had transpired earlier that night. "Can you please tell me what's going on? I don't know how much more I can take of this. Who are you?"

The old woman tenderly patted Rhea's hand. "My name is Ayewoke." She pulled food and a leather flask of water from her robes. "Eat and drink, child, slowly, mind you, and I will answer your questions if I can."

Rhea forced herself to slowly eat the food in front of her, taking small sips of the mint infused water. "Where am I?"

"You are in the kingdom of Kaldalangra, well into the territory of the King Verikhan of the DamaTalous. Specifically, you are in the rocky and desolate region known as Steinbrekka."

"That's what the other women said, too, Steinbrekka," Rhea said through a mouthful of soft cheese.

An assessing eye was cast on the woman, causing her to swallow the cheese quickly and blush. The old woman chuckled low in her throat, "So you have met the Aos Si then and lived. I should have known that by your eyes. Impressive, my child. Next you will tell me that the Malakhor came to you in your sleep."

Rhea shook her head, "I don't know what a Malakhor is, but I did wake up with a large white furry creature with big fangs curled up around me."

Ayewok sucked in a sudden breath and narrowed her eyes, staring down at the ledge. "Then you did meet the Malakhor. He is a very powerful being, and very wise in the people he chooses to help. You should not take such an encounter lightly."

"To be honest, I'm just happy he didn't eat me!"

The old woman chuckled. "Yes, well, he normally only eats people after playing with them."

Rhea choked on the bite of food she was currently chewing. "Playing with...Actually, I don't think I want to know the answer to that question."

"No, a wise person would not want to dwell too long on that thought. The Malakhor is said to be a protector who has long awaited the arrival of his particular human."

Rhea stared at her fingernails, torn and ragged, and nodded. "Then I am lucky he decided to protect me and not the other option." She glanced at the grandmotherly companion. "Could you tell me how to get home? Do you know if I could get from this world back to where I came from? Back to where I belong?"

Ayewok smiled, the action both sad and serene. "You are where you belong now. It may take a little while to get you home though. Perhaps this is meant to be your home now." She patted the young woman on the arm. "Now you go close your eyes and get some rest. I will keep the elements at bay for you for this night."

Rhea stood up slowly and gave a small bow of respect before carefully descending to the rocky ledge for the first tranquil sleep she experienced since arriving in this strange world. *I want to be home,* she thought before the darkness took her. *I want to have a home.*

~ * ~ * ~

The bright noontime sun flooded Rhea's eyelids with brilliant oranges and reds, causing the woman to stir and crack open an eye. Her stomach felt oddly full for the first time in weeks, but her throat and mouth were still parched after a long time of abuse. The woman quickly but carefully made her way down to the pool of water and took several long swallows of the clear water.

Rhea closed her eyes, and then splashed water onto her face and hair before realizing that, while the sun was bright, her skin was not burning and the heat was not as painful as it was before. Rather than the scorching inferno, the heat had turned into comfortable warmth, like when a person wraps herself in a thick blanket on a chilly day. She opened her eyes and gazed into the water, only slightly alarmed when bright blue eyes stared back from her reflection.

These were not dead eyes however, and that lifted her spirits slightly. The blue danced with the ripples of the water, alive and filled with promise. If she looked deeply enough small flecks of green could be seen around her pupil, not noticeable to the casual observer but definitely there. Her hair had settled into a deep blonde, the color of honey, and her skin had shed its red inflamed burns to reveal a light tan across her body.

She took another deep drink and settled comfortably onto the damp sand, drawing little nonsense pictures with the grains to pass the time. She felt so relaxed, so at peace that she did not notice the small creatures braving the light of the sun, and creeping closer to her position on the water.

They froze when Rhea looked up at them, rooted in their tracks by the bright blue eyes. A couple of the small animals made chitterling sounds at their companions on the edge who scampered off into the shadows of the rocks. Rhea very slowly pulled her legs under her body, ready to get up and try to run if she needed to do so.

"I see you now small creatures," she said slowly in as soothing of a voice as she could muster. "I have seen you in the moonlight and for what you truly must be. I don't know much about you, but I see that you play with one another instead of fight, and that you care for each other like a family. I see now that you are not as evil or vicious as I originally thought and are just prone to the moods of a regular animal."

The smallest of the creatures crept forward inch by inch, belly low to the floor in the manner of a dog that had been subdued by a creature higher in the pecking order. The creature did not stop until it reached the shadow created by Rhea's cloak, at which point it curled up into a tight ball like a cat, staring up at the woman with wide white eyes.

"I won't hurt you, hopefully you won't hurt me. Are you hot in this sun?" Rhea scooped some water into her hand and gently extended it towards the creature. A small pink tongue came out of the brown mouth and cautiously lapped the liquid out of her hand, fur brushing against the tips of her fingers and eyes closing in a sign of trust.

Suddenly, a terrified squeal came from the creatures further away, and they scattered into rocks as quietly as seeds in the wind. Rhea saw a shadow fall over her shoulder and turned around, slowly standing up as she realized a rider on a horse was standing just a few feet away from her.

The rider spoke softly. "Not only are you alive, but you managed to coax the Ellyn out into the daylight. Impressive, my Lady." Lianna pulled her thin cloak off her head, lips in a joyous smile and green eyes shining with unshed tears. "Come, Rhea, mother sent me to bring back your body. It will bring her great joy that I bring you back alive and whole."

Chapter Five

Steinbrekka

Amber light filled the space behind Rhea's eyelids as she stirred out of slumber. She cracked open her eyes, shielding them from the light with her hand and wondering why the blistering heat did not follow the brightness. The sky above was a clean white, with gold streaks and a beautiful eight-pointed flower suspended above her head. The woman blinked and stared up again, her brain slowly registering that she was inside a room, and curled comfortably on a soft, downy bed.

Rhea sat up slowly and looked around. If her first room was surprising then this room was beyond expectations. Larger than the average two-car garage and filled with furniture covered in thick silk cushions, the room was airy and sunlight poured through four large glass windows. An opulent chandelier hung in the center of a raised dome in the ceiling, the multi-sized crystal prisms scattering the light into small rainbows that danced across the pure white walls.

She slowly walked over to the large wardrobe located in the corner of the room using muscles that still protested from their rough treatment over the last week. The wardrobe was sixteen feet tall, and wide enough that she could step onto the sturdy wooden base and not be able to touch any of the four walls. One section of the wardrobe was filled with beautifully constructed, elaborately jeweled formal gowns reminiscent of colored wedding gowns. Another section was filled with long, full dresses made of the finest silks and embellished with simple, golden threaded designs. Colors filled the wardrobe;

golds, reds, blues and brilliant purples. Under each dress sat a pair of jeweled shoes in matching hues, daintily made and with straps so thin they appeared non-existent.

The deep rumble of voices shifted Rhea's attention to the large and intricately designed door. She hurried to it and pressed her ear upon the soft wood, straining to hear the conversation on the other side.

"Her transformation was completed, Rowan, but there is still a depth to her eyes. She appears to fit the part but I am not sure exactly what happened out there." The woman, Lianna's, voice trailed through the door.

Rowan let out a sigh. "Well, we had better hope she is smart enough to keep her mouth shut then and not let anyone know there is still something in her head. That will do her no favors, even with the blonde hair."

"I will speak with her about that when she wakes up." Lianna's voice trailed off, and then urgently whispered, "Rowan, the High Prince approaches."

Rhea scrambled back into the bed and under the soft comforter just as the sounds of a brief scuffle streamed through her door. She quickly rolled her back to the door to give her body time to slow her frantic breath and heard the thick door swing open.

"She has still not woken up, High Prince. I will be sure to call you when she does and is presentable." Lianna quickly crossed the room and Rhea felt her soft weight as she sat next to her pillow.

The Prince's deep voice gave off the distinct tone of annoyance that increased as he walked towards the bed. "Well then let us hope that she awakens soon. It has been three days and my father grows impatient."

Rhea felt a hand move the blonde hair that had fallen over her cheek and forced her expression to remain still. Then the hand was hastily removed and she sensed another body between her and the man.

Rowan stood between the bed and the Prince, every muscle poised for fight. "You will have her in your own time, Prince; you need not start while the woman is unconscious."

A haughty laugh followed. "Ah, de Nespa, I think you forget. My desire is law and I can do whatever I damn well please." Then she heard the sound of boots ringing across the marble floor and a door slamming.

Lianna smacked Rowan across the shoulder as Rhea cracked open her eyes. "Do not antagonize him, you idiot. This is going to be hard enough to manage successfully without you causing your own mess."

Green eyes blazed and then cooled as the man saw he was being watched from the bed. "Or maybe that is exactly what we need. I can make him so agitated with me that he will not notice the woman learning how she is supposed to act. He will not notice little errors or be prone to spend extra time in the company of others if he is so agitated by my behavior that all he wants to do is challenge me."

"You will not win any challenges, you know that!" Lianna turned towards the wall to collect her emotions and tried to unclench her fists. "You will not do any of us any good if he starts looking so closely at your actions that he starts realizing that he does not know everything that goes on at court!"

Rhea softly cleared her throat, breaking their conversation. "I can handle my own, but thank you for the offer. I've realized that if this is a dream I'm not waking up any time soon, so I think it is time for Lianna to teach me what I need to know."

Rowan let out a snort of disgust and stalked out of the room, muttering, "Stubborn, foolish females," over his shoulder.

"Is he always that prickly?" Rhea forced her weakened abdominal muscles to assume a seated position on the bed.

Lianna chuckled. "Only on some days, dear. Now let us get you moving and get some food into your body."

The two ladies made their way to the plush, silk armchairs and sank their feet into the soft fur rug. Lianna had brought up a tray of warm beef stew, thick hunks of freshly baked bread and a pot of strongly brewed mint tea. She ladled the stew into two decorated porcelain bowls, handed one to Rhea, and then poured the tea into the heavy ceramic mugs after dripping golden honey into the brew.

After many silent minutes Rhea swallowed the last of the stew in her bowl and relaxed into the back of the chair. "I'm guessing I wasn't supposed to survive out there, was I?"

Lianna set down her mug and shook her head slowly. "No, you were expected to survive. What was not expected was you returning whole of mind. The Transcinare is designed to drive all rational thought from the mind; to leave the individual with the basics instincts of survival but not the ability to make higher decisions or use their own logic. All people who are brought to this realm go through the Transcinare, it is the way."

"All people who are...you mean there are other people like me? There are other people who weren't born here and don't belong here?"

Lianna's stern but caring look curbed Rhea's enthusiasm. "There are other people like you, but with rare exception they were all fully transformed. They know only what they were taught after the process and nothing about their other lives or the world where they once lived. Only four people have remained mentally intact after the Transcinare, and you are one of them."

Rhea sat forward, hope born again. "And who were the others? Are they still living in this realm? Maybe together we could-"

"I cannot name them all without the risk of death, but..." Lianna leaned forward and lowered her voice, "I can tell you I was one of them. There is no hope of going back Rhea. Time does not work the same way across the land and it does not work predictably."

"Where were you from? When were you taken?"

Lianna leaned back and closed her eyes, pulling memories that had been long pushed back into the depths of her mind. "I was taken at the age of fourteen from my home in the province of Connacht, in the time of the Queen Medb. I had absent-mindedly walked into a circle of white mushrooms, we called them a fairy circle, and the next thing I knew I was falling in a glass tube and landing here. That was sixteen years ago."

Rhea stared at the woman, fresh bread in her hand forgotten. "Queen Medb...but she was part of the Ulster cycle in Celtic myth...she was rumored to have lived around the time of Christ! Lianna, I came from the year 2009. Over two thousand years have passed in our old world and only sixteen have gone by here?"

The woman shrugged. "Time moves differently for everyone. The last important person to be taken had a slip of paper upon which the number 2005 written. He has been here for 10 years by our time."

"But that's...incredible and makes no logical sense."

"It is what it is. Now, you have a choice to make." Lianna stood up and walked over to the large wardrobe in the room. "Either you can stay here and let your body rest further, or we can take a very gentle and slow walk about the castle and I can start showing you your new life."

Rhea took in a deep breath. "I may need frequent rests, but after the events of this morning I feel it would be best to learn this new life as quickly as possible." The woman slowly stood up and stiffly walked over to the wardrobe beside Lianna.

A dress the color of chocolate soon covered Rhea's emaciated body. The long sleeves and thick fabric created warmth inside the garment and the modest neckline fell just below the woman's collar bone. The full skirt brushed the ground and trailed slightly behind her as she moved, and the stitches were done with miniscule, impeccable detail. Lianna also gently placed a sheer veil of matching hue over Rhea's head, securing the fabric with crystal studded hair combs and covering the woman's long hair.

Lianna pulled a piece of sheer gray fabric from her wide sash and secured it over her own head. "The first rule of your new life is this; the head must always be covered while in public. All women of noble standing, including their servants, must always have the head covered unless they are in the sole presence of their spouse or are ordered to remove the covering by the King himself." She looked straight into Rhea's eyes. "Rhea, if the King ever tells you to do anything, you will do it. Protocol, rules, everything is thrown out the window when it comes to the King's demands. His word goes above all else so make certain you follow it, understood?"

Rhea nodded, feeling the thin fabric flutter over her shoulders and brush into her peripheral vision. "Keep head covered, obey the King. Got it."

"It is also very important to keep the rest of your body covered as well." Lianna gently draped a russet-colored angora cloak over Rhea's shoulders and clasped the mother of pearl fastener. "No one is to see your skin other than your spouse or your personal servants, understood? In the summer months the court relaxes a bit due to the heat, but make sure that you always keep your lower half covered all the way to the ground. A good rule of thumb is to watch the Princess Nyssa. When she starts showing her arms in public company, then you may consider it safe to do so as well."

The two women opened the door and walked into the hallway, passing the guard Rhea had nicknamed "The Giant" at his post just outside the bedroom door. Lianna turned and gave the man a small bow, motioning that Rhea was to remain upright. "This is Savin. He is your Komisar, or personal guard, and is here for your protection. If you ever go off the castle grounds or into a public space you must be in his presence. If you are ever viewed outside your room without his escort he will be punished for his inability to complete his duty, so do not attempt to go anywhere on your own."

Rhea nodded silently, awestruck by the elaborate hallway that had opened in front of them.   As the women slowly walked, discussing more rules and protocol, she reached her hand out to touch the walls. They had been constructed of a translucent marble with the consistency of glass. Shadowy figures in bright clothing could be seen walking along a parallel hallway in some areas, whereas in many places the wall darkened into an opaque material. Lianna explained that the darkened marble protected privacy and signified the presence of a chamber requiring such thick walls, such as a bed chamber or bathing room.

At regular intervals Rhea also found another type of room which caused her some initial confusion. The walls were the same transparent color, yet there were thin doors placed in the wall and tapestries in the interior. Many figures were seen standing by the walls or sitting in the elegant furniture but no clear details could be distinguished after the glass distortion.

Lianna looked at the subject of Rhea's fascination and smiled. "Those are courting rooms, sometimes called social rooms." She opened the door to an unoccupied room and motioned Rhea to follow her inside. "These are used for young couples who wish to have a small bit of privacy while courting. The walls are relatively soundproof and do serve to hide facial features, but still are open enough where a couple cannot be accused of relations out of wedlock." She paused and watched Rhea walk around the room, slowly taking it in. "It is also often used by friends as a place for socializing without requiring an official chaperone."

Rhea moved to the middle of the room and slowly turned around. A thick beige rug covered the floor, bright yellow chairs and couches were positioned by the side walls, and faced one another to aid conversation. A small table was placed in the center of the room and was covered by a cotton cloth of slate color. The wall hangings were brightly dyed threads woven into hunting scenes and elaborate ballroom images.

The two women left the small room and slowly moved back down the hallway. Lianna led Rhea down a wide set of gleaming marble stairs which led to a lower floor of the castle. Here the walls were a white stone, not quite as opulent as the marble above but still with enough beauty and richness to have made all of the kings in Rhea's world envious. Gold thread lined elaborate banners and tapestries gently swayed from their fastening atop of the vaulted ceiling all the way to the gleaming azure floors.

Lianna led the way through the small groups of people, with an occasional curtsey to an individual placed on their path. She led Rhea up a small flight of stairs onto a balcony overlooking the large room.

"Now, this is the Poibli Frien. This is where the Patrons of the realm gather to socialize and create a presence. There are three types of Patrons in our realm; The DamaTalous, Personae de Valeur, and the Pengesum."

Rhea gazed over the brightly clothed people below them. "The DamaTalous are the royal family members and can only be named as such by birth or marriage, and even in marriage they might not be labeled as such unless judged worthy. The Personae de Valeur are the men who gained their high status through military achievements." The woman faltered and her brow furrowed as she tried to remember the last. "I don't remember reading about the Pengesum."

"The Pengesum are those who have achieved their status through wealth alone. The Pengesari are the wives of the wealthy men, for women cannot hold their own wealth in the realm and must rely on the status of their husbands or fathers." Lianna gestured and walked through a heavy curtain to the other side of the balcony. "Here we have the Mercenes, or those who are hired by the court. Personal servants, such as me, are also included in this caste even though our social standing is almost equal with a standard Patron due to the company we keep. You also see below you the Fuldt Hus, or the house servants."

This room functioned as a large hallway, or possibly foyer, between the Poibli Frien and the main door to the court. Servants worked at a feverish pace to keep the floors swept and shined while they paid close attention to the movements of the doors. When a Patron walked through all work halted and the servants quickly moved to the sides of the room, eyes downcast and head bowed to avoid contact with the Patron.   The room was not nearly as expensively decorated, but still held Rhea in awe of its opulence. Benches and straight backed chairs were positioned against the side walls, with a small antechamber that served as a storage area for the voluminous and heavy cloaks of the Patrons.

Suddenly all movement stopped as an obvious figure of authority stepped into the room. The Fuldt Hus scattered into alcoves that appeared, almost magically, behind the floor-length embroidered panels.   Patrons suddenly turned their eyes down and lowered themselves to the floor, the women in deep curtseys that defied leg anatomy, and the men in bows low enough to brush the floor with their shortly trimmed and well-styled hair.

Lianna hissed and pulled Rhea back behind the curtain. "Get back here, that is Kofizek , the Komisar of the High Prince. We cannot let the High Prince see you walking about after this morning's insistence that you are not well."

Rhea moved back behind the curtain, parting it ever so slightly to peer through the sheer hanging in front of it. The man who entered the room behind the Komisar was the man in white whom Rhea had seen at the stables those first days after the kidnapping. He was again dressed in a snowy hued pair of soft leather pants, with a thick vest of gilded leather across the broad chest. Ice blue eyes surveyed the room and a sneer came across his features as he observed the crowd bowing in submission. He turned his head to address a patron by the wall and Rhea could barely contain her gasp of surprise and shock as his face came into full view.

"Lianna," she turned to the other woman and whispered frantically, "that's my friend Matthew, the High Prince is my Matt! The one who went missing!"

Lianna grabbed her arm in a firm grip and her eyes blazed with fear. "No, it is not. That is the High Prince Mateo Verikh de Kalda. That is all he is, Rhea."

"But it's not! That's my friend who disappeared four years ago, that's-"

The elder woman cut her off and clamped her hand over Rhea's mouth, moving her beside another curtain as the High Prince and his guard walked into the Poibli Frien. "Listen to me, Rhea. It does not matter who he used to be, or what your relationship used to be, all that matters is now. And now all he knows is that he is the High Prince, sole heir to the realm of Kaldalangra. He is ruthless, blood thirsty, and will let nothing, absolutely nothing, get in the way of his power. Your Matthew is dead. Mourn him and move on or none of us will survive."

Chapter Six

The Court

Several days later a young woman appeared at Rhea's door, looking nervous. She entered the room and dropped into a deep curtsey. "Forgive me for intruding, my Lady, but the Lady Lianna has asked that I come prepare you for dinner. "

Rhea placed the book of protocol on the table next to her and slowly rose. The short time since her return from Steinbrekka had healed most of her body, but her muscles still protested if she moved too quickly from a seated a position. "But where is Lianna? I would have thought she would have wanted to be here herself."

The servant girl wrung her hands so tightly in front of her body that Rhea feared for the small bones inside. "I do not know, my Lady. I only know that the Lady sent me here with instructions to prepare you for dinner. "

"Well then," Rhea gave the girl an encouraging smile after realizing she was terrified, "we had better get started. I'm afraid to admit I am still hopeless with the fashion of this realm." She walked over to the wardrobe and opened the wide doors. "Which dress would you suggest...Lady?"

The young girl flushed red. "Oh no, I am not a Lady, my Lady. If you wish to speak to me you can simply call me girl, or servant, or 'you there'."

Rhea took a gamble on revealing too much and asked the girl, "Well, what is your name, then? I find it difficult to speak to another person only by calling them girl or servant." She desperately hoped that her intuition was correct that Lianna would not send her a girl who would betray their secret.

The girl gave a nervous laugh. "Yes, Lianna said you would probably say that." She took a deep breath, as if about to reveal a great truth. "My name is Faina, my good Lady. I am the daughter of the washer lady Inna and am training to be a true Mercene under the instruction of the Lady Lianna." A few hesitant steps brought her beside Rhea and Faina peered into the wardrobe. "May I suggest the plum dress? It will cast your eyes into a lovely shade of blue."

Rhea smiled and pulled out the plum gown. She carefully stepped out of her current simple gown and, with Faina's assistance, donned the new dress, holding her breath as Faina tightened the corset back. Like the dress before it, the gown was floor length with a slight train that gently swept the ground behind her heels. Long silken sleeves ended at the wrist with delicate lacework, and the scoop neck of the bodice was enticing while still being modest. Intricate beadwork adorned an adjustable leather cord that sat lightly on her hips, emphasizing her figure and then draping down the contours of her outer thighs.

Both women moved over to the mirror and Rhea carefully sat down on the stool in front of Faina to get her hair styled. Faina efficiently pulled the wavy blonde locks up into a beautiful and elegant coiffed style which was secured with small jeweled pins. Then she knelt in front of Rhea and expertly applied the customary cosmetics for the realm, even though her shaky breathing betrayed her nervousness. She gently draped a violet veil over Rhea's head and gently fastened the cloth with amethyst studded clips.

Faina stepped back and gave a small smile. "You look beautiful, my Lady. Good luck at dinner. Savin will escort you to the dining hall." The girl gave a quick curtsey and swiftly exited the room.

Rhea looked in the mirror and smiled to herself, then looked at the door. *Where is Lianna that she was unable to come tonight?* A cool wave of fear rippled through her body as she realized the full implications of a dinner summons. She suspected this would be far more than the casual dinner conversations that she and Lianna often held in her room or in one of the privacy rooms.

She stepped out of the room and nodded a greeting at her Komisar, Savin. He gave her a short bow and offered his arm. "May I escort you to dinner, my Lady."

Rhea arranged her features into a smile. "I would appreciate that, good Sir."

The two walked down the hallway in silence. Finally as they neared the dining hall Rhea halted in nervousness and turned to Savin. "Who else will be present at dinner this evening?"

One of the muscles in the giant guard's jaw-line twitched. "The entire DamaTalous is scheduled to be present at dinner tonight, my Lady. The King will be delayed but will also attend."

The woman gave a quick nod and stepped forward to the door. *Best to get this over with,* she thought, *the first step is always the hardest and most frightening. Time to show there is some steel in that backbone.*

The dining hall was elaborately decorated with large murals, intricate tapestries, and small marble tables that lined the spaces by the smooth walls. Small doorways sat beside and behind many of the tapestries, and Rhea guessed that these passages must lead to various kitchens or serving rooms. In the center of the massive room a monstrous black wooden table stood with thirty sturdy and beautifully carved chairs lining both sides. The five diners who had already arrived turned as Rhea walked in, and the woman was struck with the beauty of the people seated at the table.

On the far side of the table sat familiar faces, their dark hair and complexions a stark reminder of the differences between them and their companions. Lianna sat at the table, expression tense and grave and she did not smile as she looked up at Rhea's entrance. Beside her the guard called De Nespa sat with a face of stone as he continued in hushed conversation with the beautiful blonde woman across the table from him. Next to the guard sat the Lady Risalka, whom Rhea met briefly her first day at the castle. The woman was even more stunning at the table with her hair expertly pinned upon her head and clothed in a deep blue gown.

On the near side sat two exquisite women. One turned from her conversation with De Nespa to look at the newcomer and Rhea was immediately struck by the quiet power she emitted. Shining hair the color of goldenrod swept down her back in an elaborately tied braid while bright blue eyes shone in a perfectly proportioned face. This woman alone stood up as Savin nudged Rhea toward the table and her face lit into a warm smile.

"Welcome, Rhea. We have waited quite some time for your arrival. Are you feeling well?"

Rhea curtseyed with as much grace as she could manage and quietly responded, "I am feeling quite well, my Lady, thank you."

The woman's eyes sparkled, though her words were still quite reserved. "Your placement at the table is this chair here, my dear." She gestured to the seat directly to her left, and across from Lianna, and then sat down herself.

Rhea sat down slowly, then watched as the green-eyed guard stood and had swift but inaudible words with her guard, Savin, along one of the lesser lit corners. She went to address Lianna but was silent when she saw the subtle, but very clear head shake from the woman ordering her to remain quiet.

The second blonde slowly swirled the liquid in her cup. "Shall we start taking wagers on how late dinner will be served tonight?"

A muffled snort of laughter came from the woman beside Rhea. "Quiet, Agrafina, they might hear you."

"Well, then shall we talk about our embroidery lessons that are occurring later in the afternoon?"

Then all talk silenced abruptly as a door swung open and the Komisar of the High Prince walked through the room just before his Master. All of the women quickly stood in a fluent motion, and Rhea curtseyed low with her eyes to the ground as the man walked into the room and approached the table.

Risalka was the first to straighten, and said, with her eyes lowered, "Good evening, High Prince, Heir of the great realm of Kaldalangra. I wish to present to you the Lady Rhea who will be dining with us tonight and into the future."

The man's eyes sharpened, the blue eyes seeming to pierce Rhea through her skull. "It seems to me the future will greatly depend on the outcome of the present evening. It seems quite presumptuous to assume there will be one for any person seated at this table."

Rhea kept her eyes studying the carpet as the man walked over to her, and steadied her anxious breathing by examining the tip of his finely crafted leather boots. Unyielding fingers grasped her chin firmly, and lifted her face until her eyes gazed upon his own. "Well, at the very least you are much prettier than the last one who came through. I am sure I will find some enjoyment from the process this time, even if the end result is not that which is desired." The man released her face and then turned to Lianna, "You will bring her to my waiting chamber after dinner. That is not a request."

Lianna gave a curt nod as he moved away from Rhea and sat down at the seat to her far right, next to the second blonde woman.

This must have been the cue, for now all of the women once again resumed their seats. The two guards separated, Savin seeming to meld into the wall by one of the tapestries and the other, de Nespa, returning to his seat between Lianna and Risalka.

Other men and women began to filter into the dining hall, all adorned in great finery, and all in complete silence. When the last had taken their seat Rhea counted all thirty seats were filled, with the exception of the finely gilded seat at the head of the table, recently carried in by a servant. Curiously, Lianna's side of the table still contained only those who had darker features, and Rhea supposed these were all Mercenes who were given the privilege of accompanying their Patrons to dinner. The group on Rhea's side included variations of blond hair, and the ages appeared to be between mid-twenties and late thirties.

The wide door where the High Prince entered swung open once more and all of the people at the dinner table stood as one, like a giant flock of birds lifting out of the water. Rhea followed Lianna's cue and curtseyed very deeply, eyes downcast and head bowed. In her peripheral vision she saw several of the guests drop down to their knees in reverence of the man entering, whom Rhea surmised could only be the King.

Two loud claps rang through the room and the people surrounding the table straightened and sat down at their seats. The King's great booming voice flooded through the room. "Welcome, my people. Sit and enjoy the bounty which has been provided for us on this fine night."

Food suddenly appeared on the table in front of Rhea, roasted birds, potato dishes, large baskets of breads and exotic vegetables flooded the smooth surface. A deep blush wine filled the goblets of the women while thinner amber-colored liquid welled up into the men's smaller, clear glasses. China plates so thin that they were translucent held the mountains of food from the table. Everyone moved slowly, deliberately, as if every person in the room was afraid of making a noise in the quiet, over-sized room.

After people had finished the main course, the King clapped his hands twice again and a well-dressed Mercene walked into the room. The King's booming voice rang out once again. "Bring on the entertainment, as well as the dessert!"

Almost instantaneously ten women entered the room and began to dance beside the table. Sheer fabrics highlighted their slender bodies, muscles moving in sync with music that floated out from the walls of the room. Rhea risked a guarded glanced down the table. The King and High Prince appeared fascinated with the women, entranced as they danced by the table. The blonde women beside her looked uncomfortable, keeping their eyes downcast and paying intense attention to the small pastries that had materialized on their plates. After some time the music trailed off, and the women stood in line, eyes downcast as the King rose from his seat.

"Which shall it be tonight, eh?" He boomed. "The selection is impressive; I believe I shall need your assistance, my family and subjects!"

Lips of all the women tightened and all of the women on the dark side of the table closed their eyes as their foreheads furrowed in fearful anticipation. Rhea spared a look down the table and saw that the High Prince now looked bored, de Nespa had a look of forced indifference, and the other men of the table appeared to be flushed and excited. She spared a quick glance at the King, since the women appeared to be looking that direction, but with faces carefully cleared of any emotional signs.

He was a large man, easily over six feet tall and with a powerful build. His hair had been shaved close to the head so that only fine straw stubble was visible beneath the large and richly jeweled crown. He wore a tight jerkin of black and red silk, with a deep purple cape draped over one shoulder. The man moved closer to the table and stopped behind Lianna, who had squeezed her eyes shut so tightly it almost pained Rhea to look at her.

"Shall I choose from the table tonight, my good friends? Or choose from the dancers?"

Calls went out from the males. "The dancers, my King, the dancers."

The large man let out a hearty laugh. "Ah, they have truly impressed tonight, have they?" He walked to stand behind the dancers, gesturing to each in turn as the crowd cheered the women in varying degrees of boisterous assent. Finally, he pulled one out of the line-up and pushed her towards his servant. "She is the lucky winner of the night. I will not keep her waiting for long."

The young woman walked out of the room, face void of all expression while a single, long breath seemed to be released from all other women in the room. Rhea sensed movement to her right and observed the woman next to her twisting a ring on her right hand around her finger, out of nerves or excitement she was not quite sure.

Dinner finished at a rapid pace after the selection process. The King made his royal exit, followed by the High Prince who gave Rhea one more assessing look after whispering something to the blonde directly beside him. De Nespa stood and offered his arm to the woman directly beside Rhea, escorting her out of the room without a backward glance. Lianna approached Rhea as Savin materialized from the wall and stepped behind the women as they left the room.

"I do not think he will want to do anything tonight," she furtively whispered as they walked down the hallway. "He has had too much to drink and Agrafina looks reserved, which is normally a sign that he summoned her. Just do what he says so that this first meeting will be over quickly. Savin will wait outside the door to escort you back once you leave. Make sure you wait in the hallway until he is there, it will not be safe for you after leaving the Prince's room."

Rhea nodded, focusing on moving one foot in front of the other as they walked down the gilded hallway. Her head was slightly spinning from the wine that had been offered at dinner, even though she drank sparingly and only when her still sore throat cried out for moisture. After what seemed like far too short of a walk the trio appeared in front of a large door covered in gold plates and a carved suit of arms.

"This is where I must leave you, Rhea." Lianna leaned close and whispered, "Remember not to think, not to show reason or how much of yourself you have contained. It is alright to be afraid, he will expect that and is probably looking forward to it, but do not show a reason to be afraid other than that he is the High Prince and you are humbled in his presence." She leaned closer, "and for all of our sakes, do not even think of mentioning who you think he might have been, understand?"

A quick nod, and then the door opened and Rhea was being shuffled into the receiving room. Deep couches lined the room, as well as benches and the occasional set of stools, all covered in a rich purple silk. Heavy black curtains hung over huge windows and blotted out any sign of the outside world. Two of the walls were created of doors, seven on each side, and the third wall held an elaborately decorated wooden door that seemed thick and secure.

Rhea slowly turned in the room as curiosity overtook fear and she wondered what hid behind those doors. She started to walk toward the center of the room when the black curtains were flung open and the room was filled with a blinding white light.

"Hello, little mouse. Welcome to my waiting chamber."

Her breathing quickened against her will at the flash of light and realization of the man in the room. She did the only thing she could think of in the situation, and dropped into a deep curtsey. "I thank you for this opportunity, my Prince."

Once again the leather boots appeared in front of her, and a firm grip on her jaw forced her to a standing position. She sucked in a nervous breath and she tried to remember what Lianna said, that in his mind, he was no longer her beloved Matt.

The man stood there, gave her a calculating series of looks and then took a confident step backward. "Turn around, slowly," he commanded.

Rhea obeyed, quelling the emotions threatening to bubble to the service.

"And who are you, woman?"

She desperately tried to remember the script she had worked out earlier with Lianna. "Well, my Lord, I have not yet truly discovered that. I do know that my name is Rhea, and that I am a subject in this realm, but everything else has yet to be written in my story."

He smiled then, the act hardly encouraging but only creating a tight knot of fear in Rhea's stomach. "Yes well, it will all make sense in time, have no fear of that. If you are a good little girl you may even have the great honor of becoming my Forena. That is why you are here after all. Do you know what that is, little pet?"

Rhea's breath came fast and hard as she remembered the Book of Protocol. "No, my Lord, I do not believe I have been told of that role in the court yet." She felt his warm breath as he stood just behind her, as he lightly rested his fingers on her lower arms.

"Perhaps you should read your protocol book, my dear, I suggest chapter twenty-three. It will be highly...educational." Then he abruptly moved her toward the door and opened it, addressing the guard standing in the hallway. "I am done, take her away."

Savin once again offered his arm and Rhea took it, grateful for any sort of support both for her nerves and her shaking muscles. Now she understood why she was brought to this realm, why her hair and eyes were changed and why she was taken to become a mindless puppet. She composed herself as they walked, wished Savin a good night, and blew out her single candle before she allowed the tears to fall.

Chapter Seven

The Court

In the days that followed Rhea poured over her protocol book, more certain than ever that her only chance of survival was to completely understand the interplay of the court relationship. The Forena, as she remembered reading in her first weeks here, was the consort to the High Prince. She was awarded certain privileges within the court system, but mostly was at the mercy of the High Prince's bidding every second of the day. Chapter twenty-three was an incredibly detailed account of how the Forena was to act in the presence of the High Prince, both in public and private quarters, and several passages caused a bright red to rise to Rhea's cheeks as she began to feel the full weight of this responsibility.

It also did not help her growing anxiety that Lianna seemed to have disappeared from her circle, and instead the girl, Faina, arrived in the morning to help Rhea get prepared for the day. The dark-haired woman still sat across from her at the dinner table, but refused to speak to Rhea and avoided eye contact as much as possible. She missed her talks with the other woman, always informative and filled with humor. She felt the loneliness keenly and, after several days of emotional isolation from the woman, Rhea decided she would seek her out and figure out what was wrong.

Rhea knocked on the inside of the door, a habit she developed once when startling Savin out of conversation with the green-eyed guard, then stepped out. Both men were in the hallway and turned her way as the woman stepped out of the room, nodding a polite greeting at both.

"I would like to see Lianna please. Could you tell me where she is at this time or bring her to my chambers?"

Both men cleared their throats, looking anywhere but in Rhea's direction and fingering the edges of their fitted shirts. After a long moment Savin looked up and responded, "I apologize, my lady, but we cannot reveal that information at this time or request her attendance. The woman is currently in service of another Patron and cannot be contacted until she has been released." He shifted uncomfortably on his feet. "Is her replacement not fulfilling her duties to your satisfaction?"

Rhea kept the knot from rising into her throat at the thought of not being able to see Lianna. "Oh no, she is very good. It's just that I miss…" An odd look from de Nespa caused the sentence to catch in her throat. "It's nothing. Forget I ever asked." She turned to leave and go back into her room.

Savin halted her with a gentle touch to her shoulder. "My lady, Rowan and I were just discussing the state of disrepair to the back garden. I have seen the way you look out the window, and we were wondering if perhaps you would like to view the garden?"

"A garden? I could go outside?"

The giant nodded, "As long as I accompany you, of course." He smiled at her for the first time since she was brought here and the motion softened his features. "Contrary to how it must seem, you are not a prisoner here and have the ability to go where you want, within reason."

Rhea thought about the implications of this statement as they walked silently through the corridors in an unfamiliar direction. After several minutes, Rowan opened a small wooden door and stepped aside to let Savin, and then Rhea step outside.

The bright light took Rhea by surprise and she closed her eyes briefly against the glare. She scanned the immediate area of the garden and was taken aback by the state of the foliage around her. The plants were all covered in a fine frost, causing them to become brittle and threaten to shatter at the slightest touch as the group moved along the overgrown paths. Slender saplings rose out of tufts of grass and bushes, thin and weak, bending precariously without the support of gardening stakes. Reds and pink hues of fully bloomed roses and lilies glistened under a thin frost casing and small petals littered the ground around the glass-like plants. The men stopped, and Rhea looked up at the man standing in front of her on the pathway. He seemed as old as the earth itself, with a thin, long beard that hung down to his chest, and his gray hair streaked with sections of pure white. Rhea curtseyed low, and the man smiled.

"Welcome, child, to the frosted garden. What brings you here on this fine day?"

Savin stepped forward with a respectful bow. "Good day, Dmitri. The lady was feeling a bit shut up in the castle after all this time, and we thought a walk through the garden would do her spirit well."

The older man nodded. "If the lady would like future chances of sunshine I could always find some light tasks for a young woman with castle fever. Feel free to explore, my child, just be wary of the plants. They are quite fragile as you can see."

Rhea nodded, her attention suddenly drawn to the shape of a small red dot sitting on top of a lily leaf. She carefully knelt down in front of the tall plant and looked curiously at the ladybug encased in frost. She turned to Dmitri and inquired, "How do the plants come to be this way, Sir? I see no frost or other sign of cold when I look out into the main courtyard, yet this garden seems as if it is living in the dead of winter."

Dmitri smiled sadly. "That is a very astute observation, dear Lady. The garden thaws at night to allow slight growth and enable the occupants to survive, but just. Every morning the frost coats animal and plant alike, and once almost coated my person, as well."

The woman turned back to the ladybug. "I wonder if they could be thawed with our help…" She turned back to Dmitri and looked into his eyes, surprised to see a pure white iris. "Good Sir, I have given you no indications of my nature, or any sign that you should trust me, but I would like to try to save this little ladybug. Do I have your permission? I swear to you that I will try my best not to cause harm in this place."

Dmitri nodded stiffly, and as Rhea moved closer to the leaf with its tiny occupant she did not notice the look of surprise and apprehension between the two guards. She very carefully threaded her hands between the layers of icy leaves until both lay cupped under the precious little bug, then carefully blew warm air onto the icy bug. The bug gave off a slight red glow as a layer of ice melted and then froze once again. Rhea blew a second, third, fourth time to the same results. *Please little bug, please let me save you from your prison as I cannot save myself.*

The frost slid off of the bug then; the tiny creature tumbling from the plant into Rhea's waiting hands. She drew them out of the leaves and carefully clasped them together, creating a small pocket of warm heat with the ladybug in the center. After a few anxious minutes Rhea opened her hands slightly, and saw one of the little legs wave from the center of her palm. The hands closed once again and she drew them into her cloak, lending her body heat and the heat of her thin cloak to the bug. Finally she felt a tickling sensation on her palm, and opened her hand to see the ladybug moving about her palm, gaining strength with every miniscule step.

Dmitri walked behind her, eyes wet at the sight of the ladybug moving about her palm. "I think this garden has been waiting for you, my dear woman. For the first time in my long life a creature lives during the frost time."

Rhea gasped as the ladybug suddenly spread its small red wings and flew off her hand. Her breath caught in her throat from fear it would land on a frozen plant and become trapped again. The small bug landed on a frozen leaf, and when it flew up again a small puddle of water the size of the bug was left behind, welling up into a droplet, then slowly falling down the leaf, leaving a trail of brilliant green exposed to the sunlight and free of the binding frost.

The group of people stood silently and watched as the small bug landed on several plants, leaving water drops on each plant as it landed and then once again flew off. After each landing the color of the plant blazed through the small hole in the frost, bright greens and reds, and occasional blue or white. They stood there for an hour just watching the small water droplets increase in amount as tiny parts of plants were slowly being exposed.

Savin looked up at the cloudy sky and broke the spell. "We should get you back inside, my lady. If you like, we can come back in the morning."

The woman nodded in appreciation. "I would like that very much, Savin." She gave a curtsey to the old garden keeper and followed the two men back through the door into the castle.

Chapter Eight

The Court

After only a week the state of the garden was much improved. While Dmitri reported that the frost still came every morning, it was not able to touch the parts of the flowers that had been affected by the ladybug. Rhea had attempted to warm the plants in a similar fashion but found she was unable to keep the frost from returning by her actions alone. She focused her efforts on finding the small bugs of the garden and freeing them, then watching in amazement as the small ones acted as little droplets of heat and magic, spreading through the garden to melt away the frost. Beetles, ladybugs, small grasshoppers and dragonflies, all were reanimated and worked tirelessly to release the plants around them.

Rhea's relationship with Savin also bloomed through their daily visits to the garden. She still felt the sharp grief from Lianna's unexplained absence but it was slightly dulled by the occasional smile from the stoic guard as they spent time in the private place. There was also the increased presence of the guard, Rowan. Generally a figure of silence, aloofness and invulnerability, there were times in the garden when Rhea saw him tenderly hold a newly freed leaf or caress a bright red rose finally free of the frost prison with a soft smile upon his face.

On this day Rhea decided to test the truthfulness that she was able to walk about the castle with her Komisar. She woke with the sun and dressed in thick woolen socks, a plain brown dress, and heavy leather boots. After the customary knock on the inside of the door she stepped out, surprised to see Rowan outside her door instead of Savin.

"Good morning, Lady Rhea. You are up early today."

"Oh, yes, um good morning, Rowan. I must confess I did not expect to see you here." Rhea peered down the dark hallway. "Is Savin feeling unwell?"

The man chuckled, almost revealing a smile. "Even a Komisar with the skills of Savin requires sleep, my lady. Several of us rotate the night watch so that he is able to better protect you during the day."

Rhea blushed at his words, annoyed with herself that she would have had to have such a basic function explained to her at all. "I should have realized that. My apologies. Rowan, I was wondering if I could go to the stables today. It has been quite some time since I have been around horses, and I believe the insects can do more good in the garden now than my presence."

The mask of caution once again slid over the man's features. "I am not sure that would be wise this early in the day, my Lady. The stables will not have been cleaned to Patron satisfaction this close to sunrise and not the proper place for a Lady such as yourself."

"I believe I will be quite well in that environment." Rhea hated that she could not keep the pleading tone out of her voice. "Please, Rowan, I'm just...I need something normal, and in my world dirt is normal."

Rowan gave her a curious look for several heartbeats before finally acquiescing and leaving a small cryptic message for Savin in a small notebook tucked into a stone niche as to their whereabouts.

As they stepped outside Rhea pulled her dark hood to conceal most of her face, mindful of the few people who were out and about already. The boy at the scarf stall looked at her and Rowan curiously as they passed and Rhea pretended not to notice the small leather bag that Rowan quickly pressed into the boys palm as they brushed by.

Other servant vendors were also out early that morning as customary, each setting out their wares for the day and cooking a meager breakfast over small fires. They all nodded a silent greeting as Rowan walked by their stands and the glances that followed the woman beside him were filled with both curiosity and apprehension. Rowan gave three soft taps on the stable door as the sun crested the horizon and began to spill light onto the world.

The young man Rhea saw who argued with the guard on her first day opened the door, grinning at Rowan and then looking at Rhea in fright. "I am very sorry, my Lord Rowan, but we are not yet prepared for one of such status as my Lady."

Rowan glanced at Rhea, lifted his eyebrow and smirked, and then turned back to the stable hand. "I informed the Lady of this fact and she told me she would like to see some dirt instead of marble floors." He smiled at the young man, the action seeming to warm the room and melt away the fear and doubt.

"Ah, well, then," the man ran his dirty hands nervously over his linen shirt and stammered, "We have plenty of that about here, no doubt about it." He looked at Rhea with his eyes half closed in respect and bowed low. "My name is Aleksei, my Lady. Welcome to the stable." He began to lead the couple further into the stable, describing the various rooms on their way to the place where they bed the horses.

The tack room was larger than any Rhea had previously seen in her years of riding, and filled with leather pieces that had been polished until they shone in the dim lamplight. Gold and silver strands flowed over the leather in intricate designs, whirls and family crests, and geometric designs of all sorts. Saddle blankets were fringed with thick tassels of braided silk and small jewels were inlaid into the saddles and the leather of the bridal pieces. Rhea estimated that there were hundreds of tack sets, and wondered at the amount of horses that would require such a large amount of riding gear.

She noticed a small doorway in the rear of the room. "Aleksei, where does that door lead?"

Rowan coughed to cover a chuckle. "Aleksei, would you mind giving Kalar a quick brushing and we can show her to the lady."

The boy hurried away, not bothering to conceal his look of relief at the dismissal.

Rhea's eyes followed the young man down the hallway. "I'm sorry, Rowan. I did not realize such a question would make him so uncomfortable."

The man's green eyes looked directly into her new, blue ones. "I know, my Lady. You must realize that people here do not ask such questions. People like Aleksei, the servants and the lower class; they know to respond to orders and commands and are afraid of questions. Questions are used to trap, to ensnare a person with a wrong answer which can easily result in death." He put a comforting hand on her shoulder as the blood rushed out of Rhea's face. "That room leads to the room where the personal riding equipment of the DamaTalous is stored. It is to be accessed only by their Mercenes and no eyes are to fall upon the equipment without permission of the family."

The two walked down the hallway and stopped where Aleksei was grooming a beautiful dapple gray mare. The young man smiled hesitantly at the beaming smile that came across Rhea's face. "Oh, she is so beautiful!" Rhea approached the mare slowly and offered her hand for the horse to sniff. "Look at you. Such a pretty girl, aren't you." She ran her hand slowly on the mare's forehead and the horse lowered her head into Rhea's chest for a thorough ear scratching.

While the woman was thoroughly enthralled with the mare Rowan pulled Aleksei into a side stall and the two conversed in low tones. "Aleksei, I apologize for the fright that was given to you when the Lady asked her question. She is new here and does not yet fully understand the implications of such questions."

Aleksei nodded, absent-mindedly petting the horse that occupied the stall. "I did not mean to react so poorly, Rowan, just took me by surprise is all. It is not often one such of her stature and position does not have malicious intent behind such questions." He peered between the wooden slats of the stall as the woman gave the mare a gentle kiss on the soft nose. "She is special is she not, Rowan?"

The guard's features darkened and his voice grew husky. "Yes she is, and she is also destined for the High Prince. It is only a matter of time before she can no longer be trusted."

"That is a sad thing indeed, my Lord. Is there no way you could just -"Aleksei coughed as he received a glare from the other man. "Never mind then. I apologize for overstepping."

"She is intended for the heir to the throne, Aleksei. That is what Risalka said and that is what will happen. We cannot change her purpose in this world because she seems to be a decent person."

"And because she came out of the Transcinare, and she likes dirt, and is clear intentioned, and released the Queen's frozen garden, and because I can see hints of green in her eyes, and-"

"Enough!" Rowan tried to rein back his frustration at the stable hand's words. "Enough, Aleksei. If I could spare her from this fate I would, but I cannot. It is the way it will be, just like everything else in this realm. There is no changing the life we are given, all we can do it survive each day."

Both men froze as they heard Rhea give a soft greeting towards someone behind the horse.

~ * ~ * ~

Rhea peered around the horse's shoulder once again, "Hello there. Why are you hiding in the corner?" She gave a gasp of shock as Rowan, unsheathed knife in hand, was suddenly pulling her behind him, startling the horse that was quickly restrained by the stable hand.

"Who goes there? Reveal yourself!" Rowan boomed into the stable.

Rhea pushed Rowan away from her, hand against his shoulder. "For goodness sake, it's only a cat!"

Rowan looked behind the horse as a little gray cat walked cautiously around the horse's large hooves. "A cat? A cat?" He stepped out of the stall quickly and stalked down the aisle, fuming silently and jaw muscle twitching as he attempted to regain control of his emotions.

The woman knelt down and put out her hand, pleased when the cat came over and rubbed her head against her. "Hello pretty kitty. Do you live out in the barn? I bet it's a nice place for tasty snacks and you can find a lot of warm places to nap."

The cat purred loudly, wrapping her thin body in figure eights around Rhea's legs. The woman gave her a scratch near the base of the tail and laughed. "Classic elevator butt," she said as the cat's hind end rose up in the air and her head dropped to the ground. She turned to Aleksei. "Is she always this friendly with strangers?"

Aleksei looked at the cat in wariness. "Actually, my Lady, I have not seen this cat before. All of the cats in the castle are bred to be either pure white or orange, and gray cats-" he flinched at the kindness in Rhea's eyes as she pet the feline, "well, gray cats are not allowed to live long enough to open their eyes, much less grow old enough to prowl around the stables."

Rhea picked up the cat in alarm and held her close. "But then how did she get here? She seems friendly enough that I can't imagine she was feral and just wandered in here." The cat pushed her head against Rhea's chin, put her small paws on Rhea's shoulder and softly kneaded the fabric. "I don't suppose I could keep her? If I kept her in my room, or maybe brought her out to the garden she would be safe enough, don't you think?" She turned her eyes to Rowan and the cat's yellow eyes stared at him in tandem. "She's so old and skinny. I think she wants me to help her."

Rowan gave a brisk nod and helped Rhea to her feet. "We had better get back quickly though. The last thing we want is for you to be seen wandering through the castle with a small gray cat."

They hastened toward the door with a last caress for the mare as Rhea tucked the cat as far into the folds of her cloak as she could manage. They were met at the door by the young boy from the shawl stand.

"Excuse me lady, but I thought this would be of assistance to your need." He bowed deeply and presented Rhea with a brilliant shawl, one side of the fabric brilliant shades of emerald, cobalt blue, and turquoise. The other side of the shawl was an equally fine design made of various shades of silver and grays.

When Rhea only looked at him in confusion he blushed and turned to Rowan, eyes downcast. "You see, my Lord, I thought…well. I saw your Lady having trouble with her parcel, so I was – was thinking that maybe, that is, that it might be, I mean-"

The guard put his gloved hand on the boy's chin, causing him to look up in such a similar manner to the High Prince that Rhea felt a pulse of apprehension course through her body. "Use your words, Nastasio, they are safe in this company but others will be stirring soon."

Nastasio straightened, a newly found confidence and pride in his voice. "My Lady, I see that you carry that which you wish to conceal. My mother and I agreed that your small companion would be much safer wrapped up so as to be secured out of view of the court." He extended the shawl once more and Rhea allowed him to gently wrap the cat so there was only a small hole for air and nothing more. "There you are. Now anyone will see only a Lady carrying a newly acquired shawl." He gave Rowan a sly look. "Although perhaps your guard wishes to carry the package to spare your arms from the strain."

Rowan's lip twitched as he worked to contain an emotion and gently took the shawl-wrapped cat from Rhea. He then gave the boy a stern look and glanced at the woman watching them from behind the shawl stand. "Perhaps your mother would like to come to the garden alcove when darkness falls and hear what I think about your suggestion."

Nastasio gave a hasty salute as a worried look fell across his face, then bowed deeply before hurrying across the plaza toward his mother.

They walked in silence a moment before Rhea finally said, "I could trade something to them. I don't have money, and things seem to appear for me, but maybe I could trade one of my veils for the shawl? Would that be adequate payment?"

Rowan guided her into the hallway leading to the Poibli Frien. "His mother will receive the payment for his words and actions in the traditional way. Payment methods for the boy's advice are none of your concern."

Rhea stopped short, horrified at the implication of his words. "But the boy just meant to help and is helping! And now you're talking about taking his mother into a bad situation just because he suggested you carry-"

"It is the way things are done, Rhea. That is enough." He dropped his voice lower as several servants looked their way, and then quickly bowed their heads. "Do not think you can change things, my Lady, no one has that power here but the King. Everyone of the realm has accepted that and you must, as well."

They spent the remainder of their walk in stony silence, unkind words and phrases contained as they threatened to burst from Rhea's head. After what seemed like ages they arrived at her room and, after a quick hello to Savin who was once more by the door, Rhea took her new companion inside her small sanctuary and slammed shut the door.

Chapter Nine

The Court

Dinner that night was a tense affair for all involved. Lianna looked haggard and drawn, now sitting further down the table and facing a strongly-built man in his middle years with a fierce and unforgiving face. Rowan was seated directly across from Rhea at the table and, with the exception for the rare need for civility, Rhea alternated her interactions with him between veiled looks of anger and ignoring any attempt at conversation. The blonde seated beside the High Prince also looked shaken and withdrawn, speaking only when directly addressed and merely picking at her food. The blonde next to Rhea alternated her concerned looks between Rowan and the woman next to her, once kicking the guard under the table to get his attention and narrowly missing Rhea's legs on the way.

During one lull in the conversation the blonde woman quietly said, "Rowan, it would greatly please me if you would meet with me after dinner to discuss an issue with a peasant vendor. It is of vital importance."

The man nodded but remained silent, draining his cup of brandy as he pushed away from the table. "I bid you all goodnight. Lady Nyssa, I will attend to you at your summons." He then abruptly walked out of the room.

The blonde then slightly turned toward Rhea. "I think we need to speak later, as well, Lady Rhea. I will come to your chamber after the tenth bell."

Rhea opened her mouth to protest, but then silenced it as she saw the man across from Lianna stand up and lead her roughly out of the room. Perhaps this woman could help, or at least knew what was going on with her friend. She nodded and murmured a quiet, "Yes, my Lady."

~ * ~ * ~

The tension spilled out of the dinner hall and the walls seemed to pulse with the heartbeats of the castle inhabitants. Rhea was very subtly ordered to remain confined in her room by Savin and paced in front of the window, occasionally stopping short just before tripping over the little gray cat that enjoyed walking between the woman's feet. When she looked out into the courtyard the servants also seemed to be filled with a sense of unease. They carefully set up their shops, taking special care to arrange their goods in a pleasing manner and glancing around nervously every time another movement was detected. The stable horses seemed as anxious as their human counterparts. Hooves scraped against stone as the horses danced beneath their riders and startled at every small noise or movement, poised for immediate flight at a moment's whim.

A small mew from the cat below brought Rhea's attention back to the room and she sat down on one of the trunks so her small companion could jump into her lap. "What's happening lately little cat? Do you know why everyone is so tense these days? I wish you could tell me what is happening with Lianna, or what the Prince's intentions are, or any of the millions of questions about this creepy place that are threatening to spill out of my heart."

The little cat pushed her head into the woman's chin in a feline hug, purred for a few seconds and then tilted her head to assume a thoughtful expression. Then, as if she had made a decision in her small furry head, the cat jumped off her lap, crossed the room, and nimbly leapt onto the table holding the protocol book. A quick flick of the paw resulted in the book tumbling to the floor and falling open, wrinkled pages exposed. She crouched down then, lowering her head so that it was barely above the faded writing on the pages. Her tongue flicked out and began to turn the pages of the book and did not pause as Rhea moved closer and sat down on the floor behind the animal. Finally the pages fell still, and the cat turned to give Rhea an imploring look before she settled her gray body comfortably on the woman's lap.

Rhea bent over slightly and stroked the cat with one hand, attention drawn to the writing on the page. A quiet knock sounded on the door, subtle and soft but perfectly timed to startle Rhea and cause her heart to race. She quickly stood up, placed the cat next to the bed with a quick motion for the animal to hide, and then went to the door.

"Good evening, Rhea, may I come in?" The blonde woman who had spoken to Rhea at dinner stood in front of the door, the image of royalty with perfectly coiffed hair and an immaculately pressed gown.

Rhea curtseyed low and motioned for the other woman to enter her chamber. Savin remained in the hallway, unconcerned and more intent on the dark shadows of the hallway than the new guest in her small sanctuary. She closed the door gently and turned to the woman.

"I'm afraid I quite lost track of the time and did not send for refreshments, my Lady. If it would please you I would be happy to do so now and it will be sent up in a timely manner." Rhea motioned for the woman to sit in one of the chairs as the blonde turned a slow circle, taking in the decorated chamber.

The woman turned towards Rhea, her face a blank mask of emotion. "That is quite fine, Rhea, do not worry yourself over refreshments." She walked over to the chair and her face paled as she picked up the book from the ground. "Doing some light reading? What would inspire you to peruse this chapter at this time?"

Rhea silently cursed that she forgot to close the book. "Truthfully, my Lady, the book fell from the table and that is the page which presented itself. I have yet begun to read the instructions presented." *What did this woman want,* Rhea wondered, already exhausted by the careful court dance of words and actions. *Can't she just tell me so I can get back to the book? Why is she so freaked by the page?*

"You may call me Nyssa, Rhea, I grow weary of hearing 'my Lady' every time someone speaks in my company."

"Yes my…Nyssa. I will try to remember to do so diligently."

Nyssa let out a quick sigh, breath slightly puffing up the hair so elegantly styled over her forehead. She opened her mouth to speak, and then shut it quickly as her attention was quickly drawn to the foot of the bed. "Rhea, what is that?"

Rhea turned to look at the bed and felt clammy fear surge through her body at the sight of the tiny gray paw sticking out from the safety of the bed. "It's nothing, just a…um…a small stuffed creature which I found in one of the chests, surely intended for a child but it gives me company nonetheless."

Naturally the cat chose that moment to cause mischief, and promptly retracted the paw as the two women watched. Rhea looked at Nyssa anxiously. "A mechanical…animal…toy." Rhea's breath caught in her throat as the cat fully emerged from under the bed, slowly stretched her body in a nonchalant manner, and then wound her way around the women's feet.

Rhea quickly picked her up and held her protectively against her chest. "Please, Lady Nyssa, she found me when I was in the stable and…and the guard said that she would be harmed, so I brought her here where she would be safe. Please don't hurt her, she's-" Rhea's voice cracked with emotion and she cleared her throat, "she's my only friend here and won't cause any harm."

The mask fell from Nyssa's face and revealed a person full of laughter and love; her eyes shifted to a tint of green and she reached out to pet the cat that had started to purr with such veracity that her whole body vibrated. "Relax, Rhea, I will keep her secret. How did you get her up here without anyone noticing?"

The feline squirmed out of her arms and landed lightly on the carpet, then moved to curl in front of the fireplace and looked up at the women with expectant yellow eyes.

"Well, I was with the guard, Rowan, and I was hiding her under my cloak to try to get her up here unnoticed. A young boy approached us with a shawl and gave it to me to use to wrap up the cat so that I could get her into the castle." Her expression grew serious as she remembered the rest of the night. "Then the guard threatened the boy because he suggested the guard carry the cat up instead of me, which seemed logical considering how the other Patrons interact with their guards."

Nyssa's gaze softened and she placed a hand on Rhea's shoulder. "Things are not always what they seem in this realm, Rhea. That goes for the good and the bad. Do not discount your guard for one transgression." She sat down on one of the benches and pulled her legs up closely to her chest, dress falling down in ripples to cover her body. "Is it truly so lonely for you here, Rhea? I am aware of how different this place must be from your old home, but I thought Lianna would have helped keep the darkness at bay. She may be a Mercene by birth and training but she is a good friend by nature."

Rhea fought back the tears that threatened to spill over her eyes by blinking rapidly. "Lianna has been assigned to another Patron for the past couple of weeks and I have only been able to see her at dinner. She looks so withdrawn and as if she is afraid and in pain. I'm both afraid for her and sad because of her absence."

Nyssa nodded and put her chin on her knees, toying with the ring on her finger. "What of your other servants? Do you not like the company of Faina, Savin, or," she paused and smiled slightly, "the guard, Rowan."

"Oh I like them very much. Faina is very competent and Savin and Rowan are very good at what they do. It's just, different. I'm used to having friends, real friends, not servants who have to act amicable and pleasant."

The other woman's finger came to rest on a small design carved into the trunk below her. "And this room?" she asked, looking intently at Rhea, "Does this room suit you?"

Rhea looked around and a smile lit upon her lips. "It is a beautiful room Nyssa, and far more than I would have expected given how I came to be here. The clothing is beyond belief and I continue to find small little ladybugs and butterflies carved into the furniture which makes me smile. It seems like the room for someone far more important and loved than just a kidnapped girl from a different world."

Nyssa smiled sadly. "Yes, it was once the room of the most wonderful woman ever. But, I think you do not give yourself enough credit. This room is yours now, and seems to have adapted quite nicely to its new inhabitant." She stood up, straightening the rumples of her gown and gave Rhea a small squeeze of encouragement on the shoulder before walking to the door.

"Get your rest, Rhea, tomorrow morning we will see the Kontorist and try to get your friend back."

Chapter Ten

The Court

The wing of the Kontorist's office was large, yet surprisingly simple in design. An expansive waiting room was adorned only with a series of benches that reminded Rhea of rows of church pews. The sun had just crested the horizon so Rhea was surprised to see the room was already filled with the residents of the realm, Patron and lower classes alike. Opulently dressed Patrons sat in the front pews closest to the door, most looking relatively calm and collected and rather bored. The servants' place in the chamber was further back, a clear delineation of power and status between the two castes. Most of the servants looked terrified and could be seen wringing their hands, glancing around the room nervously, and holding small babies closely to their chests.

Nyssa motioned for Rhea and her guard, Savin, to step forward through the center aisle straight to the door. She glanced at the guard under her eyelashes, the perfect image of demure obedience beneath her veiled head. "I have come with a prospective member of the DamaTalous. Allow us to enter."

The guard gave a curt nod, motioning for Savin to remain standing by the door as the ladies entered. Once inside, Nyssa turned to Rhea and whispered, "Standard procedure, no guards are allowed in the room except the Komisar of the Kontorist."

Rhea nodded and focused on moving one foot in front of the other. The room held very few types of finery and instead of elaborate tapestries and wall décor, the walls were covered with large bookcases and heavy chests. The room reminded her of her archaeology lab, how far away that seemed, with the cases of site reports, field notebooks, and walls of maps.

The Kontorist was a small man, the white and feathery hair an indicator that he was a man of great age. Small spectacles perched delicately on his nose and his right finger tips were smudged from a lifetime of exposure to the black ink of his trade. The extremely spacious desk he was perched behind held large stacks of paper, which were then whisked away by several young assistants to be sorted into appropriate folders and drawers along the bookcases and chests.

"Who is the sponsor?" The man did not even look up as he moved a fresh sheet of parchment in front of his newly inked pen.

"Nyssa Verikh de DamaTalous." Nyssa spoke clearly, causing the Kontorist to jerk his head up quickly and stare at the women intently.

"Ah, Nyssa, it has been some time since I have seen you here." He released a small, quick smile before returning to the mask of indifference. "Name of the applicant."

Once again Nyssa spoke as she signaled Rhea to remain silent. "Rhea Aralia."

"Eye color, age, place of origin, caste, distinct identifiers..." The questions rattled off at a speed that made Rhea's head swim. She paused for a moment to wonder how Nyssa knew the answer to all of these questions, but decided in the end it did not matter and she did not care.

The elderly man finished the last piece of information with a flourish and handed the paper to an assistant to be blotted and dried. "And is there anything else I can do for you, dear Lady?"

Nyssa graced the man with a smile. "There is, good sir. Now that Lady Rhea has been added to the files of the realm, she wishes to establish her personal Mercenes."

The man nodded, rifled through the papers and pulled out a sheet. "Very well, very well, and completely expected. And who, pray tell, is the Komisar?"

"Savin de Caislean."

"Yes, yes, understandable, and the primary lady in waiting?"

"The Lady Lianna de Dhome, daughter of the Washitza Risalka de Dhome."

Intensely bright eyes stared up into Nyssa's with keen interest. "Is that so? I will have my assistant release her from her current assignment then."

Nyssa nodded. "It is so. Lady Lianna's assistant is to be Faina, daughter of Inna. I also require you to document a secondary Komisar for the Lady."

He hissed under his breath, grabbed another sheet of paper and mumbled, "What game are you playing here Lady, assigning all of these high status Mercenes and guards to a - ."

"Rowan de Nespa will be the secondary Komisar. This is not negotiable. None of this is up for discussion."

Sharp eyes pierced through the air as the man stared at Nyssa and slowly wrote the name onto the parchment. "This is most unorthodox, Lady Nyssa."

She bestowed upon him another smile, both warm and calculating, and a second at his assistant. "I am aware of that, my good sir. I trust your wife is feeling well?"

He shuffled his papers and handed the newest parchment to the assistant to dry. "Yes, yes, quite well thank you. I was just commenting on the situation. No need to get in a mood. Well then, that is quite done. Rhea Aralia has been added to the Patron list of the DamaTalous and now has listed in her household one Savin de Caislean, Rowan de Nespa, Lianna de Dhome, and Faina daughter of Inna."

Both women gave a deep curtsey of respect before leaving the room, gathering Savin who looked oddly anxious and uneasy. The three walked down several hallways before Nyssa pulled them into one of the parley rooms. The moment the door closed she quickly gave Savin a hug before pulling Rhea into a brief embrace.

~ * ~ * ~

"He did it! I knew he would but did not hope to guess he would have put up so little of a fuss about the whole thing. It is in the papers! Savin, you are officially Rhea's Komisar with Rowan as your lieutenant. The Kontorist's guard will fetch Lianna this evening and she will occupy the room beside yours, Rhea. All you need to do is tap thrice on the small bell by the fireplace and she will be at your side."

"Ok wait." Rhea rubbed the back of neck. "What does this mean now? Why did we put it into writing instead of just going like we are now? I'm not following the situation."

Savin smiled down at her. "Nyssa just gave us immense protection and moved us up a couple of notches in the caste system by putting this in writing. Without having it on paper I can act as your Komisar, but if challenged by an individual of higher caste than myself, which is most male Patrons, I would have to acquiesce to their demands. Because Nyssa went on record as your sponsor, and listed me as your official Komisar, the only people who can challenge my presence in your life are the King and the High Prince."

Nyssa also smiled. "It also means that they cannot be called into service of anyone else, which is the situation Lianna finds herself in currently. They will serve you and you alone unless you dismiss them from your service and go on documentation as enabling any other Patron the use of their services."

All three fell silent as the door to the room opened and Rowan slid inside. Savin gave the man a wide grin. "Just wait until you hear what Lady Nyssa has been busy doing today!"

Rowan shook his head, features grave and breath heavy. "The Catturra has begun. Unless we can get out of this castle immediately we will have to report to the armory with everyone else."

Savin shook his head. "No, Rowan. We are bound to protect the Lady Rhea. We go where she goes unless she orders us to leave her side."

"In an ideal world, yes, but unless that has been ratified by the Kontorist..." His voice trailed off at the grin shared between Savin and Nyssa. "You were able to get it ratified? All of us? Who is listed as her sponsor?"

"I am on the record as her sponsor." Nyssa laughed. "As to the first question, the Kontorist owes me a few favors. He has repaid part of his debt today." She let out a squeak of breath as Rowan came over and hugged her tightly, then kissed her on her cheek.

Both men dropped to one knee in front of the women. "What would you have us do on this day, my Lady? Your will is my life."

Rhea bit her lip and looked to Nyssa in confusion. "Um, I, I don't know. Nyssa, what would I have them do?"

"Violence roams the earth tomorrow. I require both of you to remain outside Rhea's door and use your own discrepancy for rest. Lianna will join us tonight for dinner. Tomorrow, Rhea and I will both fall victim to food poisoning from the breakfast meal and be unable to receive any guests for quite some time."

The men nodded and escorted the ladies back to Rhea's room. Nyssa gave Rhea a small hug before leaving to be escorted back to her quarters by Rowan. "Try to get some rest before Lianna comes. The next few days will be trying and you will be greatly needed."

Chapter Eleven

The Court

The cat's claws digging into her shoulder awoke Rhea from her rest as Savin knocked urgently on the door. Rhea sat up and called for him to come in as she rubbed the sleep from her eyes. When he did she bolted out of the bed to help him support Lianna, who looked as if she were too fragile to stand.

"Lianna! What happened? Who did this to her?"

Savin gently laid Lianna down on one of the plush couches, carefully propping her head on a down pillow. "The Kontorist's assistant gave the Patron permission to keep her until sunset after telling him that she was now ratified into your service. He was less than pleased that he would not be able to call on her when he so desired and now this was the result."

Rhea gently pushed his large body out of the way and took inventory of Lianna's condition. Her face was various shades of blue and purple, with deep bruises covering her skin and rising into her hairline. Her neck showed similar bruising, along with a deep, linear mark that looked as if a rope had been tightly wrapped around her neck and pulled with enough force to darken and break the skin.

Nyssa rushed into the room then, barely glancing at Savin or Rhea as she kneeled beside the couch and placed a soft hand on Lianna's face. "It is okay, Lianna. It is going to be okay now. We are going to take care of you and this will never happen again." She turned to Rhea and Savin and quietly said, "Rhea, could you please tell Rowan to fetch her mother. Savin, lean her up so I can undo the buttons on her dress."

Rhea rushed to the door, unsurprised to see Rowan pacing outside. "Nyssa said to go get Risalka."

"How bad is it?"

Rhea bit her lip as the tears started to fall. "We've only seen her face, but I think it's bad."

The man hurried down the hallway and Rhea stepped back into the room, frozen in action at the sight of Lianna's body. A whip had been methodically applied to her back, the welts angry and red, the skin split and bloody in areas where there was overlap. Her arms and legs were covered with small burns as if someone placed hot coals onto her skin and left them on the flesh. Small, precise lacerations lined her upper torso, giving her skin a spider web-like appearance beneath their tangle of bloody lines.

Risalka pushed past her then, and Savin stepped back to allow the wise woman better access to Lianna's body. She methodically placed poultices and thick pastes onto the various wounds, instructed Nyssa to press a cold cloth to Lianna's face, and began to clean off the dried blood from the wounds as Lianna cried out in pain. "It looks bad, but he has done much worse. She will recover quickly enough but you were wise to call me so hastily, child."

Lianna turned her head and gestured with weak fingers for Rhea to come near her couch. Rhea hurried over and dropped to her knees, gently taking Lianna's hand between hers. "It will be okay. This isn't going to happen to you ever again, I promise."

Lianna whispered, "Ratified? Me and you?"

Rhea nodded as tears fell down her cheeks. "Everything is ratified. Nyssa took care of everything."

Lianna smiled weakly. "Then when I sleep tonight I will be at peace."

Rhea stood up and backed out of the way as Risalka continued to treat the wounds, replacing bandages and poultices. Risalka looked up at her and smiled. "She will fully recover, Rhea, and it will be fine in due time. This is not your fault and now you have the power to make the rest of her life a good one."

As Rhea backed up she bumped into Savin, and instinctively turned towards him to hide her tears. He carefully wrapped a strong arm around her, shielding her from the sight of her friend's mutilated body, and the evidence of how men treat women in the court. "She will be okay, Lady. We are in your care now so she will be just fine."

<u>Chapter Twelve</u>

The Court

Morning dawned early and Rhea awoke to the sound of horses' hooves as they clanged across the courtyard. She hastily jumped out of the bed and peered out the window to see what was causing the commotion. Soldiers filled the courtyard like an ant swarm, metal armor shining from the early sun rays and horses covered with thick, protective padding over their vulnerable faces, necks, and bodies. The High Prince could be seen in the front of the line as he waved his sword high in the air, yelling encouragement at the men before the massive swarm pushed through the city gates and beyond Rhea's vision.

She backed up and went over to the couch where Lianna still slept off her wounds, the small, furry, gray cat curled at her side. Rhea bent down and gently kissed her friend's forehead, grateful that she had been returned, even if not unharmed. "You are safe now, Lianna. I don't really know how things work around here, but they all said that you were safe now and I believe them."

The woman gave a weak smile and her eyes fluttered open. "Trust them, good." Her voice trembled and she slowly patted Rhea's hand where it rested beside hers. "Green eyes good, black eyes, be careful."

Rhea nodded. "I will be. You rest today and get stronger. Now it's my turn to take care of you."

Lianna smiled as the cat gently crawled onto her chest and began to purr, sending a gentle frequency of healing through her. "Glad cat found you." She halted after each phrase to catch her breath. "Go with Nyssa today. I will be fine."

As if on cue, there was a knock on the door and Nyssa entered, dressed in a gray split overdress and dark charcoal cloak. She walked over to check on Lianna's condition first, then handed Rhea a bundle of clothing. "These should fit you. Put them on with haste and we must be on our way. Aleksei will have the horses ready for us and I will explain on the way."

She quickly put on the charcoal gray pants, split dress, and cloak and felt as if she had already blended into the stone of the castle that surrounded her. "Should we leave Lianna here alone? She's still very weak. What if something happens to her?"

"You go on, Rowan will stay." Lianna summoned a bit of energy to wave off the women. "Cat protect me." She chuckled softly and then winced as the motion pulled at some of her newly healed wounds.

"There you have it. Rowan will stay here to guard her. Savin will ride with us." The women walked out the door cautiously, Nyssa shaking her head in an amused manner when she saw Savin dressed in similar muted tones of clothing. "I should have known you could not go anywhere without him."

The three quickly walked down the empty corridor, ducking into empty rooms and alcoves at the sound of another approaching. Nyssa slipped into a small wooden door towards the end of a hallway and motioned the others through before it quietly latched shut behind them. They cautiously picked their way down a very steep flight of curved and uneven stairs, and then Nyssa quietly mimicked the sound of a small owl.

An echo came through the door from the outside, deeper in resonance, and Nyssa pushed open the door so the trio could slip outside.

Aleksei stood just outside the door with three horses, all of a dappled gray hue. The mare from before instantly recognized Rhea and pushed forward, only to be calmed down when Rhea gave her a gentle forehead rub and a kiss on the velvety muzzle. Nyssa quickly mounted her gelding as Savin gave Rhea a leg up and then mounted his own horse. The three quietly moved along the edge of the wall, the only sound the muffled clop of the horses' hooves on the grassy surface. Aleksei silently stepped through the small gap in the hedges just large enough for a man and horse to pass through and led them out of the castle walls.

Nyssa rode point, holding her excited gelding to a slow and silent walk as they entered the woods surrounding that section of castle. No one spoke, and even the horses seemed to sense the urgency for silence as they picked their careful way along the thin, barely visible path through the forest. The sun was halfway into the sky when they finally emerged from the forest, and Nyssa gave her horse his head, the stride quickly lengthening into a ground eating canter as they crossed the open ground. Savin kept his senses alert and his eyes continuously scanned the horizon around the riders in an attempt to detect any other humans before they saw the small party.

After several moments they reached the edge of Steinbrekka and the riders slowed their barely winded horses to a careful trot as they entered the craggy area. Rhea took the time to look around the area, surprised at the ability of the horses and riders to have been able to come through this path with only the moonlight to guide their way. Sharp rocks stuck out of the cliff walls at jagged angles and threatened to unseat an incautious rider. Fragments of shale slid beneath the horses careful hooves, and Rhea adjusted her grip so that she held the reins loosely in one hand while using the other to aid her balance on the horse as she tightly gripped the front of her saddle.

They came up to the pool then, and the horses stopped to take long gulps of the cool water. The sun was well into the sky now and Rhea estimated they had been on their journey for several hours. Always Savin and Nyssa kept their eyes on the horizon, muscles tightening with anxiety that seemed to increase at every step. The party paused at the top of a hill and Nyssa pulled out a small eye scope before methodically scanning the open area below that lay in their path.

She turned to the other riders. "It looks like they have already ridden back this way so we should be safe. We are going to hug close to the edges of the flats, though, just in case there is a stray rider or scout coming up from behind."

Once again the horses ran, their riders mindful of any unexpected guests and intending to limit the view in the dangerous open area. Hooves flew over the soil, hardened and baked by the sun and hot temperatures of the area. Nyssa slowed her horse after a rocky cairn appeared and scanned the woods carefully, contemplating the numerous deer trails which seemed to litter the woods. After a few long moments of careful study, she turned her horse onto a specific trail, and guided Rhea and Savin into the dark forest.

Here, Nyssa slowed the gelding beneath her as the horse grew increasingly excited. The creature snorted, tossed his head, trotted in place and made small whinnies of happiness to himself. Rhea and Savin's mounts were far quieter and simply focused their energy on the walk through the forest as they ignored their excited friend in front of them.

They reached the edge of the forest and Nyssa had to firmly rein her dancing gelding to a stop, snorts and hooves sounding their annoyance to anyone who would listen. The three anxiously sat there staring into the distance for many long minutes as Nyssa's breath grew heavier, and the look of barely-contained panic increased in her eyes.

Rhea could see a small village in the distance, about 100 paces from where they stood waiting. There was smoke rising from the rooftops, and whether the smoke came from controlled and desired cooking fires or was the product of arson, Rhea could not determine. The ground around the village had been churned into thick dust and studded with hoof prints and the rusty color of already dried blood could be clearly seen as it stained the ground between the houses.

After quite some time a figure walked out of the village and headed toward the party. He was a well-muscled man, easily over six feet tall and built like a fighter. His muscles bulged as he moved and sweat glowed off of his arms as it was reflected in the sunlight. The man had a noticeable limp, and a bright crimson cloth could be seen wrapped around his left shoulder, the blood slowly seeping underneath the bandage to drip down his arm.

Nyssa let out a cry of distress and flew down from her horse before she ran across the final distance to the man. They exchanged a few words and then Rhea was astonished to see the large man wrap the dainty woman into his muscular arms in embrace. After a long moment the two walked back to where Rhea and Savin were standing with the horses while tears streamed down Nyssa's face.

"It was too close that time, Savin." The man spoke with a thick accent, similar to what Rhea would suspect of an Italian man in her world. "They got too close to the children, too close to our secret areas."

Savin nodded. "It looks like they got too close to you as well, Sebast."

Sebast shrugged. "I let them get too close. This is true. They are getting smarter and coming quieter. We barely had time to get everyone out before we were surrounded." The man looked at Rhea, "And who is this?"

Nyssa shifted her weight under his arm, "This is Rhea. She can be trusted, have no fears about her."

The man nodded. "Then welcome to Asimina, Rhea. I am afraid you have come at a poor time, although there never really is a good time here."

Rhea gave a small curtsey to the man. "Thank you. If there is anything I can do to help, please let me know."

Nyssa gave a weak smile. "For right now we need to get Sebast in a safe place and check on the others. Savin, can you help him to the hut? Rhea will come with me."

Savin walked over and, with some protests from Sebast, supported the man's weight as they walked into the woods. Nyssa wiped the blood off her hand onto her dress and sighed, "Let us go then and see what damage has been caused this time. We will leave the horses here; they will not go beyond the wood line without us."

The village was the image of desolation, desperation and a place that had been treated cruelly for a lengthy time period. Dwellings were crudely-created structures with grass thatch roofs supported by four foundational posts that stood about eight feet high. Thin mats made of woven grass and twigs formed the walls and Rhea could see where thin scraps of fabric were roughly sewn together to form patches over the multiple holes. There were no functional doors and Rhea could see people huddled in the corners of the hut that gave the most privacy from the outside viewer.

As they approached, many children began to slowly come out of the huts before running over to embrace Nyssa. She hugged them all close and wiped tears as they began to talk simultaneously about what had happened earlier. Women slowly followed suit, however, many remained at the doors to their homes, wary of the unknown woman who had arrived in their village during such a dangerous time. Nyssa looked as both a queen and a saint as she walked through the increasing throng of women and children. Everyone received an embrace, a kind word, the reassurance that it was over for the day and that they were safe now.

Savin approached again, and after he informed Nyssa that Sebast was comfortably, if reluctantly, resting he walked back to the horses and began to pull the thick saddle bags from their backs. These he brought over and placed in front of Nyssa who had encouraged all to gather in the dusty center of the village. Rhea's eyes opened in surprise as the woman began to pull out supplies from the bags - blankets, shirts, pants, dried pieces of meats and fruits, grains and several loaves of bread that had been made earlier that morning. One of the women began to cry at the sight of a thick wheel of cheese and a bag of rice.

Rhea realized this was intended to feed the entire village, this amount of food that back home would have supported a family of four for a week, perhaps two, if they stretched it out through careful rationing and planning. She was astonished and humbled as she realized not a single person rushed ahead or reached for the food.

Instead, everyone sat still with their want for the supplies only seen in the shimmer in their eyes. Nyssa passed out the supplies methodically and asked each family unit what supplies they had left from last time, or if any sickness was present among their members. Women with children were given priorities with the supplies, along with any person showing signs of immediate illness. Malnutrition could be seen on all of the women; the lines of their bones clearly seen under the skin, hair rough in texture and dull in color, and the children's bloated bellies amplified by the stick thin limbs they curled around their bodies.

Finally all of the supplies were gone and Nyssa kissed the foreheads of the women who did not receive any of the supplies. "Have faith. I will return soon. Changes are in the wind and this life will not last forever." The women nodded slightly and walked back to their huts where they curled up to sleep, for they had no energy to do anything else.

Savin moved to the edge of a central hut and picked up a thick, sturdy wooden rod, then held it steady as several village women slid bark buckets with woven grass handles onto the poles. After twenty had been added Nyssa waved the women away, and motioned for Rhea to follow Savin and her down the steep path to a nearby water hole.

Rhea dipped the first bucket into the muddy water. "What is this place, Nyssa? Why does no one help them?"

Nyssa dipped a bucket and carefully balanced it on the rod on Savin's broad shoulders. "This is the village of Asimina. The King considers everyone who is not of the castle to be a Skov, or outsider. They are not privileged to any assistance through food, medicine, or the basics of human life. To add to their injury they also are regularly plundered to help supplement the supplies and to support the barbaric entertainments encouraged by my father."

"Your father? Who is he to hold such power?"

Savin chuckled low and assumed a sheepish expression when Nyssa glared at him. "Her father is the king."

"Oh." Rhea quietly placed another bucket upon the rod. "I would have never made that connection. You seem to be so kind and giving and he's - well, he doesn't seem to hold the same values in such high regard."

At this both of her companions laughed and Nyssa dipped the last bucket. "I think that is one of the most polite ways I have heard that to be phrased. You are correct, however. My father and I hold very different values in importance. He is not aware of this, however, and it is imperative that you keep my secret, as well."

"Oh, of course. It's too bad your brother doesn't seem to hold those values." Rhea thought of the High Prince's actions at that first dinner and his constant, seemingly unwanted, advances he made toward Agrafina, the blonde usually seated beside him at dinner.

Nyssa glanced over at Rhea. "My brother does not?"

Rhea blushed bright red. "I apologize for any slight for that was not my intent. I just noticed that he was leading the group of men who left this morning, I'm assuming for here, and thought-"

"Oh, Mateo," Nyssa cut her off. "Yes, well, he is the King's protégé and bends to his whims quite easily. One can hardly blame him. If you go against the King in any way, either your heritage is forfeit or your life. If he enjoys the duties that fall into his daily conduct, the better for him I suppose."

Savin grunted as the weight of the final bucket went onto his shoulders and the three began walking up the path back toward the village. Nyssa moved to walk beside him on the path and inquired about Sebast.

"Oh, he will recover," Savin said without worry. "The arm wound is the result of a rather nasty knife, but it has been cleaned and bandaged and should heal well enough as long as he tries to not over use the limb. The rest are mostly superficial bruises and scrapes which should heal on their own. He received a solid blow to his kneecap which is the cause of the limp but that should work itself out as long as he is careful in his movements for a bit."

She nodded and bit her lip as her eyes began to water with emotion. "Thank you, Savin, as always, for coming here with me."

He gave her an encouraging smile. "We do what we can, when we can and that is all we can do. These people would have been dead a long time ago if it were not for you, Lady."

Nyssa looked up at the spindly women who waited at the top of the path for their water. "But is it truly better this way, Savin? They are living only on what I can sneak out here and the nuts they can find from rodent stashes. No one over the age of thirty survived last winter and no babies are able to be kept alive long enough to grow into children. Am I just cruelly prolonging their suffering?" She began to cry then, silent tears falling onto the dusty ground.

Rhea put an arm around her waist. "You are doing the right thing, Nyssa, and this is not your fault. A people cannot rebuild if they are all dead, and as long as there are a few survivors in the end these people can have a new beginning one day. I'll help you as much as I can, even if it's just to help sneak more food from the kitchens or more fabrics from the washroom. They chose to accept your help and continue what existence they have; you just give them the option to live another day and be there to welcome the possibility of a new future. Otherwise, the only path they would take would assuredly lead to death."

Nyssa sniffled but gave a small smile at that. "Thank you, I needed to hear that."

"You are doing wonderful things here, Nyssa. I know it's hard to see that, but you really are."

They reached the village and Savin put down the buckets as women slowly drifted out of their shaded huts to gather water and take it back to their dwellings. They returned a few minutes later with the buckets empty, and reverently placed the buckets back onto Savin's shoulders.

The trio collected water for the rest of the daylight hours, making countless trips to the small waterhole and back to the village. Rhea learned that Nyssa and Savin came out here once a month at least, and tried for twice a month if they were able to slip out unnoticed. With the exception of Sebast, none of the inhabitants of the village had the strength to carry water, so they would try to carry up as much water as they could physically bear to limit the amount of trips that would be made once they left. Rhea also discovered that physical exhaustion could be pushed quite far when a small child looked at her with such misery and pain in his eyes. Back home the children she knew always demanded the latest toy, the best candy, the most realistic toy cell phone or for their rooms to be decorated with the latest movie theme. Here, all they wanted was a sip of water and a bite of food and even if these did not come, they would not voice a complaint or cry, merely walk away and accept that they do not always get what they want or need.

Savin and Rhea walked in the twilight over to the horses while Nyssa ducked into the small hut where Sebast lay with his injuries. Savin looked at Rhea, face smudged with mud and dirt, arms that hung limp from overuse, and he gently wrapped his arm around her waist. "You did a good thing today, Lady Rhea. Thank you for helping us."

Rhea smiled at him and leaned into his solid body, glad to accept the help as her aching body walked toward the horses and dreaded the ride home. "How did you first come to this village, Savin?"

He grew thoughtful. "Well, it has been years now, probably close to sixteen or so. Nyssa had slipped out of the castle and I followed her. Stupid really, I was fifteen at the time and just begun my guard training, but I thought I could protect her. She was twelve, far too young to know any of the atrocities that occurred under her father's rule and did not understand why she was ordered to remain inside on certain days. I followed her and was able to convince her to hide from view just as the first wave of soldiers came through with the men of Asimina. There were many more back then, it was a different time. The men were strong and plentiful, babies were abundant and the women had good muscle and healthy fat on their bodies.

We hid until the soldiers rode by, then Nyssa insisted on seeing from where they came. There were old men and women comforting the younger women. Back then only the fittest of the men were taken for the games of the court and the rest were left in peace. Generally most of the men came back, battered and bruised, but alive. Sebast was a youth who took charge even then, and the elders made sure he was kept out of sight from the soldiers. They had already known then that he was needed to care for the village when the other men were gone. Four years older than Nyssa, the man was far beyond his sixteen years. He did the heavy work while the men were gone and recovering, carried water and food, hunted the animals that still roamed the woods, and organized plans to put a stop to the raiding of the village. He and Nyssa struck an uneasy friendship. She was fascinated by a person who was different than all others in her structured world, and he was impressed by her willingness to help a stranger.

When he turned twenty it turned to survival and I saw the friendship grow to something more. Fewer men returned from the games and women and children grew leaner. Sebast spent all of his time and energy to evade capture because early on the village recognized he may be all they had left. Nyssa began to bring them supplies to help, but it was futile in the end. The population dropped almost fifty percent by the time Nyssa was twenty and now this is all you see left from what was once a thriving culture."

Rhea paused as Savin carefully helped her onto her mare. "I understand the need for secrecy, Savin. Horrible crimes have been committed here and if anyone knew about Nyssa," she shivered, "well, I don't think their bond would be smiled upon in the court now would it?"

The man waited until he saw Nyssa emerge from the hut and walk towards them, face already composed as she transformed back into the court doll everyone thought was her true self. "No, having a romantic relationship below your status would be met with by death for the lower status, and immediate expulsion from the realm for the higher. Once you added the punishment for aiding a man declared an enemy of the realm and you would have death for both parties and any who were aware of the action. Here you only commit to people who are deemed worthy in the eyes of the realm."

"How would you know who is acceptable? There seem to be so many layers of protocol and status it makes your mind spin."

Nyssa accepted Savin's help and mounted her gelding. "Oh do not worry about that. The Kontorist will figure that out for you and present a list of those suitable for consideration. Now we had better hurry back before Rowan gets worried and decides to come looking for us."

Chapter Thirteen

The Court

Lianna's health improved quickly and once again the two women began to take slow walks through the castle, this time at the pace set by Lianna's weak muscles. They further discussed the intricacies of the court as they spent time in Poibli Frien and Lianna pointed out men from the Kontorist's list of suitable matches to Rhea.

"Of course," she said, "the whole list is a moot point once the High Prince shows interest in you and I am certain he will. Once he expresses attraction towards someone they become untouchable forever in the realm."

Rhea leaned back against one of the large columns and stared out into the room thoughtfully. "Is that what will happen to Agrafina if he takes an interest in me? I noticed that he spends a lot of time looking her way and she is seated next to him at dinner. I don't know her that well, but she looks so withdrawn and upset lately that I worry for her."

A sad smile played across Lianna's face. "I think you two would be good friends in any other world, Rhea. Yes, if the Prince turns his affections your way, Agrafina will be cast out of eligibility for any other match. Any man who aligns himself with her romantically will be at risk of expulsion from the kingdom or death."

"But she can't be much older than me. What if she wants to have a family? She can't just be left alone for the rest of her life?"

"She is in her late twenties and reaching the end of her eligible period regardless of the Prince's actions. Rhea, what people want does not have a bearing here, only what will happen according to the rules. From what I hear, the Prince has been talking about you in increasing amounts which is deeply worrying to her, and you now see why. Maybe a future tied to the Prince is not the best future, but at least there is a chance of having children to love and people to surround you."

"What about you, Lianna? Do you get a list as well?"

Lianna gave a harsh laugh, "No. Any female who is of my particular status is to be left available to the men of the court. If any non-arranged relationship is discovered the man will be executed and the woman will be expelled from the court." She gave Rhea a look of gratitude. "You may think that I am a person, Rhea, and I am greatly appreciative of that, but to everyone else I am just a body here to serve their whims."

Rhea gave her friend a subtle squeeze on the arm. "Not anymore, Nyssa made sure of that. I may still be learning how everything works but we are going to wrap you in so many layers of protection that no one will touch you."

Lianna smiled softly. "I heard from Savin that you have visited the garden."

Rhea paused at the sudden change of topic. "Yes, he and Rowan have been taking me there. It's beautiful, Lianna. Do you want to go see it?"

She nodded. "I would like that very much. I feel like it has been quite a long time since I have seen living beauty and not the artificial world that surrounds us."

The two women walked down the long corridors and slipped out the small door to the garden. Rhea stood back and smiled as Lianna's eyes grew wide, her amazement at the garden transparent on her face.

"Rhea, it is so beautiful. There is no frost anywhere and look at how much has grown! Where did these benches come from? And I know that fountain in the corner over there has not been there all of this time? Hello, Dmitri, you are looking well."

Dmitri nodded a quiet hello and smiled at the two women. His facial features had softened with the improvement of the garden, and while he was still quite old, there was a new twinkle in his eyes and laughter in his smile.

"Some new improvements have been springing up overnight it seems. This garden is once again being used by some people of the court, mostly friends of Nyssa and Rowan. Their whispered hopes and prayers have slowly built what you see here. It is a testament to the purity of the hearts that have built this garden that none with malice or evil intentions are able to see the changes. I was speaking with Lady Agrafina just yesterday and she said the High Prince was questioning why she wanted to spend time in the frozen wasteland of the garden. This is a good thing. This is now a sanctuary for those who are deserving of rest and peace."

Rhea smiled and slowly walked the garden paths as her companions babbled to each other excitedly. The garden had changed drastically over such a short time. The largest change was the very size of the garden. It had started out a small space, and Rhea could easily walk every step of the four main paths easily and quickly. Now the garden was a large expanse of beautifully landscaped foliage and decorations, with an intricate pathway system that would take hours to explore. Trees grew tall and bloomed while their leaves spread wide as they reached for the sun above, freed from the debilitating frost of earlier years. Tiny flowers could be seen on the newly formed fruit trees, hints of the produce that would be joining the garden's living residents.

Many animals now called the garden home as well. Insects were still the main occupants and Rhea could not take a step without seeing a brilliantly colored butterfly, shimmering dragonfly, or bright ladybug. Honey bees flew from flower to flower, ignoring the people as they buzzed past on their way to their secreted hives. Birds chirped in the treetops and even small rodents, foxes, and squirrels poked their noses out of the foliage to look at Rhea as she walked by.

She paused in one area of the garden, mystified at the sense of waiting that seemed to flow from the surrounding plants and animals. She stood in the center of a perfect circle created by cherry trees, the small pink buds dotting the branches with their beauty. The thick grass under her feet was soft to the touch and a healthy deep green. Rose bushes grew on one side of the circle and their endless blooms gave bright reds, whites, pinks and even some purples a wall of color.

"What are you waiting for?" Rhea quietly asked the space. "Why does it seem as if you are patiently waiting for me to do something?" She lowered herself onto the grass in the center of the circle and stared up at the clouds that floated past her vision. Warm sunlight filled the circle and Rhea closed her eyes as the heat began to seep into her skin, began to warm her body and soul. She was suddenly gripped with such a sense of loneliness she could not control the tears as they seeped out of the corners of her tightly closed eyes. *How long has it been since I have been able to lie in the sun at my university? How long has it been since I've felt warm and safe?"*

An uncomfortable coughed preceded the voice. "Are you injured, my Lady? Is everything alright?"

Rhea quickly brushed away her tears and looked up at Rowan's concerned face. "I'm fine, Rowan, just enjoying the sunshine and looking at the clouds."

Rowan looked upward, dubious at her words. "Looking at the clouds? Are you worried about rain falling? The day seems quite clear."

"Well, no, I'm just looking at them. Haven't you ever looked up at the clouds and picked out shapes, or wondered if people were living up there?" Rhea blushed at his look of incredulity. "Well, never mind then. Forget I said anything."

The man looked into the garden for a minute and swallowed hard, then looked back at Rhea. "Ok, how do you see shapes in the clouds?"

She smiled at the softness that had entered his voice. "Well, first you have to lie down so you don't get a sore neck." Rhea held back her amusement as the dignified guard lay down on the grass beside her and gave her a look that plainly conveyed his skeptical amusement.

"Ok, so now we just look up at the clouds and see if there are any recognizable shapes. For example, I think that one up there looks kind of like a bunny. There are two long ears on a little round body, and a little tuft of a tail." She glanced at Rowan and saw the outer corner of his lip twitch, a habit she had noticed when it seemed as if he were struggling to maintain a stoic expression.

"Or there's that cloud over there, to our left. That one looks like a turtle with a big oval shell and little legs and a head and a tail."

Rowan still looked unimpressed. "And why are we laying on the ground picking out shapes in the clouds?"

Rhea absent-mindedly removed her veil and smiled as she felt the sunlight touch her head and warm her hair. "Because it's fun, and silly, and relaxing to just lie in the sun and not think about everything else happening in the world."

The man stared through the trees towards the entrance to the castle and abruptly got to his feet. "Well, some of us cannot afford to spend our time on such frivolity. Replace your veil. It is not seemly to remove it in the presence of anyone other than your spouse." He stalked off through the winds.

She rolled her eyes at his behavior and looked at a small grasshopper that had landed on her stomach. "Don't worry, little grasshopper, he's always an ass. I still think it's fun to lay in the sun and spend my time on 'such frivolity'."

The sound of Savin's angry voice floated through the garden and Rhea rose to her feet, repositioning the veil onto her head before brushing off the small pieces of grass that clung to the material of her dress. She placed a hand on one of the trees at the edge of the circle. "I'll be back in just a little time and we'll figure out what needs to go into this space." She looked at the group as she approached their location by the door. Savin and Rowan were exchanging heated words while Lianna and Dmitri stood by uncomfortably.

"Is something wrong, gentlemen?" Rhea approached the group and the conversation immediately came to a halt.

"Nothing," both men spat out in sync.

"Alright, then. Thank you for the day in the garden, Dmitri. It was enjoyable. We will see you again before very long. Lianna, will you accompany me inside while these two continue talking angrily about nothing?" She curtseyed and walked through the door as Lianna chuckled behind her.

The men hurried to catch up and Rowan took his position ahead of the women while Savin lingered behind. Once they reached the door Rowan bowed and, after he informed Rhea he would be preoccupied for the evening, stormed down the hallway.

Rhea turned to Savin. "What was that about back in the garden?"

"It was nothing, Rhea. Do not be concerned."

"Anytime you and Rowan start raising your voices it concerns me, Savin."

"It was nothing. Now may I suggest you get changed before dinner?" Savin gestured her forward, clearly not intending to talk about the prior conversation.

Rhea bristled at the second slight to her person in one day. "And just what is wrong with my appearance exactly. Is it not satisfactory to the standards of the realm? Would I be an embarrassment at dinner?"

Savin could not help but release the smile he held in for the entire walk down the corridor. "No offense intended, my Lady, but you have a bit of green on the back of your person where any man with a pulse would certainly notice."

She blushed bright red as Lianna laughed. "Well, then, thank you for your consideration. We will see you for dinner." The two women slipped inside the door as Savin released the chuckle he had been restraining.

Chapter Fourteen

The Court

"Lianna, I'm going to the stables for a bit today. Would you like to come or stay here and relax?"

Lianna looked at Rhea from her position on the thick chair with the gray cat curled up asleep in her lap. "If it is fine with you I would prefer to stay here in front of the fire and read away the afternoon."

Rhea smiled. "Of course that's ok. I'll take Savin with me and ask Rowan if he will stand watch for you."

"I think it would be better if it were the other way around."

Rhea groaned softly. "But Rowan is such a stick in the mud."

Lianna looked up, brows furrowed in confusion. "He's a what?"

"Oh you know the phrase, stick in the mud." Rhea looked over as Lianna just raised her eyebrows. "Ok, maybe you don't. He just, he doesn't know how to have fun or relax or let his hair-" she stopped herself before saying another common phrase Lianna likely was not familiar with. "He doesn't know how to just be normal."

"That is true. He has not had an easy life, Rhea, and normal for him is far different than normal would be for anyone else, even in this realm." Lianna looked at Rhea through her eyelashes. "However,

I did notice a particular grass stain on the back of his trousers that day in the garden as well."

Color rose on Rhea's cheeks. "I was just looking at the clouds, and thought he would have fun looking at them, too. Then he let me know exactly how stupid he thought that was and that was that."

"I see." Lianna smiled as the conversation between the men in the garden began to make a bit more sense.

Rhea puffed out a frustrated sigh. "Ugh, fine. I'll take Rowan if it means that much to you."

She walked out the door, almost bumping into the man who was having an animated conversation with Savin. She caught the words "it does not work like that," before the conversation fell silent. "I'm going to the stable. Rowan, you are coming with me." Rhea began to walk down the hallway before he had a chance to reply.

Rowan caught up to her when she was five paces down the hallway. "Why are we going to the stable today?"

"Because I want to go to the stable today. I thought since I have such a frivolous and carefree life, I might as well enjoy it before something changes."

Rowan let out a frustrated sigh. "Then let us go to the stable, my Lady."

Tense silence followed them to the stable and Rhea was grateful to see Aleksei with a smile on his face. "Hello, my Lady Rhea, what brings you here today?"

"I just need to do something other than sit in my room or listen to how stupid some people consider me to be. Is Kalar in her stall?"

Aleksei opened his mouth to ask a question and then changed his mind. "Yes, she is, my Lady. She has had quite a romp in the dirt, too, so she will give you plenty of distraction if that is what you have come for."

"Thank you." She swept down the long hallway, grabbed some brushes on the way, and ducked into the stall before either male had a chance to follow her.

Aleksei stood at the end of the hallway with Rowan, interested in what had made Rhea so upset. "So...my Lord"

"Do not ask, Aleksei."

"I am just wondering is all, Sir. I do not think I have ever seen the Lady quite so rattled, and you seem to be quite agitated yourself, if you do not mind my saying so."

"I said drop it," Rowan growled under his breath. "It is nothing worth talking about." His attention was suddenly drawn to two servants standing outside the stall beside Kalar's. "Aleksei, what are they doing?"

"Ah, no." Aleksei paled and quickly hurried down the long row of stalls.

~ * ~ * ~

Rhea crouched down beside the stall as the voices of two strange men began to speak just outside Kalar's stall. She peered through a little chink in the wood and was astonished to see two men of the servant class. One she recognized as a stall vendor, a small, frail man with white hair and a large selection of veils and fans often sought after by the wealthier female Patrons.

"'Allo, Aniketo. 'Ow is your Lady doing?"

A taller, better dressed man laughed sharply, "Oh the old bag is doing as well as ever, Mikhail. She has grown particularly fond of your amber veils."

"Ah, but 'aven't I noticed! I must refold the veils five times, yes I must, from her visits alone! Of course, these stingy wenches won't want to purchase the veils after they have been, ruffled, as they say."

Aniketo snorted. "Yes, yes I know. Do not worry. I have slipped a little extra out of her purse to compensate for your lost sales, my friend. I will not let your family starve because she cannot keep her bejeweled fingers off of everything shiny or pricey."

A hefty leather bag was exchanged and Rhea heard the metallic rustling of coin as the man opened the bag. "Ah, thank you, my friend. You make an old man 'appy and his belly full."

Rhea saw Aleksei hurrying down the aisle and both of the men instantly fell silent and still as stone. She quickly grabbed the tool to clean Kalar's hoof and bent over. "Excuse me, is there anyone nearby?" she called out. "Could someone please help me with this hoof?"

Aleksei ducked into the stall while the two men held their breath in the aisle. "My Lady?"

"Oh hello, Aleksei, I didn't know there was someone that close to me! I have been unable to get Kalar to pick up her hoof for me and have been trying for forever it seems."

The stable boy smiled as Kalar responded instantly to his touch. "My Lady...I do not suppose you heard-"

Rhea looked into Aleksei's eyes. "I heard nothing worth sharing, Aleksei, nothing at all."

He nodded and stuck his arm out of the stall to wave away the two men. "I give you my thanks, my Lady, from the bottom of my horse hair covered heart."

She laughed as he stepped back out of the stall and turned back to brushing the horse. Kalar was finally gleaming when Rhea heard a whinny of fear come from a stall further down the row. She poked her head out into the aisle but did not see Rowan or Aleksei within view.

I hope the poor thing didn't hurt itself, she thought as she carefully latched the door behind her and hurried down the row toward the distressed animal. The rows of stalls continued far into the back of the stable and Rhea noticed that most of the stalls were now empty of occupants. The snorting horse continued, the sound growing louder as the woman approached the back of the stable. Finally she saw a large stall with a gilded leather halter and lead hanging on the door and Rhea peeked inside.

The large, black horse whinnied in fear and rose high on her hinds legs, striking out at the small creatures that danced below her feet. Rhea recognized them as the small catlike creatures from Steinbrekka and carefully slid open the door to step inside. The creatures scattered into thin air as Rhea's foot crossed the threshold and the mare stood still, though her muscles still trembled from fear. Her deep brown eye stared down at Rhea, the white corners reflected her inner desire to run away from the terrors found in her stall.

"Hey there, girl, easy now. It's ok now, they're gone." Rhea slowly took off her veil and carefully placed it on the stall door. "No one will hurt you. I won't even touch you if you don't want me to. I'll just stand here a moment and make sure the creatures don't come back to hurt you again." She slowly stepped forward, holding out her palm with a small amount of grain she had found in the bottom of the feed bucket.

The horse slowly inched her head forward, and Rhea's heart skipped a beat as she saw the one aqua eye. "You're the pretty girl I saw before, aren't you? Those creatures scared me, too, at first. Do they come here often and bother you, or was this a one-time thing?" Rhea held herself very still as the horse cautiously snuffled around her hand and gently took the small grains between velvet soft lips.

Why is this wonderful creature kept so far back in the stable, she wondered, *and how often do those creatures come to harass her? She looks like she hasn't been groomed in days nor had the stall changed out, yet this is the horse that the High Prince rides?* Rhea found herself lost in thought as she slowly began to rub the forehead of the mare, dirt falling off in clods where it had been caked onto the soft fur.

She looked around the stall and found a coarse brush tossed into the corner. "Hey, pretty girl, will you let me clean you up a little bit? I promise that I won't hurt you and you will feel much better." She gently placed the brush high on the horse's neck and softly began to hum as she worked the dirt off of the trembling mare. The shining black color of the fur began to show through the dirt and the woman was delighted to see a small triangle of white on the horse's chest. All of her black animals at home had that little spot of white, and Rhea was once told by an old woman that it was to protect against evil and witches.

What an odd lady she was, Rhea mused as she brushed over the white mark until it shone. She had taken a new litter of kittens into the veterinarian's office for their first vaccinations and the elderly woman had been standing outside with her dog. Rhea was not surprised that the lady made a ward against evil with her hands as she passed with the small black cats, for the office was located in a highly superstitious community, but was confused when the woman then sighed and said, "Oh good, they have the protective mark." She then told Rhea that she had always been raised that animals that were fully black in color were the familiars of the devil, but some had been saved by the angels during birth. Those animals, forever protected against evil forces, could be recognized by the white mark the angels pressed onto their chest.

Rhea heard the footstep outside the stall just seconds before the horse, then suddenly felt herself being firmly pushed back into the corner of the stall by the creature's muscular shoulders. The horse braced for a fight, feet spread, nostrils flaring, and ears pinned straight back on the head.

"Whoa, Kata, easy girl. It is only me." Rowan stepped into the stall slowly, arms held loosely at his sides with the palms towards the horse. "Do you have Rhea hiding in there, pretty girl? We have been missing her and are very worried."

Rhea gave a gentle push on the horse's shoulder but the mare would not budge. "I'm here in the corner," she said softly. "Apparently she wants to keep me here for some reason."

Rowan peered around the horse's head. "Are you hurt? You should not have come in here."

"Well there wasn't a sign saying not to come in and no, I'm not hurt. We were doing just fine until you came by and scared her."

He rolled his eyes but kept his tone even so as not to scare the horse further. "Do you realize whose horse this is or how much trouble we would be in if you were spotted in here by the High Prince or one of his men? Do you think you are going to tame all the wild horses, as well as become a master gardener? What next? Do you intend on making the star constellations shift in the sky, as well? You cannot fix the problems of this realm, my Lady."

Rhea felt the angry flush of heat fill her body. "I heard a horse in trouble and came to help. It's not my fault, or her fault, that her stall was filled with small creatures biting at her feet and that no one else was paying attention to her calls. If the High Prince cared so much about her or came here to check on her frequently, she wouldn't have been in this state of disarray and fear to begin with. As for the rest, if you are going to insist on mocking and degrading me every time I say or do anything, then maybe I should tell the Kontorist I don't need you as a Komisar after all and simply entrust my well-being into Savin's care since he holds it in higher regard anyway!"

The man backed out of the stall then with eyes that glittered like polished emeralds. He kept his voice low but the rage in the undertones scared Rhea out of her own anger. "My job is to keep you safe, my Lady, and it seems that you are trying to make that job as difficult as possible."

Rhea gently moved the horse to the side and slipped out of the stall. "Then I apologize for making your job so difficult, Komisar Rowan. Maybe you should have thought about that before you kidnapped me and brought me here in the first place."

She ran down the empty aisle of stalls, pausing only to pull her cloak over her head to conceal her hair before she stalked across the courtyard and back to her room.

~ * ~ * ~

Lianna jumped up from the chair, the cat spilling off her lap with a hiss. "What happened? Where is your veil?"

Rhea angrily dashed the tears falling through the dust on her cheek. "Oh, I must have left it in the stable. Nothing's wrong. No, that's a lie. Everything is wrong. I shouldn't be here, Lianna. I should be at home sorting through artifacts and wearing jeans and having a normal life instead of being part of this circus act. I should be eating mac and cheese for dinner and worrying about having enough money to pay my rent. I should be watching stupid reality TV shows and studying and wondering why I could never hold a guy's attention for longer than a few weeks. I shouldn't have to deal with people constantly gaping at me, or insulting me, or dealing with people violating and using other people just because they feel like they can." Rhea's control on her emotions finally broke and she threw a glass across the room, and then sat down abruptly as it shattered and buried her face in her arms to sob.

Savin rushed into the room in panic at the sound of the shattered glass. "What was that? Is everything ok?" He saw Lianna frozen in shock and Rhea curled against the wall. He slowly walked over and sat down beside the woman as she shook in anger and shock. "Rhea, what is wrong?"

"Nothing," she choked out. "It's nothing. It will pass and there is nothing you can do. I'm fine."

Lianna walked over and knelt in front of her. "Rhea, from what you were saying it is not fine at all. When did this happen? Tell us everything." Rhea shook her head and Lianna took her hand and squeezed it. "We are here to help you, Rhea. Please trust us and tell us."

Rhea took a shaky breath and talked into her arms. "It's just that every time I'm with him all he does it insult me. He'll say that I'm stupid, or that I don't understand the world, or that I need to just accept the way that things are." She sniffed and Savin put his steady arm around her shoulders as encouragement. "I'm not that stupid you know. I know that I'm not going home, and I know that things are pretty screwed up here, but he doesn't need to be so mean about it." She blinked her eyes against the newly formed tears. "And he doesn't have to punish servants just because they are being nice to me. I would think someone in his position would be glad that any kindness was shown to other people. I wouldn't have suspected him of being cruel but I guess it has just been well hidden."

Savin's arm tightened around her shoulders and he forced himself to steady his breathing. "Mateo did this? When have you been alone with him?"

She gave a harsh laugh. "No, not Mateo. He's been creepy but has largely ignored me. I'm talking about Rowan."

The man carefully moved his arm from around her shoulders and slowly stood up. "If you will excuse me, ladies, I will return shortly after having a discussion with Komisar Rowan." He walked out the door and closed it behind him with delicate care. Then the wall shook with a tremendous force and he could be heard running down the hallway.

"Oh no." Lianna stood up quickly and looked outside the door. She turned to Rhea. "Okay, I need to know everything now and quickly. Every word, every action, every detail of what has occurred."

Rhea nodded and started from the beginning, a hard knot growing in the pit of her stomach. She told her about the night of the abduction, of their exchanges in hallways and in the garden. She told her about the boy with the shawl and the man's response when the boy suggested her guard carry the shawl.

Lianna listened quietly to all the stories, eyes widening slightly in surprise at the events that occurred earlier that night in the stable. She cursed when she jumped at the knock on the door. "Come in. What is it?"

The rich, deep voice that filled the room flooded the women with terror. "Now is that the way that you have been trained to respond to me? I should certainly hope not, or you will need to be newly trained."

Both women quickly fell to deep curtseys as the High Prince walked over towards them. Lianna pushed back the wave of fear-driven nausea long enough to reply, "Forgive me, my esteemed High Prince. I was not expecting it to be a person of your status outside Lady Rhea's humble door."

He laughed and lifted Rhea's face up. "I was going to ask your Komisar to announce my presence but it seems that both of the faithful-" his tone showed the irony of that word in the circumstances, "-guards you have employed are elsewhere."

Rhea swallowed the thickening lump in her throat. "I believe there was a disturbance they felt needed attending and that I was safe enough in my room."

The blonde man smiled, cold and calculated. "Yes, well, their loss is my gain. Tonight the formal dinner has been cancelled and I would like for you to join me in my dining chamber."

"Yes, my Lord."

"And wear the russet gown from the other day. It shows off your skin beautifully."

"Yes, my Lord."

"I will expect you in fifteen minutes. Is that enough time for you to make yourself presentable in such a manner as to be acceptable company in my chambers?"

Rhea took a shaky breath. "Yes, my Lord, thank you."

~ * ~ * ~

Lianna walked Rhea to the High Prince's chamber, waited until she heard the door lock click shut, and then set off down the hallway to search for Savin and Rowan. *Please, oh please do not let this be too bad,* she pleaded as she hurried down one hallway and then another. She cursed softly as her foot slid in a wet patch on the stone floor, then again as she realized she had slipped on a small area of blood that led to the door of the garden.

She entered the courtyard and stood in a state of shock at the sight of the two muscular men locked together in struggle. She could see Dmitri standing just off the garden path, the man obviously concerned but unable to prevent the growing aggression. Lianna jumped to the side as Rowan stumbled into her, Savin thundering behind.

"Savin, what-" Rowan's words sputtered out as Savin's curled fist connected with his jaw. He quickly pivoted and threw up his hands in self-defense. "What are you so angry about!"

Savin growled in response and surged forward, neck muscles bunching and strained with rage. His fingers dug into Rowan's tunic as he snarled, "How dare you upset her! How dare you make her cry or feel like she is not welcome." His strong hands pushed backward and shoved Rowan hard against the stone wall.

Rowan tucked a knee and slammed it into Savin's abdomen in an attempt to gain space. "Get off of me!" He grunted as he released a quick jab and slid out of the giant's grip.

Savin turned and caught his opponent by the back of his collar. His knuckles connected to the man's tender ribs with a sharp crack. Rowan tripped and landed ungracefully on the leaf-covered path.

"Savin, talk to me." Rowan scrambled backwards away from the heavy boots of his friend.

"You treated her like the mud on your boot. You, of all people. Maybe they are right. You are just like your father."

Lianna felt the momentary silence that fell over the garden at the words. They hung in the air, heavy and filled with venom. She stepped forward to intercede but was frozen in place by the cold fury that flashed through Rowan's green eyes.

Rowan launched himself onto his feet and the two men were locked in a desperate battle for domination, driven by rage and passion. Rowan swung. Savin blocked. Savin connected an elbow to Rowan's cheek and received a knee to the groin in return.

Savin's right fist crunched into Rowan's nose, temporarily dazing the smaller man with the blow. Rowan shook his head clear and took a step backward to regain his balance.

Lianna gasped as Savin shoved Rowan into the stone wall with enough force to rain loose mortar down upon their heads. The soil under their feet shifted with their weight and a small salamander fled from its foundation home.

The muscles on Savin's forearm bulged and swelled as it pushed against Rowan's vulnerable neck and jugular vein. Rowan's fingers clawed ineffectually in return, gouging, scratching, desperate to break the increasing pressure.

Lianna watched in growing panic as Rowan's face began to turn crimson, and then, in desperation, threw a bucket of water intended for the roses onto Savin's head in an attempt to break his concentration. Both men paused for a moment from the shock of the icy water and Lianna took advantage of the precious time. A quick shove had Savin back near Dmitri, and she moved in front of Rowan on the wall, unceremoniously toppling him sideways onto the grass. "Are you two done yet?"

"Is he still breathing?" Savin growled.

Rowan held up his hands in a passive gesture to Lianna's angry glare and took in a shaky breath. "I still do not know what is going on. He came out of nowhere and started swinging at me." He gingerly touched his lip and the cut that had opened on his cheek during the scuffle. "If Savin is just jealous because Rhea asked me to the stable today and not him then he needs to take it up with her. It hardly warrants the insults he has hurled my way."

Savin roared in anger and surged forward again, only stopped by the presence of the woman between the men. "Sit down, Savin!" Lianna demanded before she turned to Rowan. "What is your problem with Rhea? Why are you giving her such a hard time? What has she done to earn your sharp tongue?"

He laughed cruelly. "Oh, so this is what this is about? Rhea told you about what happened at the stable and this is why my longest and truest *friend* is trying to kill me?"

The other man shook off Dmitri's hand. "Oh yes, we know about the stable, and punishing the shawl vendor for being kind."

"I do not follow. What are you talking about?"

Lianna cleared her throat. "We need to talk, all of you. You also need to know that while we are talking, Rhea is being lost to all of us. Mateo showed up right after you left and she is currently dining with him. You had better pray he reveals his true colors to her or we may have lost every part of her forever."

Suddenly Nyssa burst into the garden, rage aimed directly toward Rowan. "What in the name of the Gods did you do?"

Rowan held a cloth Dmitri gave him to his lip. "I was simply spending some time enjoying the sun shining down through the trees when Savin came out here, raging like a stuck bull, and attacked me. I have yet to be informed of what has happened and why everyone seems to be directing their malice in my direction."

Nyssa hissed in low tones. "What is going on is that you have antagonized our only hope of a future. Now she is having dinner with Mateo, and I am starting to get the feeling that he knows she is not fully gone. Why did you try to make her angry? Why did you work to push her away from our cause?"

"I was not doing anything of the sort!"

Lianna paced the garden with her brow furrowed, "Okay, shouting is not going to help. How do we fix this?"

Three pairs of eyes looked at her with undisguised hope. Finally Nyssa sighed. "I think the only way is to not do anything to make it worse. Savin and Lianna, you keep along this same path. Rowan," she glared at the man gingerly stretching his shoulder, "you just stay away from her as much as possible until I can figure out some way to convince her that you are not just a condescending, arrogant fool."

~ * ~ * ~

Rhea chewed on her tender piece of chicken slowly as she thought about the events that had already transpired that evening. To say that this dinner was not what she expected would downplay the irregularity of the world as she knew it. The attitude of the High Prince seemed more subdued than usual, less arrogant and a bit more relaxed. So far he had not made one inappropriate comment and instead had treated Rhea like an esteemed guest in his personal dining space.

The space was certainly suitable for a man of his status. One entered through the waiting room, where Rhea had been previously, and then passed through a door in the wall to enter the dining chamber. A finely carved wooden table stood in the center of the room with seating for four, and an impressive array of food was laid out on the gold threaded table cloth. Sheer gold curtains let sunlight into the room and gave the entire room a bright yellow glow.

The man took a long drink from his cup, then sat it down and looked across the table at Rhea. "You will have to forgive my earlier actions, my dear. It was not my intent to frighten you. It is rare that we get one of your unique beauty brought to this realm, and I found myself quite overwhelmed with emotion."

Rhea allowed herself a small smile. "Thank you for the compliment, my Lord. I must admit learning my new place has been a bit stressful at times. I am grateful for the help of my personal servants, particularly Lianna."

He raised his eyebrow. "Ah, yes. Lianna is quite well instructed in the ways of the court. I had hoped that I had made the correct choice in assigning her to your person when you first came to the realm."

"Oh, I had not realized that had been due to your good judgment." Rhea silenced herself in a moment of confusion and quickly composed her face into a neutral to happy expression. "Thank you, my Lord for your impeccable insight."

His pale hand waved nonchalantly. "I do what I can for the residents of the realm to the capacity that I am able." He leaned forward on the table, face arranged in an expression he used to use often as Matt just before beginning to gossip. "May I confide in you, Rhea? It would be my head if this opinion were to spread to the court."

She gave a quick nod and felt flush with anxiety and longing for her old friend. "Of course, my Prince. You have my word."

"It is difficult, sometimes, to help everyone see what is necessary in this realm. My father has his way of ruling and I cannot deviate from that path. It pains me, at times, to do what is necessary for the good of the people. This is especially true when the people are not aware of the constant negotiation and danger which is kept behind closed doors."

Rhea nodded again, unsure of the proper response to such an unexpected statement. "I do not envy you your responsibilities, my Lord."

He smiled and stood from the table. "The hour grows late already, my Lady. I believe it is time to return you to your Komisar. If you like, I could have a small discussion with the man about the proper protocol for being in such a privileged position. I assure you that it does not include leaving his lady's side and running off with no regard for her safekeeping at the first signs of conflict."

She felt her face grow warm and ducked her head. "I assure you it was a one-time transgression, my Lord. I will speak with him and impress that it is not to occur again."

Rhea stood up and allowed the man to lead her out of the room and found Savin as he waited outside the door. She turned back and curtseyed to the High Prince. "Thank you very much for dinner, my Lord, it was truly a pleasure."

Chapter Fifteen

The Court

Rhea slowly wandered through the garden, cloak pulled tightly against her body to keep out in the chill that came with the turn of the seasons. The garden foliage had begun its natural morphing as the weather turned, leaves curling and dropping off the summer flowers while the winter blooms just began to peek open and show their colors.

The past few weeks had turned her world upside down, and she smiled to herself as she remembered the sunset horseback ride she had taken with the High Prince the night prior. *Mateo,* she reminded herself, as that night the man had asked her to just call him by his name in private. A far cry from the arrogant ruler she once thought he was, the man treated her like a delicate doll in both actions and words. Whenever they talked, there was no judgment, no insults and she found herself relaxing while in his company.

Her guard Rowan had all but disappeared ever since their confrontation in the stable and Savin seemed drawn and gaunt. The two men had shown a strained relationship, as if a chasm had opened between them and neither knew how to create a bridge. Their interactions were strictly professional, and rarely were they together when it was not required by duty. Rowan was in the garden currently, but stood by the door to guard the garden entrance while Rhea strolled along the individual paths.

Nyssa stepped into an intersection and smiled at Rhea. "The air is getting cold now. I am anticipating it will only be a few more weeks until the first snow covers the ground."

Rhea smiled back at her companion. "Does court change much during the winter seasons? I already miss the bright colors of the vendors in the courtyard and being able to take a ride around the walls every day."

She shrugged. "It will not change too drastically. We do have several events in which your assistance would be much appreciated, if you would be up to it."

"Oh? What events?"

"The largest is a wedding to join two of the wealthier Patron families. It will be occurring the day before the full moon and, as the Princess of the realm; I was put in charge of the whole affair. I could greatly use an extra mind and set of hands for both the planning and the execution."

"Oh, I would be delighted to help!" Rhea practically bounced in excitement. She had attended very few weddings in her life and the idea of a wedding in this strange place was intriguing. "Where will the wedding take place? Wait, the full moon; but that is tomorrow!"

"The groom's family wishes for it to take place at their villa, just outside the main castle walls. I will be going there in a few hours. Would you accompany me on the journey?"

Rhea bit her lip in disappointment. "Well, I was supposed to have dinner with Mat-um, the Prince tonight." Her face brightened at the thought of seeing the house of a wealthy Patron and spending some time out of the castle. "I'll have Savin give him my regards and reschedule for tomorrow. I'm sure he'll understand this once."

Nyssa gave her a curious look. "Well then, as long as he agrees we will ride out in two hours. We will probably be walking around quite a bit so dress for comfort more than elegance." She walked out the garden path.

Rhea practically skipped down the path towards the large clearing she had found months earlier. She still received some pangs of heartache when she remembered that she came to this place by kidnapping, but she had to admit to herself that her situation had certainly improved in the recent months. Mateo and Agrafina seemed to have a tense relationship but still sat next to one another during dinner so Rhea felt able to enjoy a companionship of her old friend without the obligations of the Forena position or the guilt from taking him away from Agrafina's affections.

She was about to step into the cleared area when soft voices belonging to a male and a female filtered through the trees. Rhea quietly slid behind one of the large trees and, using muscles she had not tested since high school, carefully climbed up the branches and perched about twelve feet off the ground. The thick branches and leaves successfully covered her person and she pushed her back flat against the thick trunk as she tucked her arms around her knees.

A woman stepped under the branch and shifted her weight from leg to leg as she waited for her companion. Several moments later Nastasio walked up with a small brown package clutched protectively in his hand.

"Hello, Nastasio, it is good to see you well." The woman's voice was hushed but her love for the boy could be heard in the tone. She looked around furtively and then gave the boy a quick hug.

"Hi, Alma. I brought a shawl for you. Mother said that you deserved a special present for your birthday since we knew that your Patron would not do anything."

Alma hugged him again and wiped tears from her eyes as she took the package. "You and mama are the best, Nasta. Thank you." She handed him a small bag of coins that jingled as he slid it into his deep pocket. "Here is the payment for the last three shawls that she purchased. I am sorry it took so long to get the money, you know how it is."

The boy shrugged. "You do what you can. We know that."

"How is mother? Is her health getting any better or does she still suffer from the cough of last season?"

"She still coughs. We have petitioned time and time again for the physician to come see her but he refuses. He says that the cough has settled into her lungs and there is nothing he can do to fix her."

"Oh, Nasta," her voice wavered, "what will happen to you? I wish I could take you into the court with me, but the Lady would never allow me to do so."

"I will be okay, Alma. You do not worry about me. I am eight, and almost a man grown after all. You just keep yourself out of trouble."

She nodded and gave him another quick hug. "I need to get back soon. She is napping but will wake up soon. I love you, Nasta, take care of yourself and mother."

He hugged her back. "We love you too, Alma. I will see you again when we can."

Up in the tree, Rhea carefully freed a hand to wipe the tears that had begun to fall from her eyes. It had not occurred to her that a single family could span the different levels of servitude and would be cut off from one another. She began to realize how the payment for goods among the different classes worked in this realm. The Patrons would take whatever they wanted from the servant vendors, and then it appeared their personal Mercenes would settle the debt with the vendor during a secret meeting after the event. This way the Patrons always felt as if they were having their wants handed to them without consequence.

I wonder if that is why the stable was so tense that day, she thought as she lowered herself out of the tree. *I overheard those two servants talking and they were worried I would say something. I wonder how to get an exchange started. I would still like to give Nastasio something for the shawl he gave me.*

She was lost in thought as she walked back towards the door, not noticing the wide clearing until she had walked out of the tree cover. A smile lit up her lips at the small benches and fountain set to one side of the clearing. She also found a small stone storage unit with a thick wooden lid and curiosity encouraged her to look inside. Inside the chest was a small supply of blankets that ranged from very lightweight to the thicker materials she anticipated would be commonly used during the winter months. There were also a few soft pillows as well.

Rhea pulled out one of the medium weight blankets and a pillow and laid it down in the center of the clearing, then settled herself onto the chilly ground. She supposed she could take five minutes to stare at the sky before she would have to get changed to ride out with Nyssa to the villa. She was quickly disappointed by the lack of clouds in the sky on that day and packed the blanket away as the air brought goose bumps to her exposed hands and face.

She walked back to Savin and then the pair headed back inside the large castle to prepare for a day of hard work. Rhea slipped into a taupe, split overdress with a pair of sturdy woven pants underneath. She had learned that this outfit was deemed suitable for women to wear while riding or working and took every chance she could get to wear pants, though she still longed for a pair of comfortable jeans.

A few minutes later she stepped out of the door just as Nyssa walked up in a similar manner of dress. Rhea was not pleased to see Rowan but greeted him with politeness before taking Savin's arm as he offered to escort her to the stables.

Rowan and Nyssa walked behind in similar fashion, and Rowan gave a small sigh then whispered, "What am I doing here, Nyssa? You do not need me to help get things ready if Savin is going as well."

Nyssa patted his arm. "I miss your company, Rowan. You have been occupied recently and I feel you growing distant from those who appreciate you."

He shrugged. "There seems to hardly be a point anymore. You were right, Nyssa, when you said that I may have ruined our one hope. I have seen the way she looks at Mateo and every day she slides deeper into his web of deceit."

"Well, it is not truly over until she accepts the position so keep yourself sharp and pull yourself together. Maybe our original plan will not be reasonable to execute but we can always find another way. You and Savin need time away from the castle as well. I hate seeing you two at odds." She smiled as she added, "Besides, I thought you would rather enjoy seeing Rhea in a different setting."

Chapter Sixteen

The Villa

The party arrived at the villa and found the preparations for the festivities already in full swing. Nyssa was instantly pounced upon by a middle-aged woman holding what looked eerily similar to the clipboard that held Rhea's inventory notes from the archaeology lab ages ago.

"Lady Nyssa, thank goodness that you have arrived! The flowers have been dropped off just minutes ago and Lady Kira has been beside herself in anxiety wondering how we were to get all of this finished in time." She turned towards the two men. "You two go assist the other men with the placement of the tables and chairs and such. Off with you now." She clapped her hands for emphasis.

Both men nodded and hurried off towards the area where the other men were milling about, grateful not to have been pulled into a conversation about daisies and color coordination. Rhea watched as Savin was greeted with pats on the back, handshakes and wide smiles and wondered for a moment why Rowan received such a cool and terse reception in his wake.

Nyssa was mumbling to herself as she scratched notes onto the clipboard with the pencil provided and Rhea followed her over to the table filled with flowers. The princess of the realm took one sweeping look of her choices and quickly pulled several bunches into quick but elegant arrangements. "Do this arrangement until we have run out. Save one each for the bride, her sister, and her mother and place the rest at intervals around the tables."

She gave Rhea a quick smile and took her arm. "We are going to go check on Kira and see if we can alleviate her fears about the day. Send Savin to contact me if you need us."

Desba waved them off and began to gather the flowers in a furious whirlwind of productivity.

The two stepped into the house to find a woman in her early twenties sprawled on the couch with her hands over her eyes. She moved her hand slightly when she heard the door open and popped up to hug Nyssa, then sank on the couch again as tears built up in her eyes. "What am I going to do, Nyssa? I do not know what to do!"

Nyssa sat down on the couch beside her and put a comforting arm around the younger woman's shoulder. "Well, first thing tomorrow I will be here and we will get you all dressed up. Then you are going to walk out to where Akaeno will be standing and you two will tell those in attendance that you are promising to a political alliance."

"Not that part! I know that part of the day, the ceremony and all." The woman dabbed at her blue eyes with a pink tinted piece of cloth. "I mean the after part. I do not know how to be a wife, or the wedding night, later on, how to-"she burst into tears again.

Nyssa laughed then and gave the woman a hug. "Oh, sweet heart, do not be worried about that part. You and Akaeno will figure it out just fine." She gave the woman a stern look. "You have been chaste, have you not?"

The woman nodded so quickly that Rhea was amazed her head did not topple from her shoulders. "Oh yes, Lady Nyssa. I have been waiting for this day for five years now and we would not dare do anything that would jeopardize either of our families. I just," she bit her lip, "what if we cannot figure it out? What if I cannot bear him children?" The woman looked absolutely horrified and close to fainting.

Rhea quickly jumped up and grabbed a cloth from the dressing table, dipped it in a water basin and gently pressed it to Kira's brow. "Take a deep breath now. Everything will be just fine."

Nyssa smiled her thanks at Rhea. "She is right, you know. You found something rare, Kira. You found a man who is within your status but who also loves you dearly. You will figure it out together, probably with a little laughter, and if we need to address the second issue then we will. There is no point in worrying about that now. You two will have many years to enjoy one another before you need to really worry about children and heirs. Both of your families are secure within their caste enough to give you a bit of breathing time."

Kira sniffled and wiped her eyes again. "Yes, I suppose you are right, as you always are." She turned towards Rhea, "And thank you as well. I do not know what has gotten into me."

Rhea smiled, "Oh, just bridal jitters. I hear it happens to the best of women. My name is Rhea, by the way, and I'm a friend of Nyssa's. She brought me out here today to help you with the preparations for tomorrow."

"Oh! It is so nice of you to come all the way out here for a stranger. Would you like a tour? It is not my villa yet in legal terms but I am sure Akaeno's family won't mind me showing Princess Nyssa and a friend of hers around the estate."

Nyssa laughed and stood up, then helped to pull both women to their feet. "I had better get back out there before Desba begins losing hair from worry, but you two go ahead." She gave Rhea a quick hug and whispered, "You can trust her, she is a friend," before hurrying out the front door.

The two women stared at each other in a moment of awkward silence before Kira cheerfully linked arms with Rhea. "Well then, let us go start at the front door!"

The stone villa was, to Rhea, massive in size and spectacular in design. The residence itself consisted of a main dining room, kitchen, receiving room, and spacious formal room. Kira explained that if the weather had not cooperated with clear skies the joining would have happened in this room as opposed to the outdoors. As the main ceremony can occur outdoors this room was set up in preparation for a large group of diners. Tables ringed the perimeter of the room and the large serving dishes and pots were already organized and placed to best display the food that would come later the next day.

As they walked through the expansive and perfectly manicured gardens Kira began to open up to Rhea and tell her a bit more about her life. She had been born in a nearby villa and lived her entire life as a Pengesare, or daughter of a wealthy man. Her betrothed also grew up as a Pengesare but also had been steadily acquiring his own wealth throughout his thirty years. The couple met five years earlier and instantly struck a spark, but were careful to keep their attraction away from the prying eyes and ears of the court Patrons. While both were legally suited to one another and their parents approved of the match, it was not uncommon for other Patrons to create false affections for entertainment.

Rhea found herself relaxing at the villa and very much enjoying the company of the young woman serving as her escort of the estate. She also noticed that every time they came within eyeshot of her soon-to-be husband, Kira would suddenly blush and her face glow with joy.

The women suppressed smiles as the groom, busy setting up chairs with the other men and, distracted by the view of his future wife, attempted to set one of the chairs on top of one already placed.

"Oh, he must be nervous too." Kira took one last look at him from under her lashes before the women moved away. "I have never seen him do something that silly, at least not in the company of others! I wonder what is causing him to be so nervous."

"I suspect the same thing that you were nervous about earlier."

Kira looked at her in amazement. "But why would he be nervous about that?"

Rhea chuckled. "Well, ultimately he's the one who could keep the night from happening if he were too nervous."

Kira gave her a wide eyed look and Rhea cleared her throat before responding. "Um, never mind. I'm sure both of you will be just fine and you have nothing to worry about."

The women finished the tour and came back to the main area where Nyssa and Desba were putting the finishing touches on the decorations. Kira clapped her hands in joy. "It looks absolutely beautiful! I cannot believe how much you have accomplished in such a short time."

Nyssa looked up from placing the flower stems in a bag to be composted and smiled back. "You deserve it, Kira. You have been nothing but a wonderful friend and helping with your wedding is the least I could do."

Desba made a sound of disapproval at the exchange of affection and moved to the next table.

Nyssa finished the last of the flowers and brushed her hands off. "Well, we should go check on the men and start to head back. We will have to be up early to come back out her tomorrow."

Kira smiled again. "Nyssa, what do you think about you and Rhea staying here tonight? We have plenty of space in the room I am using and we can always pull in another bed or two. Send one of the guards home for the things you will need and then they can return and we can spend the night catching up before I have to take up my wifely duties."

Her enthusiasm was infectious and the women could not help but smile in return. "That sounds like a perfect plan, Kira. We will send Savin back and keep Rowan out here, if that is acceptable with the men of the household."

Kira faltered, "Oh. I, um. Let me go confirm that with Akaeno's father and I will be right back."

Rhea watched curiously as the happy bride went to the group of men and pulled her betrothed's father aside. They had a quick conversation and, after a few dark looks toward Rowan by the man, she came back. "He said that was fine, but that he would have to stay outside."

Nyssa's eyes grew cold. "He is not a guard dog to be kept outside at night and tossed a bone to chew."

"I know that, Nyssa! I know that, but you know how people are with Rowan."

Nyssa pursed her lips together and took several deep breaths to push down her temper. "Yes, I know. I will never accept it, but I know. Let me go talk to him and Savin and see what we can figure out."

Rhea glanced at Kira while she watched Nyssa confer with the two men, anger rising on both of their faces but also some other emotion darkened Rowan's skin. "How are people with Rowan, Kira? I am new here and unfamiliar with all of the nuances."

"Oh, well, most people here distrust him, because of his color, you see. The royal family is all blonde hair and blue eyes and pale skin, like the King and Princess Nyssa."

"Well, sure. But most of the Mercenes are not. I mean, some of them are but then you have my main Mercene, Lianna, who is both dark of hair and eyes."

Kira gave her an odd look. "Mercenes can be any shade. They are not expected to be pure of appearance like the High Patrons or the DamaTalous."

"But if Rowan is a guard then why would it matter what color his hair is?"

Savin stepped up then, Rowan and Nyssa at his back, and said bitterly, "Because there is rank in every social marker and that is the way his cards fell on the day of his birth. I am going back to the castle to get the items needed by yourself and Lady Nyssa. She has given me an extensive list, but is there anything additional you would require?"

Rhea took the list and carefully scanned the items. "I don't believe there is anything to add. Nyssa certainly is thorough!"

Nyssa laughed. "Yes, well, it comes with the position. I have arranged for Rowan to stay in the stable with the rest of the Fuldt Rolig." She paused and looked at Rhea to clarify. "Those are the stable hands. He will require seeing us to bed of course and making sure we are secure in our lodgings before he will retire."

Rowan looked troubled but nodded his agreement. "I do not wish to cause any interruptions to your joyous occasion, Lady Kira, but as you know I hold the safety of my Lady Nyssa and Lady Rhea as first and foremost."

She smiled. "But of course I understand, Rowan. I will see to it that all in the stable receive extra rations tonight on your behalf."

He bowed stiffly and set off for the stable to discuss the arrangement with the current workers and residents of the large complex. Rhea wondered about the cryptic stories of his status but barely had time to give it more than a moment's thought before being bustled off to nervous activity by her new acquaintance.

Chapter Seventeen

The Villa

"You look absolutely stunning in that dress, Nyssa." Rhea fastened the final buttons and smoothed the fabric of the high neck. Nyssa was clad in a deep indigo gown with a lengthy train that trailed behind her as she moved around the room, the gown meant to signify her status in the DamaTalous. The high neck was created by careful lacework and the long sleeves were purple dyed lace that flared at the wrist and fell just to the fingertips.

Rhea carefully traced the intricate beadwork design on her own dress of a dark jade-hued silk. "What is the plan for today, Nyssa? I've never been to such a fancy wedding in my own time, much less one for people of a high status in a place like this. What do we do?"

Nyssa carefully placed her veil on her head before she loosely settled a light lavender veil onto Rhea's carefully styled hair. "Well, for the most part we just sit quietly and look moderately content. Not happy, mind you, just content. Because there is always a ceremony when the King arrives there will be an order to the guest entrance. The King will escort me down and we will take our places, then Mateo will follow behind him and the rest of the royal family and those held in high favor of the King. Rowan will be your escort for the day, do not give me that look, and Savin will be escorting Lianna."

"What about Agrafina? If Mateo walks in alone who will be her escort and really, shouldn't he be escorting her?"

A sharp look preceded the words. "Until Mateo declares an official Forena he will not be obligated to escort anyone. 'Fina is more or less his toy unless he makes her that offer and holds no more status than a regular Patron. Less really, because she is not allowed the regular freedoms of a regular Patron since she always has to be available for his every need, no matter the time."

"Oh, I see. I'm sorry if I hit a sore spot, Nyssa."

She smiled then, although it was a smile tinged with sadness. "No, you are fine, Rhea. I just feel like I have known you so long that I forget you are not from here and new to all the politics."

The women heard a burst of excited giggling from the hallway and Nyssa smiled. "That would be the bride starting her walk outside. We had better get moving and go greet our escorts so we do not hold up the ceremony."

Rhea stood for a moment in awe of her surroundings as the two women stepped outside. Family members and personal servants had been busy during the night and the decorations now included hundreds of beautifully dyed and skillfully draped ribbons hanging from every available place. Glass lanterns lined the wooden structure created by a marble fountain with smooth flooring that reminded Rhea of the dance floors described to her by friends who attended weddings. The chairs were set up in perfect rows and forced the viewer's eye to an intricately built gazebo, which had been erected for the day. A holy man in elaborate, heavy, golden robes stood in the structure with a large book in hand looking rather impatient.

The men from the court arrived then, dressed in golden clothing and their horses' hooves dancing upon the ground. Rhea fell into the required deep curtsy as the King and High Prince dismounted and walked over. The King graced the crowd with a rare smile and held out his arm to escort Nyssa to their seats. Rhea heard him murmur, "Perhaps this will encourage you to finally accept a suitor of your own," and felt a pang of sadness for her friend's relationship that could never be more than secret.

The High Prince stopped in front of her and treated her to a smile. "Hello, Rhea. I have missed you during my lonely dinner. We will have to find some time tonight to talk about some arrangements I have pondering for our future."

Rhea nodded graciously. "Yes, my Lord, whatever you wish."

Agrafina walked by then with a group of high status Patrons from the court. She was dressed in a beautiful silver gown with small embroidered embellishments of golden thread. Her veil was ivory and the edge was trimmed with precious gems that twinkled in the sunlight. The woman glanced at Rhea, the look filled with enmity and hostility, before settling into her designated seat.

Rhea was surprised at the sight of her friends dressed in their finest for the wedding. Lianna's wounds had fully healed and tonight she was the epitome of the elegant Mercene. She could have easily fit in with the Patrons with her finely tailored gown and perfect looks if it were not for her hair and eye color betraying her status.

Savin stepped beside Lianna dressed in an incredibly fitted pair of brown pants and a sable leather vest. His long hair had been tied up into a neat knot at the back of his head and he looked like much more than just a guard. He bowed deep to Rhea and kissed her hand before complimenting her looks. Then he turned to Lianna and offered his arm as they went to sit in their assigned section towards the middle of the chaired area.

Lianna looked up at Savin as they walked and Rhea felt her stomach flip at the sight. Her friend showed so much love and admiration in that look that she wondered how she never saw it before. She was also a bit unsettled that the flip had the familiar feeling of rejection from all of the times her crushes would ask if her friends were single or not.

"You look very beautiful tonight, Rhea."

She turned to the low voice and was shocked to feel her stomach flip the other way. Rowan stood in front of her, arm offered to escort her to their seats next to Lianna and Savin. As they walked

144

she used her peripheral vision to take in this man who looked a total stranger.

He was wearing well-fitted black cotton pants, tall black leather boots and a white shirt under an impeccably well-made hunter green leather vest. His dark hair had been tied into a neat ponytail at the nape of his neck. Rhea refused to admit to herself how well his clothing revealed the body it covered and began to wonder if she had been up too late listening to stories and advice given for Kira's wedding night.

"So, ah, how was your night?" Rhea sat down in her seat between Rowan and Lianna and crossed her hands in her lap.

Rowan shrugged, eyes focused on Nyssa sitting straight and tense by the King. "It was a typical night in the stables - hay, dust, and the conversations of the working men of the villa. How was your night in the company of the bride-to-be?"

Rhea could feel her cheeks turning that familiar shade of pink and focused on brushing some non-existent dirt off of her shoe. "Oh, the same, minus the hay and dust, just the silly talk of women."

Lianna coughed to cover up the laugh that threatened to burst from her mouth and Savin winked at Rhea, causing the blush to deepen from a pink to a deeper red. The holy man clapped his hands then and signaled for silence as the father of the bride walked down the aisle between the seats, his daughter close behind him.

They exchanged the words, traditional according to Lianna, where the new husband promised to keep his new wife safe, to provide for her, and to take responsibility for her actions. The father of the bride provided a list of assets she would bring to her new husband as well as his assurances that she would prove fertile and provide an heir to the estate in short order. Kira stood quietly between the two men, eyes downcast to hide the glow of joy she felt that she was finally able to become the wife of Akaeno.

Rhea took the time to subtly scan the faces around her and take in the audience. The royal family was present, along with many of the Patrons whom, she assumed, were of the same social standing as either the bride or groom. All of the Patrons were dressed in brightly colored silk gowns embellished with pounds of jewels and layers of fabric. The Patrons sat in perfect silence throughout the ceremony, eyes staring at the couple in the front and faces alternating between looks of boredom and anxiety.

Rhea gently nudged Rowan's knee with her right hand and whispered close to his ear. "Why is it that some of the Patrons look so anxious?"

He glanced around and then bent his head so that none but her could hear. "Most of the Patrons only view this wedding as a political allegiance and not a match between two people. They are already preoccupied with how this new allegiance will affect their trade, their social standing, and their own future political matches."

She nodded and quickly cast her eyes down as the Patron a few rows in front of them turned around and glared at the couple for their whispers. She caught Rowan stifle a laugh at the look and adjust his long legs in the short space between the rows. She moved her head closer and dropped her voice even lower. "Why are the Mercenes not looking concerned?"

His breath slightly tickled her ear as he responded. "All Mercenes present have been formally assigned to a Patron. In addition the bride and groom have kept the same Mercenes for over five years so they are not worried about movement or loss of status because of the wedding."

Rhea nodded again and focused on the remainder of the ceremony, feeling a small tug on her heart as the groom kissed his new bride on the cheek and the couple walked between the chairs to leave.

The King followed next with Nyssa; then Mateo walked down the aisle with a soft glance for Rhea and a dangerous look for the man next to her. After they entered the large room where the food was located, the Patrons also rose and filed out of the yard, flanked by the Mercenes and lesser Patrons behind them.

Rowan turned to Savin. "Do you want to go find us a seat at the tables and I will escort the women inside for the feast?"

Savin nodded with a probing look at Rhea. "Certainly." He stepped close to Rowan so the women could not hear his next words. "Rowan, be careful around the High Prince. I saw that look he gave you and it did not bode well. I do not want to see you hurt."

The dark haired man gave Savin a smirk and a small bow. "But of course. Am I not always cautious? The only one who can surprise me or best me in combat is yourself." He sobered at the concerned look in Savin's eye. "I have forgiven for you the bruises, Savin. Thank you for the warning. I will be careful." He turned to escort the women into the large receiving chamber.

Rhea was astounded by the amount of food laid out on the tables before her. Eight large, stuffed turkeys were placed on silver platters, one on each table, surrounded by deep serving dishes of potatoes, puddings, and vegetables. Fish covered in a berry sauce and large beef sides were available for those who strayed from the turkey and one of the tables was filled with pastries of all sorts. She followed Lianna's example and took only the tiniest amount of each type of food, so as not to offend the maker of the food, as Lianna explained before they entered. Rowan carried both of their plates to the table where Savin sat and glared at any who tried to slide onto the bench he had claimed as theirs.

The King, High Prince, Nyssa and the rest of the royal family sat at a large and elaborately decorated table next to the newly married couple. A table cloth of pure, bleached, white satin draped to the floor and the dishes were gilded with gold. Crystal goblets were filled with a deep blush wine of which the King and High Prince greatly enjoyed. Nyssa looked more reserved, sipping her wine and barely touching her food, while looking wistfully at the table that held her friends.

The tables surrounding Rhea and her companions were of a much more relaxed countenance. Polite manners still were observed but the Patrons and Mercenes were able to speak among one another and an occasional ribald joke could be heard down a table.

After a good amount of time the large pile of food began to subside and court tunes were struck up on the side of the marble dance floor. The groom led his bride out onto the floor; then bowed deeply as the King took her hand and the groom led Nyssa in the customary first dance. The music came to an end after a few moments and the groom eagerly took the hand of his bride and swept her up with a jaunty waltz as the members of their household stepped onto the dance floor.

Rhea gave a low curtsey as the High Prince stepped in front of her small party. "My Lord, I hope you are enjoying your time here."

He smiled at Rhea, earning a few dubious looks from her party and extended his hand. "I would enjoy it doubly more if you would grace me with a dance."

"I, um, well. I would like that very much; however, I am afraid I would just embarrass a man of your standing as I have never been instructed in the graceful manner of court dance."

His expression faltered but a moment, and then the smile once again fell on his lips. "Well, that is truly a shame. Perhaps we shall have to spend some time rectifying that problem in my chambers. Come walk with me instead, Rhea."

She nodded and felt his warm hand through the material on her back as he led her away from the table and toward the side of the dance floor. They would walk in this manner every day when they were in Virginia. Matt would escort Rhea home from work when they had a closing shift together, and every time a person walked by his hand would stray to her back as a protective gesture. They stood for a moment watching the couples dance before Rhea broke the silence. "Mateo," she inquired quietly, "I noticed that the Lady Nyssa is acting as the King's guest on this occasion, is that customary?"

"Quite. Ever since the Queen's death he has refused to consider an official consort and instead is content to have Nyssa as a stand-in for any duties which would fall onto the Queen. In addition, she would gain the throne if any tragedy was to befall the King or myself, and we make sure to screen any potential suitors thoroughly." He glanced at the woman, mesmerized by the dancing, and smiled slyly. "We choose only the best of the realm for the Lady Nyssa."

Rhea, distracted by the colors and whirling fabrics did not hear the sarcasm in his tone. "Oh, that is understandable." She processed this information, trying to view the stoic and seemingly somber woman in front of her with the one who ran barefoot through the garden or toiled to carry water for the less fortunate.

Her body leaned closer to the man as his hand gently caressed her hair from above the veil. "Have you given any thought to your future position in the court, Rhea?"

"I admit I have not. I have received the list of appropriate suitors from the Komisar, but find myself unable to have eyes for any of them at this time."

"I have missed you greatly over this past week, Rhea."

She smiled at the affection in his voice and felt his hand close over hers. "I have missed you as well, Mateo. It seems that my life here is made of bursts of business and then nothingness." *I missed you for years when you went missing, and now I have you back.*

His hand slowly slid up to her elbow, the act comforting and familiar. For a moment Rhea heard Matt's voice under the tone of the High Prince. "I could fix that, Rhea. I could make it so that you would answer to no one, and your every wish would be granted."

Rhea looked up at the man, seeing her old friend's face on his, the shining eyes and the easy smile. "I think I could enjoy a life with you, Mateo, but first I need to become more adept at the ways of this court." Her hand slipped into his, warm and comforting. *It would not be so hard to help you remember who you once were,* she thought. *I could have my friend back, and then we could find a way home.*

149

He cocked his head to the side then, hesitating before smiling and gently touching his lips to the back of her hand. "A well thought answer, my love. I will give you all the time you need. Ah look, Nyssa has been released from her Queenly duties and could use some assistance."

Rhea gave a quick curtsey and a brilliant smile before she hurried over to Nyssa to help her with a small tear in the bride's gown.

Chapter Eighteen

Asimina

"He told you what?" Nyssa glanced over at Rhea as they quickly tightened the girths on their simple leather saddles.

"He told me that he found a loop hole in the court protocol! I told him I was unwilling to accept the title if it meant 'Fina would be doomed, and he found an amendment that allowed her to regain her status in the court."

"Well, that is unlike him. It seems you must have truly melted his heart for him to have been willing to search for such a - loop hole – as you call it. I must admit in all of my years I have never heard of this amendment, but perhaps it was created solely for this purpose in recent days. What exactly were you talking about to bring up that subject?" The woman swung onto her gelding and waited for Rhea and Rowan to mount before quickly ducking through the hidden gate behind the stable.

"We've been talking about the position of Forena since the wedding and I told him that I wasn't able to accept the position if it meant 'Fina would be an outcast." She gave her friend a quizzical look. "We talk about a lot of things, is that such a surprise? He is, well, he was my best friend. He told me the things he does are for duty and duty only, and not personal pleasure so he would be more than willing to search for a way to make the transition easier on all involved."

During one of the slow stretches between the castle and Asimina, Rowan raised his voice to be heard through the growing wind. "And what makes you believe him when he talks such sweet words? When he says that he does not do these things for his own personal gain?"

Nyssa turned in the saddle to shoot him a dark look as Rhea shrugged.

"I don't have a reason to not believe him. Mateo has been nothing but an honest gentleman since he called me for dinner. He has never once said or done anything to make me suspect he is being deceitful. He is slightly more polite, more…sophisticated, but other than that he is my friend all over again." Rhea glanced back at Rowan, confused at the darkness that settled over his face. "Where is Savin anyway?"

Rowan began to reply but was cut off by Nyssa. "Savin was unable to extricate himself from the party this time. He went with the other men."

"He went with…Oh, Nyssa you can't be serious!"

"He went with them but will do nothing to aid their goal. If anything they are likely making slow time to the village. He is a skilled rider and will be able to cause his horse to kick up dust the entire way there without any visible command. It will give the village time to react and protect their people."

Rowan called up the line. "Unlike your darling Prince. He is likely riding head of the line as usual, expressing his extreme disgust at the delay of grabbing new play things."

Rhea reined in her horse sharply and turned in the saddle. "And just what did Mateo do to you to give you so much hatred of the man, de Nespa? Did he kick your dog? Spit in your food? Steal the woman you loved? It is not his fault you are of a lower status."

Nyssa spun around then, too, jaw dropped and eyes wide that Rhea would have chosen such a direct attack on Rowan's darkening mood.

The man carefully cleared his throat several times, hands flexing on the reins and chest still as death. Finally he looked up at the two women and forced a smile onto his face. "Perhaps all of the above. I will not speak of him again, my Lady."

A huge breath of relief gusted from Nyssa's chest then and she turned back to the front just in time to see a giant bird silhouetted against the sun. "Rowan! Look out!" she screamed.

The bird slammed into Rowan with enough force to stagger his horse sideways into a nearby tree. He kept his seat only through his grip on the thick leather saddle and the tree trunk that his right side was pinned against. The large russet hawk settled onto Rowan's leather-clad arm and began to preen its feathers.

"Was that entrance dramatic enough for you, Faulks? I thought we had a discussion on smooth landings last time?" Rowan looped the reins of his terrified horse around his arm and ran his free hand down the mane in a soothing gesture.

Rhea looked at the bird in amazement while Nyssa shook in her saddle with laughter. "Well, maybe Faulks was just angry that it has been so long since last time."

The bird swiveled its head around and Rhea could have sworn she saw one of those majestic amber eyes wink at Nyssa before the bird rubbed its head against Rowan's chest.

The man scratched the large raptor on the neck, ruffling its feathers in the process. "Yes, well. It has been a while since I have been able to get out of the castle and have some quality man-to-hawk time." He looked up at the sun as it dipped past the midday point. "They should be there by now. We should make up time and ride."

The hawk obediently moved down his arm to perch those strong talons into the thick leather pommel of the saddle. Rowan gave the horse one last pat before plunging into the canyon as quickly as safety would allow behind the two women.

They arrived at Asimina shortly after the soldiers from the castle had left. Sebast quickly made his way across the field, uninjured, and gave a deep bow to Rowan before pulling Nyssa into an embrace. He was clad in the usual light cotton shirt and heavy pants and gave Rhea a brief smile before turning back towards the village.

"Thank the spirits for Savin. He and his little dancing horse kicked up so much dust that all five men were able to escape into the woods. Most of the women and children were able to run as well just in case they decided to add them to the list. I believe the King will be quite unsatisfied with his entertainment today!"

The four arrived in the village, then, and Rhea received a glimpse of what the village must have been like before being decimated by this practice. While there were not many men, each one was working diligently to patch the shelters, helping carry water from the river and pounding some corn into coarse flour.

Rhea recognized many of the women and children from her last visit, and her heart sank as she remembered faces that were now not seen among the crowd. A small boy tugged on her sleeve and looked up with eyes wide. "Up, circle please."

She almost cried at the simple command and complied instantly, picking up the small boy and spinning in a circle until a squeal of laughter escaped from his lungs. Other children made their way over then, and Rhea treated them all to a hug or a quick spin, ending in the center of the village.

A man from the village walked up to where Sebast and Rowan were standing and watched the woman with the children. "She is doing more for those children right now than we have been able to do in a while."

Sebast nodded, eyes travelling from Rhea with the children to Nyssa helping the women to patch garments. "They are certainly two incredible women." He glanced at Rowan. "Maybe it is a good thing you brought her here, Rowan."

Rowan scuffed a heel into the dirt. "That has yet to be determined."

The third man chuckled at the expression on Rowan's face. "It is not every day you find a woman of her beauty who is willing to come here, work, and then spread joy in the simplest of ways."

Rowan growled under his breath. "Okay, I hear you. Rhea is an amazing woman who will do our realm a lot of good. She has also been claimed by the High Prince as a potential Forena and, for some insane reason, has decided he is a good person at heart, forced to do unpleasant things by the King while I do nothing but cause her emotional pain. What do you want me to do?"

The men fell quiet then and Nyssa glanced over in concern. She could not hear the words but knew Rowan's tone of voice well enough to know that they were not joyful phrases coming out of his mouth. She distributed the last cloak to the women and walked over to where the winded Rhea put the last child down with a smile.

"Walk with me, friend, so we can gather some fruit for the people."

A cool breeze cut through the hot air as the two women approached a small orchard. Rhea's eyes lit up as she saw the rows of apple and pear trees covering the ground. "How did these come to be here?"

Nyssa smiled and picked a ripe apple from the first tree. "This was our project from a few years ago. Rowan and Savin helped me sneak out seeds and saplings and would ride here every other day to water the young plants and help them to grow. This is the first year they have provided fruit. I wanted to make sure they did before telling the villagers about the small grove."

Rhea grinned and walked to the nearby pear tree, pulling the branches down toward her so that she could pluck the ripe fruit and fill her basket. "Nyssa, what if we took some of the fruit to a friendly farm and asked if we could use their kitchen to can it? I don't know anything about canning or making jelly, but I know my grandmother used to do it every year because she bought entirely too much produce when it was at peak season."

"That is a fabulous idea! I will have Aleksei do it and say it is a present for a sweetheart. He knows not to ask questions and I trust him with my life." Her smile faded and she turned to her friend. "Rhea, I hope that this is not something that needs to be spoken, but you are being careful to keep this from Mateo, are you not?"

Rhea filled her basket with the last pear and hefted it up to her shoulder to carry back to the village. "Of course, Nyssa. Why would you think such a thing?"

The woman shrugged. "I just was not sure since, well, since you and Mateo have grown so close. I worried that you may have forgotten that he would not be happy if he knew what we were doing out here."

"I know that, Nyssa. You all are my best friends and I would never betray Sebast or his village. Whenever Mateo mentions Asimina I just give him a blank look and change the subject."

Nyssa smiled as if a huge weight had been lifted from her shoulders. "Thank you, Rhea. I had hoped you remained as true as I knew you to be, but was worried."

Rhea gave her friend's hand an affectionate squeeze. "I won't ever do anything to put you in danger, Nyssa. You are far too dear too me, and I would be a mess without you or the others."

It was a short walk back to the village and both women laughed with joy at the expression on the faces of the villagers. Sebast hurried over to carry the basket, eyes wide with amazement at the contents.

"Where did you get these?" His eyes narrowed at Nyssa and he tilted his head to the side in suspicion. "You did not steal them did you?"

She laughed. "Technically yes, but the saplings and seeds were taken years ago and never missed. I just wanted to make sure the orchard would bear fruit before showing it to you."

One of the bolder women stepped forward, eyes glistening with tears as she looked at the small treasures. "An orchard? There are more?"

"Oh yes, much more. Your village now has an orchard with fifty apple trees, ten pear trees and six sweet cherry trees. Rhea came up with the idea of preserving the extra fruit so I will have a trusted friend see to it that the surplus gets dried, canned, or jellied and you will be able to have the bounty the entire year."

Rowan took out a small hunting knife and carefully cut a few of the apples and pears the women had brought back into bite-sized pieces, then walked around the village center to make sure that every person received a taste. He then walked over to where Nyssa was standing at the edge of the circle, eyes glistening with unshed tears of joy.

"You would have made Queen Sula proud, Nyssa. She shines through in everything you do."

She sniffled and wiped a tear that escaped from her eye. "Thank you. It just never feels like enough."

"We do what we can do with what we have been given."

"Yes, we do."

Chapter Nineteen

The Court

Rhea woke the next day to violent shaking from her friend Lianna and loud cries from the cat. "Lianna, what's wrong? I was having a wonderful dream about eating macaroni and cheese and going to see a movie."

"We have to get dressed, we have to go outside." Lianna was white as a ghost and already throwing on a simple gown and pulling out a grey cotton dress for Rhea.

Rhea quickly stepped into the dress as she picked up the desperation in the woman's energy. "Why? What's going on?"

Lianna fastened their veils with two quick pins just as Savin banged on the door twice. "We are coming, Savin! Is Rowan out there already?" She unlocked and swung open the door to find both men present.

Rhea stifled a deep yawn and glanced outside. "Wait, it's still dark outside. Will someone please tell me what's going on?"

Savin took the lead down the hallway and the women fell in behind him. Rowan stepped to the side of Rhea and quietly said, "Zelkhova and his men are setting up whipping posts. Something must have happened yesterday, something bad."

"Who is Zelkhova?"

Lianna glanced back and whispered, "He is in charge of punishments and executions."

"Oh," Rhea paled. "But why so early?"

Rowan spoke under his breath as they stepped through a door into the edge of the courtyard. "That way they have time to clean up the mess before the daily routine gets underway."

Nyssa was at their side then, a vision of outward calm even though her eyes reflected the turmoil within. "Listen to me well, for I must speak quickly. Whatever you do, stay here at the edge, stay quiet, and do not try to be a hero. The man will be compensated as best I can and, as usual, this is a situation where honesty will do the greater good no favors." She gave the men a stern look and then hurried away, arriving at her original spot just seconds before the King and High Prince arrived in fully-dressed glory.

The man called Zelkhova stepped in front of a wooden structure assembled in the courtyard. The man was not impressive in height or build, but had arms as firm as tree trunks and muscles that rippled with every motion. The wooden structure consisted of two tall poles, roughly eight feet in height and the width of telephone poles. Thick, rough ropes were secured at the top of the poles and finely shaven saw dust was placed between them in a two-inch bed.

Light from nearby torches and lanterns cast his face into an eerie and menacing half-lit state. Short, white, spiky hair was perfectly groomed on his head and eyes the color of dark coal gleamed in his face. He turned to the crowd and his nasal tone rang out across the courtyard. "Bring the man!"

Two guards came forward then with a shirtless man between them. The man was one of the land, with dirt stains on his pants and scars crisscrossed against his bared chest. Unkempt sandy brown hair fell in front of his eyes, damp with sweat and what Rhea suspected was the glint of wet blood.

The landlet was stopped in front of Zelkhova and forced to his knees. "Speak your name, landlet!"

"My name is Ito, my Lord."

"And do you accept the guilt and consequences for the offense of minor conspiracy?"

"I accept the guilt and consequence, merciful Lord."

"Then you admit to warning the Skov village to the approach of our people!"

The crowd seemed to hold its breath, and Rhea slid her hand onto Savin's arm in alarm.

"I do, my Lord."

The breath released and the crowd was suddenly filled with noise and movement. Anger rose in the voices and gestures of the men and women present. The majority of those present were enraged over the offense and the Patrons called for justice. The quieter anger was that of the people who proclaimed the man's innocence and the wrongness of the punishment.

Rhea tightened her hand as Savin began to move. "No, Savin, Nyssa said stay put." She saw Rowan move closer to the large man until he was close enough to get a hand on Savin's elbow.

The guard stared at Rhea with grief and anger in his eyes. "It is not right for him to take the punishment for something I did. This is not right."

"Better him than you," Lianna hissed under her breath. "He knows what he is admitting to and what the consequence would be. You know what will happen if you step forward, Savin, and then what will happen to us!"

He stepped back then, visibly forcing his muscles to relax. "I know, I know. It still is not right."

Lianna squeezed his arm. "Is not that always the way of the realm, Savin?"

A rumble of anticipation forced Rhea's eyes towards the platform. The man was tied between the poles now, arms extended far above his head and to the side. Zelkhova stood between him and the crowd and Rhea flinched as the leather whip cut through the man's tan skin and sent trails of bright crimson down to the sawdust. The Patrons cheered, clapping and shouting with each lash, each time the whip sliced down and split the skin across the man's back. The servants and lower class stood silently, casting uneasy glances at the sight of the well-known and even-tempered man in such condition.

The man bore his pain in near silence, allowing only the smallest of groans to escape from his lips as leather crossed already lacerated flesh. His biceps and forearms strained with the pain, fingers digging into the ropes that chafed the thin skin around his wrists in an attempt to stay standing. His breath began to come with difficulty, the harsh rasping sound echoing through the courtyard and bouncing from the tall, stone walls.

Rhea turned to Rowan, unshed tears welling in her eyes at the cruelty. "What would the punishment for Savin have been? This seems barbaric enough."

Rowan swallowed hard. "If a guard was given the charges it would have been treason to the crown, punishable by immediate beheading."

She felt the world get hazy then and reached out to the side to grab Rowan's strong arm. He wrapped an arm around her waist to hold her steady as she wavered. "Rhea? Rhea, focus on my voice."

The voice was comforting, deep, and she felt drawn to it. Rhea clawed her way out of the hazy blackness that was threatening to overtake her and took a shaky breath. Her eyes focused on the worried face that was now in front of her. "Okay. I'm okay. When did it get so cold?"

Rowan took off his light cloak and wrapped it around her shoulders, leaving his arm for support as he carefully led her out of the large crowd. They found a hay bale at the perimeter of the crowd and she sat down hard, breathing fast and leaning on the man for support. "I've never done that before."

"You have probably never been in a situation like this before either."

She shook her head, regretting the action when small white dots danced before her eyes. Rowan's hand was warm as it rubbed between her shoulder blades and she used that warmth to anchor herself and while sucking in deep breaths. Her face felt clammy, cold and damp and she felt the edges of her veil sticking to her cheeks before she pulled it behind her ears.

"Easy now. Focus on your breathing. If you need to let yourself sink into the darkness I am right here and will not let you fall. No one will blame you or think badly. None will harm you."

This time the head shake was done slowly. "I think I'll be okay. I just need to sit a moment." Rhea focused on the ground in front of her as her face gradually warmed and her hands stopped shaking. She looked at Rowan. "Thank you for being here."

"It is what I am here for after all. I may have been a bad Komisar in the past but I do not intend to repeat that mistake again."

There was some pleading in his eyes, something that the man wanted to convey. Rhea started to ask him what he meant when the sight of cream-colored boots stepped onto the pebbles to which she had averted her attention.

"Lady Rhea, are you unwell? I saw your Komisar lead you over here and was worried for your well-being."

Rhea smiled up at Mateo. "I will be fine, High Prince. Just a moment of faintness is all. Luckily for me Komisar de Nespa was there to keep me on my feet."

The man gave a false smile unseen by Rhea. "Oh, lucky indeed." He extended a gloved hand towards the woman and gently tugged her hand. "Come with me, Rhea. There is no point in you remaining in this dusty courtyard. Come with me and we will get you some rest and refreshment. Your Komisar can wait by the door."

She let herself be pulled up and guided inside, feeling slightly better but still shaky on her feet. Rhea focused on putting one foot in front of the other as they walked down the hallways to Mateo's waiting chamber. He held open the door to allow Rhea to pass through, gave Rowan a dark look and then swung the door shut with him still standing on the threshold.

Rhea sank down on a nearby plush couch, letting herself sink into the fabric cushions and resting her head against the tall back headrest. "Forgive me for my weakness, my Prince. I have never been in a situation of that sort before and reacted poorly."

Mateo shook his head and brought her a cup filled with clear, cold water. "I should have asked Father to place you by myself and the Princess. Who knows what the lesser beings around you were whispering to cause such a fright."

A sip of cold water cleared her head and refreshed Rhea further. "Why the punishment? What is that village that a warning of our approach would cause such a response?"

Mateo stared out the window at the rising sun. "Asimina is a curse on our people. The village is filled with sickness and death, and the only way for their people to survive is with our help. We go there when able to remove the sickest of the men and make sure that they do not pass the illness to others. We have been taking care of them since the beginning of my memories and rarely have we had such a mess as we did today."

Rhea looked at him curiously, trying to put her experiences at the village to his description. "I see. Then the men are brought back here for nursing?"

A sad look flitted across his face. "If only it were that simple. No, Rhea, this village is beyond repair that any of us can give. The men are brought here and put into a contest, a great honor as their final contribution to life on this plane of existence. Without the games

163

our gods will not give us rain for crops, or children to continue our line. We are lucky in that way. If it were not for an already ailing village with the ability to spread their disease throughout the land, we would have to begin sacrificing our own people to the spirits."

"Is there not another way? One that doesn't involve killing people?"

"You sound as if you are personally vested in these people, Rhea." Mateo's voice was calm, soothing, almost hypnotic to Rhea's tired mind. "Have you seen the people of Asimina?"

Rhea barely pulled herself out of the fatigue induced trance before answering. "That's a silly question. I don't even know where this village must be. My only experience out of the castle walls was at the Lady Kira's wedding, after all. In my world killing is viewed as an abysmal act, is all, so it is hard for me to come to terms with the necessity of the action."

"Ah, yes, a fabulous wedding." His blue eyes softened. "Rhea, have you given more thought to my consideration? I have spoken with Agrafina and she is agreeable to the arrangements." He kneeled in front of Rhea and tenderly placed her hand over his heart. "You have changed something in me, you beautiful woman from another world. It is as if I have known you for a lifetime instead of such a short time."

"I need a little more time, my sweet Prince, just a little bit more time."

Chapter Twenty

The Court

"You seem distracted today, Lady Rhea. Is everything alright?"

Rhea jumped at the voice and laid a hand on Kalar to sooth the mare she spooked. "I'm fine, Aleksei. I just have a lot on my mind is all."

A grin lit the young man's face. "I should say so! You have been brushing that spot on Kalar for so long that the coat is as shiny as a new mirror."

She stammered out, "Yes, well, I guess I've been going through the motion without realizing what I was doing."

Aleksei leaned against the side of the stall. "It seems to me there is another female in this stable who is a bit on edge today. I was wondering if you would do me a favor and take Kataolya into the practice yard. She is a bit full of herself for riding but seems to like you much more than the stable lads. She could use a bit of companionship, a gentle hand, and some time in the sun."

"I would be happy to take her out." She gave the gray mare a gentle pat and a kiss on the nose before carefully latching the stall behind her. She walked a step behind Aleksei down the long vacant corridor that led the other mare's stall.

"Aleksei," she asked, "I was wondering if you could tell me where the mare came from. She doesn't seem like any of the other horses I've seen in the stable."

He shook his head sadly as he remembered. "Ah, she is a beauty and one of a kind. She used to be the Queen's horse, from the moment she was born. Queen Sula found her out in Steinbrekka, wee little slip of a horse, maybe two months old at that point. She found a nursing mare with milk enough for two and kept that little filly alive by sheer will alone. Horse was a perfectly behaved angel at that point. The Lady would ride sidesaddle throughout crowds and Kata would just step daintily about any stray feet and keep the Queen from harm. My pop even has great stories of the Lady Nyssa being thrown on the horses back when she was just a babe and Kata proudly walking her around the exercise ring as if she were the Princess's own mamma."

"That's hard to believe, given her behavior now. She seems like a wild thing." Rhea thought of a detail, "but Aleksei, if Nyssa was riding on the mare when she was baby, that means the mare is over twenty years old!"

He smiled, "They make them long lasting in Steinbrekka. According to my pop, the Queen brought the girl to us, oh, twenty-seven years ago, give or take a year. Then she just went crazy when the Queen left this earth. One of her eyes turned dark and gray started to be seen in her mane and tail. Suddenly she was afraid of everyone and unwilling for anyone to touch her or approach. The High Prince insists on riding her on occasion, using whips and spurs to make her behave, but the rest of us, well, we let her be. No point in stressing the old girl now unless we absolutely have to do so after all. She has earned a bit of peace and quiet. I just wish her inner demons would not torment her so badly as they do."

They reached the stall and Rhea slowly stepped in front of the door. The mare was covered in a thin layer of dust and hay was tangled in the graying mane. Whites showed in her eyes as they moved closer to the stall and she backed into the far corner of the enclosure.

"Hey pretty girl, no need to be scared of me." Rhea kept her voice low and smooth, "I'm not going to hurt you or do anything that will scare you." She pulled a small stool over and sat just outside the door, with her side to the mare, giving Aleksei a small wave goodbye. "I once had a horse who was very scared of everything, but you didn't know that. She was a good mare. We called her Callie. She was a chestnut, with her coat and body being a bright red that rippled in the sun. Her past career was as a racehorse, you see, but she hurt herself early on so they turned her into a breeding mare instead." She shook her head sadly as she remembered the first day the mare had arrived at the barn.

"She was a mess, even worse than you. She came to us with a little filly that arrived to the farm dead in the trailer. The poor momma was beside herself in anger and fear. Everyone who tried to open the door would get attacked, but you could hardly blame her. She was just defending her baby, after all. She didn't know we were just there to help her. We just opened the door and left the trailer in the field so she could come and go as she pleased. She came out, eventually, and we were able to bury the foal." Tears started to fall. "Someone had done something horrible to her and I think she just snapped. It took me months before she would let me approach her, and then more months before I could lay a hand on her neck."

She sniffed and smiled to herself as she felt a cautious pair of lips moving along her hair. "But she came around eventually. It took years, but she came around. We found her a good home with a rich old lady who wanted a beautiful horse to look at and who hired a caretaker who worked with rescue cases. Her days were spent trotting around a lush green field and being admired by everyone who passed."

Rhea carefully turned and saw the horse looking at her quizzically. "Can I pet you now beautiful girl? Would that be okay?" She lifted her hand slowly, making sure the mare saw every movement of every finger for several seconds before moving closer to the lowered head. When she was just one inch away she held her hand still, then smiled as the mare dropped her forehead into the woman's hand.

"That's a good girl." She rubbed the head in gentle circles, slowly moving the other hand to move down the mare's neck in slow even strokes. "Do you think we could have a little brushing?" She picked up a nearby brush and held it up to the horse for inspection. After no outward objection from the mare the woman slowly stood and walked into the stall, then began to lightly groom the dust off.

The mare visibly relaxed then, shifting her weight off one of her hind legs and letting the head droop down. After quite some time Rhea looked down to realize that she was covered with more dust than the horse.

"I bet you could use some exercise time, maybe a bask in the sun. Will you let me put a harness and lead rope on you, sweet girl? It looks as if your stall opens up to a small fenced in area where we could go." She picked up the light cloth harness that had been left outside the stall and held it out to the mare for inspection.

Kataolya backed up then, tension slowly seeping back into that powerful body. Rhea lowered the harness and leaned back against the wall, willing calm into her every expression. "We're doing this on your own time, sweetheart. Let me know when you are ready."

Calm rippled through the muscles of the mare and she moved forward to poke her nose through the halter. Rhea slowly and gently fastened the slipknot ties and then moved back a foot. "See? Now we're attached to each other." She looked at the door and felt a moment of apprehension. "You aren't going to run away if I open this door are you? I don't think I would survive for very long if I lost the Queen's horse."

She took a deep breath and opened the door, then stepped outside and slightly to the left so the mare could follow. "Come on girl, let's get you some sun."

The sun trickled down the black mare's clean mane as she slowly stepped out onto the grass. Rhea braced herself for the wild burst of energy she expected from a horse that had been cooped up in a stall for far too long and was surprised when the mare simply stood half out of the stall and trembled.

"Hey now, it's okay. The sun is our friend and we like to feel it beating on our backs." She encouraged the mare to take a few more steps into the pasture. "See, this is good." Rhea moved beside her and ran a hand down the warm fur. "Not so scary, is it?" A few more steps had the mare completely out and in the sunlight.

Aleksei and Savin stood off to the side of the pasture in the shade of a large round bale of hay. "She got her outside without a fight. I may have suggested it, but I was not thinking it would happen so smoothly."

Savin softly grinned. "Well, she is sleeping in the Queen's room and wore her cloak at Steinbrekka. Maybe the horse is drawn to the scent?"

The stable hand snorted, disturbing a group of nearby foals lounging in the shade. "After ten years? I doubt that." He hesitated. "Is Rowan still being surly?"

A sigh escaped Savin's lips. "No, he is on his best behavior now that he realized he cannot push her. For all her bravado and charisma I think on the inside she is a very scared woman just trying to find small joys in the day. The problem is now Mateo has become interested and has offered her the position of Forena."

Aleksei's breath caught in his throat. "How? She does not seem like the type to enjoy his brand of hospitality."

The larger man hesitated. "He has changed, at least when she is around. She asks him questions, makes requests, and he actually considers them before answering."

"Well, that is just...really?" Aleksei looked at the man in disbelief. "I guess if I think back, he has not taken out Kataolya since Rhea first came here and has been sticking to his white stallion instead." He scratched his head. "What would that mean for us?"

"That is just it. None of us know what it would mean for us. I just cannot put the two personalities together when I think of the High Prince. I just, I have this nagging feeling that something is amiss. As if I can sense the guillotine above our heads but cannot yet see the blade or the executioner."

A smile grew on Aleksei's face as he watched the woman slightly lean her weight onto the mare's back, and the mare accepting the action. "I am sure it has, but has it occurred to you that he might have some grand scheme?" He frowned slightly. "That he might have some plot that he is going to pull her into that will be the destruction of us all?"

"It has, but he seems genuine around her, almost human."

"Then either she truly has the ability to change our world, or we are in much greater danger than we ever anticipated."

Chapter Twenty-One

The Court

For several hours Rhea tossed and turned in her bed, unable to sleep or quiet her racing mind. Something was happening that day but she did not know what. All day people had been elusive, tense, and Mateo had quickly left their dinner after his Komisar stepped in with his riding cloak billowing. The mounted party of ten left the castle walls shortly after, the white stallion shining in the lead.

Lianna had disappeared that day, as well, only returning for a few brief hours of sleep before taking off down a narrow hallway. Rowan stood outside Rhea's door and Savin was nowhere to be found. Finally Rhea gave up on sleep and pulled on a dark blue dress, then knocked on the door once and swung it open.

"Rowan, what is going on today? I can feel something in the very air."

The man sighed and stared at the ceiling a moment. "May I enter your chamber? It is best not to discuss such matters in the hallway."

"Well, sure, come in." Rhea stepped back, a bit startled that he would ask permission when, as Komisar, he had access to her room at any time.

"We found a man on the lake beach today, washed ashore. Alive, but just barely. The men went out to fetch him and Lianna has been busy with her mother preparing remedies to try to repair his body. We think that he is from your time. We found one of those little cards with his name and picture like the day we found you."

"Oh! Could I see him? I may not be able to help very much with the healing, well, besides carrying water or fetching things, but I may be able to get some information out of him." Rhea slid into her court shoes as she spoke.

Rowan hesitated. "With respect, I do not think that is the best idea, my Lady."

Her face darkened. "Because I'm helpless and weak?"

His eyes widened. "No! Not- you are not helpless and weak." A tired hand ran through his hair. "It is because all people who enter this realm from the other must go through the process, similar to the one you went through." He put a soft hand on her shoulder. "Rhea, even if he lives from these wounds to the body and mind, it is very likely he will not live through the Transcinare. I do not want his potential death to weigh heavily on your conscious if you try to help him."

Rhea stood speechless for several minutes as she processed the information before she gathered her courage. "Even knowing this, I still would like to go see him. I need to do it, to remind myself that this is not my home, not where I belong. I've gotten too comfortable here and have forgotten too much of my past life."

Silence filled the room for several long minutes until Rowan finally sighed and handed the woman her cloak. "Savin may punch me again for it, but alright, let us go down and see him."

The prisoner sat in a small room, bare of any decoration or furniture with the exception of a small wooden cot. Lianna sat to one side, carefully wiping away the worst of the blood and adding healing poultices onto the deepest of the wounds. She cast a look of unease towards Rowan as he entered with Rhea.

"I do not think he will live to go to Steinbrekka. He spent too much time under the water and a part of his mind broke at the crossing."

Rhea kneeled beside her friend and placed a hand to the man's fevered brow. "Where did he come from?"

Lianna shrugged. "The lake is all that we know. People come through the lake all the time and we find odd bits of debris on the shore. Pieces of boats, large pieces of metal, but very rarely do we have a survivor."

"Large pieces of metal?" Rhea looked down as the man stirred on the hard bench. "Hi there, my name is Rhea. I'm from Virginia, in the United States. Where are you from?"

The injured man made an effort to swallow then whispered, "Sailing to Bahamas. Crew said not to go through triangle but I thought it was just a myth." He looked up into her eyes. "A hole opened in the water, and we couldn't escape. One minute it was clear sailing and then the water turned white, and then there was this hole. There was crying and screaming and then nothing." His chest spasmed as he began to cough.

Lianna put a calm hand on his shoulder. "That was good. You did well to tell your story. Rest now and get back your strength."

Rowan led Rhea off to the side as the man closed his eyes, it seemed for the last time. "What did he mean?"

Rhea wiped a tear off of her cheek and slumped back against the doorframe. "The Bermuda Triangle, or Devil's Triangle. It's a section of water where a bunch of boats and planes were reported to have mysteriously disappeared. Most people think it's just a myth, or bad reporting, but some think the area is possessed by aliens or supernatural forces."

Rowan looked at her blankly. "I do not understand what you are saying."

She sighed and shook her head. "Just a strange thing from my world that is apparently dumping things into your world."

All three people in the room jumped as the door banged open and Savin entered. "They got a girl. Your mother needs you Lianna, and you, as well, Rhea."

Lianna looked down as the man's chest ceased to move. "Well, hopefully he is at peace now. Let us go to the girl and hope she will fare better than this poor soul."

They quickly walked down a long and dark hallway, soft slippers scraping and stepping lightly upon the stone floor. Rowan held open a door and the women entered the room. Rhea remembered this chamber from her arrival at this realm, the first time she had met Lianna and was being prepared for her Transcinare. He shut the door behind them and remained in the hallway with Savin.

Rhea walked in cautiously as she took in the shivering, trembling, young woman standing by Risalka. Her hair was a deep black, with hazel eyes set into a pale face. She was clad in ripped jeans and a t-shirt and appeared to be missing her left shoe.

"We are to bathe and clothe her, and then show her to the room. She will start her trial tomorrow." Risalka turned to the door, "The High Prince has required Rowan to attend as escort, along with myself and the guard Sarkan."

"Tomorrow?" Lianna blinked and stared incredulously at the woman in front of her, "Are they sure that they want her to start tomorrow?"

Risalka nodded. "That is the instruction of which I have received."

Lianna nodded as well and the two women got to work on the terrified woman while Rhea tried to keep her mind occupied.

"Where are you from?"

A soft and shaky voice answered, "From Washington. We went to see the hole, and dad told me not to get to close but something kept pulling me closer to the edge. Then I was falling and woke up in a glass box with strange men around me." Sobs began to rack her body as she whimpered, "I want to go home. I don't know where I am or what I did or what you people want but I want to go home now. My dad doesn't have a lot of money but he'll give you every penny if you just send me home. I swear I won't tell anyone about this and I'll never go near the hole again and I'll never, ever, disobey my father again if you just let me go home."

Rhea looked away from the pain in the girl's eyes as she remembered her own frantic haggling for her life months and months ago. She put on a false smile and made a decision. "We will get you home sweetheart." She ignored the angry grumble from the other women and glared them into silence. "We have to wait a little bit though. The elevator takes a long time to travel up and down so it's going to take a little bit. For right now you just let us clean you up and get you warm and then we'll talk about getting you home, okay?"

The tears subsided and the girl gave a small smile. "Okay. I can wait for a little bit if it means we are going home and I can see my dog again."

<u>Chapter Twenty-Two</u>

The Court

Rowan spent the day pacing a circular path in Rhea's chamber, stopping only to pet the gray cat who insisted on winding around his feet. "Why do I have to go? I hate going to Steinbrekka. Why does he not take Brokkan, or Eitri, or any of the other guards who do not mind that dismal place and horrid task?"

Lianna snapped at him, "Why do you think? Obviously you angered or irritated someone important and this is what they decided was a suitable punishment for you. Now stop pacing, it is giving me a headache."

Rhea slipped into the room. "I tried to talk to Mateo but he wouldn't budge. He said it was better for her to get it over with now before she has had time to scare herself into fits. He did agree to withhold the poisoned food and give her proper sustenance before she leaves."

Her friends' eyes rolled as Lianna helped Rowan to fasten a leather armband. "The benevolent Master. Oh, never mind that we are sending a girl to her death, as long as she is not poisoned before she leaves."

Rhea flinched. "He's doing what he can to give her a chance. It's not his fault that the King gives orders he must follow."

"Oh, sure, orders." Whatever Lianna was about to say was cut short with a sharp look from Rowan.

"You know that every time a person rides to Steinbrekka there is a chance they will not return. Do me a favor and let my last memory not be of you two fighting or defending the High Prince."

Rhea's eyes suddenly filled with tears. "But all you have to do is ride there and back. She's the one who gets dropped off, right?"

The other woman shook her head. "No. Every person who steps into Steinbrekka at night feels the pull of its creatures, and the pull of death. Some seem to have more defenses than others. Risalka has never been attacked by the creatures or felt the pull of the pool, but we have lost many guards to that forsaken place."

Rowan buckled his leather armor before he donned his deep black cloak and gave Lianna a quick hug. He then turned to Rhea. "You take care of that cat, and of Kataolya. Tell Nyssa - tell her I am sorry for screwing everything up, in case I do not come back."

"In case you do not come back?" Lianna followed him out of the room. "You had better come back, Rowan, or I will make an end to you myself!" She yelled down the hallway after his retreating figure.

Savin moved her into the room and held the Mercene as her tears began to fall. "He has had a bad premonition all week. Bad dreams, bad feelings. Nyssa asked him what was wrong but of course he would not share his burdens with her."

Rhea stood with her forehead on the cold window, watching the cloaked figures mount horses and move toward the gate. *Bad dreams?* She thought. *I had plenty of those last night. A large black shadow attacking someone, huge fangs that dripped with blood.* She shuddered at the memory and bent down to stroke the gray cat down the length of her back.

Lianna began to pace the room then, twisting her fingers with such fierceness that Rhea worried for the small bones. "He should not be out there. They should not be making him go out there. I just have a feeling something is going to go horribly wrong."

A sudden urge prompted Rhea to blurt out, "Lianna, shall we go and wait the night in the garden?"

A nod and the three left the room and walked down towards the garden. Savin sat Lianna down on a bench by the door and held her as she cried. Rhea glanced at them and moved off into the dense foliage.

Sometimes I think she loves Rowan as much as she has affection for Savin. I will have to check with Nyssa and see if there is any way to safely remove them from duty so that they could start a romance and family.

Her feet walked along the path as Rhea sank deeper into a feeling of unrest, a feeling that she was supposed to be doing something on this night. The path came to an abrupt halt in front of a small stone gate, one that had not existed during her last garden visit. Rhea looked back the direction from where she came as she heard Nyssa's clear voice floating through the garden. After she took in a deep breath she quietly swung open the gate and slipped out of the garden.

She followed a pathway then, destination unknown but feeling the world approving her choice of actions. She kept her footsteps light, for though no other people could be seen through the thick foliage walls on either side of the path, she was unsure if a person could stand just on the other side. The path ended at a tall plank wall and Rhea's hand found a wooden doorway just in front of her. Rhea carefully swung it open, surprised to find herself in an abandoned hallway of the stable. A few careful steps revealed that the stable residents, human and equine, slept soundly while Rhea quickly and quietly made her way to the nearest horse.

Rhea stopped for a moment then, surprised to see a simple black leather saddle and matching bridle hanging outside of Kataolya's stall next to a small saddle bag. The horse was uneasy, and began to push her strong chest against the stall door once she realized Rhea was outside.

"Easy girl, easy. Quiet now or we'll wake up everyone. Do you know where we need to go? Can you take me there? I know this will be scary but we have to do it." She slipped into the stall and gently placed the saddle onto the mare's back before sliding the bridle onto her head. "Did you let Aleksei brush you today, sweet girl? You look nice and clean and your stall also looks shiny and fresh."

She walked out of the stall and then paused to figure out how to get the horse out of the stable without alerting everyone who might still be awake. She noticed another door then, set in the shadows, just big enough for a horse to fit through. She smoothly swung into the saddle and the two left the stable silent as the night.

~ * ~ * ~

Kataolya knew the way and Rhea focused on keeping her seat as the horse plunged onto the path to Steinbrekka. The horse was perfectly behaved and often shifted her weight just in time to spare the rider from a sharp tumble onto a boulder or craggy rock formation. The moon shone down from the black sky, illuminating the rocks and plunging others into inky darkness. After much time had passed, Rhea gathered up the reins and encouraged the horse to slow her pace slightly, for she sensed they were on the edge of the mystic place. Kataolya slowed to a smooth trot as they moved through the shadowed tree ring surrounding the open space with the large pool of water.

They stopped at the edge of the tree ring, and both horse and rider stopped to catch their breath as voices drifted down from the top of the mountain. Rhea could see the four riders then, slowly walking towards the tall rocky ledge. One of the figures, a guard based on his height and build, lifted the woman onto the ledge and Risalka followed them onto the large, flat butte.

There was a nervous energy around the land that night. The small creatures that Rhea saw at her arrival milled around the horses,

179

snapping at legs and trying to scale the cliff wall. Bones were scattered across the area by the water hole, and Rhea shuddered to think of how they got there. She had not been aware of any people arriving in the realm but she thought back to all of the times Lianna was tense, or Savin acted upset and it was plausible that they had successfully kept these events from her for quite some time.

A sudden shift in the wind brought a swirling dust cloud around the party and Rhea watched in horror as Rowan was lifted off his horse and dropped to the hard ground. Instantly, he was surrounded by the small creatures as he regained his footing and attempted to make his way back to the horse.

The horses bolted then, and even steadfast Kataolya stood trembling beneath Rhea as her very nature told her to flee from the squirming mass of tiny, fanged creatures. Then the creatures scattered as quickly as they had swarmed and created a deep circle of snapping fangs with the bloodied man in the center. Rowan managed to pull out his sword and took a defensive stance, only daring to swing when a creature came close enough to bite.

A cry of alarm stuck in Rhea's throat as the brush in front of Rowan began to sway and part. The creature that emerged into the light of the moon towered over the bodies of the Ellyn and its back came well to Rowan's shoulders. The cat looked as if it were a thing made of nightmares, with a large and muscled body, thick head, and twelve-inch fangs that glinted in the moonlight as it roared a challenge at the man.

Rowan braced his feet then and took a fighting stance. A small creature flew at the back of his knee, causing his legs to buckle. He fell hard onto one knee, bracing himself on the upright sword.

Rhea stifled a scream as she felt something push against her back, and spun in the saddle to find the small gray cat perched on the horse's rump with her eyes on the girl.

"Where did you come from? Oh, that doesn't matter. I wish you could tell me what to do, little cat."

A quick head bob and the gray cat was streaking across the space between the woman and the man, scattering the small vicious creatures under her nimble feet. Rhea whispered, "Well, I guess that's a pretty clear sign," and clung tightly to the mare as they plunged into the moonlit circle behind the gray feline streak.

Several long seconds later they reached the clearing and Rhea flung herself from the still-moving horse, running the last few steps toward Rowan and pulling him to his feet. His face was covered in a web of small scrapes and cuts, and his sleeve ran red with blood.

"You crazy woman." His voice rasped out of a tightened chest. "You will get yourself killed. Why did you come here?"

The horse screamed a challenge then and they whipped around to see the giant cat moving towards them Body low to the ground, it stalked forward on silent, massive paws. A loud hiss came from the small cat and Rhea resolved that she would not allow her small companion to be eaten by a creature whose paw was the size of her body. She stepped between the cat and the creature and raised her voice.

"My name is Rhea Aralia. I have been to Steinbrekka and left my own person. I have met with the Aos Si, the Malakhor, and the old woman Ayewok. You will not harm my companions!"

Her courage failed as the great cat roared again and moved ever closer, large tongue licking thick lips in anticipation. Rowan edged in front of her, sword pointed at the crouched predator. "You are more important, Rhea. Get on the horse and get out of here. The world does not need me."

"No, Rowan. The world does need you. You know as well as I do that our friends would be lost without you."

The black shadow pounced, claws outstretched and salivating at the easy kill. Rowan braced himself for the impact of the cat on the blade while trying to push the woman further away from danger. Then there was a second snarl, and a flash of white met the black mass and the two creatures were rolling through the throng of scattering creatures.

Rhea watched in amazement as the large tiger who had sheltered her during her earlier ordeal pinned the attacker down and snarled a command. She stepped slowly in front of Rowan then, the man protesting behind her and stared at the two large felines walking toward her. The little gray cat hissed again before abruptly sitting down on Rhea's foot and fixing the two giant cats with her little yellow eyes.

The Malakhor snarled once more, and the black feline quickly lowered himself to the ground and slid toward the woman on his side, offering Rhea his belly. The gray cat walked up to the Malakhor without a care in the world and began to purr as she rubbed her body along the giant pillars of legs.

"I thank you for saving me once again, great cat." Rhea addressed the Malakhor. "I know I hardly have room to ask more favors of you, but if you could help the girl up there stay alive I would greatly appreciate it."

He lowered his head reverently and, after the black cat slipped back into the forest, he calmly jumped onto the ledge and climbed the path to the woman.

The smaller black creatures backed away from the couple, blending into the shadows. Rowan swung onto Kataolya's back, stiff and clumsily

. "Rhea, you should not have come here. You could have been killed."

She gently placed the little gray cat on the saddle in front of him and then settled on Kataolya with the help of a high rock. She placed her hand on Rowan's shoulder and said gently, "Well, you shouldn't have come here, either."

"It is not like I had a choice. I was ordered-"

"Yes, I know, you were ordered to do it. Did it ever occur to you to say no? Did it ever occur to you to just not show up? " Rhea felt his back tense and she moved her hand to sit on her leg. "You could have just told me, and I would have talked to Mateo for you."

He laughed then, harsh and cruel. "Oh, yes, your precious Mateo. I am sure that would have gone so well." His voice dropped lower as the horse danced in unease underneath them. "You should ask him who ordered for me to ride out here tonight. I can tell you that it was not the King."

They rode along in a heavy silence then, Rhea's arms loosely wrapped around his waist for balance as Kataolya carefully followed the path back to the castle. As the side of the castle wall loomed into view Rhea softly asked him, "Why didn't you ask Nyssa to intervene? She would have the authority to change the order, right?"

He dismounted quickly then and walked a few paces in front of the horse as he collected his thoughts. "Because the last time I asked Nyssa to intervene on my behalf, she was almost killed. Because I was informed that the next time Nyssa intervenes with the King or the High Prince on my behalf, she *would* be killed." The man turned to face her and Rhea saw the truth in his eyes.

"You love her, don't you, Rowan? Is that why you volunteered to be my guard, because it would mean you could be around her more? Even though you know how she feels about Sebast..."

"I love her because she is my-" The phrase burst out of his lips and only the sharp hissing of the gray cat cut him short. He took a deep breath. "My queen, or the closest thing we have to a true Queen. She is the only chance we have for a future that is not blanketed by oppression and death. We need her desperately, all of us."

Chapter Twenty-Three

The Court

"The woman survived?" Rhea glanced up from the needlework she was attempting as Lianna bounced into the room.

"She did! It was very doubtful the week that she returned, but she is completely healed now. Oh, she has assuredly been mentally scarred by the experience, but she came back alive and her wounds will heal. Mother says Inna can find her a place with the washer women and she will be happy enough. She is learning quickly and has good fingers for sewing and mending."

"She could probably teach me a thing or two." Rhea scrunched her face in annoyance as she held up the botched needlework.

Lianna laughed. "You are doing just fine." She pulled out some of the stitches and showed Rhea an easier way to execute them. "So I hear through the servant line that you spent the night with Mateo?"

Rhea blushed. "It was nothing like that. We were up late talking and I fell asleep on his couch since I've been so tired lately." She glanced up Lianna. "Rowan certainly didn't look happy in the morning though."

"No, I suppose not. Rhea, did you talk to Mateo about that night?"

"Yes. He said that Rowan must have misunderstood. He was never ordered to go to Steinbrekka and could have always just refused the guard detail, especially now that he is a Komisar and not just a common guard." Her eyebrow raised at the look Lianna was giving her. "What?"

The cat came over and jumped on Lianna's lap. After she stared into those wide eyes for a moment Lianna smiled somewhat sadly. "Well, I guess I just do not think of him as a common guard is all. It is certainly not an easy vocation."

"No, I guess not. He definitely has his own way of expressing himself, that's for sure."

"What do you mean by that? Has he been behaving poorly again?"

"Oh, no, not at all." Rhea put her work down in her lap and sighed. "He's just been distant is all. I guess I got used to his rude words and attitude, and now that it's gone I find myself wondering where he went."

Lianna snorted, then covered her mouth as she laughed. "It sounds to me like you are growing new feelings towards him."

Rhea rolled her eyes. "Oh, please. Mateo is the only one I'm interested in right now, partly out of self-preservation. I can't imagine having eyes for another man while the offer of Forena is on the table would go over too well." She looked out the window and smiled as Mateo mounted his stallion and then waved at her window. "No, they are just two very different people and I got used to dealing with both of them on a regular basis."

"Uh-huh…as you would say, 'I'm not buying it'." Lianna looked up at her. "How are they different?"

"Well, Mateo is such a gentleman. He is always opening doors for me, helping me with things, complimenting how I look. Rowan on the other hand is like that pesky little brother always pulling on your braid when your mom isn't looking. Plus, he just, oh, I don't know

185

how to describe it. He just always seems like he is on the outskirt of society, you know? He certainly wasn't on my list of acceptable suitors, that's for sure. I don't know how to act around him and everything I say upsets him."

A gentle tapping and Nyssa walked into the room. Both women jumped up at the look on her face. "Nyssa, what's wrong?" they said in tandem.

She walked over to the bed and sat down, tears streaking down her face. "She died. Nastasio's mother, the shawl lady. Her cough grew to be too much and she could not catch her breath and she died."

Rhea felt her heart drop as she thought about the young boy selling shawls. "But what will happen to him? Can his sister take him into her care?"

Lianna glanced from Nyssa to Rhea. "How do you know he had a sister?"

"A little bird told me?"

Nyssa picked at a piece of invisible dirt from her skirt. "Her Patron will not accept him because he is too old to be trained in the ways of the court. We, everyone, have been ordered to stay away from him and let him fend for himself." Fresh tears flowed down her face.

"But, you can't fend for yourself at that age! How is he going to cook or get food or sew new clothing?" Rhea shook her head. "Let me go talk to Mateo."

Nyssa gave a harsh laugh through the tears. "Talk to Mateo? Do you really think he will fix any of this? Face reality, Rhea. I do not know what he is telling you, but Mateo is the one who is ordering all of this. He is the one who ordered Rowan to Steinbrekka, he is the one who is ordering everyone to ignore Nasta, and he is the one who ordered your kidnapping in the first place. All of his explanations to you are lies to keep you complacent."

Rhea's jaw twitched, in anger or sadness she was not sure. "I don't believe you. I have asked him about all of those things and he has given me a reasonable explanation for offense, along with an apology for my kidnapping. Most were misunderstandings because people interpreted his requests incorrectly, or things that he regretted afterward."

Lianna looked between the two women with concern as Nyssa replied, "You can think what you want. You do not know this man nearly as well as you think you do, Rhea."

She stood. "No, Nyssa, maybe it is you who doesn't know him. Matt has been my best friend for years and years and every time I talk to Mateo my old friend shines through more and more. He's not this tyrannical monster that you make him out to be. He's a kind, gentle, loving person who saved me from more scrapes and accidents and alcohol-induced mistakes than I can count!"

Nyssa looked at her curiously then and softened her tone. "Yes, I guess you are right in that account. He has been here for so long in our time that I forget you two have a history together in your own realm." She took a shaky breath. "Will you two come to the funeral with me? No one else in the family will go, and I do not think I can bear it on my own."

~ * ~ * ~

The funeral was a hasty and somber event held in a light gray rain. Nastasio stood alone by the shallow grave carved out of the earth for his mother. Rowan stood a few paces away with a shovel in hand, and eyes downcast to hide his grief. As Rhea looked around she realized that Nyssa was the only noble woman in attendance, and Nastasio's sister had not been allowed to attend the funeral.

Nyssa walked up to the young boy and wrapped her arms around him as he finally broke down sobbing. The rest of the mourners slowly drifted away until it was only Nyssa and her friends who remained. Rhea realized how truly alone this boy would be, and how hard his young life had suddenly become. She walked over to where Nyssa stood with the boy in her embrace.

Rhea squatted down until she was face to face with the young boy. "Nasta, I will buy every shawl I can to help you. If you need anything just come to the garden and let me know and I'll do what I can."

He sniffed. "Thank you, Lady Rhea. I was actually wondering, well," he glanced at Rowan and Nyssa talking quietly to the side, "Rowan is taking me away. Could you come with us? I know it is not my place to ask but you remind me of my sister, and ...and...."

Tears filled her eyes and she nodded, feeling as if someone had shoved a cotton ball down her throat. "Let me double check with Rowan, but yes, I'll come with you."

Chapter Twenty-Four

The Court

"Make sure you pack light, but pack as much as you need. Definitely an extra simple dress, extra boots, a blanket, any toiletries you might need. Rowan will take care of the food and anything needed for the horses." Lianna carefully rolled items and placed them into saddle bags that were held open by Faina.

Rhea pulled on a pair of light but sturdy riding boots. "How long should I plan on being away? This sounds like more than a day trip."

Faina answered in her soft, shy manner. "If you are going to the village of lost souls, then it is probably going to be several days travel, a couple of days to settle Nastasio, and then a few days to return. They will likely have garments for you in the village, but they would not be favorable while traveling."

"Village of lost souls?"

"He will explain more once you get out of the castle gates." Lianna glanced out of the window to check on the progress of the men and horses. "Once you pass Asimina, be sure to take off your veil and stow it safely in your pack. Outside of the castle, covering your head for no reason is considered an insult and causes distrust. I have packed a few shawls in case the wind gets bad or a sand storm blows up and you need protection. There are also many of the shawls from Nastasio so that the community knows he has goods to offer and hopefully will smooth his entrance into his new life."

Rhea looked out the window and saw the horses were saddled and the men were talking with Nastasio. "Time to go then." She gave the other women a hug and picked up her pack to walk outside.

It only took a few minutes to get her pack settled on the dappled gray mare and then Rhea mounted. Nastasio looked at the bay gelding in front of him with doubt and a bit of fear. He put one hand on the horse and then jumped back as the gelding restlessly shifted its weight.

"I am sorry, my Lord. I have never been taught to ride a horse before. I did not realize they were so big." Nastasio stood several feet away from the horse, small white teeth biting his lip enough to bleed as he tried to work the courage to mount.

Rhea moved her horse beside Rowan and suggested, "Perhaps he could ride double with me on Kalar? I'm sure she could hold his slight weight and then I could help him balance."

He contemplated the idea and then frowned. "No, if we run into trouble you need to be able to make a quick escape. He can ride with me."

A quick hand on his shoulder stopped the words as he turned to the boy. "Rowan, if we run into trouble on the way, you need to be able to defend us. You can hardly do that if you have him on your horse as well."

Rowan cursed then as he knew her logic was sound, but still was uneasy with the thought of any escape being hindered. "All right. The boy rides with you, and we can use his mount to carry the extra goods and lighten the loads from our horses." He gave her a look of concern. "Be watchful as we go, and if I say to run, then I want you to run without asking questions or looking back."

She nodded and moved her horse closer to where the boy stood and gave a reassuring smile. "You're going to ride with me, Nasta. Don't worry, I'll keep you from falling. Kalar is a good horse and will take good care of us." The boy barely had time to catch his breath before Savin swung him up onto the mare behind Rhea. "Hold tight to my waist and let me know if you feel unbalanced, ok?"

She felt his small head nod at her back and reached behind to give his knee a small pat of encouragement. The party moved forward with Rowan with the extra mount in the lead, and Rhea riding behind with her passenger. They crossed the wide courtyard at a sedate walk, Rowan looking increasingly nervous as they walked past the wide gate and received nods from the guards.

He slowed his horse so that he rode beside Rhea. "Rhea, what did you tell Mateo about today?"

"I told him that I wanted to see the mysterious lake for myself. Since he will be busy for the next few weeks and won't be able to spend time with me, it only made sense for you to go as a guide."

His pent-up breath released in a low whistle and he smiled. "Good. He will not think twice about sending guards to follow us then. If anyone reports that we have the boy with us, they will probably just assume we are going to leave him there so the court will not have to witness his last days." He glanced over to see her astonished expression. "You should not look so surprised. I would not do it myself but it would not be the first time an orphan or widow was taken out of the castle walls with no impending return."

Nastasio's small voice piped up. "That is why I was so happy when Lady Nyssa said Rowan would take me to Kylassame! It may not be home, but at least I have a chance!"

Rhea felt her eyes well up at the joy in his voice. *It is a true tragedy that such a small boy should be so excited just to get a chance to be alive.* "Rowan, could you tell me more about this place we are heading, Kylassame?"

He shrugged. "There is not much of a story to tell. The people of Albadarl, we will pass by on the way to Kylassame, told me that strangers were building structures a day's travel to the east, so I went to investigate and evaluate if they were a threat. I do not know how they got here, but they had the most peculiar names and manner of

191

dress when they first arrived. We had to help them learn how to do everything, hunting and sewing and cooking and all. It has been three years since they have first arrived and they have built themselves a nice little working community."

As the sun rose to mid-day they passed Asimina and Rhea waved at the women and men who came to watch as they rode by. Rowan took one of the larger saddle bags from the gelding and passed it off to Sebast as they passed with a smile.

Rhea glanced at Rowan and saw the tension slowly lift off his shoulders every step they took away from the castle. He still looked around with careful eyes, but seemed less afraid of an impending attack. "Rowan, before we left, Lianna told me to remove my veil once we passed Asimina because it could be taken as an insult by the people outside of the castle. Is that true?"

Color rose to his cheeks. "Yes, that is truth. I cannot believe I did not think to tell you that myself. The last thing I want is for you or the people to feel uncomfortable."

She smiled. "Well, it's not like you wear a veil on a regular basis to have remembered such a womanly detail."

"Still, if anything happens to you out here a lot of people would have my life. I should have thought of that." He became introspective, trying to remember what else she would need to know about the cultures they would visit. "When we ride by Albadarl we will probably not see any people, but if we do, do not be alarmed. They are small in stature and bear the markings of their ancestors. They may look fierce, and certainly are if threatened, but they mostly keep to themselves and away from anyone not accepted into their clan." He went deep into thought again. "And the people in Kylassame like to hug. They are a very, how did you put it that one time, touchy feely group."

The woman laughed. "Did you just say 'touchy feely', Komisar Rowan de Nespa? Next I'll have to teach you the word, 'thing-a-ma-jig'."

He gave her a skeptical look and shook his head, not bothering to cover the smile that had spread to his eyes. "First, you have to learn to dance, then we can work on other strange phrases."

"No deal! I don't dance. I already told you and Mateo that."

A small voice from behind her chimed in, "I do not see why not, Lady Rhea. I think you would make a great dancer if you tried it."

She stuck her tongue out at Rowan for starting the topic since she could not turn around to face the boy. "Not going to happen. My friends back home have been trying for years without success."

~ * ~ * ~

Several hours later they reached a small copse of trees and Rowan grew silent as he stared at the edges. He held his finger to his lips and the party silently rode up to an area with a series of stacked vertical and horizontal stones. He dismounted softly and slid a large saddle bag from his gelding, carefully placing it on a flat piece of limestone while Rhea looked on from a few feet away.

A small man appeared in front of the stone and nodded his head in respect towards Rowan, then gave an expression of curiosity in the direction of Rhea. He was most extraordinary in appearance. He was short in stature, as Rowan had explained, coming to a height roughly the equivalent of Rhea's waist. The man was covered in a loose fitted garment made of woven leaves and grasses with small decorations created of berries and carved wood. Elaborate geometric designs covered his dark face, the yellow ink standing out against the ebony skin. A series of elaborately placed small scars traced from the base of his skull, onto his shoulders, and flowed down his arms, giving his skin the texture and appearance of tree bark.

Rowan lowered himself to one knee and bowed his head in respect. "Elder Wekesa, I did not expect you to be at the edge at this hour of the day."

The elder clasped his hands in front of him and continued to look at Rhea. "The leaves told me you were taking a journey this way. They also told me that you would have a woman I needed to see." He tilted his head sideways and his bright eyes shifted to Nastasio. "They failed to tell me that the woman had a son."

Nastasio blurted out, "She is not my real mom, just a friend who is being a mom because I just lost mine. She and Rowan are taking me to a safe place."

Eyes the color of milk chocolate turned back towards Rowan. "Ah, so you are journeying elsewhere then, and not directly to us."

Rowan nodded. "We are taking the boy to Kylassame, as the castle has become dangerous for him. I have not been here in some time so I thought to drop off some provisions on the way."

"Ah. In that case I invite you to spend a night with us on your way back to the castle." Once again the clear eyes fell onto Rhea. "She is as beautiful as the seer foretold but much lighter in color than we had anticipated."

"I will explain as we pass through on our return, Elder."

"Ah, yes, well." The man grinned, showing a mouth of glistening white teeth. "I shall not keep you from your journey any longer then." He nodded at the group once again and then disappeared back into the tree cover as quickly as he had stepped out, leaving an empty space where the bag of provisions had just been.

The three rode in silence for quite some time after the encounter. Rowan opened his mouth to speak on several occasions but silence emerged every time, and Rhea was still a bit stunned at the entire episode. Little Nastasio had dosed off and she could feel his body relaxed against her back, arms loosely wrapped around her waist for balance, as the horses trotted along.

As the sun began to set the party reached a small cave and Rowan pulled his gelding to a halt. "We will sleep here for the night, then continue on in the morning. The village has scouts positioned this far away who will see us. They will see the fire tonight and know to expect us soon."

Rhea gently shook Nastasio's arm to wake the boy and was grateful for Rowan's help with dismounting. She was not used to riding for such long stretches of time and she held onto the stirrup for a few minutes as she tried to get taxed leg muscles to support her standing weight once again.

She walked into the small cave and found evidence that it had been previously utilized and was quite suited to being a temporary shelter. A small circle of stone sat in the center of the cave under a conveniently positioned smoke hole in the cave ceiling. Rowan already had coaxed a small flame to grow and consume the small twigs and kindling he had placed in the circle. A small leather scrap was rigged under the ceiling opening so that it could be closed in the event of poor weather. Body-length pole bed frames with ropes woven across the span were quickly covered with thick furs that Rowan removed from a series of stone cubbyholes located in the back of the cave.

He pulled out a small pot and poured water into it, waiting for it to come to a boil before emptying the contents of one pack into the container. He glanced up at Rhea. "We will eat and then get some rest. You and Nastasio take the beds. I will be just outside so just call if you need anything."

Rhea watched and became fascinated by the contents of the pot. Dehydrated beef rapidly grew moist with water and swelled along with some grains, carrots, some green herbs, and potatoes. A pouch that was the size of a small hand had expanded enough to feed the three of them very comfortably and with little inconvenience to the travel. She took a tentative bite and was pleasantly surprised by the taste. Both the broth and the contents had a good flavor and texture and the warm food eased the ache in her tired muscles.

Nastasio had barely finished his last bite of food before curling up on one of the beds and closing his eyes. Rhea yawned but forced herself outside to help with rinsing out the dishes.

"It's so quiet out here," she remarked as she looked into the dark sky. While the woods around them rustled with the usual noises of the forest and small creatures could be heard running along the paths, the lack of human voices gave an otherworldly feel to the night. She picked up a dish and began to rinse out the contents with a bit of water from their supply.

Rowan gave her a cautious smile. "You do not have to do that, Rhea. Go sleep, I will take care of it."

She shook her head even though the wide yawn betrayed her weariness. "I'm fine. You made the dinner so I might as well help clean it up. That's what my mom always taught me anyway."

"And did you always listen to your mother?"

"Hardly ever. I never understood how hard it was to run a household until I moved out of hers." Rhea smiled sadly. "I hope she has found peace with my absence. I can't help but wonder how much time has passed or if she is still up searching, or waiting for my body to turn up."

Rowan gently took the cleaned plate from her hand. "I am sorry for any pain that was caused bringing you here, Rhea, but I am not sorry that you are here. Go get some sleep; it will be an early morning and a busy day."

Chapter Twenty-Five

Kylassame

She awoke the next morning to the sound of a very excited Nastasio talking to Rowan outside the cave entrance. "So we will be there today? Do you think they will like me? What if they do not like me? Are there other people my age there? Will they like my shawls or think they are stupid? Are you sure they will like me? "

Rhea quietly stepped to the doorway and looked outside as Rowan ruffled the boy's hair and smiled. "What if they do not like you?" He exclaimed. "That is just a nonsense thought. Of course they are going to like you! What would make you think such a thing?"

Nastasio scrunched up his face. "No one back at the castle liked me very much. Why would here be any different?"

Rowan tapped him on the chest. "Because here, people are not stupid or superficial. They see more than just the color of your hair or the shade of your skin. They do not look at people as belonging to a certain rank. People are just people and as long as you are good in your heart and honest to your neighbor then that is all they care about."

The boy's eyes lit up. "You mean like you? And like Lady Nyssa and Lianna and Rhea?"

"Exactly!" Rowan glanced up and blushed when he saw Rhea standing at the doorway with a soft grin on her face. "Would you like a cup of hot tea before we get started?" He rose and handed her a small leather mug filled with a steaming brew.

Nastasio jumped up. "I will go get the horses ready!" He bounded down the short pathway to where the horses stood, while Rhea and Rowan sat balanced on their heels with their mugs.

The woman took a sip of the tea. "He seems to be in a much better mood today."

Rowan shrugged. "I may have told him that at the village they have dogs trained to do tricks for treats. Young boys are easily distracted for short amounts of time." He hesitated before adding, "Rhea, I know I probably do not need to tell you this, but-"

"No, I won't tell anyone about anything we hear, say, or see on this journey." She winked at him. "I'm one of the good ones, remember?"

He let himself laugh then, the rare and joyous sound carrying far into the forest beyond.

~ * ~ * ~

It was a short ride to the edge of the valley. Rhea looked around at the dense forest surrounding them and wondered where the entrance to this valley lay. The trees grew thick, and behind the foliage was a solid wall of rock.

Rowan led them down the edge of the trees, then began to walk down an unmarked trail through the foliage. A crack appeared in the wall, barely larger than the gelding Rowan rode, and they slipped into the darkness.

Sound bounced all around them, the steady clip-clop of the horses' hooves striking in counterpoint with the dripping of water falling from the steep walls. Far above the light of the blue sky could barely be seen, a narrow ribbon above them.

Nastasio tightened his grip on Rhea's waist as they traveled through the narrow passage and she murmured reassurance. Rowan called back gently, "Just a little longer and we will be out."

A small light appeared in front of Rowan then, casting a halo glow around the outline of his upper body. Gradually the light began to spread, and the narrow tunnel opened to a wide funnel that met a wide expanse of open land.

Rhea felt her body relaxing as they stood on the edge of the valley rim and the land of the valley spread as far as she could see. The horses walked down the gently winding path to a wide, green expanse of land. Blue skies spread over the horizon with just a few white puffy clouds marring the smooth sky. Grass muffled the sounds of the horses' hooves on the path and Rhea could feel Nastasio quivering with excitement behind her.

"Look, Rhea!" The boy pointed down into the valley. "I can see the dogs down there!"

Rhea looked down at the village and smiled at the image. The houses reminded her of a small sea-side village she once visited. White-washed stucco walls were topped with red clay shingles and bright purple doors. Small flower gardens surrounded the walls of the house and were showing the last bit of bloom before the winter frosts began to sink their teeth into the valley. Beyond the houses agricultural fields extended as far as Rhea could see, and as she watched a bright green flag was waved from the top of a tall building. People from the fields put down their buckets and baskets then and ran back to the village, milling about the center in excited anticipation.

Rowan rode at the front and waved to the man who came to greet him. "Good morning, Justin! How are you on this fine day?"

Justin shook his hand heartily. "All the better now that you have joined us, my friend!" The man was equal height with Rowan but had a slighter build. Dark denim jeans covered his legs and Rhea was shocked to see a shirt with a familiar company logo on the front. Curly red hair covered the man's head and his brown eyes shone with laughter. "And you have brought us company!"

Rhea smiled to hide her nerves as the man strode over and shook her hand, as well. "It is a pleasure to meet you, Justin. My name is Rhea and this young man behind me is Nastasio."

He shook Nastasio's hand. "Pleasure to meet you, young man. I see you have been lucky enough to score the coveted position in transportation of this visit." The compliment was greeted with a blank stare by the boy. The man cleared his throat and whispered to the boy in a tone just audible to the woman, "That means you got lucky that you got to hold the lady's waist the whole way here."

"Oh! Yes, sir. I agree. Rhea is the best lady there is out there."

Rhea felt the familiar warmth rising to her cheeks. "Enough about me, tell me about this village. It is beautiful." She swung off her horse after the man helped Nastasio down.

Justin offered an arm to her as Rowan rounded up the horses and took them to a nearby barn. "My dear and welcome woman, this is the village of Kylassame! A grand village of its own uniqueness and one that could never be replicated even if a million men set their minds to do so. Here you will find a band of refugees from this world and beyond, all coexisting and for the most part peacefully living. I am the current acting Governor if you will, and in charge of things for the time being."

"It's so beautiful and joyful." Rhea looked around with wide eyes. Clothes lines were strung between windows and carried an array of bright fabrics in every shade of color imaginable. Ribbons fluttered in the breeze from their positions on doorways and curtains rippled in the open windows of the homes. Children ran throughout the streets, carefully avoiding the adults and mindful not to get in the way as they chased balls and threw hoops to one another.

Nastasio shrank behind Rhea and slid his small hand into hers for comfort. The excitement of the arrival was now dwarfed by fear of the unknown, and he clung to the back of Rhea's skirt in an attempt to make himself invisible.

The man took this in out of the corner of his eye and waved at a nearby woman. "Daisy, would you mind taking this young woman and her young protector to get a bit of water and freshen up while I get everything settled with Rowan?"

Daisy smiled at the group and her personality shone every bit as brightly as the flower from which she was named. "Why, hello there. My name is Daisy Mae and welcome to our village. Come on up and we'll have you feeling fresh and clean in no time!"

"Thank you, we appreciate that." Rhea smiled at the energetic woman as she bustled them into a large house. The woman looked to be in her mid-thirties and had a trim, slender body. Light brown hair was pulled up into a loose bun on the top of her head and held in place by a bright piece of yellow ribbon. She was wearing a yellow sundress that touched the top of her knees and dainty cloth slippers protected her feet from the pebble pathway.

She led them to a small room upstairs and Rhea was surprised to see a small sink with a faucet. "You have sinks!"

Daisy smiled. "Well, of course. Jhoni was a plumber in his old life and he managed to get everything rigged with the streams outside using gravity. I won't pretend to understand it, but I certainly do appreciate it!" She closed the door lightly behind her so the two could have some privacy.

Rhea showed Nastasio how the faucet worked and immediately felt rejuvenated after splashing the clear water on her face and washing off the travel dust from her neck. She pulled the curtain to the side and a slow smile spread on her face as she watched Rowan and Justin walk through the village.

Rowan had a smile for every person, a handshake or a hug for the more familiar. The men each waited their turn to tell Rowan in loud excited voices about their latest inventions, crop harvest, or marriages. The younger women stared at him from the outside of the circle while a few of the older ones said things that made a bright red blush rise to his cheeks.

Rhea walked out of the room with Nastasio's hand squeezing hers tightly. She met Daisy in the living room and the woman handed out two glasses with lemonade. "Have a bit to drink while we walk you over to Rowan's dwelling. Nastasio will be staying with you two until we find a better arrangement and you go back to Kalda."

They stepped out into the street where Rowan's pride and joy in this place was plain to see. Nastasio tightened his grip on Rhea's hand and she squeezed his in encouragement. Rowan's voice carried over the excited voices of the crowd as he said, "My friends, there will be much time for talking and celebrating. Allow me and my companions to go air out the house and we will meet you for dinner!"

A very pretty auburn-haired woman approached Rowan. She looked to be in her early twenties and slim with curves in the right places. Her eyes shone at Rowan and she blinked her long lashes as she stepped close to the man. "Oh, Rowan, we've been airing and cleaning the house since we saw your signal last night. We would always be prepared for you."

"Well, thank you, Amanda, I appreciate that." He gave her a kiss on the cheek and extricated himself and his companions from the crowd.

Nastasio moved between the taller bodies of his two guardians and took one hand in each of his. "There are so many people here. How will I remember everyone? Who will I stay with once you leave?" The excitement from earlier turned to an overwhelming anxiety and deep fear.

Rowan smiled down at him. "Well, I have some people in mind but I need to speak with them tonight. They are wonderful and friendly and have children your age to introduce you to everyone. I know it seems a bit scary right now but it will get easier quickly."

The boy gave a quivering smile. "Okay, I trust you."

They turned onto a small pathway and stood in front of a small, one-story, stucco house. A large, sprawling, roofed porch contained many chairs, benches, and hanging seats and Rhea supposed it was a popular place to sit and talk on warm days. They stepped inside and Rhea was astonished at the simple elegance of the house.

Rowan went to check that the extra rooms had been aired out and gave Rhea free reign to explore. The house had several walls on the interior, all covered in beautiful tapestries and weavings. She stepped into the kitchen area and found a decent set of cookware, a large sturdy table and a set of finely sharpened knives. Opposite to the kitchen were three bedrooms with doors made of thick and supple leather that covered the space from floor to ceiling.

Rhea looked into the first bedroom and decided this must be the room where Rowan would stay when he occupied this house. The furniture was sturdy and the thick grass mattress was large enough to comfortably sleep three people. An intricately sewed quilt was smoothed over the mattress and reflected bright blues, greens, and reds onto the white walls. Thick fur rugs lined the floors and a small glass vase of flowers had been placed on a well crafted wooden table. A large wardrobe occupied the space on one wall and there was an oversized mirror sitting atop a heavy wooden dresser.

The next room was slightly smaller and less decorated. A thinner mattress was covered by a light blue cotton blanket. A fluffed pillow encased in green woven cotton sat against the wall. A small dresser and wardrobe stood against one wall and blue curtains blew in the light breeze that flowed through the window.

Rowan was in the third room and Rhea pulled back the dyed linen fabric hanging in the doorway quietly as she took in his movements. He seemed nervous, plumping the pillows on the bed that were covered in a pink silk and smoothing the already perfectly flat patchwork quilt that covered a double wide mattress. Tapestries hung on the wall and Rhea could make out scenes of women dancing, riding horses, and splashing in a stream. A delicately made dresser was topped with an oval mirror, framed in intricately woven twigs and polished to shine in the sunlight.

She dropped the curtain and stepped back into the main room. Nastasio sat huddled in the corner with his arms around his knees and his eyes were deep pools of unease. Rhea squatted beside him. "You okay, Nasta?"

He shook his head and gulped to keep from crying. "I am scared, Rhea. It is better than anything I had in the castle, but this place is so strange and new."

Rhea slid down so that she was sitting next to him and pulled the boy into her lap to hold him close. "I know, sweetheart, I know. This is all new and exciting for you and a little overwhelming. I bet in no time you are going to have a lot of friends though. These people look really nice, and you liked the drink that Miss Daisy gave you right?"

He nodded and smiled through the sniffles. "Yeah, it was good."

"And you know that Rowan wouldn't put you in a situation where something bad would happen to you, right?"

"I guess so."

"I'll tell you what, let's go sit on those fun-looking chairs on the porch and spend some time just looking at the people before we have to go talk with them. Maybe then they won't seem quite so strange or scary. Does that sound like a good idea?"

"Yeah!"

They walked out onto the porch and Rhea took Nastasio over to one of the swings. The boys eyes lit up as Rhea gave him a small push and the swing moved forward. A happy peal of laughter rang from his mouth and Rhea smiled as she sat down in a rocking chair beside him.

The village bustled with activity, yet still glowed with deep peace and contentment. After the initial commotion, people kept to their own, as if they understood that Rowan would like some space once he entered his house. Medium-sized dogs, mostly hounds from their appearance, milled around the feet of the residents. Nastasio laughed as one of the dogs stood on his hind legs on command, then turned around in a circle while on two feet.

Rhea noticed a young couple walk up the pathway to the house, nervous excitement radiating from their faces.

"Hello. We have come to speak with Rowan," the man said with a smile to Rhea.

She smiled back through her nervousness. "He's just inside, let me go get him."

Rowan followed her back out and his face lit up at the sight of the couple. "Lily! David! I am glad to see the two of you still speaking to one another. Are you married yet or still being stubborn?"

The red-haired woman smiled shyly. "Well, that's why we came here. We would like to formally invite you and your family to our wedding, which will happen tomorrow at sunset."

"Tomorrow! That is fabulous!" Rowan jumped down the steps and embraced the man, then gave the blushing woman a kiss on the cheek. "I'm glad we had such good timing that we can be a part of the excitement."

Lily, still flushed, looked at Nastasio on the swing. "I was also asked to speak with you on behalf of my sister. I'm sure you already have people in mind for the boy, but she lost her youngest son several months ago and has a free room already set up for a young boy. I told her I would speak to you on her behalf."

Rowan's face fell. "Oh, Lily, I am so sorry to hear about that. I know how much your sister loved her little boy."

She nodded and blinked back the tears threatening to spill out. "We're all adjusting. We've missed you, Rowan."

"It has been a little busy in Kalda," Rowan said with a guilty look.

He was treated to a bright smile. "We'll have to make up for lost time in the next few days then. Remind you of why you love us and then maybe you won't leave for so long!" She winked as David took her hand and gently led her away from the cabin.

Rhea looked at the retreating couple. "All the mess with me has kept you away from this wonderful place."

He grunted. "Being at the court has been more important recently than being here. They can take care of themselves if they need to do so." He smiled again. "Come, let me show you two to your rooms."

As she had suspected, Rhea was to be housed in the most feminine of the rooms, with Nastasio in the smaller room and Rowan in the large master room. After a relaxed dinner by the grand stone fireplace Rowan took a few more visitors and Rhea listened to their stories while Nastasio sat curled on her lap. The people here truly did seem to get along in peace, with petty squabbles being quickly and fairly settled by the Governor on duty. Couples brought newborn babes to be kissed on the forehead and a young man about Rowan's age sat for several hours telling bawdy tales that had tears of laughter streaming down Rhea's face.

During one lull in stories Rhea felt a small shudder go through the boy on her lap and gave him a hug. "What's wrong, Nasta? Still worried?"

He nodded his head and sniffled before he said, almost inaudibly, "I am still scared, Rhea. What is going to happen when Rowan leaves me all alone? I do not want to be alone. I have never lived a day without having Rowan or Nyssa around."

Rhea picked up a brightly colored shawl from the table next to her and wrapped it around the boy, hiding everything but his face from the men who had glanced over, one in curiosity and one with a look of a lion ready to defend his young. Rhea slightly shook her head at Rowan and his friend continued with a story of the women who had planned bets on which one would be in Rowan's house by the end of the night.

"You aren't going to be alone, sweetie, not anymore. It's true that Rowan and I will have to go back to the castle, but you are going to be surrounded by so many friends and so many people who love you here. A bunch of people can't wait to meet you, and I know I saw quite a few boys your age with wishful looks on their faces who would probably love to get a chance to show you their toys and their puppies."

"I do not like that Amanda girl. She keeps making silly expressions when she is around Rowan."

Rhea stifled a laugh at this quick change in thought. "Now, Nasta, anyone can look at Rowan however they want as long as it's not in a bad way. Maybe she likes him and misses him while he's gone."

The boy looked unconvinced. "Well, I think you should look at him that way."

Rhea sucked in a breath and coughed as she swallowed wrong. "I don't think that would be a good idea, Nasta. The High Prince made me an offer that I will probably accept when we get back, for me to stand at his side." She got her breathing under control and ignored the men staring at her face as it turned from a light pink to a tomato red.

Nastasio plucked at a stray string on his shirt. "Well, I think Rowan is better than the High Prince."

"I think that the High Prince is on my list of suitable companions while Rowan is not, even though maybe he should be."

"Well, I think that list is stupid and you and Rowan should look at each other that way."

"Well, I think it's time to stop talking about this and go to bed."

He whined, "But I don't want to go to bed," through a deep yawn.

Rhea adjusted her arms so she was supporting his weight and stood up. "Come on now, let's go lie down and rest our heads."

After some time Nastasio was sound asleep and Rhea walked out onto the porch to find Rowan staring off into the night. He smiled up at her and pushed a cup of steaming liquid towards her on the small outdoor table. "Did he end up going to sleep easily?"

She accepted the mug with a smile and sighed as the sweet mint tea touched her lips. "After a story or two. Oh, and after I checked under the bed for monsters and assassins."

Rowan chuckled and took a drink out of his own mug, feet propped on the porch railing in front of his chair. "You can hardly blame him for being wary. He has had a hard life already and has learned not to trust strangers."

Rhea stared at the stars that sparkled in the sky and blew over the liquid in her cup. "Mm. It's not a bad thing to learn." She glanced at Rowan. "Strangers do have a tendency for kidnapping you and all."

Crickets chirped in the thick silence before Rowan responded, "Yeah, I guess they do." He stood up to walk inside, then paused at the doorway. "Rhea, if I am gone before you wake up I am just tending to local matters before the wedding celebration gets underway. There is plenty of food in the freezer box and cabinets or you can go down to Daisy's house and she will have something to share. Sleep well and know that I will be close if you need assistance, my Lady."

She sighed and leaned her head back against the top of the rocking chair frame. *Why did I say that? This visit had been so nice with no harsh words or hurt feelings, and then I had to go and say that.* A cool breeze went through the porch and she lifted her face, marveling at the feel of her hair blowing around her face after so many months confined to a veil. *It doesn't matter in the long run anyway. Once I get back I'll let Matt - Mateo, know that I've accepted his offer as long as Agrafina is okay with it. From the sounds of it, she'd be more than happy to have some freedom and not have to worry so much about his company.* She stood up and looked over the peaceful village with a sigh. *Besides, I was brought here for Mateo, that's been clear since the start even if I didn't realize it until recently. It's the best path for all of us. There's no sense in dreaming of a different future, especially now that I've seen how people don't ever get out of this world.*

Rhea did dream that night, though, as she lay curled with her head on a soft downy pillow with the scent of lavender from the quilt filling her senses. She did not remember what the dream was about but felt a rush of regret when a small scratching on her leather door hanging pulled her out of the slumber. She sat up and focused on making her breathing even as she called out, "I'm awake."

A small head poked around the door and Nastasio edged into the room. "Rhea, I cannot sleep. Could I maybe sleep in the bed with you? I promise I will not kick you."

She scooted to the side and patted the covers, smiling at the boy as he raced across the room and jumped onto the bed. "There is room for two in this big bed. Having nightmares?"

He curled up into a tight ball beside her and small eyes looked into hers. "Not really. I'm just scared and lonely and…"

Rhea hugged him. "And you've never slept in a room by yourself before?" she guessed quietly.

He started to sob then and Rhea found out his entire sad story. The boy's father had been taken in for punishment for stealing a loaf of bread when Nastasio was only two and the man never came back.

The older sister then began to serve the Patrons as an additional part of the punishment since the father did not survive for what the King considered the entire payment. The mother and Nastasio lost their house soon after, and he had spent half of his young life sleeping in a rough, leaking tent with his mother behind their vendor stand.

Rhea sang him lullabies until the small boy's sobs turned to hiccups and then finally subsided as his breath grew heavy with sleep. She carefully tucked him in and then laid her own head on the pillow and slipped into sleep with the feeling that this was exactly where she was meant to be.

Chapter Twenty-Six

Kylassame

"Oh, Rhea, you look so cute!" Cassie sat on the bed and clapped her hands. The woman had shyly approached the house an hour earlier and asked Rowan if Rhea would like to borrow a dress for the wedding.

Rhea turned around in front of the little mirror in the room. The sundress fit her perfectly and the bright green color brought out the small green flecks in her blue eyes. The dress was cut to flare out as she turned, and fell just above her knees in the front, then dipping down to mid-calf in the back. The halter top showed a well-developed upper body that tapered down the narrow waist, and the brilliant green and blue shawl that Nastasio had given her so long ago would keep the chill out as the night got cooler.

"Now put on the heels! And then I want to do your hair." Cassie bounced while seated on the bed and then bit the inside of her lip. "Sorry, I've just always wanted to have someone my age that I could do this with. My older sisters always exchanged clothes and did makeovers and stuff but told me to go away."

Rhea laughed and stepped into the strappy peep-toe heels. "Oh, don't apologize. It's just been so long that I've worn this type of clothing that it is feeling a bit strange and, well, incredibly revealing." She sat down on the chair in front of the mirror and Cassie picked up a brush.

"Where are you from anyway? You have the coloring but not the prissy attitude of the rest of the court. Judging from the accent I would say you are American." She brushed out the blonde hair and then pulled the sides up to show off Rhea's face and then fall in ringlets down the back of her neck.

"You are right. Virginia, actually. What about you?" Rhea loved the look of the tiny yellow flowers that Cassie braided into her hair.

"Texas, for me. Heard a strange noise at night outside my cousin's farm, went walking, then BAM, here I was. I woke up just outside the valley and hid in a cave for a while, then Rowan found me and brought me here and here I happily stayed."

A knock on the door frame announced Nastasio's arrival and the boy's face peeked around the curtain. "Lady Rhea, Miss Daisy sent me to tell you to tell Miss Cassie that if you did not hurry up you would have to sit in the back and would not be able to see anything." He straightened his back. "Oh, and that I was to be your official escort for the night! Unless you tell me to go away, and then I can."

Rhea raised an eyebrow and grinned at the woman next to her. No one would have believed this was the same scared boy who had crawled into her bed for comfort the night before. "Well, we had better be on our way then! We can't be getting bad seats to a wedding!"

He offered his small arms and both women graciously took one as they allowed their small escort to lead them to the wedding grounds.

Rhea's eyes grew wide in wonder as she stared at the small clearing. Hay bales had been dragged into neat rows where people were scattered about, conversing in excited chatter. Ribbons were tied to every available tree branch and fluttered in the wind like small flags, and small paper lanterns with tea candles surrounded the clearing to give light once the sun set below the horizon.

Cassie laughed and gave Rhea's arm a squeeze. "All the men are looking at you. I knew that dress would be a hit!"

She looked around and felt the constant pink color rising as she realized that most of the men were indeed looking her way with appreciation in their eyes. Justin walked over then and told their young escort he was free to run and play with the boys.

He walked with the women to a set of hay bales near the front of the action. "Here you are, darlin's. Daisy said to save a seat up front since this is the first time our visitor has been here for a festivity, especially one as grand as this. We should be starting any time now."

Rhea was still focused on Nastasio, who was now happily running around playing a game with the other boys that involved much happy laughter and wooden hoops. "It's incredible how relaxed he is today. What did you do?"

Justin tried to hold back the smile that became a smirk. "Myself? Not a thing. Rowan brought him down to the creek this morning and introduced him to some of the boys. A bit shy to begin with but before long he was running and jumping and splashing away with the best of them."

"He looks happy, carefree, almost like a kid his age should look. Who's that?" Rhea nodded her chin towards a young woman who approached the boy and shook his hand.

Cassie waved Justin away and took over. "Oh, that would be Deliah, Lily's older sister. She's one of the mothers who would be more than happy to offer the boy a proper home with love and laughter. She lost one of her boys a few months ago and has plenty of space and funds to help out someone in need."

Rhea made a mental note to go introduce herself to the woman and then turned toward the sounds of harps and flutes that paraded down the space between the bales. Musicians of all ages danced down the aisle with their instruments, faces painted in bright designs and ribbons tied to their hair. Skirts of the female players whirled around their legs and small specks of glitter twinkled in the evening sun as their hair tossed in the movements of the breeze and the dance.

Rowan stepped lively behind the musicians and Rhea gasped as she saw him; a small nudge and conciliatory wink from Cassie reminded her to replace her gaze of astonishment with a smile.

The man looked completely different than the court guard to which she had grown accustomed. A bright green shirt flowed loosely over his chest and enhanced his muscular shoulders and trim waist. His arms were uncovered from the elbow down and small grass and flower bracelets had been woven and carefully placed in multitudes upon both wrists. His legs were clad in dark brown buckskin pants covered with small embroidered flowers, trees, and forest creatures. Beaded soft leather moccasins covered his feet up to the ankle and muffled the sound of his progress through the audience as he moved toward the front of the clearing.

His face was what shocked her most though, and caused her heart to race a little faster as he walked by. The eyes that were normally shadowed with reservation or anxiety shone a clear and bright green in the sun. His hair was left untied and flowed in shaggy waves around his head. His face was illustrated as well, a deep forest green mask painted around his eyes with small sparkling accents across the forehead and temples.

"Wow," Cassie murmured on her hay bale perch. "He looks incredible and every bit royalty. It's going to be a long wait to get a dance with our prince tonight!"

Rhea could only nod, spellbound and speechless as the man stood under an arbor made of living tree saplings and turned toward the large crowd.

"Welcome, my friends and family of my soul," his smooth voice rang out. "Welcome to this joyous occasion. As you have probably been hearing for the last year," he paused for the twitters of laughter to subside, "we are here to join David and Lily together in marriage and celebrate their joy. Has anyone been able to locate the groom on this fine morning?"

Laughter rang out as the groom, splendid looking in a bright blue pair of fitted cotton trousers and white shirt was dragged up to the front of the assembly by a stern-looking mother. "Here he is! I found him a-cowering in the bushes, scared a-mighty at the thought of meeting Lily's father."

The audience rang out in glee and Cassie turned to Rhea. "David and Lily have been sweethearts ever since they were little. They've been waiting for this day for ages because David wanted to be able to have their own house built before they had the wedding."

David stood in front of Rowan, face lit in a giant smile. "I am here and ready for instruction!"

Rowan clapped the man on the back and turned him to face the crowd. "What advice have we for this young man who is about to become a husband!"

Male voices rang out across the clearing. "The lady is always right!" "Never leave the house angry!" "Never criticize the woman's cooking unless you want to eat leather!" "Communicate, dear boy, communicate!" "'Maybe' almost always means 'no'!"

When the din hushed down Rowan turned toward the man. "Here is the most important of advice. Never take your new wife for granted. Every morning you tell her hello, and every night you remind her how much you love her. There will surely be squabbles, arguments, times when you test the patience of one another, but none of that matters in the end. A true man will always be there to support his wife and offer her aid, comfort, and his very soul if that is what she needs. Never look to another woman for comfort or pleasure for this woman you are pledging your life to holds all that you need in this world."

David nodded solemnly. "I promise to remember these things and to be a good husband to her." He bowed once toward Rowan, once toward the audience, and then went to stand in a small grove of trees.

Rowan's voice rang out over the crowd once again. "Tell me the young lady has not heard this advice and fled the village!"

A circle of girls dressed in matching blue sundresses chattered and giggled their way down the aisle, a blushing Lily dressed in a white knee-length dress at their center. She looked splendid with small designs painted on her face, outlined in pale purples and blues with traces of glitter around her eyes. Long hair cascaded down her back, decorated with smaller roses and a few giant flowers that shared her name.

Lily reached the front of the audience and one by one the girls bowed to Rowan. "We found her hiding in the flower fields, my Lord!"

Cassie clapped her hands and cheered with the crowd. "They've spent the last five hours getting ready, of course."

Rhea nodded, eyes fixated on the green man in front as he tenderly took Lily's trembling hands, the only outward sign of her nervousness of the occasion. "Darling Lily, you come to us a beautiful maiden and will leave a beautiful bride. It has been my honor watching you grow into this wonderful woman." He turned to the crowd and once again asked the question. "What advice have we for this woman!"

This time female voices rang out, filled with laughter. "Remember that you are always right!" "Cook him a good dinner but teach him how to make a grilled cheese sandwich!" "Always tell him why you are upset." "Let him have some time alone." "Don't make him wear pink shirts!"

Lily laughed then, the clear sound ringing across the glade as a peal of pure joy and happiness. She turned towards Rowan and he looked at her with a loving smile across his face.

"Lily, remember these things. Remember never to take your husband for granted, and to keep the same standard for yourself. A good meal on the table and a warm smile will do wonders for a man's spirit and the spirit of the household. Never hold your tongue out of spite and make sure to share if you are ever upset about anything in the marriage. Keep in mind that men want to fix problems, and let him know if you just need to be upset about something that cannot be fixed."

She nodded then and her eyes darted to the grove of trees where David was now standing. The groom walked over and took her hand in front of Rowan and the audience. "I will remember these things so I can be the best wife he will ever have, and the only one he will ever want." She laughed nervously.

Rowan beamed at the crowd. "You have heard the advice offered and the acceptance. Do you, the village of Kylassame, accept the marriage of this couple and promise to do everything needed to maintain their marriage?"

The clearing vibrated with the raucous, "We do," that rang happily from the lips of man, woman, and child alike.

He looked at the couple then and in a voice so low that only the row where Rhea was seated could hear him said. "Remember to love each other above all. Never take your love or your life for granted, for both can wane with time and be all too short. Praise the spirits daily for allowing you to come together and spend the rest of your lives with the one who belongs to your heart. Do not worry so much about children yet, you are still young and need to spend time enjoying one another first. Before the children there is only the two of you as husband and wife, and after the children have moved to find loves of their own, it will only be the two of you as husband and wife. Cherish every moment, every touch, and every piece of emotion that crosses through your path."

His eyes twinkled. "Village of Kylassame, I give you a new couple! If they do not object, it is now time to seal the pact with a kiss."

The crowd cheered and tossed ribbons, confetti, and streamers into the air as the couple kissed in the front of the hay bales. Rhea was surprised to find tears blurring her vision and wiped them away, not wanting to draw attention to herself during such a touching moment.

People jumped up then and women flooded the arbor to hug the bride while the men pulled the hay bales to form a large circle under the tree canopy. The musicians settled upon a small platform and teenage boys gleefully ran around the edge of the clearing with torches and candles to light the various lanterns and small bonfires.

Music filled the grove and Rhea watched from the edge of the clearing as Amanda and Rowan swept into a rousing dance. He looked relaxed, happy, included, and Rhea could not help but feel a pang of guilt at the knowledge that she had kept him from this joyful village for so long.

"Penny for your thoughts?" A shorter, plump man with a jolly face stepped beside Rhea and stood, foot tapping in time to the music.

"Ah, it's nothing worth sharing. I have a tendency to get lost in my mind is all."

The man extended a hand. "The name's Jhoni. I'm the master plumber here and one of the original five who came to set up this village. Tell me now, what's a pretty girl like you doing over on the outskirts while men stumble over their feet trying to get the courage to ask you to dance?"

"I don't dance, sir. I've never have been good at it and have managed to avoid it for a long time."

Jhoni scratched the gray stubble on his chin. "Well now, that seems quite a pity to me. Beautiful woman like you all dressed like a beautiful forest spirit and with no one able to appreciate that splendor?" He stared at the dancing couples and shook his head at Amanda's displays of affection towards Rowan. "I wish that girl would leave that poor man alone and find some other man to pester."

Rhea looked at him in surprise. "He looks content enough from where I'm standing."

A deep chuckle sounded deep from the man's chest. "He's a good leader, Rowan is. Never leads them on but never hurts their feelings either. Oh, she'll go to sleep happy tonight, but not in his bed like she plans. Well, I guess I should say if he finds who he's been scanning the crowd for she won't be in his bed. If that woman doesn't reveal herself to him," he shrugged, "well, a man's a man after all. Can't see a man like him taking a woman like her for a romp, but it wouldn't be the first time she swayed a man's affections."

Rhea accepted a glass of liquid from Daisy and clinked glasses with Jhoni before taking a deep draught of the sweet, alcoholic drink. "You know him well, do you?"

Jhoni nodded his head. "He's a good man, that Rowan. It's no wonder the ladies fawn over him, you couldn't do any better than that if you spent a lifetime searching. Honest, straight forward, a man who appreciates the little things in life like bees buzzing or a flower blooming. He's our rock, our heart, you might say, our defender against the world out there."

She took another sip of the drink, already feeling the alcohol coursing through her system in a happy, carefree way. "That doesn't sound like the man I've had the pleasure of dealing with." She glanced at the man next to her. "I'm sorry, that came out wrong. I should not speak so ill of a man you hold so highly."

"No apology necessary, lass. We pride ourselves on independent thinking here, after all. I do wonder, though, how do you get the impression he is anything but my description?"

"Oh, just stupid things, really. He's always been sharp with me, and he was the one who kidnapped me in the first place." She accepted another cup from Justin, who winked as he walked by. "He writes off most of the things I do as trivial fancies and has a tendency to yell when I do something to displease him. I've always gotten the impression his duty as a court guard is a great inconvenience.

219

Although after being here for just a day, I can see how it would be considered such. I wouldn't want to be there, either, if I had this village as another option."

Jhoni swirled the liquid around in his cup and then drained it. "Ah, you've only seen the court face of the man then. Life has dealt him a hard hand, worse than most I've met. Mother died when he was little, then he was practically left for dead and stripped of any status he might have had. When it comes to the castle and their cursed court, he's left fighting for whatever scrap of respect he might get off the floor." He spat onto the ground in contempt. "Ah, lass, now you must forgive me. I get a little heated when thinking of how the court has treated a man who has been so good to us."

Rhea shook her head and smiled. "Speaking freely, remember?"

Jhoni laughed again. "Ah, yes, and I'd better go speak freely to my wife or she will threaten to withhold my dinner tomorrow. You have a good evening, Rhea, and try to have fun."

A man slightly older than herself sidled over into the space left by Jhoni and gave her a shy smile. "Hello, Rhea, I was wondering if you would grace me with a dance."

Rhea took a sip of her drink and smiled shyly. "I'm afraid I don't dance, but I thank you for the offer."

"Well, then, would you care to accompany me to the food spread? My name is Liam, by the way." He extended his hand.

"I would like that very much." She shook his hand and then walked with him towards a table that had been set out with a variety of items. Cheeses had been artistically arranged on plates with cured meats, fresh fruits were scattered throughout the table and small sandwiches offered a great variety of taste choices. She was also pleasantly surprised to see a large crock of macaroni and cheese, a spinach quiche, and what looked suspiciously like potato salad.

"What brings you to our village, Rhea?" Liam guided her over to two empty hay bales with their drinks balanced precariously on his plate.

"Well, Nasta, the boy, needed to come here and asked me to come with him. You can't really say no to an eight year old who is scared, so here I am." Rhea happily took a bite of macaroni and cheese, sighing in pleasure at the taste of the warm, melted cheese.

Liam chuckled as he watched the boy sprinting around the edge of the circle with a group of eight other boys. "No, that you can't. We've all been wondering, are you and Rowan a couple?"

She laughed cautiously. "No, we are not. He is my Komisar at the court." She glanced at Liam's blank expression, "an acquaintance is all. He looks out for me and keeps me safe from harm."

The man visibly relaxed then and took a swig of his drink. "Well then, you had better be prepared to turn down a few dance offers! A beautiful woman like you doesn't come around often."

A heat rose onto Rhea's face and she nervously twirled a finger around a stray curl that had escaped the pins. "I can't imagine why. I'm certainly not the prettiest girl here and will probably be leaving tomorrow or the next day, after all."

He gave her a curious look and gently placed his warm hand on her cheek. "Rhea, you give yourself too little credit. You are a beautiful woman and if Rowan has not claimed you yet he is a fool." He dropped his hand and nervously laughed. "But hey, his loss is my only chance of a gain."

Another young man walked over then and introduced himself as Simon, caretaker of the sheep. Before Rhea realized she was completely at ease with her company and drawing a larger crowd as she began to tell the story of how she came to this realm.

"Wait, wait, wait. So you managed a kick on one of the guards?" One of the young men looked at her in awe. "I've seen those guards and wouldn't want to tangle with them!"

"Well, it's not like I really had a choice. I just wanted to get away, although I guess it didn't work too well." She swayed slightly on the hay bale and smiled at Liam as he put an arm out to steady her. "Sorry, I think this is the first alcohol I've had in large quantities in quite some time."

Liam smiled and gave her shoulder a squeeze. "I can truthfully say it is my pleasure to hold you steady."

Simon cleared his throat then and Liam glanced up to see Daisy smiling and Rowan looking their way with an unreadable expression. Liam smiled at him and shrugged; Rhea was unclaimed after all. "I want to know more about owning rats as pets!"

Before Rhea could begin she looked up and saw Nastasio standing in front of her, breathless and grinning. "Miss Rhea, I hereby formally request your presence as a partner in a dance." He bowed and then grabbed her hand. "Miss Daisy said if I ask that way you can't say no!"

Rhea laughed but let him pull her to a standing position. "I think I've already informed everyone here multiple times that I do not dance."

Daisy had walked over then and took Rhea's free hand. "Oh, come on now, it's a circle dance so no one will be judging you. Come on, come on. One little dance is all and then we will let you be."

She looked back at the men with a helpless grin and shrugged. "It looks like I should have worked on my dance request rebuttal a bit more diligently."

They stepped out into the center of a large circle and Nastasio and Daisy joined hands with the people around them. Rhea laughed in delight as the large group of people spun in circles, exchanged partners, and no one seemed to notice if she missed a step. Liam slid in next to her when the next dance began and before she knew it she was dancing with the man as he twirled her in circles and led her through the simple steps.

After a few songs Rhea curtseyed to her partner and turned away to remove herself from the dance floor. Before she got two steps away the form of Rowan appeared in front of her with a wary smile on his face. "Will you honor me with a dance as well, Rhea?"

She gazed up at his face, glistening with perspiration from the dancing and eyes that were joyful if wary. "But wouldn't dancing be something frivolous?" *Shut up, stop doing that.*

He licked his lips and reached out to take her hand, placing the other on her back as the musicians started a slow tune with a waltz rhythm. "Yes, it would. I am learning to appreciate the frivolous things in life."

Rhea smiled, the alcohol making her feel carefree and daring, and focused a moment on getting her unsteady feet to follow his steps as they slowly moved around the circle of dancers. "You are a surprisingly good dancer for a guard. Did Nyssa teach you?"

His hand tightened ever so slightly on her back, then relaxed again. "No, my mother. It has been a long time since it has been put to practice in a waltz, however."

Unbelieving eyes met his and Rhea could not help but notice how the rising moon was reflected in the bright green irises. "After seeing how the women here fawn over you, I find that very hard to believe."

He chuckled. "Amanda is the only one with serious intentions, and I am quite certain her intentions shift to the next available man the second that I leave the village."

"I don't know, Rowan. I think you might have something here. I'd be fine at the court now, you know, you could always live here permanently. You wouldn't have to worry about the High Prince or unreasonable demands of the court." His eyes got a far off look and Rhea motioned to where a group of women were gathered. "You know any of them would be more than happy with you. You could have a family of your own and not ever have to worry about court protocol or being poorly treated again."

Those green eyes looked down at her and he absently brushed away a leaf that had floated onto her bare shoulder. "I could say the same for you. I am sure that Liam would be more than happy to offer you a place in his household, or any of the other men whom you held captivated by your innocent charms."

Rhea licked her lips and blushed. "Ah, well, um," she stammered. "That's different. I'm just the new girl, the prime meat, the tenderloin, if you will."

His smile grew crooked at the attempt to keep in the laughter. "Something tells me people are not thinking of beef portions when they look at you, Rhea." He tightened his arm as she tripped on a step and went off balance. "Do you want to go sit down? I know of a quiet place where we can go until you regain your bearings."

"I think that might be a good idea." She let him keep his arm on her waist to steady her steps as they walked out of the clearing of dancers and down a moonlit path.

"Do you always take lonely girls out onto moonlit paths, Rowan?" She shook her head and looked up at him in the darkness. "I'm sorry. I don't know why I keep saying these things. I don't mean them."

Rowan laughed it off and helped her step over a fallen branch that had blocked the path. "Of course I do not always take girls down these paths. I just thought that you would appreciate the end of the path a bit more than standing in the center of the dance circle, at least until your head cleared."

A disbelieving face looked up at him."Uh huh, I'm not buying that one, de Nespa. I think you just wanted to get me away from the men, my new admirers." His back stiffened and he removed his hand from her back. Rhea glanced at him curiously, sobered by the sudden distance, a feeling of loss settling in her stomach. "Did I hit a little close to home?"

"I have seen what happens in court when a woman lets down her guard and is surrounded by men." Rowan's voice became guarded.

Rhea reached down to squeeze his hand. "We are not at the court. What happens in Kylassame?"

He looked down at the twined hands and smiled. "If she is unclaimed, her male relatives step in." Kind eyes looked her way as they stepped out of the tree line into a small clearing. "And if she is you, then I, as the village protector, step in so that you can clear your head until you know what you want."

Rhea let out a long breath as they walked into the circular clearing and saw the sky above. The moon was hidden by a large mountain peak and here the stars shone so clearly Rhea wondered if she could reach up and pluck them from the sky. A soft bed of clover and ivy covered the ground and the last of the season's wildflowers waved in the breeze, filling the small meadow with their sweet scent.

"Rowan, this place is beautiful! How did you find it?" Rhea turned in a slow circle and stared at the twinkling lights in the trees as small forest creatures peered at the couple.

"I have spent a long time in this clearing, running from the demons in my mind. I thought you would appreciate the quiet beauty of the place." He carefully removed a heavy quilted blanket from a hidden wooden chest and laid it in the middle of the clearing. "Come look."

Rhea lowered herself onto the blanket beside him and leaned back on her elbows, face pointed at the sky. She gasped as the first streak of light crossed the sky, then lay fully back with her head cradled in her hands as more and more meteor flashes filled the sky.

"Oh, Rowan, this is incredible! There are so many shooting stars and look at all of the constellations! There's Ursa Major and Ursa Minor and Cassiopeia. The only one missing is Orion, or the one I call 'the Rudolph stars' because they come out around the holiday time."

Rowan leaned back then and allowed himself to look up. "Which one are those? I have forgotten them over the years."

Rhea moved so her head was next to his and then pointed at the sky. "Those stars there are Ursa Major, which means the Big Bear. We also call it the Big Dipper. Then those ones are Ursa Minor, or Little Bear, also the Little Dipper. There is Cassiopeia over there. She was an arrogant and vain queen and because she compared her daughter to the gods she was-"

"Tossed into the sky for all of eternity. She is the warning for the Queens who think themselves above human kind. I remember my mother telling me about that one." Rowan brushed a hand to his eyes and then smiled as he turned to Rhea. "Tell me more about the missing constellation."

"Oh, well, Orion is a really well-known one because his belt is made of three stars in a perfectly straight line. He's also called the hunter. But every time I see the stars I think of a reindeer, or maybe a horse. There are four legs and a back and a neck and a tail, and in the winter a shiny nose that reminds me of the story of Rudolph." She sighed. "If I were back in my world, I might be seeing it right now."

Rowan rolled onto his side and propped his head on his hand as he stared down at Rhea. "After the garden, I am starting to think that you could make this constellation appear in the sky, Rhea."

She laughed softly, then felt her heart begin to flutter against her chest as she realized how close his face was to hers and could not stop herself from nervously licking her lips. "Why haven't you gotten married, Rowan? Why haven't you run away from the court and just lived your life here?"

His free hand gently ran through her hair as he answered. "I've never met a woman I could wed, who could remind me why knowing about the stars was important, who understood the need for the mask of Komisar de Nespa, while letting me just be Rowan."

Rhea sighed in happiness as his lips met hers while the stars danced above them.

Chapter Twenty-Seven

Kylassame

"I feel like we haven't had girl talk since the wedding! I heard that Rowan kissed you, what else happened?" Cassie carefully folded one of Rhea's colored shawls and placed it in the bag.

Rhea turned red and spread the newly washed sheet on her bed. "Nothing else happened, thank you very much! We were drunk, so don't go starting any rumors or looking too deeply into it."

"Oh, yeah, ok, I believe you." Cassie rolled her eyes and pointed to the small jade necklace resting on Rhea's neck. "*You* were very drunk, I will give you that, but *he* was sober. You're telling me him giving you that gift meant nothing?"

The necklace felt cool on Rhea's skin. "I'm sure it's just some silly thing he picked up."

"You don't know him very well, do you?"

An exasperated sigh escaped her lips. "No, I suppose I don't, although before we came, I thought I did. Now, I'm just confused."

"He's a good guy, Rhea. He's loyal and caring, protective and always an advocate for the less fortunate. I'm not telling you this but between him and his, uh, Nyssa, they take care of over ten outcast villages around the castle grounds. He does whatever he can to protect his people and is never selfish. He just does what needs to be done. He is a man of deep emotion and not one to just throw affections at random women just because he feels like it."

Rhea felt a piece of her heart sink and a slice of happiness float away without reason. "I can see that now. I'm not denying any of that."

"But you dismiss his affection as a flight of fancy? Something that just happened and can be ignored?"

"It's complicated, okay?" Rhea looked around the room to make sure it was left in the same condition as when they arrived to the village. They had spent a week here with Nastasio to help him adjust to his new home with Deliah, and Rhea had let herself become too accustomed to the welcoming house, the easy breakfasts at the big table with Rowan and the feel of his body when he embraced her.

"Yeah, yeah, yeah. When is love not complicated?" Cassie packed the last article of clothing in the bag and made sure it was securely tied shut. "I'm going to miss you, Rhea. I wish the two of you could just stay here and not go back to court."

Rhea gave her new friend a hug, surprised at the break in her voice when she said, "I'm going to miss you too, Cassie. I wish we could stay, really I do. Court is complicated though and there are things we need to do back in Kalda. Keep an eye on Nasta for me, will you?"

She nodded and grabbed one of Rhea's bags to help bring it to where the horses were tethered out front. Nastasio was enveloped in Rowan's arms while Deliah stood to the side.

"You be good, okay? Listen to Miss Deliah and stay out of trouble. If you ever need anything, you let Justin know and he will find a way to get the message to me." He gave the boy a kiss on the forehead and embraced Deliah. "Thank you for accepting him. It means so much to me that he is in your capable hands."

The woman managed a stiff nod and turned away with Nastasio as the tears started to fall. Daisy walked over to Rhea then and gave the woman a big hug.

"You take care of yourself now and take care of that man over there. We'll be here if you ever need an escape."

Rhea hugged her back, surprised as her vision began to blur with tears. "I'll miss all of you. You are a good people and this is a good place. I hope I can come back one day."

Rowan walked her horse over then and carefully secured the saddle bags onto their mounts. He helped Rhea mount and let his hand linger on her leg as she found the stirrup. "Ready to go?"

She turned towards the bright house with its wide porch and shook her head. "No, but I don't think I'll ever be ready to leave here." With a last wave, the pair left the village of souls and headed back along the path to the court of Kaldalangra.

Chapter Twenty-Eight

Kaldalangran Mountains

"You're kidding me! Nyssa actually put a frog in the Queen's bed? That doesn't seem like it fits the rules of the court." Rhea stared at him with wide eyes as she dipped a piece of bread in the soup bubbling on the fire.

"That is what she did. I forget why; I think she was told she could not go outside because of the weather or something. She was kept in her chambers for a week and the only thing she was allowed to do to pass the time was embroidery or weaving." Rowan sat with his back to the wide tree trunk that made up one support of their tent.

"You've known her awhile then? When did you come to the court?"

Rowan stretched out a leg and Rhea couldn't help but notice how his muscles rippled under the fabric. "We were both born there. I am a few years older so I have technically known her for her entire life."

"What about Faulks? Where did he come from?" Rhea gestured to where the hawk was seated on a large branch that had been brought in to keep him out of the rain. He had joined them once they passed the cave where they rested on their first journey. Rhea supposed they should have made it to Albadarl by now, but the driving rain forced them into making shelter at mid-day.

Rowan handed her a cup filled with a hot tea. "He was a present for my fifth birthday. Of course, he was a bit smaller back then as well. Once my position at court – changed - he flew out of the castle grounds and into the sky. I thought he had deserted me, but when I was old enough to get out of the walls there he was, just waiting for me. The first time I followed him to try to catch him again, he led me straight to Albadarl."

"He sure is special." The stone around her neck shifted its slight weight and Rhea touched it gently. "Rowan, can I ask where you got this necklace? It's beautiful and I've never seen this color of jade before. It almost looks like a little ladybug."

The green eyes looked at the necklace and then out of the tent opening into the rain. "I found the stone in a stream when I was four. My tutor was skilled at stone craft and gave it the shape. I gave it to my mother for her birthday." His voice cracked and he cleared his throat. "She gave it back to me when she got sick, for safe keeping. The next day she went to sleep and never woke up."

Rhea's eyes filled with tears and she moved to wrap her arms around his shoulders as the stoic man's facade crumbled. "Rowan, I am so sorry that happened. I know if she saw you now, and all the work you've been doing to help people, she would be so incredibly proud of you."

His fingers gripped onto her arms and he laid his head on her shoulder as the sobs began to rack his body. She held the man close and whispered words of comfort while gently running her fingers through his dark hair. They sat entwined for several moments, Rowan mumbling out the hurt and the pain that had been held in for the years following his mother's death. Rhea gently stroked his cheek, his arm, his back, giving comfort as well she could and holding the tears from her own eyes as she absorbed his grief and let it wash over her.

She held him thus until he began to take even breaths and wiped his eyes. "I am sorry, Rhea. I have not cried like that since she died." He pulled his legs up and rested his arms on his knees. "Some brave guard I am."

"You *are* a brave guard. It's okay to be human and have deep feelings."

He looked at her with such intensity that a wave of warmth swept through her body. "Having feelings has always been dangerous in this place. People die because of their feelings."

Rhea laid her head against his shoulder as she felt a twinge of sadness. "Only in the court, and we're not back in the court yet."

He smiled and kissed her temple gently. "Then I will just have to hope the rain never stops."

She nodded and pulled the thick blanket over her shoulders to keep out the damp chill brought on by the rain. She curled under the blanket and smiled as Rowan moved in and held her close against him. "Goodnight, Rowan."

"Goodnight, Rhea."

Chapter Twenty-Nine

Albadarl

They arrived at Albadarl a few hours after the sun rose and the rain dissipated to a fine drizzle. Once again they halted at the limestone slabs and waited until the Elder moved out from the protection of the trees.

He looked at the pair with those dark brown eyes and smiled. "You are a bit delayed in reaching our village, Rowan. We had received news that you left Kylassame with plenty of time to be here for dinner. Did you experience trouble on your journey?"

Rowan dismounted and knelt on one knee in front of the Elder. "Just a rain storm, honorable one. We thought it wise to make camp and wait a day for better weather."

A petite woman with the same dark skin as the Elder stepped forward. "Yes, we suspected you would appreciate a bit of time in the rain." Her eyes twinkled as brightly as the mica torc around her neck. "However we perhaps did not time it quite right. The intent was for you to have more time in Kylassame, not be stranded on the path."

Rhea slid off of her horse and curtseyed. "I am honored to meet you. My name is Rhea."

The woman watched her with wide eyes before turning to the man. "This is the one? I had thought she would be darker-natured."

Rowan stood and moved next to Rhea with a fierce, protective look in his eyes. "Her true nature has much darker hair and eyes. Risalka bestowed the light hair and you can have a discussion with the Aos Si about her eyes."

Vigorous nods from the couple. "Yes, yes. They did such things for protection we suppose."

Elder Wekesa turned toward his companion. "This is my daughter, Chasike. Please come join us for a meal before you continue on your way."

Rowan brought the horses a short way into the woods and then tethered them to a branch where Faulks could keep watch and give warning of intruders. The group walked down a narrow deer path that opened up into a large glade filled with large grass huts.

A powerfully built man approached as they entered the glade. He reached the group and nodded in respect toward the newcomers, shaved head barely reaching up to Rhea's chest. "Welcome to Albadarl, Rowan, Lady Rhea. We have awaited your visit since we heard you were taking the journey to Kylassame. I regret we cannot give you quite the joyous occasion we had planned due to frequent circumstance."

Rowan looked over the village and noticed the rust color on the fallen leaves and the lack of peace that usually came with Albadarl. "What happened here, Emeku? How bad is it?"

Emeku looked up at the man, a grave expression filled with pain adding ferocity to the tattooed designs on his face. "The White Plague appeared shortly after your departure, my Lord. Several of our children were out of the trees and were caught." His jaw muscle tensed and Rhea saw tears building in Chasike's eyes. "They got Kibwe with their swords, my Lord. The White Plague himself struck the blow."

Rowan sucked in a quick breath. "Is he..." he trailed off, unable to say the word while he remembered the couple's youngest child the first day he saw the boy swinging from the trees.

234

Chasike stepped forward and bowed her head. "He lives, my Lord, but the leg was cut completely off. He is in our tent. I know it would greatly raise his spirits if you would sit by his bed for a time."

He nodded and gently took Rhea's hand as he walked toward the largest of the huts. "It would be good for you to be there, Rhea. You have a way of calming children."

She ran her tongue over the roof of her dry mouth and followed him into the low ceiling hut. The child was lying on a thick, grass woven cot towards the back wall of the enclosure with a heavy fur covering his bare body. The boy looked to be about ten years old and had several small tattoo swirls on his shoulders and chest.

He opened his eyes and gave a painful smile. "Rowan, they said you would come."

Rowan sank to his knees beside the cot and took the small boys hand in his own. "I am here now. We will stay for the night and make sure that the men do not come back. I brought my friend with me. Her name is Rhea."

Kibwe looked up at Rhea and nodded. "Hello, Rhea. I would offer to show you how to swing through the trees but I will have to re-teach myself." He glanced down at his leg. "At least it was a clean cut, right, Rowan? It could have been much worse."

The man just nodded, throat too caught with emotion to release a sound. After a moment he cleared his throat and asked, "how many more were injured, Kibwe? Did you recognize the people who came?"

Kibwe closed his eyes against the pain that shot through his body and thought. "Sefu, Tafar, Uduak and Lekan escaped with wounds less than mine. Paki and Rudo were cut down and did not come back. I grabbed a piece of the Plague's stirrup before I fell." The boy reached under the fur mattress and pulled out a small leather ornament, pure white with gold thread embroidery. He started to reach down toward his foot then stopped, and his voice trembled.

"Rowan, my foot itches. How does something itch when it does not exist anymore?"

Rhea's heart fell at the sight of the stirrup piece and the tremble in the young boy's voice. How many times had she looked at the beauty of Mateo's riding gear while spending her time idling in the stable? Her mind reached for a reasonable explanation for why this occurred, and she began to breathe harshly when she realized there could be no justifying this attack.

Chasike came into the tent then and ushered the couple outside. "Kibwe needs his medicine and some sleep now. Thank you for coming here, Rowan, and you, as well, Rhea."

They walked around the village for quite some time then, and Rowan took Rhea to visit every family present. Two of the houses were covered in a layer of black ash and he explained that those were the families who had lost children in the attack. The huts that housed the injured had red sashes hung from the door and it was explained to Rhea that the intensity of the crimson was in correlation to the severity of the wound.

The rest of the injured children fared far better than Kibwe. They explained to Rowan how they had gone out into the open on a dare by Paki. They only went out five feet and thought it would be safe enough. Suddenly the White Plague and ten of his men had surrounded them with their swords drawn. They laughed as the children attempted to flee and cut down the two immediately. Then Kibwe threw himself onto the White Plague with his small hunting knife and the other children were able to scatter under the legs of the horses to safety. Kibwe's leg was severed by the leader, who then picked up their friend by the shirt and tossed him at the woods. "He said it was a warning to stay in the forest where the magical freaks like us belonged."

By the end of the story Rhea's face was wet with tears that she had to blink away in order to finish bandaging one child's arm, and examined the bruises on another from one of the horse's powerful hooves. Rowan kneeled throughout the story, head bowed in complete silence, his face grim and dark with every word that came from the children.

The exhausted couple finally walked out of the last hut and Rhea blinked at the fireflies that had filled the clearing of the village. "The White Plague is Mateo, isn't he? He's the one who did this."

Rowan glanced at her and put an arm around her waist for support, then withdrew it nervously. "Yes, he is."

Rhea looked around as the women went about cleaning up the camp and started to prepare the evening meal for their guests. She reached out and slid her fingers into Rowan's hand, cherishing the warmth and the security she felt when he was touching her. "What can we do to help them?"

"Not much now. Give them time to grieve and help clean wounds. We will go back to the court at first light." Rowan led her to a smaller hut set back in the village and held the woven door hanging to the side as she stepped through. "It is not much, but welcome to my Albadarl home. It is usually a much more welcoming place and happier atmosphere." He shook his head and his free hand balled into a fist. "Why did they go outside? Why did they have to be there when he was riding through? Why was he riding through this late? If we had delayed on our way to Kylassame…"

She sat in front of the small fire and curled her knees up to her chest. "I still can't believe that Mateo would do this, but I hardly can deny this when I'm here and seeing the results. It just doesn't mesh with the man I know."

Rowan sat behind her and stared into the hearth that one of the village women had built in the hut prior to their arrival. "The man you know is not the High Prince. The man you know from your Virginia does not exist anymore, Rhea. He is the High Prince, a man who causes fear and pain upon those who cannot defend themselves. This man is dangerous, and I fear for you when we return."

"What's going to happen when we get back to the court, Rowan?" She leaned against his broad chest and felt his arms close protectively around her. "What do we do once we get back?"

She felt his chest rise as he took a deep breath in the moment of heavy silence. "I do not know, Rhea. I do not have the status to try to court you openly and I am not willing to take the risk of you being punished." He touched his lips to her hair and Rhea sighed. "As your guard, I will be able to interact with you but moments like these will be gone except if we slip away to visit the villages. They do not care about the status or the politics involved; they just want people to be happy."

"Is this what it's like for Nyssa?" Rhea whispered as she stared at Rowan's tan hand laying over her pale one. "You just wait for the little snippets of happiness and suffer the rest of the time?"

Rowan's lips were lightly touching her neck then and Rhea sank into him as he replied. "She does what she has to for the court. People like us do not get to love openly. We fear for the day she is forced to wed, when the King will not accept her delays any longer."

Sleep did not come easy that night, as they lay curled in a cot of woven branches. Rowan's hand casually stroked the side of Rhea's body through her thin gown and he wiped the tears that fell from her eyes. "It is okay, dear one. It will be okay. We just need to be strong and persevere."

Rhea nodded but knew it was a lie. The second that she had arrived at the village and seen what Mateo had done to the children she knew what path she needed to take. *The only way to stop this is to tie myself to Mateo. If that happens I will never be able to see Rowan this way again, never get to feel him against me or see that confident smile. Coming to any of the villages will be out of the question and I will miss those people so much. Rowan will hate me, and never be able to understand why I'm doing this but I can't let more people die if there's something within my power.* More tears flowed down her face and she curled tighter into the security of Rowan's body as she felt her heart break. *Tomorrow I'll take the first step to Forena and protecting these people.*

Chapter Thirty

The Court

Lianna gave the miserable woman in front of her an incredulous look. "You seriously told Rowan you were going to accept the Forena position? Are you insane? I would have thought some time away from the castle would have cleared your head from all of Mateo's games."

Rhea sat hunched on the stone bench in the garden, red rimmed eyes fixed on where Rowan was talking with Savin further down on the path. "I know about Mateo's games. I know about what he's doing and this is the only way that I can stop it. If I'm-" her breath caught and she struggled to regain her composure. "A man will tell a woman who shares his bed much more than he will tell a casual acquaintance or sister. Then I can let others know what he has planned and we can give the villages more warning."

"And Rowan? Where does he fit into this plan of yours?"

Rhea did not try to stop the tears that traced a chilly path down her face. "And the week we had will be locked up forever in my head as a cherished memory to banish the dark nights. That's just the way it has to be. Maybe he and Agrafina can find happiness together."

"The man wants you, Rhea. He has not wanted someone in his entire life, but now he wants you."

Rhea stood up abruptly and angrily replied. "You think I don't realize that? You think I don't want to spend every day in his company and every night in his arms? You don't think I realized how different he is when he doesn't have his court mask on or how right it feels to be with him at Kylassame? I'm not a robot who can make these decisions and not feel anything." The anger was immediately replaced by a heart-wrenching sadness and Rhea turned her face away with a suppressed sob as Savin approached the women.

"My Ladies, Nyssa has requested your presence in her chamber. It appears that the High Prince has ordered a raid for Asimina to commence immediately." Savin looked over to where Rowan paced along the garden path. "Rowan and I have been ordered to attend this raid and you are to stay with Lady Nyssa under the protection of Kofizek."

"Kofizek?" Lianna slipped a hand on Savin's muscular arm as they stepped out of the garden and made their way toward Nyssa's chamber in the royal sector. "But why would Kofizek be guarding Nyssa, or us?"

Savin dropped his voice and looked backward to where Rowan and Rhea were having sharp words with one another. "I do not know, Lianna and I do not like it. We have had no time to warn the village and Nyssa has been under Kofizek's thumb for the last three days so she has not been able to get word to Sebast. I fear this is nothing but a trap for all of us."

Lianna gripped his arm tightly. "Be careful out there, Savin. You and Rowan both. I do not like the feel of this day and the way this has been kept so secretive. There is too much misery in the air already."

Savin pasted a confident smile on his face. "Do not worry about us. We have got the experience to make it out whole."

Both turned simultaneously as Rhea spat out, "of course it wouldn't be better if you died, you stubborn man," toward Rowan.

Lianna glanced at Savin. "Are you certain about that? If Rowan is as distracted lately as Rhea has been, you may have a harder time of it than you anticipate."

"I will keep a careful eye on him. You two watch your own backs and take care of Nyssa. She is going to be a wreck today."

"I think the entire room will be filled with wrecks today, Savin." She glanced back to see Rowan's hand brush over Rhea's cheek as he gently wiped away a tear. She gave the giant man's arm a squeeze. "Please come back, and bring him back, and please be careful."

They arrived at Nyssa's chamber quickly and the men walked away after ensuring the women's' safety with the Komisar of the High Prince.

Nyssa was seated on a long, plush couch, face blotched with red as the two women entered the chamber. Each sat down beside her, took one of her hands and for a moment they simply sat in silent misery as they listened to the sounds of horses being saddled and mounted in the courtyard.

Rhea walked over to the window and pressed her hand against the glass. She found it easy to pick out Rowan's body in the large contingency of guards, partially because he rode next to Savin who towered above the other men, and partially because she had been well acquainted with the outline of his strong build. The High Prince turned at the front of the line and his drawn sword glinted in the sunlight as he gave the command for them to be off.

"Rhea, did you hear me?" Nyssa looked toward the woman.

"Sorry, my head was elsewhere."

Nyssa twisted the ring on her finger as she stared at the window behind Rhea. "He truly does love you, I want you to know that. Rowan, I mean. He told me to make sure you knew that in case something like this ever happened. Something where the chance of return was…diminished."

Rhea looked up at the ceiling as she felt the water pooling in her eyes and willed herself not to cry more tears. "They will come back. Savin and Rowan will come back safe and Sebast will be safe. That's the way this has to turn out."

Lianna placed a kind hand on Nyssa's to halt the spinning progress of the ring. "Nyssa, you are either going to wear a hole through your finger or thin the metal until it disintegrates if you keep that up."

A deep sigh of sadness as she responded, "I know. I cannot help it though. I guess I am hoping that mother's spirit will tell me what to do if I spin her ring. The King keeps threatening to remove it from my person so I have had to make sure I do not fidget with it when I am around him."

"Do you think he misses her?" Lianna took a turn by the window and stared at the dust cloud rising. The men were riding hard and fast and it seemed as if they were already halfway to Asimina.

Nyssa shook her head. "I think he has gone far beyond the point of missing her." She looked over at Rhea, who stood watching the small fire in the room. "It was not always like this here, with fear and death constantly hanging in the air. The King was never a warm man, or the kind of father you would run to with a bruised knee, but he was a decent man. When he would get ideas that were brutal or too beyond normal, Mother would rein him in again just like an unruly horse. Then she got sick and we realized just how much she held him together. Every day that her condition worsened he would sink deeper into his grief, and it became more and more obvious that she was the only thing in his world that really mattered or gave him joy. Her opinion was the only one that mattered and that he would listen to when he got into his moods. Then her life slipped away and any mercy in his soul disappeared. Causing misery and pain was the only thing that filled the void and he soon turned into the man he is today." She wiped the tears from her eyes. "Everything would have been fine if she just recovered, if she had stayed with us and not left us all alone."

Lianna put an arm around her friend's shoulder. "We cannot change what happened. All we can do is try to keep pushing until we can get a better future. The King cannot live forever and maybe, just maybe, Rhea can temper Mateo's eventual rule the same way the Queen did the King."

She shook her head. "That is our only hope right now." Nyssa glanced at Rhea as the woman's face paled and another tear fell down her cheek. "I know that is probably not what you want to hear, but it is the truth."

Rhea watched as the tear fell onto the back of her hand. "I know that. That is why I told Rowan what we wanted was impossible. I have to get closer to Mateo in order to reach him. I also know that Matt is still hidden in there somewhere. If I can just find that part of him, the part of him that I know remembers his old life then everything will be okay. He and I can find a way to go home and you can lead this land and make it what it needs to be."

Lianna stepped to the window again and saw the huge dust cloud that arose in the distance and the flashes of lights from the sun-lit swords wielded by the soldiers. "They have reached Asimina. Not much longer now."

Nyssa nodded tensely. "This should be much faster than the usual raids since they had no warning time and no one would dare to delay their progress on this occasion." A shudder went through her body. "I did not know it was possible to be this afraid. You know what they will do if they catch Sebast."

The other two women nodded. A man who had eluded the castle's elite guard for nearly two decades would not get kind treatment upon capture. The King constantly spoke to Nyssa about the renegade and the various torture methods that would be used if he were ever to be caught alive. Every silent minute that passed Nyssa remembered his words and felt the hole in her chest grow larger and larger.

"I do not know if I can keep up the court mask if he dies. I do not think I could continue pretending not to care. How can I keep from betraying all the people who depend on me?" Nyssa whispered into the air.

Silence fell on the chamber then as all three women stared at the approaching dust cloud. A sharp rap on the door caused them to jump and Kofizek walked into the chamber, disapproval at their window position and swollen eyes written clearly on his face.

"My Ladies, your presence is required at the Festival. I will escort you." He sneered and then held open the door for the three women to walk into the hallway.

Chapter Thirty-One

The Court

The Festival arena shocked Rhea with its size and gory splendor. Row after row of benches surrounded the center area, which she guessed to be about fifty yards wide and covered with thin, brightly dyed material that flapped in the slight breeze. Designed to keep the worst of the sun from touching the Patrons, the fabric gave a cool environment to those who sat below the awning. It seemed as if every person in the realm had gathered already and Rhea felt a momentary touch of nausea as she realized the expressions on their faces were created of excitement and anticipation for the events to come. Plaster walls of gleaming white with rust-colored patches surrounded the area with a twenty foot high wall, with vividly painted murals depicting men fighting and dying in the field of battle. A thick layer of brick-colored sand created the arena floor that had been fastidiously raked until even.

The three women entered and were ushered to a special box, close enough to see the blank expressions on the faces of the servants as they finished raking the arena sand and arranging the weapon racks. The King was already seated in a grand throne of gold and silver with Agrafina sitting quietly in a smaller golden chair in the row before him. She looked up and offered Nyssa a forced smile of encouragement before she noticed Rhea and her features darkened.

Agrafina took Nyssa's hand in hers and gave it a gentle squeeze as she whispered, "I have been praying for you ever since I found out we would have a surprise game today. I swear I knew nothing of his plans. Maybe they never found him."

Nyssa squeezed back and attempted a small smile of reassurance. "I know. You have always been like a sister to me. "

The King clapped a hand on Nyssa's shoulder as the crowd began to grow excited at the sound of hoof beats on the stones surrounding the arena. "It will be a good show today. I do not believe the crowd has been this enthusiastic in quite some time."

Nyssa merely nodded in response as her white face stared at the door where, Rhea assumed, the captive men would enter the arena.

The High Prince stepped into the booth then and Rhea watched out of the corner of her eye as he stopped next to the King and whispered in his ear. The triumph in both expressions caused her to involuntarily grip Nyssa's hand next to her. She cast a worried look around the arena for Savin and Rowan, hoping her feigned look of disinterest would cover her true intentions.

They appeared then, sliding into the empty designated spaces in front of the women and kneeling to prevent the view from being blocked for those behind. Rhea saw that they were both covered in sweat, dust, and not a small amount of blood. She longed to reach out and touch Rowan but, after a stern reminder to herself that such an action would not be tolerated, settled for greeting her two guards casually.

King Verikhan stood then with a ceremonial flourish that immediately quieted the crowd, now almost to a frenzy with the level of anticipation for the event. His powerful voice boomed across the crowd. "My people, my subjects, I bid you welcome. The High Prince has led a successful raid on the cesspool known as Asimina and returned with great entertainment for your pleasure and a suitable offering to our Gods."

The High Prince stood then, perfect in his white riding ensemble and sword that gleamed golden in the sun, and extended an arm of respect towards the King as he addressed the audience. "I thank you for the acknowledgment, great King. Today was a successful day thanks to the full participation of the soldiers and guard forces of our great kingdom!" He paused as a roar from the crowd deafened ears. "We have returned on this day with the traitor who has eluded capture and held our great realm captive to the spiteful wills of the malevolent spirits. Behold, the mysterious ghost man of Asimina!"

Voices rose in anger and condemnation as a tall man covered in blood and bruises was shoved into the arena with his hands tied in front of him. Rhea saw Nyssa sway slightly beside her before the woman willed her body still. The only source of distress that Rhea could detect was the labored breath from her chest, and the way her throat quivered as the Princess of the realm struggled to contain her forbidden emotions in front of the subjects.

Sebast stepped to the center of the ring and found Nyssa's eyes immediately. There was no hate and no judgment in that stare, only sadness and futility. The muscular man stood tall in the ring despite his wounds and turned slowly, silently mapping every entrance or exit that could be used against him. Soon the ring flooded with the other men of Asimina, as well as heavily armored guards from the castle.

Rhea jumped as she felt a heavy hand rest on her shoulder and the High Prince's voice filled her ear. "I am glad you finally were feeling well enough to come view the Festival, Rhea. The crowd watches their future Forena with pride and curiosity. Remember that, for it would not do you well if you were to faint in the midst of their favored entertainment and religious ceremony."

She nodded acknowledgement, then took a few deep breaths and willed her heart to a regular beat as the High Prince sat back and the trumpet blew for the games to begin.

It was an immediate slaughter of the older men. They were given short sticks with which to defend themselves while the soldiers savagely attacked with razor sharp sabers and knives. The soldiers took their time as a man dressed in finery in the stands told the story of the day in a great booming voice.

"The realm has been infected with a curse, my dear subjects!" A man received a brutal slice to the arm, nearly severing it from the body. "This curse has existed since the time we remember, and inflicted by those who did not pay honor to our true Gods." Another man fell as a soldier's sword swung through his vertebrae. "The only way to cleanse this curse is by releasing the blood of the infected and sending their tainted souls to the next life." A third man fell with a cry as his leg was severed at the knee.

Rhea kept her vision focused on Sebast as she realized how the brutality of the games worked. The man was given no sticks, no weapons of defense and his hands remained tightly bound by thick cord. He managed to dodge the attacks from the guards with minor injury, his abilities and strength resulting in immediate survival. After a short time the immediate action halted, and the audience held its breath as they realized the tall man was the only man of Asimina left standing in the ring.

She held her breath as the first guard advanced. *If only he could be freed from the ropes, he would stand a chance. If he had his hands free he could move and get some sticks, or perhaps steal a sword.* Rhea closed her eyes to think about what the man could do to save himself; about if there was anything she could do, fervently hoping with all of her being that he would emerge from this contest alive.

A gasp rose from the crowd as the man dodged a swing of the sword and maneuvered his hands so that the sharp blade slid through the rope, completely severing it between his two hands. A quick pivot and roll and he grabbed two of the short sticks in his hands and had his back to the empty side of the arena. Another quick roll and he was shoving two more sticks into the small knife holsters built onto his boots, emptied when the guard seized his knives upon capture.

He tossed his loose hair back from his eyes and carefully watched the guards as he dodged and parried the blows from their swords. The defensive sticks were cut shorter with every swipe and he continued to roll and slide across the sand to retrieve additional weapons for protection. Then a wild strike from a guard opened Sebast's calf and sent him crashing to the sand.

A pause in the movement had the crowd holding their breath, and then Sebast rolled to the side and knocked the guard's legs from under his body. The armored man toppled and Sebast took the precious moment to knock the man's helmet heavily with the stick. The man fell still and the sharp sword was now in Sebast's capable hands. He braced himself for battle, injured leg resting lightly in front with the brunt of his weight being held by his steady back leg.

The King growled behind the women and exchanged angry words with the son seated next to him. After the second guard fell to the sword in Sebast's hand the King stood and bellowed, "That is enough for the Gods!"

A poignant hush fell over the crowd as the guards formed a wide circle around the man. The High Prince stood and glared down into the arena. "You offend the Gods by your flagrant disrespect for the realm. However, I am a man of appreciation for great fighting skill. Drop your weapon and the guard will not harm you. This is the will of the Gods as spoken through my person."

Nyssa tensed beside Rhea, her entire body strung as tightly as a harp string as she watched Sebast look around the circle of guards, glance once at her, and then lay the sword down.

Immediately, the guards were upon him and within seconds his hands had been firmly secured behind his back and legs manacled with heavy iron chains. He was dragged to his feet and pushed awkwardly to the edge of the arena to be within low talking distance of the High Prince.

The High Prince looked over the arena railing with contempt. "You will spend your days in the dungeon for your treason and blasphemy to the Gods. I hope you enjoyed your display of disrespect for it will be your last time in the sun."

Sebast merely looked at the man with unreadable eyes. If he showed fear, anxiety, or distress about his situation one would not be able to tell. He walked out calmly with the circle of guards as Nyssa trembled beside Rhea.

The King stood then and left abruptly, the High Prince following with his Komisar at his heels. The four women stood then and Nyssa softly said, "I think I would like to spend some time in the garden." Her vacant eyes stared at the space that her beloved had occupied not moments before. "Please come with me, I do not think I can bear to be on my own right now."

~ * ~ * ~

Rhea walked over to where Lianna was carefully bandaging a deep gash on Savin's arm and sat next to Rowan on the bench. "I'm glad you came back in one piece," she whispered.

He glanced over at her and shrugged, then winced as the movement tugged at a wrenched muscle in his shoulder. "It was an effort. The guards enjoyed laying the traps on the way back and then sending us out on scouting missions to walk straight into them. It is safe to say they were none too pleased when we returned, even if we were a bit more bruised and bloodied than when we left."

Lianna slid a clean bowl of water and soft rag over toward Rhea. "Here, those wounds need to be cleaned and you know the men will not do it themselves." She and Savin moved off of the bench then and down the forest path with the man's hand lightly resting upon the small of her back.

Rhea dipped the cloth into the water and gently pushed aside Rowan's hair to dab at the dried wound on the side of his temple. "You came back though. That's all that matters."

He flinched slightly as she pulled the ripped collar of his shirt to the side to clean the knife laceration across his chest. "Rhea, you should not be involved with me, not after this. Savin and I were targeted on this raid, and it would kill me if something happened to you because of it." He took her hand in his and held onto it for a long moment before he sighed and released it. "I wish it could be different, Rhea, I do, and I know I was harsh on you for your decision. I want you to be happy, and if happy is unattainable, then you should at least be alive. I will ask to be permanently removed as your Komisar, and to be assigned an outpost position so we will not be forced to torture ourselves with what cannot ever be."

Rhea blinked back the tears as he stood and moved to meet Savin with a small nod, and then walked down the path back in their direction with Lianna. Savin stood in front of Rhea and gave a polite bow. "My Lady. I ask your permission that Komisar Rowan and I be excused from duty on this evening. We will send a suitable replacement to guard you." The formality then dropped out of his pose, and he looked at the corner of the garden where the distant form of Nyssa could be seen curled into a small ball. "Take care of her, both of you. Let her know that this will be rectified. Sebast will not die in that dungeon."

The women nodded and watched soberly as they walked out of the garden and Dmitri moved to sit as a quiet guard at the entrance. The men moved with purpose and confidence, but under it all Rhea could not help but wonder why their parting felt more like a permanent goodbye than simply requesting a night off from duty.

Lianna broke her concentration as she cleared her throat. "I am going to go talk to Nyssa."

Rhea looked toward her retreating form and then turned down a different path and allowed her feet to wander. The King had located Nyssa in the hallway and explained the punishment that would be carried out on their prisoner for his disobedience to the Gods. Lianna told Rhea that the King did this often, as Nyssa would be the heiress to the realm if anything were to happen to the High Prince. Rhea wondered how such a sweet woman could bear the weight of such cruelty and still continue down her path of goodness and compassion.

She stopped as she walked into the large clearing in the garden and saw the form of Agrafina lying prone on the ground. Rhea quietly walked over and sat beside her, encouraged when the woman did not move away. "I'm sorry if I have caused you any grief, Agrafina. I only wanted to do what is best for the realm and the future of its people."

She gave a harsh laugh and turned her tear-stricken face toward Rhea. "I know. I knew that one day this would happen, even though I never knew who the person who drove my demise would be. I am not mad at you, not truly, just the situation and my own stupidity for getting involved with him in the first place."

"But Mateo promised that you wouldn't lose your status and you would be free to pursue other relationships."

A look of pity met Rhea's eyes as Agrafina turned her way. "You will learn how he really is soon enough, Rhea. He speaks with a honeyed voice and makes promises that he never intends to keep. I will likely be allowed to remain at the court, perhaps to be his mistress when you are with child." She laughed at Rhea's look of surprise. "Please, you thought he would be faithful? He is the High Prince. I will survive but I will never be allowed to court another man or have my own family."

Rhea lay back down on the grass and felt as if all of the hope had finally fled from her body. "I'm sorry, 'Fina, really I am."

"I know you are. You do not do this for love. None of us do anything for love here." Agrafina reached out and took Rhea's hand in a gesture of friendship. A small laugh escaped her body. "I swear the clouds are mocking us, that one almost looks like a heart with a giant crack down the middle."

Rhea followed her eyes into the sky and was startled at how accurate of a description that was. "I didn't think anyone else here looked at clouds and saw images."

"Oh, very few people do these days. Queen Sula would always bring us out here as young children and play games with cloud shapes. For Rowan every cloud looked like a dragon, or horse, or turtles, while Nyssa and I saw unicorns, kittens, and dresses."

The longing for the past in Agrafina's voice could be heard so Rhea pressed on, glad to have something to consider other than the recent events of the day. "Tell me about the Queen, 'Fina. I've heard a little bit from Nyssa, but I hear such joy mixed with the sadness when she is mentioned."

Agrafina smiled then. "Oh, she was beautiful, the most beautiful woman on earth. She had dark brown hair that shone in the sun and always smelled like lavender. You always knew when she was happy because her hazel eyes would twinkle and she would get this little sly smile, like she always knew what you were about to say before you said it. Animals loved her too. There was the horse of course; I think you have met her. Then, there was also a little gray kitten. She was born the runt of the litter and the mom kept pushing her away. Well, Queen Sula convinced the mother cat to take in the little baby and then kept her safe in her room until she was old enough to defend herself. And she loved ladybugs, dragonflies, any of the prettier bugs. She said they brought good luck and she was forever carving small ladybugs into the furniture in her room because it would make her children squeal in happiness every time they found a new little surprise. I have never seen a woman with such love for her children as the Queen."

Rhea sat up in surprise. "Children? I know that Mateo was brought here, so did she have a child other than Nyssa? What happened to them?"

Agrafina gave a low laugh and slowly rose to her feet. "You really are clueless sometimes! Her second child has been here all along. You need only cast off your blinders to see him." She straightened her dress and walked out of the glade.

Chapter Thirty-Two

The Court

Soft whinnies and the sounds of sleeping horses filled the stable as Rhea sat in the corner of Kataolya's stall. It was well after midnight and, with the exception of Aleksei who was working the night shift, the entire staff of the stable was deep in slumber. The woman found that she could not sleep that night and after a series of troubling dreams pushed her to panic, she made the decision to slip out of her room and into the stable for the comfort only dirt and hay could provide. Even Kataolya was deep in slumber and offered her back for Rhea's comfort as the horse lay curled in the middle of the freshly cleaned stall.

"It's too still tonight, Kata," she whispered to the sleepy mare. "It's too still, like the moment before chaos erupts." She shook her head. "Maybe I'm just making things up though. It's not unreasonable for the men to want a night off, especially after a day like today, well, yesterday. They are probably just holed up in a safe place getting some much needed sleep. They had a long day and the last thing they need are some worried females pestering them, right?"

A soft footfall outside of the stall caused the horse to open her eyes and Rhea held her breath until a familiar young woman stepped just in front of the stall and spoke quietly with head bowed. "Hello, Lady Rhea. I know that you do not know me, and that it is quite an unacceptable hour for one of my status to approach, and I do apologize for the timing and intrusion."

Rhea waited until it became apparent the woman was going to stand silent with her head bowed until she said something. "That is quite all right. What can I assist you with at this late hour?"

The woman's face lifted up and her eyes shimmered with equal amounts of worry and hope. "My name is Alma, my Lady. Nastasio is my little brother. I heard that Lord Rowan took him to a safe place and was wondering if you knew anything of his condition?" Her voice choked with emotion and she stammered out, "I begged my Patron to take him in, he is my family, but she would not. She would not even let me go to our mother's funeral. I could never forgive myself if he was really left at the lake or in the woods or taken away from the city to be dumped like they are saying in the court."

Rhea stood and gave the horse a gentle pat of reassurance before stepping into the aisle to lay a comforting hand on the woman's arm. "Nastasio is doing well, Alma; you have no reason to worry. He was taken in by a wonderful family who had just lost a little boy of their own and will be incredibly loved and cared for in a village filled with joy and life." The happiness she felt at Kylassame and the time where the world felt almost normal tugged sharply at her heart.

Alma took a shaky breath and stepped forward to embrace the woman. "Thank you. Thank you so much, my Lady."

Both women stiffened at the sound of the stable door opening down the hallway and light footsteps quickly approached their location. Aleksei rounded the corner and stopped abruptly in front of Rhea to catch his breath.

"Lady Rhea, there has been trouble. We need to get you back into the castle now." He grabbed her hand and tugged her down the hallway.

Lianna burst through the side door, white as a ghost. "There is no time to go back inside. If anyone asks, we heard a commotion in the stable and went to check and make sure your mare was quite alright and that Aleksei was still on guard."

Rhea straightened her veil and brushed the dirt off of her dress as the small party hurried out of the stable door and approached the courtyard. "What's going on? Is it Sebast?"

Both women came to an abrupt halt at the sight of punishment devices in the courtyard and the crowd that slowly grew as word spread throughout the castle. The whipping posts had already been erected but next to them stood a shorter set of poles with heavy chains attached, about the height of a man's shoulder.

The High Prince walked out then, and Rhea could immediately sense the fury that radiated from his body like heat waves. The crowd scrambled to obey protocol in time as he stalked toward the area where the structures were erected. Nyssa walked in behind him, pale and shaking and stopped to stand in the crowd by Agrafina.

He stepped up onto a platform and the venom in his voice caused the crowd to shrink back in fear. "This past day has seen a great victory, a blasphemer to the Gods, and now treason to the crown. The man of Asimina has escaped from his cell and his fate by those close to the heart of the realm. Fear not, for we will find him and bring him back and right the supernatural wrong. Now I call upon you, Patrons of the great Kaldalangra, to observe the punishments as witnesses and return the balance of our desecrated court!

Lianna let out a cry as the limp form of Savin was brought forth, carried between two large guards who looked greatly disturbed by their load. Rhea forced the white stars that clouded her vision to clear and clutched her friend's hand in a desperate grip. "He can't be dead. He and Rowan took the night off and are not...If he is here, then where is Rowan?" She focused on his chest as she tried to discern the slightest indication of breath and a hard knot formed over her heart.

Risalka stepped quietly behind the two women, face hidden by a deep cloak. "He lives, but barely." The small gray cat stealthily moved from behind the cloak folds to take shelter under the volume of Rhea's dress and curled her warm body around the woman's ankle.

They watched in horror as Savin's body was dumped next to the shorter of the poles into a pile of straw that had been filled with thorny nettles. A bucket of water was thrown onto his face and the large man coughed, then opened his eyes and fought to gain his focus. Blood slowly trailed down the side of his head from a large wound, punctures and lacerations covered his unclothed upper body and his knees were horribly swollen and disfigured. His eyes carefully met Lianna's in apology and his head bowed in sadness and pain.

The High Prince once again addressed the crowd, who had grown uneasy at the state of a well-known and widely-liked guard. "He is not the only traitor to the crown, for a man could not accomplish such a feat of treason without assistance. Bring the second man out for questioning!"

Rhea cried out in dismay and went to surge forward as Rowan limped into the courtyard between two armed guards. The firm hand of Risalka wrapped itself in the back of Rhea's dress and pulled the woman back with a sharp whisper, "There is nothing you can do now. It is not yet the time; it is not yet the place." She felt sharp claws through the thin leather of her shoes as the cat seemed to echo the sentiment.

The men stopped with Rowan and moved just off to the side of Savin. It was apparent that the men had not seen each other since the escape and Rowan's face looked dangerous and feral at the sight of his friend. Rowan's own body bore the marks of recent fists and knives, and he held his left leg awkwardly under his body as he stood to face the High Prince and the crowd.

"Savin de Caislean, do you name this man, Rowan de Nespa, as your accomplice in the crime of treason to the DamaTalous and court of Kaldalangra?" The crowd held their breath as Zelkhova walked toward the two men.

Savin's eyes focused on Rowan's face for a long moment before turning back to the High Prince. "I do not name him such. I bear the sole responsibility of the crime. He is innocent of any charges and should be released. I bear the sole punishment for releasing the man of Asimina."

Rowan surged forward with a cry of denial as he shook off the hands that restrained him. He fell onto the thorny straw next to Savin and exchanged heated words before the guards dragged him off and began to attach the green-eyed man's wrists to the manacles on the whipping poles.

A malicious smile spread across the High Prince's features. "Brave words from a foolish, dying man. Guards, turn de Nespa around. I want the people to see his face as he receives the punishment a man of his standing bears for treason. The guard protects him but valued and trusted sources have attested to his involvement in the crime and it is enough evidence to convict."

Rhea felt her breathing quicken dangerously as the man she loved was turned and stripped of his shirt and protective vest. At the first blow of a heavy club to the man's left knee she willed herself to be calm, to breathe evenly, because she knew that if she fainted now she would never forgive herself. *Be strong. Be strong and stand tall. Let this blow over like a sharp wind and not cause lasting damage. Please, please,* tears rolled off her cheeks and fell to the dry earth below. *Please, let him be okay and come back to my side. I will do anything if they both will be fine and be able to come back to where they belong.*

The audience jumped as one as the tail of the whip sliced through the air and cracked across Rowan's back. Rhea forced her body still as his green eyes found hers in the audience, and she held his gaze fiercely in an attempt to give him any comfort or encouragement. He did not flinch while the leather cut into his back time and time again, and he kept his eyes focused on the woman he had brought to this realm.

The beaten man beside him staggered to his feet as the sawdust below Rowan's feet began to stain with the blood that dripped from his body. "I take his punishment," Savin cried out hoarsely. "Punish me, but leave him alone. It is not right to do this to him without a confession and Queen Sula turns in her grave at your mockery of justice!"

Sharp silence filled the crowd then and Rowan broke his connection with Rhea to look around the stilled crowd. A shuffling of feet, a nervous cough, a murmured statement of dissent, the sounds of a mob suddenly grown insecure with their intent filled the courtyard.

Zelkhova looked over and, with a nod of permission from the High Prince, coiled the whip around his arm. "It is acceptable for the guard to take on the rest of the punishment." He stepped up in front of Rowan and slammed a gloved fist into his unprotected kidneys before walking over to where Savin struggled to stand on the straw.

The man looked upon the broken and bloody guard with disinterest and boredom showed on his features as he roughly pushed Savin to the center of the poles and fastened the manacles over the giant wrists. The whip snapped open and hissed through the air before it slashed across the large man's exposed back. Savin dug his palms into the chains attached to his wrists and focused on staying upright as the whip sang across already open wounds and pushed the small thorns of the nettle into exposed skin and flesh.

After some time Zelkhova turned to his assistants. "Leave de Nespa until the sunrise so he may see the sacrifice made on his behalf. Leave the guard here until his flesh rots from the bones." A malicious grin, then the man brought a heavy boot down onto Savin's knee to send the leg crashing out from under the man.

Rhea realized the full extent of the punishment after this act. The manacles would allow a man to stand in little discomfort between the poles, wrists contained at just above waist height. Yet when his broken body failed him he would be unable to bear his weight upon his knees on the stinging bed below, and his full weight would be taken by the wrists encased in iron. The manacles themselves were

259

sharp enough that they cut into the thin skin around the hands and wrists, and she felt a sense of dread as she realized it would only be a matter of time before they severed the life-giving veins found there.

Lianna turned toward Risalka and began to cry in earnest then, hidden within the deep folds of her mother's black cloak as the cat moved from Rhea to curl around Risalka's feet. She had seen this punishment issued before to servants and wayward guards and knew that none of them survived the night. Rhea put a hand of encouragement on her friend's shoulder before she slipped back into the castle with her mother's support.

The crowd filed out of the courtyard then, uneasy and conflicted by the events of the day. Among the nervous mutterings Rhea could pick up curious phrases.

"Not right that he should be punished without confession. Not him. No matter how far in status he has fallen."

"He did not flinch at all! How is that possible?"

"Savin's a good guard. How could he betray us like this?"

She approached Savin first and stepped lightly onto the straw as he lifted his head and flexed his hands. Her feet immediately felt the sting of the nettles even through the thick soles of her shoes and she could see the tiny thorns protruding from Savin's body from where he was dropped. Rhea moved close and put her shoulder under the man's broad arm, lending her small power to his legs as he forced himself upright and into a standing position to ease the pressure on his bloody wrists.

The eyes that stared back at her were the eyes of a man who had already lost the battle, empty and in pain. Rhea put a soft hand to his cheek and was thankful that only her flushed skin reflected her terror. "Komisar Savin de Caislean, I order you to not give up. You are not to spend your last moments in this courtyard and I fully expect you to be able to return to my service in one week time. Is this understood?"

Savin's eyes blazed with a spark of hope as he drew off of Rhea's strength, then his eyelids fluttered as his surge ebbed away and was replaced with grim determination. "I understand, my Lady. I will do my best be available for your service at that time."

Rhea nodded and turned to Rowan, tied between the two posts with the blood slowly drying in rust-colored rivers across his back. She tenderly moved the hair that had fallen over his eyes and tucked it behind his ears. "That applies to you as well, Komisar Rowan de Nespa. You are to report to my chambers the moment you are released from your bonds. Is that understood?"

Rowan shook his head and looked at the ground, unable to meet her eyes. "Rhea, I am not going to live until sunrise, not after tonight. The last thing the King needs or expects was for public sympathy to turn my way after something like this. I want you to go to your chamber tonight, hang a thick blanket over the window, and not look out for any reason. We are not going to make it out of this, Savin nor I. I can only hope that Sebast traveled far enough to make the cause worthy of our deaths."

His eyes met hers and filled with tears he refused to shed in public. "I want you to go to Kylassame, Rhea. Nyssa can get you to Albadarl and Faulks will guide you the rest of the way. Liam is a good man and would support you in my stead. You are in danger here and you need to get away as soon as you are able."

She shook her head. "I will not accept that; I refuse. Neither one of you will die, that is not the way that-"she choked down a sob and blinked her eyes rapidly at the pressure of tears, "that just isn't an option. I will see both of you when the sun rises. That is not a request."

Rhea turned around and forced herself to slowly walk towards the castle. Snow began to fall around her and she looked up at the sky for answers. Three stars in a perfect row twinkled back at her and Rhea swallowed hard to keep the tears at bay as she approached the castle door. She remembered that night in the glade when Rowan and she kissed in the moonlight. *If I can change the stars, surely I can change the outcome of this night.*

The High Prince watched her from the steps, arms across his chest, shoulder leaning against the cold stone and a look of indifference upon his face. "Touching moment, to say the least. We will have to find you new guards of course. I doubt the large one will last another hour and the less significant of the two will likely find a similar fate. He has angered many influential members of the court over his pathetic life and is just standing there defenseless and strung out like a wild animal."

Rhea let the anger that heated her body burn away the tears and strengthen her resolve. "Mateo Verikh de Kalda, these men are to be alive come morning and they are to return to my service when they are physically able. That is not a request, and that is not a plea. My title of Forena demands that I am granted such a request if made."

A slow, lazy, and malevolent smile crossed the High Prince's fair features. "Is that so? I assume you have then read about the payment for the request?"

"I am well aware."

He laughed and looked at where Rowan stood, wide-eyed and horror-stricken, straining between the posts after hearing the exchange. "Well then, let us go back to my chamber."

Chapter Thirty-Three

The Court

Rhea awoke as the strong rays of sun fell across her eyelids and stifled the groan as she forced them open. Her entire body throbbed and, as she stared at the bruises across her wrists, the events of the past night rushed back into her memory. She had been surprised at Mateo's actions, and that the one thing she had assumed he would demand was left undone. He had been content enough to take his wrath out upon her outer body, the blows and small slices from his rings scarring her pale skin, the bruises from his hands darkening the skin of her wrists and neck. She had expected more, especially after he ordered her to step out from her overdress upon entering the room.

Her muscles screamed as she sat up in the bed and swung her legs over the side. She rose unsteadily and her legs shook as she slowly shuffled to the dresser with the washing basin and vanity. The dresser provided a solid support and she lightly rested her hands on the side of the strong furniture before she carefully splashed the water on her face and ran a trembling hand through her tangled hair.

The window in the room looked out on the courtyard and Rhea stumbled over to look out of the glass. Her heart twisted and froze as she saw the workers taking down the poles before sweeping the blood-stained straw and sawdust into wheelbarrows to discard. A thin layer of white snow was filled with footprints, large drag marks and horse tracks. Aleksei could be seen breaking ice from one of the outer horse troughs, glancing occasionally at the nearby scene.

"Do not worry, they both live, if barely. Your precious guards are in the care of Risalka now. Surprisingly, Rowan was barely touched over the night, although Savin is still on the brink of death. Now it is up to the skills of the healers to decide their fate and none of my concern. They were both breathing at sunrise and thus I have met my end of the bargain." Mateo had entered into the room silently and stepped behind Rhea. "You took last night well. If it was not so against your usual character, I would have thought you rather enjoyed it." He laughed at the shudder of fear that rippled through the woman's body.

"I am but a servant of the realm. I do what is necessary for the greater good of the realm." Rhea willed steadiness into her tone and tried to quell her trembling as his hand slid down her exposed skin.

Mateo's breath felt hot in her ear. "And what of Asimina, or Albadarl? Will you do what is necessary for them?"

Through a mouth that felt like it was stuffed with cotton she replied, "I have no idea of what you reference. Asimina is but a town to be used to our benefit. The other is unknown to me." She straightened her aching back and turned with what she hoped was a coy smile. "What is Albadarl, another place of miscreants and disease?"

He laughed and trailed his hand down her bare shoulder and arm. "A place of miniature freaks. They are like little magical fruits to be picked out of the trees for your own use. Every time one is killed their blood nourishes the Gods and strengthens our armies." His hand slid across her collarbone and stopped at the stone that hung from her neck.

Rhea swallowed hard and smiled at him sweetly. "A trinket that Lianna found for me in the market, my Lord."

His hand closed around the stone and Rhea's body jerked forward as the necklace was ripped from around her neck, cutting deeply into the tender skin before breaking loose. "How many times have you lied to me, Rhea? I have been told about this stone ever since I can remember. A ladybug amulet made for the Queen by her cursed son. A Queen who betrayed the territory and forgot the way that Royalty should function, thus sending the entire realm into insanity. A derelict Queen who thought she was no better than the rest of her subjects!" His fist fell across her face with enough force that sent Rhea backwards into the side of a large wardrobe.

"I would not dare to lie to you, my Lord. I was unaware of that history of the necklace." She stammered, the sinking feeling of realization of a mystery in her heart firming her resolve and lending her strength. "I thought it was simply a pretty stone." She refused not to flinch in front of him as he flung the stone across the room to crash against the thick wall.

"Get dressed. The King has ordered an early dinner and wishes us to attend. I will send the girl, Faina in to assist you and Kofizek will escort you to the dining hall."

Rhea murmured assent and watched carefully as he left the room, then listened to the footsteps as he walked away from the door. Quickly she scurried to where the stone necklace had fallen between two chests and, with a whispered apology for the treatment it received, retied the broken string around her neck. She would have to be more careful in the future and be sure to remove it before Mateo had a chance to see it.

Her legs gave out their strength then and Rhea let herself sink to the floor in the corner. *How could she have been so stupid as to think the High Prince had changed?* She realized now that it was all just an act to buy her affection, or an attempt to get information about his rivals from her once he had her trust. The Matt she had known had disappeared completely last night as he inflicted one brutal blow after another upon her after bolting shut the door.

She laid her cheek against the cool, stone wall and gently clasped the small stone in her fingers. According to Mateo, the son of the Queen made this necklace. Rowan had told her that he had made this necklace for his mother. Her mind refused to make the connection that seemed too unreal given the man's treatment by the realm. It made no sense that if he were the child of the beloved Queen, that he would have been thrown away like rubbish. Maybe Mateo was told the wrong story, or maybe Rowan was lying to her with his story and stole the necklace from the true son of the Queen.

Faina entered slowly, and gave a gasp of alarm when she saw Rhea on the floor. "Oh, dear Lady, you are injured! Should I call for the court physician?"

Rhea smiled, the action tugging at the tender skin on her cheek where the man had struck her. "I will be fine, Faina. Help me out of this corner and into a dress please. I cannot afford to anger the High Prince by being late to dinner."

Faina extended her hand and gently tugged Rhea into a standing position. After a furtive glance at the door she dropped her voice very low and leaned towards her Patron, "My Lady, Rowan said he will see you at dinner. Savin is still going in between the worlds of the living and the dead but Risalka thinks he will pull through, although it will be some time before Savin can be moved. Risalka had him placed in your room so, well, I guess we will make arrangements for you to sleep elsewhere in the meantime. Lianna said she will be glad to give up her bed."

Rhea carefully stepped into the emerald green dress that had been draped on the bed and held up her long hair while Faina finished doing up the delicate buttons. "I don't think I am going anywhere, Faina. It is very likely that I will remain here with the High Prince until he discards me for another. Savin is welcome to the room. Hopefully the happiness of the room will help heal him as it healed me."

The young woman carefully placed a bleached white veil upon Rhea's head and secured it with decorated pins of ladybug design before placing a sheer green face veil across the worst of the bruises. "It is going to be difficult for Rowan to see you in this condition, my Lady. It may be necessary for you to formally dismiss him from your service so as to avoid conflict with the High Prince."

She shook her head slowly. "I don't think I have the strength to do that, Faina. I don't think I am strong enough to send him away."

"You could always banish him from the court for his actions as the final punishment. As his Patron, you have the authority to do such a thing. He would go to his village, maybe the one who took in Nastasio. I suppose they would take him in, as well, would they not?"

Rhea found herself unable to nod her head in agreement even knowing that the girl was right. He would be happy in Kylassame, and more importantly, he would be safe. If he remained here it would only be a matter of time before his temper erupted and his fury over Mateo's actions resulted in disaster.

"Forgive me if I am talking out of turn, dear Lady, I do not mean to offend." Faina looked alarmed at Rhea's haunted eyes in the mirror.

A pause, then Rhea heard herself agreeing with her young helper as she resigned herself to a bleak existence.

~ * ~ * ~

Rhea entered the grand dining hall with her head high and made a forced effort to ignore the stares and whispers of the Patrons already present at the dinner. Her dress and veil covered the worst of the bruises but the discoloration could still be seen in areas through the sheer areas of fabric. She moved slowly in an attempt to limit the pain spreading through her hips and back from the slow application of the thick leather belt from the previous night.

Lianna was not present at dinner that night and Rhea assumed she chose to remain at Savin's side in fear of the worst outcome. Agrafina occupied the space directly across from the empty chair of the High Prince and had a jet black veil fastened to fully conceal the blond locks as an outward sign of her degraded status in the realm.

Nyssa sat to the left of the King and gestured for Rhea to occupy the seat two down from her, as the seat between them would be reserved for the High Prince. Rhea was a bit startled at the change in seating arrangement but tried to assume an air of indifference as Rowan slowly limped into the room and took a seat across from hers.

"Komisar de Nespa, I am pleased to see you have returned to duty."

He inclined his head, the court mask fully in place once again and refusing to meet her eyes. "It is my honor, my Lady. I apologize for the inconvenience my unwise actions have brought upon you and this court."

The King entered then, followed by the High Prince and their Komisar. The King turned his piercing blue eyes upon Rhea. "Well, you look well enough for having gone through your first night as Forena." He shot a dark look toward Mateo. "Do not tell me this woman is making you soft, my true son and heir to the realm."

Mateo chuckled and stepped over to Rhea to pull the concealing veil from her face and pulled down the neckline of the gown, fully revealing her bruises to those present. "I think you will find my actions quite unchanged, Your Eminence. She is just a bit shy about exhibiting evidence of her new position at the moment. She certainly seemed to enjoy the night as much as I." He leaned forward to place a hand intimately upon her body and placed a kiss on her lips, a mockery of tenderness with its coldness.

Rhea put on a feigned smile and melted into her chair with as much grace as she could manage. She glanced across the table to where Rowan sat in obvious anger and felt a pang of jealousy and sadness as she realized Agrafina's hand was resting on his leg, tethering him to the chair as he fought to control the rage rising in his heart.

King Verikhan laughed heartily as he looked down the table. "Such discord I see at the table tonight! Have heart, for today will be a joyous day. Today the hunting horn will sound and the heir to the

Kingdom will ride to dominate the creatures of Steinbrekka as I did so many years ago. And then," his blue eyes twinkled with malice, "and then the beginning of the continuation of my line. My heir will take his new brood mare to the chamber to get her with child."

The High Prince chuckled. "I rejoice in this day and await the horn then, my Lord and father. Have no fear, my dear," he turned to Rhea and ran a hand up her thigh, "you will enjoy it quite as much as you enjoyed last night's little fun."

Rhea managed a stiff nod and focused on the empty plate in front of her. Heavy tears threatened to spill over her cheeks and she rapidly blinked to hold them at bay. *This is necessary,* she told herself. *If I don't do this too many people will die. Too many people will be punished. It is better I take the punishment. I can survive this when they may not.*

The food began to arrive then and she nodded politely at the servant who placed the choicest morsels onto her plate. "My Prince," she gently placed a hand on Mateo's arm, "would it be permissible for the Lady Nyssa to come to your chambers tonight to help me prepare for your pleasure?"

Blue eyes twinkled as the High Prince witnessed the quick flash of rage in the eyes of the man across the table. "But of course, my dear. Do be sure that your Komisar escorts you and remains in the chamber as your chaperone as you ladies discuss the finer details of breeding. I would hate for harm to come to you in my chambers while I am otherwise engaged."

Rhea took a shuddering breath and dared to glance at Rowan. "As Komisar Savin is still unavailable for duty, I will require your presence, Komisar Rowan."

He swallowed hard, jaw muscle clenched as he growled out, "Yes, my Lady."

Tense silence then fell over the table, broken only by the occasional deep chuckle of malicious joy that rumbled from the throats of the High Prince and the King. Rhea ate her food slowly, unable to allow her mind to think of what would happen when the food ceased to arrive and dinner would be completed.

Just as the final course was being set upon the table the horn sounded, a bellow deep and ominous as it vibrated throughout the stone walls of the court. An expression of surprised longing crossed Rowan's face, and Rhea was startled back from her dark thoughts by the quickening need to move that the horn brought to her soul, as if something had pushed her heart closer to the surface of her skin and quickened her blood in the veins. She placed a hand over her heart, brushing against the hidden stone under her dress and took a shaky breath. As Rowan fought the influence, she found herself fighting not to encourage him to follow the call, to go to Steinbrekka, follow the yearning she saw in his eyes and to meet with the creatures.

"You think you would have a chance, de Nespa?" The High Prince laughed harshly as he stood and carefully placed his napkin upon the table. "The court well knows what occurred on your last visit to Steinbrekka. It was a good thing the Lady Rhea was there to save you. No, this day has always been mine, and mine alone. I do request that you do me a boon, however. Keep an eye on my mare will you? I will need her available immediately primed and readied when I return." He moved beside Rhea then and slid his fingers down her throat to follow the line of her shoulders, eyes black as coal fixed on Rowan and enjoying the man's misery.

Rhea refused to breathe until the man stalked out of the room assured of his victory and self-importance. Rowan still looked pained and another wave of jealousy rode through Rhea's body as Agrafina placed a calming hand on his shoulder and whispered softly into his ear.

King Verikhan rose and clapped his hands for attention. "My Patrons, let us take refreshments in the entertainment room for the time being. The family will stay here to await the High Prince's return and we shall be alerted of his triumph shortly." He extended a hand toward Agrafina. "My Dear, I request your attendance."

Nyssa paled as Agrafina slowly stood up and followed the King into the room, softly closing the door behind the last Patron. The Princess let out a deep breath and looked around the room after she realized that she, Rhea, and Rowan were the only people left at the table.

"He hurt you." The stark pain in Rowan's voice forced Rhea to look up and meet his eyes across the table.

She looked back down at the cup filled with wine in front of her. "I'll survive. It is necessary to protect the realm, and to protect you."

Rowan stood up and walked over to crouch next to Rhea. "It is too much to ask of you. This is too much." His fingers gently traced the dark outline of Mateo's fist upon her cheek. "There is no excuse for this, Rhea. There is no validation for this abuse."

She took a deep breath, wincing at the soreness in her ribs as she did so. "It was my fault for resisting him at first. It will be okay, Rowan. I will adapt to his brand of passion over time and-"

"No!" He stood and gripped the edge of the table with such aggression his fingers paled and stiffened as the wood surface cracked. He forced himself to calm his anger and sat down in the chair between the two women. "No, it is not right and it is not your fault. Nothing like this could ever be your fault. He has the blame and he alone. We need to get you out of here, now, while no one is watching."

"Rowan, I appreciate your concern but please, I can't handle this right now." She took a shaky breath and gave in to the urge to touch his hand. "You know what is about to happen, what is going to happen tonight. It simply must be." Rhea sighed, surprised at the futility she heard in her own voice. "Listen to me, Rowan. I want you to leave. I want you to go to Kylassame with Lianna and Savin and disappear. Our situation is only serving to act as torture for both of us, and I don't want to cause you any more pain." Her voice broke and she took an unsteady breath. "Go to the village, marry a sweet girl like Amanda, and forget all about me."

Nyssa stood then, her expression a mixture of shock and fury. "Just leave you alone here? You really think that he would do that? It would be more of a torture for him to pretend to just live another life and try to push you out of his mind." She looked at the door and steely resolve sang through her voice. "You will both leave, right now, while everyone else is occupied. You get on the horses and you ride as fast and as hard as you can to Kylassame and never look back."

The couple stood and stared at her in shock for a moment before Rowan softly responded with, "I am not about to leave you here for the wolves, as much as the idea of getting away from this life forever gives me joy. I am not leaving either one of you here. Either we all go, or we all stay."

King Verikhan burst into the room then, red faced and out of breath. "He returns! He returns already. This is the sign of a great victory!"

Rowan stared helplessly at the door and moved to position himself behind Rhea, hands resting lightly on her chair to take the pressure off of the injured knee that had begun to pulse in time with his heart.

Nyssa was the first to cry out as the High Prince staggered into the room. Blood trailed down his chest, creating rivulets of crimson and rust as it dripped onto the floor. His face had gone alabaster white and as he moved closer, the family saw a small black creature perched upon his shoulder, onyx claws sinking into the thin fabric of the shirt and soft flesh of the Prince as he staggered to a stop in front of the table.

The creature was small, roughly the size of a large bird but with the form of a cat. Shiny black fur coated the small body and pointed ears moved in response to the surprised outcries in the room. Glittering red eyes rested above a long, thin, fox-like nose and long fingerlike paws were tipped with razor sharp talons. The creature opened its mouth to speak and needle sharp fangs glinted against the darkness as a sibilant tongue darted forward to taste the air.

"You send an imposter to answer the call to Steinbrekka? I had my doubts when you were allowed to leave Steinbrekka, Verikhan, and doubts more when you slaughtered her creatures. I had thought our chosen Queen would have calmed you to raise the next generation in the correct manner of the DamaTalous. I see we were gravely mistaken."

The voice was low and ominous, the accent a mixture of all the sounds in the animal kingdom. His red eyes slid to where Rhea was sitting and smoke hissed from his mouth. "You dare to defile the Lady we chose!" The claws dug angrily into the skin of Mateo's shoulder and blood ran anew.

The King rose to full height but did not leave the protection afforded by the giant table. "You dare to spill the blood of the true heir of the realm! Be gone vile creature! Be gone from my sight! I command you to leave this room and go back to the shadows where your kind belongs."

Nyssa began to spin her mother's ring in a frenzy and whispered, "On the day of the true betrayal, the Gormellyn will arise. The Gormellyn will choose the true heir. The Gormellyn will destroy all of those in his path. Spirits help us."

The Gormellyn smiled and the thin red tongue traced the edges of its lips. "It is good of you to remember me, daughter of the beloved Queen. It seems to me the blood of the true heir was spilled long before I was called from my slumber." He shifted his stance and curled closer to Mateo's neck and extended a long talon towards the man's throat. "You defy the natural order of the realm, Verikhan. You hunt our creatures and taint our land with poisoned flesh and blood. You dare to defile the Lord and our chosen Lady." He placed his snout close to Mateo's ear. "Did you truly think you were the heir to the throne, White Prince?"

Mateo nodded and planted his feet firmly beneath him. "I have been raised High Prince Mateo Verikh de Kalda. I am the rightful leader of the throne and the heir to the realm."

The creature hissed again and pinned his eyes on Rowan. "Foolish man, foolish, foolish false prince of this cursed court. Was it you then who ordered the Lord to be whipped like a dog? Was it you who created the bruises on the Lady? Was it you who tore Sula's amulet from the Lady's throat? Oh yes, false prince, I see all from my shadowed home."

Mateo nodded and paled further as the creature dug his claws into the tender skin between the neck and shoulder and casually shredded the muscles below. The Gormellyn turned to the King, still standing defiant and unmoving as the life blood of his prized heir flowed onto the stone floor.

"Did you really think you could break the line, foolish King Verikhan? The line of succession is only created by the blood. You have two options, Verikhan. Either you may allow the pure-hearted Lady Nyssa to assume the throne, or that of the cast away Lord Rowan. What shall you decide?" A talon leisurely traced a bloody path along Mateo's face as the Gormellyn waited for an answer.

The King looked at Rowan with disgust. "No ruler of my realm will ever come from his tainted being. I chose Mateo as my heir, and it is he who will breed the girl."

Red eyes rapidly shrunk into mere pin pricks and again the talons slashed, brutally ripping open the muscles of Mateo's chest and causing shreds of the thick doublet to fall like confetti. The creature opened its mouth wide and began to clamp the sharp teeth around Mateo's throat.

Rhea abruptly stood and willed calm into her voice. "Venerable Gormellyn, you will stop this at once."

The sharp teeth retreated from the throat, leaving small, bloody pinpricks where they had begun to penetrate. The creature looked over at her with a sly smile. "And who are you to ask such a thing of me?"

She took a deep breath. "I am the Lady Rhea Aralia. I have met the wise woman Ayewok, the Aos Si, and the Malakhor of Steinbrekka. I have sat in the company of the Ellyn and been nourished with the water from the sacred pool." Calm eyes stared at the creature that now looked at the woman triumphantly. "I am not of a position to make demands from a creature of your standing, but I ask of you, please, to stop this bloodshed."

He licked his lips again and the small black head tilted sideways in consideration. "Will you approach me and allow me to taste of your flesh? I promise you I will spare this man if you do." Lips curled in a smile as Rhea gave a stiff nod. "Ah, then the Lady of Steinbrekka has truly come back to us in you. Come closer."

Rhea hitched a shaky breath and walked around the table. When she was but a few feet from the creature Rowan slid between her and the High Prince. He looked at the creature through steady green eyes. "You will not touch the Lady without going through me. I take any harm or ill will intended for her by you or your subjects."

A hiss briefly rang from the creature as it launched himself from Mateo's shoulder and settled onto Rowan's cotton shirt. "You are a very wise man, or very foolish, I think."

Rowan stood very still and glanced carefully at the creature perched lightly on his shoulder. "I believe it is safe to say that I am made up of a bit of both. I protect and serve the Lady, be the action wise or foolish. Her will is my life and my soul belongs to her."

The Gormellyn's mouth opened and the small red tongue ran across the jugular vein of Rowan's neck. He yawned then and curled his body into a cat-like ball. "A good answer Prince of the Trees. A very good answer indeed." He tucked his pointed face into the bushy tail and stared behind the man into the bright eyes of the woman. "If you want to save the man you knew, this is your only chance. I promise not to kill Rowan in the meantime."

Rhea gave a bow of respect. "I thank you for that. He is very dear to my heart and I would be quite distraught if any harm would to fall upon him." She stepped up to Mateo and carefully draped one of his torn arms around her shoulders, encouraged to see Nyssa step under the other arm. They saw the King retreat from the dining chamber as they helped the wounded man hobble out, and Rowan remained, staring at the creature on his shoulder in amazement.

Chapter Thirty-Four

The Court

"Remember freshman year when we both worked at the bookstore? You would walk me home every night after work and my boyfriend hated you. Remember when we went to Meg's party and we drank way too much and ended up camping out in the woods all night?" She carefully dabbed at the oozing punctures around the man's collarbone. "We had a lot of fun back then, especially before the classes started getting harder and more demanding. I still think about that theatre class when we had to listen to German opera while hung over from the night before. That was a time to remember."

Risalka entered the room and came to sit by the bedside with her healing supplies, gray cat at her heels. "I heard he returned with the Gormellyn. I am surprised he is not missing limbs."

Nyssa balled the destroyed shirt and tossed it into the discard bin. "He was about to be missing his throat when Rhea stepped in and challenged the creature."

Rhea shrugged. "I don't know what I was thinking. He could have just as easily torn me apart but I just had to do something."

"Yes, well, the Gormellyn is ruled by his nature and his nature is to punish imposters. While you may have different colored eyes and hair, you are still very much yourself in spirit, and thus safe from his retribution."

Rhea moved to the end of the bed and placed Mateo's head on her lap as Risalka began to administer her tinctures and expertly sew flaps of skin back in place. "The creature is with Rowan right now. Will he be safe or do I need to go back there and do...something?"

Risalka gave a slight smile. "Ah, Rowan has always been who he is supposed to be, those around him have just refused to acknowledge him as such. He has nothing to fear from the Gormellyn. Put your hands on Mateo's forehead Rhea, gently now to avoid the bruises and cuts, and think of your life prior to now while I heal the flesh as best I can.

Rhea gave her a dubious look but placed her hands on his forehead gently. She thought about the night that her friend disappeared, remembered every detail about his face, his voice, and the feelings that flowed through both of them. Memories of lunches and dinners shared between class and work filled her thoughts and she remembered how he held her when her first love left her heart broken. Tears slowly dripped onto the man's face as she thought about their one date when they went to a restaurant specializing in tea, then danced throughout the walking area of a downtown mall in the rain.

"I know you are in there somewhere Matt," she whispered as she stroked his temples. "I know that you can hear me, that under it all you are still the man I grew up with. I'll easily forgive you for everything if you just come back. We'll find a way to go home and start over."

The little gray cat sat in front of Rhea and gave a small meow, then lifted her small front legs up to rest her paws and chin on Rhea's knee. "Hello, little cat. You always seem to turn up when people need comfort. If I didn't know better I would think you were either an omen of good or a bringing of bad."

The cat tilted her head to the side and gave Rhea an incredulous look before furiously licking the tip of her tail. Rhea let herself laugh then, and took a second to stroke the cat on the head. "I know, that's a silly thought. You're just a cat after all."

Rowan stood in the doorway for a few moments and watched as Rhea stroked his nemesis' short blonde hair, tenderness and love brightly shining through her tears. He glanced at the creature on his shoulder. *She may have feared the man he was here, but she loved the man that he used to be, did she not?*

It seems so, the Gormellyn thought back as he stared inquisitively at the couple on the bed. *I would not have expected her to stand up for one who had given so much abuse. I certainly did not expect her to offer herself for the chance of his safety. She is a special lady and far more than we could have guessed when my children met her at Steinbrekka.*

Rowan swallowed hard as Rhea bent forward and placed a gentle kiss on an untouched part of Mateo's forehead. *The King is unwilling to bend with his rule, I know that and you know that. He would never allow me to touch the throne while he lives and he is smart enough to know that Nyssa's first act as Regent would be to place me in power.*

Then he will die without an heir and the kingdom will arrange itself after he has left. Do not fear for that, Prince. One way or another, the terror he has nurtured will die with him.

He shook his head gently so as not to dislodge the creature. *Some acts will never be forgotten and the fear will likely never die. Too many people grew fat and rich under his policies and his rules and it will be difficult to turn them.* He sighed. *Mateo must rule, even if he does it as the man he was in the other world. The people need a strong Queen and they have already accepted Rhea as that person. She is the one who is important, not I.*

The Gormellyn shrugged his small shoulders. *That would be quite difficult indeed. There is a way to send them back and Mateo, at least, must go for he does not fit into the rhythm of this land. He was never meant to come here and is not part of the balance. If Rhea is not to rule at your side then it is best that she go as well. She was brought here to be your Queen, not just another person or Patron in the court. If she is not part of your life then she will not be here at all. Nyssa will be acceptable as she is the daughter of our beloved Sula.*

Rowan felt his breathing hitch as the man on the bed slowly opened his eyes and curled his fingers around Rhea's hand. She was smiling through her tears then, and Rowan felt his heart had shattered into pieces as the High Prince disappeared and was replaced with the friend Rhea had loved for so many years.

He slowly and silently backed out of the door. "I guess the only answer then is for them both to go back. I had prepared myself to lose her to the High Prince, little did I suspect I would lose her to the man he once was."

Rhea stared down at the aqua eyes that looked up in confusion.

"Rhea? Where are we? Why do I feel like I just got run over by a bus?" Matt struggled to sit up on the bed and then fell back in agony as the action stretched the recent stitches.

"Shh, lay down now. It's a very long story and once you have regained some strength I will tell it to you in full. You were…attacked. These are friends who will help you get better."

He nodded and then started up again as he looked at Rhea's face. "Rhea! Someone has hit you! Who has done such a thing? I'll strangle him with my own hands."

She shook her head and stroked his short hair away from his face. "I think that would prove quite impossible. It was someone who is gone now and that is all that matters."

Chapter Thirty-Five

The Court

The winter season had settled over the land and Rhea absent-mindedly pushed at the snow on the garden path with her boot. Risalka was going to bring Matt to the garden today, for he had finally healed from his wounds sufficiently to allow light movement. Every day he had grown stronger and every day he had reclaimed more of his memories from his old life. They tried to keep his presence limited in the court until a plan could be formulated and simply told the King that his appointed heir was going to recover and left it at that.

She walked into the clearing and smiled softly when she saw the familiar back of Rowan standing in the circle. He had grown reclusive that week and seemed as if he were pulled deep inside his thoughts. The fact that he was the son of the King and a Prince of the realm still seemed incredible to her but she noticed it now in his actions, words, and very essence.

He was standing quietly in the clearing as his unfocused eyes stared at the wintry clouds above. Rhea was almost upon him before he heard her soft boots crunch in the snow and turned around to greet her. "Today is the day he comes to the garden then?"

"Do you mind?" She stopped next to him and looked up at his face. "It is your garden after all, Prince Rowan de Nespa. Why did no one ever tell me about you? Here I've just been treating you like a guard when I should have given you far more respect."

He laughed at that, clipped and hollow. "Nothing is mine here, Rhea. If anything this garden belongs to you, for you brought it back to life. Anyone who you desire is welcome to set foot in this area, and anyone you want out of your life can be easily sent away."

Rhea heard the subtle trace of sadness and futility in his words and slowly reached for his hand, surprised when he drew his away at her touch. "Rowan, I know there have been many changes here in the last week and it's difficult. It has been a trying time for all of us." She took a deep breath of the chilled air. "I think you should come and meet Matt as himself. Mateo is gone, forever, and I really think the two of you would hit it off."

"I suppose next you will ask me to rip out my own heart too. I suppose some things never change." Rowan focused on a bird nearby and refused to look at the woman who silently stood beside him. *I would do it too if you asked me. I would do anything for you.*

An exasperated sigh sounded next to him and Rowan turned his head at the sound of Rhea's footsteps moving away from him. She paused at the edge of the clearing and half turned her body towards him. "Is this how it is going to be again? Biting comments to hide feelings? I would never ask you to cut out your own heart, Rowan, all I want is for you to meet my friend. I don't see why that is such a difficult thing to do."

She walked quickly back through the garden and fought the wetness that turned icy against her eyes. *After all we have gone through and it's back to this. What is wrong with him? I know that we still aren't able to be physically close in public while at court, but there is nothing keeping him from visiting me in the privacy of my own chamber. Yet he has been as distant as ever,* she thought as she watched the small snow birds flitting through the bushes. The last of the autumn blooms fell from the trees to add splashes of pinks and reds to the white blanket of the garden.

By the time she reached the bench by the entrance of the garden Matt had settled comfortably on a cushion and Risalka had placed a thick blanket over his shoulders to keep out the chill. His eyes lit up as Rhea approached, and he held out a side of the blanket so that it could cover her body, as well.

"The people here dress weirdly, and use strange vocabulary, but Risalka seems pretty nice." He paused and gazed around at the winter blooms. "I think everyone hates me, though. Her daughter came in once and the hatred in her eyes was plain to see, and the man with the green eyes seems to avoid me whenever possible."

Rhea took his hand in hers. "They just don't know you yet. They know who you have been, but that wasn't the real you and they will learn that eventually."

He lifted a hand and gently traced the faded bruise on his friend's face, then his hand fell to the still visible marks on her neck as they showed through the fabric. "I did this, didn't I, Rhea? I did this to you, and that's why they hate me."

She took a deep breath and watched the white cloud that formed in the blue sky as she slowly blew out the air into the cold day. "Yes, you did this before you got your mind back. You also ordered the death of Lianna's, that's the woman you referred to earlier, well, you ordered the death of her sweetheart." Her pulse raced as the still fresh memories of the fear and pain of that night came rushing back. "You ordered the death of Rowan, too. You've had a lot of people killed in your name."

Matt's voice failed him then, and it took some moments for him to croak. "What happened to me, Rhea, that I could have done such a thing?"

Rhea put her arm around him for emotional support. "You were kidnapped, about five years ago our time, and about ten years ago in this realm's time. You were brainwashed and trained to be the High Prince Mateo, the heir to the throne here. You thought that's who you were, and all you had ever been." A tear fell down her cheek and she dashed at it angrily. "They had completely changed you and you didn't remember any of your old life and were pretty evil."

Agrafina walked into the garden then and paused at the sight of the couple as they sat so intimately on the bench. Her body was held tense and she blinked rapidly, then approached the couple nervously. "I am glad to see you back on your feet, my Lord. I wish the two of you well." She curtseyed and then hurried away to the clearing where Rowan stood with his back to the couple.

Rhea closed her eyes and counted to ten before opening them again to see Matt's confusion. "She loved you, still does I think. You didn't treat her very well, but you two were a couple for a long time. When I came here, you chose me over her, and, well, I guess I should tell you that we're technically engaged, or were, before you remembered who you were and forgot who you were supposed to be."

Matt stroked her hand absent-mindedly with his thumb as he stared at the beautiful blonde woman standing awkwardly with the green-eyed man. "I think I remember her. I remember that she always smelled like roses, and her hair was softer than anything I've felt before." He looked back at Rhea, "Did I...did I do this," he gestured at Rhea's face, "to her, too?"

"I don't know. Not while I was here, but I don't know about what happened between the two of you before me."

A nod was followed by a weary sigh. "I think it's time to go back inside, Rhea. Risalka said it was important not to tire myself out while I was still healing. My head feels all fuzzy from everything you've told me."

She embraced him gently and felt the shudder of emotion course through his body from the revelations. "It will get easier once you've had time to process it. Now that you're back, we can figure out a way to go home."

Rhea stood up carefully and helped Matt to his feet in the snow. They took a few awkward steps before she realized that her own healing body was not much support for the man. She closed her eyes to prepare for the worst and slowly turned around as Matt leaned against a nearby tree.

"Rowan, could you please help me get Matt back to his room? I can't bear his weight alone."

Rowan's eyes showed a potent mix of emotional pain and anger at the request, but after Agrafina put a hand on his shoulder and whispered something in his ear he walked over, every step forced. "Of course, my Lady. Your wish is my command."

The bitter response stuck in Rhea's throat as she managed a strangled, "Thank you," and Rowan edged her away to take Mateo's weight onto his own nearly-healed body.

Agrafina walked over then and held Rhea back as the men left for the chamber. "We are all broken in different ways right now, Rhea. His leg is going to be hurting for a bit, and his heart, I suspect. It would be wise to remember that."

Rhea quietly cursed in frustration as her emotions rose from the deep hole where they had hid and sat back down on the bench. "Yeah, well, his isn't the only one."

The other woman gave her a disbelieving look. "Oh, please, you are going to get everything you have ever wanted. Your friend is back in his old mind so once he is healed you can figure out a way to go back to your world. Rowan is not stupid, and he has seen how you look at Matt. He heard you talking to the man in the chamber and knows how well the two of you go together, the depth of the memories you shared. The fact that this side of Matt has love for you, which is not hidden, only serves to pour salt into the wound."

"I did love Matt once, that much is true. You probably wouldn't believe me, but the only time we even kissed was actually the night he got kidnapped and taken here. Yes, we have made great memories together, but does Rowan think the time I've spent with him means nothing?"

Agrafina chewed on her lower lip in thought and sighed. "Every night while I am alone, I cry." She laughed in disbelief of her own words. "Despite everything he did, I loved Mateo. It was easier to see you with him when I knew that you were unhappy too, to know that I was put aside for politics and not for emotions. Now I get to see you with someone who looks like the man I love but who does not even know I existed in his life. That hurts."

Rhea stood up then and took the woman's hand so that she had to rise, as well. "Then you come back with me and help me get some food into him and convince him to get some sleep. He may not be the man that you knew, but he is a much better one. And he may not remember a lot, 'Fina, so don't be shocked if you mention an event or something and get a blank stare, but I do think he remembers you, the important, soul deep, parts of you."

"I do not think I can, Rhea. He is not the same person, probably for the better, but I still cannot. He is going to go away and there is nothing left for him here." She looked at the door, then back at Rhea. "You'd better hurry up if you want to catch them. I'm not sure how much Rowan's good will can last without you there as a buffer. He has been beaten and degraded for far too many years."

Rhea hurried down the hallway and reached Matt's door just as Rowan was stepping back into the hallway. "Did you guys make it back okay?" She braced a hand against the cold stone wall as she tried to catch her breath.

Rowan looked at her through guarded eyes and sighed. "I did not kill him, beat him, or otherwise hurt him while not in your presence, my Lady."

"Oh, just stop with the 'my Lady' crap, Rowan. The question was meant for you, too. I should have realized that you were still healing from your attack, as well, and found someone else to do the job."

He gave a stiff bow. "I apologize that I was unable to return fully capable of service to you, my Lady."

Tears of anger, frustration, and sadness began to fall from Rhea's eyes to drop onto the stone floor. "I don't want service from you, Rowan." She twisted her fingers into his tunic as the man's eyes darkened and he turned to leave. "I don't want a formal service from you. I just want you. I want the man who protects me, and comforts me, and loves me. I want the man I found at Kylassame, the one who fits me perfectly and brings me so much joy that my heart could burst with happiness. That's all I want, Rowan de Nespa, just you."

His chest rose and fell rapidly then and there were several pauses as he opened his mouth but seemed unable to find the words. "He can do all of that, too, Rhea. He will not cut you with harsh words when he does not know how to express himself. He can hold you without the hesitancy born of a lifetime of being told a person is not good enough. He also will know what you are talking about when you say things like 'computer' and 'television'."

"So what? What about when I talk about the people at Albadarl, or the women of Asimina, or the games, of Faulks, or Steinbrekka? How could he understand about our time at Kylassame and the happiness that flows out of that village? He won't get why I would carve ladybugs into furniture or burst into giggles while watching clouds. He won't understand any of that, Rowan, and that is part of my history now, as well."

Rowan stared into her face and she saw a desperation and sadness deeply settled into his eyes. "There is one way this story is going to end now, and that is with the two of you going back to your world, figuring out a story to tell your people, and then just remembering us as one crazy nightmare."

Rhea's hand fell slack against her side as her mind raced. "We can go back? I thought no one could go back? I was just telling him that to buy some time."

Rowan stared at the ceiling and then closed his eyes as he nodded. "Yes. The Gormellyn says he knows how to get you back there. I am going to meet with him tonight in Steinbrekka so we can figure out the details and respond to Steinbrekka's call the correct way."

"Is it going to be dangerous?"

He shrugged and refused to meet her eyes. "Probably. Most things involving that place are fairly dangerous."

She closed the gap between them then and wrapped her arms around his waist so that her head rested on his chest. "Be careful. Please be careful and come back, Rowan. I don't think I would ever be the same if something happened to you out there."

His arms slowly came around her and he let himself enjoy the feel of her in his arms for that moment. "I will try, Rhea. I do not know what is waiting for me at Steinbrekka to make any promises. It is hard for me to ride there with a clear head knowing that everything I learn will aid in your leaving."

"Well, we won't focus on that part then. You just focus on going there, and doing what you need to do, and then coming back. Everything else is purely circumstantial and we'll figure it out when it needs to be figured out."

He leaned down to kiss her gently then. "Be careful here, Rhea. I hate leaving you here without anyone to protect you. Stay in the room with Mateo and Risalka whenever possible and be wary of the rest of the court, especially those in service to the King or Zelkhova."

"I will. I'll be waiting for your return."

Chapter Thirty-Six

The Court

Two days was all it took for her to break her promise to Rowan to remain in the safety of her room. On the second day she felt a calling to go to the garden that was so severe she could not resist her feet from following the path. Coupled with a frantic message from the Mercene Alma, Rhea made the decision to slide into the garden at nightfall when the rest of the court would be asleep.

Rhea had spent some time walking through the ankle deep snow and silently touching the plants and trees that made up the special place. It was only after she had walked toward the back of the garden when she felt the prickle of warning as the hair stood up on her neck. *Why wasn't Alma waiting at the garden entrance for me? The night feels too cold, too still.* She made the quick decision to go back inside and turned to walk when she heard a small sound from the clearing.

"Alma? Is that you?" She stepped forward slowly, aware of the small set of footprints that led to the clearing from a small side path. Rhea hesitated at the tree line when the woman was not seen, then let out a relieved sigh and stepped forward once she saw where Alma waited leaning against a tree at the edge of the clearing.

"Alma, you had me nervous for a moment. What is so important that this could not wait for a few days? I have told you all that I know of your brother."

Rhea stepped closer as the woman kept silent. Her heart began to pound a frenzied beat as the realized the red dye lacing through the brown tunic was not dye at all, but the result of a small knife protruding from the woman's chest.

She spun around then, and as her foot slid in the slippery snow she saw Kofizek step into the clearing. Rhea forced herself to be calm and think. "Hello, Kofizek. Did Mateo instruct you to come to the garden on this night? Something evil has befallen the Mercene Alma and I would greatly appreciate your help in bearing her body to her Patron."

Kofizek merely stared at her with those glittering black eyes and smiled. Rhea saw the slightest of nods and then felt thick arms wrap around her chest as the world became black.

~ * ~ * ~

The feel of a cold draft against her neck startled Rhea back into consciousness. She opened her eyes slowly and was surprised to see rough stone beneath her hands and tilted her head at the sound of coughing beside her. Savin was slouched against the wall to her side, arms held extended at shoulder level by thick steel around his wrist. A small candle lantern hung on the wall beside him and his eyes were closed in exhaustion and pain.

Rhea gave a small cry and stood up, then swayed as small white dots filled her vision. "Savin! What are you doing down here? Where are we? What have they done to you?"

Savin's eyes cracked open and he coughed. "Down below. Do I look bad? I do not feel too bad, just a bit numb in the arms. I got dumped in here yesterday and they brought you in about four hours ago."

"But why are we in here? Alma's dead. Why is Alma dead?" Rhea leaned against the slick stone wall and slid down close to Savin, unable to clear the fuzzy feeling in her head.

"Not sure. Probably Mateo's orders. Rowan will get us out soon." Savin closed his eyes and laid his head against the side of the wall as he tried to relax his arm muscles.

Rhea shook her head and wrapped her arms around her drawn-up knees. "No to both accounts. I don't know how much you've been told, but Mateo is gone. The Gormellyn attacked him and while we were healing him everything that made up Mateo left and only my old friend Matt had returned. And Rowan is in Steinbrekka with the Gormellyn." She cursed softly. "He's going to kill me. He told me to stay in my room and not wander, and look where I am now."

A shadow fell across the bars on the door as the heavy metal screeched against the wood floor. Rhea narrowed her eyes as Kofizek and Zelkhova walked through the door and stood just inside the cell walls.

"It is a pity we can't just keep both of you in here. It seems as if that would be the best answer to our current problem." Kofizek glanced at Savin as if the man were no more than mud beneath his shoe.

Zelkhova's nasally tone filled the cell. "We must follow orders." He looked toward Rhea and extended a hand. "Come with us, girl. The King would like to see you."

Rhea slowly stood up but kept her back to the solid wall. "If the King wanted to see me, he could have simply asked. There was no need to kill the Mercene or dump us in this cell."

The two men smiled and Kofizek nodded. "This is very true. The way it was carried out offered more entertainment for the rest of the court. The Mercene was asking too many questions to be allowed to continue breathing. Now, will you come with us to see the King?"

"Why would I want to do that?"

Zelkhova pointed at Savin. "Because if you do not, his life is forfeit."

Rhea paled and put a hand on Savin's shoulder. "Well then, I suppose I have no choice, and yes, I will go with you." She stepped into the dimly lit hallway and followed Zelkhova down the black path with Kofizek at her back.

She walked in silence until they stepped over a small threshold and re-entered the opulent marble hallways of the castle. "Mateo will not be pleased with this turn of events. I am surprised the King would do such a thing to the Forena as was done to my person."

Kofizek chuckled. "Mateo is still infirmed and under the care of Risalka. He is as weak as a babe and losing his mental edge. No. The King is no longer investing the future of the realm in Mateo."

Rhea gently bit her lip to keep the panic at bay. "Then how does the King expect to continue his rule of the realm? Certainly he doesn't expect to live forever. I suppose he will pass it on to his daughter in the end?"

The men remained silent as the small party moved through a series of barred doors surrounded by heavy guards. Rhea assumed this was the area of the castle reserved for the King. The lanterns of the hallways were covered in gold leaf and thick fur rugs lined the marble hallways. Zelkhova stopped in front of a heavily crafted bronze door and tilted his head to the large guards standing in the hallway. The larger of the two swung open and Rhea was shoved inside the room.

King Verikhan's back faced her as she stumbled in and righted herself on the thick carpeting. Rhea glanced up at him before dropping into a deep curtsey as the man turned to acknowledge her arrival. Her eyes traced the movements of his shadow on the floor as he walked across the room and stopped in front of her.

"Hello, Rhea. I apologize for the manner in which you were brought here, but it was a necessary action. You may rise now, girl, and have the honor of looking upon my face."

Rhea swallowed the fear that rose in her throat and straightened her back. "Of course, you know the best action to take in the realm, my Lord King. I am but your servant."

The man smiled then, malicious and hungry. "Ah yes, yes you are. Tell me, girl, why is it that you suppose I have brought you into my private chamber?"

Her heart threatened to burst through her chest as Rhea replied. "I am quite unsure, my Lord. I had thought you would prefer I remain with your heir, the High Prince, to ensure his full recovery."

Blackness fell over the King's face, "Ah, I think not. I have no doubt that even now the Washitza, Risalka is whispering vicious lies into his healing ears to turn him against the realm. No, my stupid girl, if the monster that attacked my heir made something perfectly clear for me it was the true message. A true heir can only be created through the bloodline. As I refuse to allow the roadside scum Rowan to gain a chance at my kingdom, there is but one other path."

Rhea whispered. "Nyssa could rule. She would be through the bloodline."

The King stepped closer toward Rhea and she was forced to crane her neck to meet his gaze, their height difference was so great. "Nyssa, as the ruler? Ah, that would be rich. I can see it now. First day of rule she pardons all of the prisoners, claims equality among castes, and throws open the doors of the castle to the wretched souls beyond the gates." His large hand slid under Rhea's loose hair and firmly cupped the base of her skull. "Oh no, my dear, I will just have to make an heir myself. What do you say to that?"

Dense cotton filled Rhea's mouth as she realized the intent of the large man pressed against her. Her eyes grew wide with fright as his second hand fell to rest on the small of her back and pulled her close against him. She tried to stammer out an answer, to stall for time, but found that she was incapable of speech.

"So excited that you are rendered mute, I see? Yet when I look into those beautiful blue eyes, I see no joy at this prospect." He twisted his hand into her long hair and smiled at the cry as he tilted the head back at a vicious angle.

"Do not worry, little girl, you will have plenty of time to warm up to the idea. I am not a man who wastes a good broodmare when I see one, and the women have informed me that right now is not the ideal time for my heir to be conceived." His hand traveled from her hair down her spine, causing Rhea's nerves to dance with fright.

"Besides, an heir must be created only after following the correct protocol. I have no doubt that you will complete the tasks in a satisfactory manner. Would you like me to inform you of the proceedings so that you will not be surprised? I do hope that you remember that if I sense any form of hesitation or lack of...enthusiasm on your part, your precious remaining Komisar will be locked in the dungeon until the flesh falls from his bones."

Rhea stammered out an affirmative response, so afraid that she found herself immobile in the man's grip.

He smiled at her and turned her so that the two faced the mirror, his body pressed against her back and his cold blue eyes staring into her frightened gaze. "First my private maid servant will wash you. You will be fully cleansed, for nothing is allowed to be presented for the King's consumption without having been soaped, rinsed, and cooked. Then my personal clothier, Nikolae, will come and take your measurements to create your garments, much improved in style and function for your new role in the court. You will model your first dress at the celebratory Festival, which will mark the day of conception, and then I will have the immense pleasure of ripping it from your body that night."

Her body spasmed as fear thrust an iron fist into her stomach and twisted. Rhea took everything she had learned about self-control to keep herself from fainting and collapsing in front of the man.

"But before that is the most important part of the night. You see, Rhea, while I have no doubt that my prior Heir apparent fully used your beautiful body while you were in his custody, I cannot tolerate any doubts or rumors of paternity. Zelkhova will do an inspection on the morrow to inform me of when the best time for the Festival will be. Then you will have a rather intimate inspection with the man upon rising the morning of that festival to be sure that you have not been with any man recently, and I assure you that it will be quite thorough. Although," his hand slid down to rest just below the corset of her dress, "some of my past breeders have found that bit of protocol quite enjoyable, as well."

The man spun Rhea around then and quickly moved her into a room connected to the central waiting room in which she stood. An ungentle shove sprawled Rhea onto the silk-covered bed and she turned in fright to see the room empty, the great door closing, and the thick bolt locking from the outside.

Chapter Thirty-Seven

The Court

There were five hundred and seven blocks of marble used to create the walls of Rhea's room. She knew this because she had counted each block several times over the last seven days. The hatch marks she had incised on the small bedside table with a hairpin reminded her that today was the day of the festival, and of Zelkhova's earlier inspection. Her chest heaved with a suppressed sob as she rolled onto her side and stared at the ladybug necklace that she had laid on the pillow next to her head.

Rowan was dead, destroyed by the creatures of Steinbrekka. No one believed the news when the guard Brokkan rode into the castle, and Nyssa quickly rode out in the dark of night to shed light on the King's elaborate lie. She returned red-eyed and pale, and reported that the news was certainly true. The rocks of Steinbrekka were covered in blood, and tattered shreds of his clothing were scattered throughout the area. The horse he rode stood nervously at the edge of the wood and bolted towards her when Nyssa stepped out of the tree line. The stirrups of the saddle had been slashed, and the horse had several shallow lacerations and punctures scattered over his shoulders and haunches. Nyssa knew that the gelding would have never left his master unless in death.

Rhea closed her eyes against the tears and tried to steer her thoughts away from the man. Nyssa had given her the message on her second day of confinement and Rhea was amazed that she had more tears to cry. She received little food and water while bolted into this gilded cell and could feel her body weakening a little bit more every day. Her spirit had shattered with the news of Rowan and she felt numb, as if she were simply occupying a body devoid of emotions other than grief. What she wanted no longer had bearing in her life and she saw no potential in the future.

There was a gentle rap on the door and she lifted her head warily as Faina entered the room and gave her Patron a curtsey. Her eyes were rimmed with pink and slightly swollen with suppressed tears that welled up with the sight of the grieving Rhea.

"Hello, my Lady. I have come to prepare you for the Festival."

Rhea sat up and rubbed at her eyes with the back of her hand. "Faina! I had thought he would have sent someone unknown to me to get me ready for the butcher's block."

Faina flinched and walked over to the small wardrobe in the room. "Well, he has Savin and Mateo, Matt, locked up, and with Rowan...well, he feels more confident in the future, I suppose." She walked over to Rhea with a sheer jade gown and helped her off the bed. "Risalka told me to let you know, we are all praying for a swift pregnancy and a son. Then he will let you go, and he will find someone else to entertain him."

Rhea nodded then, muted and amazed that her vibrant life had come down to producing a son. Of all the worries and fears she had carried through her adult life, getting pregnant quickly and producing a child of a particular sex had not entered her mind. She stared at the sheer fabric and was even more dismayed that it dipped low in the front and did not allow for her stone necklace to be worn; even that small comfort was to be stripped away.

Faina gently picked up the necklace from the bed and looked at Rhea. "We knew that you would want to keep this close to you as long as possible. We created a small pocket space in the bodice boning where no one would see or feel such a thing, with the exception of you. If you will allow it I will quickly sew the stone into the space while you wash up."

She nodded and more tears flowed at her friend's thoughtfulness. "Thank you, Faina, and thank the others when you see them. I cannot bear to part with it now. It's all I have to remember a better time and when I felt truly loved." Her voice broke and she quickly dashed her face with cold water from the wash bowl to try to lessen the bright pink hue of her face.

A few minutes later Faina held open the dress and Rhea gave a small smile when she saw that the stone was truly hidden in the bodice. She stepped into the dress and held her hair out of the way while Faina did up the miniscule pearl buttons with nimble fingers.

"My Lady, I know that it is not exactly appropriate in this situation, but you look beautiful. I also thought you would want to know about all of the secret protections we have built into the dress for you. We thought they might help a little." Faina gently moved Rhea over to the small stool by the mirror and began to carefully plait her hair.

"First, we created the pocket space for your stone from Rowan, knowing you would want that close to your heart. The long sash of the dress was made with the shawl that Nastasio gifted you so many months ago, and is simply covered with the fabric of the dress so that the brilliant hues are hidden away safely. There is a bit of cat fur from the little gray lady sewed into the edge embroidery as well as hair from Lianna, Nyssa, Savin, and myself. On the hem of the bottom of the dress, out of sight, are the embroidered images of the Malakhor, Gormellyn, and the two mares who have taken an otherworldly affection to you. Nyssa also sewed tiny ladybugs, butterflies, and dragonflies onto the fabric of the interior of the gown in the less sheer areas, especially the interior of the wide sleeves, so that you could be reminded of kindness."

As the young woman talked, Rhea turned over the various pieces of the dress and felt a smile form at the subtle additions to the dress. Most were so small and finely done that a person would never notice if they had not looked for the special designs, and Rhea felt a small boost to her spirits at the thoughtfulness of her friends.

Faina finished with the elegant hair style and carefully applied subtle cosmetics to Rhea's eyes, cheeks and lips. "There. I have even applied a few extra sharp pins so hopefully anyone removing the veil in haste will receive a little reminder of why it is important to be gentle with a lady such as yourself!"

Rhea nodded and carefully stood, unsteady in the high heeled shoes that had been provided for the day. "I suppose we should just go and get this over with. Will you be able to accompany me to the Festival grounds?" She looked down and felt a rush of heat cover her face at the indecency of the fabric in which she was clad.

"Of course, my Lady. You will need someone to help you from toppling over after all. Once we arrive at the games, I will show you to your seat and then take my place with the other house staff."

The two heard the large bolt of the door slide open then and stepped into the waiting room. Rhea felt her stomach heave at the memories of the last time she was in that room and they quickly hurried into the hallway. The thin stone-tipped heeled shoes clicked and echoed throughout the castle as the women walked through the hallways, careful to not slip and turn an ankle on the smooth marble floor. Rhea gripped the long skirts of her outfit in one hand while the other rested on Faina's arm, offered as support from the awkward shoes.

"Faina, is there word of Sebast?" Rhea whispered to keep the words from floating down the hallway along with the clicks.

"He is tucked somewhere safe. Asimina will have to make due without him until his injuries heal and this story plays out. It has been difficult for them, but they will manage." She hesitated as she said, "Rhea, it is likely that they will throw anyone they can find into this game. None of this is your fault. I want you to know that going into the Festival."

Rhea nodded and squinted as the women stepped out into the sunlit corridor and made their way to the Festival games. The guard Brokkan approached them as they entered the gate and gave a deep bow to Rhea.

"My Lady, I just wanted to extend my condolences for Komisar Rowan. He was a good man and is sorely missed among the guards and servants." The man glanced at Rhea's outfit and then firmly established his view onto her face.

She nodded her gratitude and rapidly blinked her eyes to fight the new tears from falling. "Thank you, Brokkan. I appreciate your kind words in such trying times."

The women stepped through the doorway to the Festival and Faina led her Patron down the narrow hallway to the royal box. Nyssa was seated already with Agrafina and the only remaining seat was positioned in front of the King's throne. Nyssa gave Rhea a quick squeeze of encouragement as she sat down and even Agrafina took her hand momentarily for comfort.

The King entered the stands then with a company of guards and the crowd immediately silenced in anticipation. He was clad in a long white shirt, gleaming white trousers and a brilliant wine colored tunic that managed to reflect the sunlight and caused more than one member of the audience to shield their eyes. The imposing man stood and raised his hands to the crowd.

"Welcome, my people. Welcome to the Royal Festival. My dear subjects, you have witnessed the great despairs of our realm in these past weeks and for that, I am sickened and saddened. The betrayal of our people by the guards Savin and Rowan, and then the attack on our dear High Prince have taken a toll on our community that must be avenged. I am standing before you today to tell you that it will be rectified and the future will once again be bright. Tonight I take the former Forena to my bed and will provide this powerful realm with an untouched and unchallenged future!"

The crowd roared and Rhea felt unkind hands lift her to a standing position for inspection, her barely clad figure visible to the roaming eyes of the frenzied crowd. She stilled her mind, looked past the leering glares of the men and sat down the second the pressure from the hands abated.

The King sat as well, then leaned forward to place his hand firmly around the back of the woman's neck. "You tremble like a rabbit caught in a snare. Had I known you had such a strong reaction to the events of the day, we would have had more preparation time, perhaps more exposure to such events."

Rhea felt every muscle freeze as his hands ran down her shoulder blades and trailed down her sides, then finally rested firmly on her hips as the King's breath whispered in her ear.

"Yes, that is right, little girl. Just freeze and everything will be fine. Just let it happen and only these people will die. If you fight, or protest, I will kill everyone dear to your heart. Oh yes, I know who they are, and it will all be because of you."

Her heart beat frantically, pushing against her chest like bird wings until she felt the coolness of the hidden stone against her skin. She quelled the panic then and instead forced her attention forward into the area, forward as the guards began to open the door and as she tried to ignore the roving hands of the man behind her.

The doors opened and a large group of men and women were herded into the arena. Rhea felt her heart drop and saw tears well in Nyssa's eyes as she recognized many of the women from Asimina, men from Albadarl, and beloved children from the market enter the arena in a daze. She turned around in her chair to face the King, her blue eyes ablaze with anger.

"This is not right! I have never spoken directly against the ways of you and your people, but putting women and children into this is beyond barbaric."

He chuckled then and the tips of his fierce lips curved in smile. "Yes, well, this is a special occasion, after all. It seems that all of the men of Asimina have disappeared, so spilling the blood of the women is all that is left. The events of the day require the sick blood of Asimina, the magical powers from the aberrations of Albadarl, and the blood of the innocent from our own realm. Now, one more word from you, and I start throwing your servants into the arena." His eyes began to move slowly down Rhea's body and, as his body began to visibly respond, Rhea whipped around and sat down abruptly.

The gong sounded and the guards entered the arena. Panic ensued as the victims scattered in an attempt to run from their pursuers, futile in the oval area. Rhea closed her eyes tightly and tried to convince herself that this was not truth.

I'm not here, I'm not. This is just an insane nightmare. This whole thing is just an insane nightmare. Matt was never kidnapped and I was never kidnapped and Rowan is just an imaginary person I made in my head because I was lonely and wanted some romance in my life. I'm not here at all. I'm really sitting in the woods where I grew up, the place next to the stream. It's a spring day and the ferns are just starting to unfurl, and the daffodils are just starting to show their glimpses of yellow to the world.

The woods were alive with sounds as birds and small creatures moved through the underbrush around Rhea. She still wore an oddly sheer outfit, but now the pictures of the insects, the mystical creatures, and the stone ladybug shone brightly through as if woven with deeply dyed golden threads. Rhea no longer cared about the fabric of the gown, for she was alone out in these woods and felt unwatched, private, and at peace.

A deer hopped over the burbling stream beside her and stopped for a cooling drink, soft muzzle dipping into the water and sending small ripples in the slight current. Rhea smiled at the velvety fur and then grinned widely as her old gray-striped tabby cat came to curl up beside her in the moss. It had been eight years since she had seen her precious Kitty, not the most original of names but certainly a cat who was beyond duplication. The feline head butted her leg, then began to thoroughly lick Rhea's hand with her sandpaper tongue as the woman tried to pet the soft fur.

She heard a tiny splash and Rhea peered down into the water, pleased at the small frogs that swam throughout the steam below. As a teenager she would spend hours watching the frogs as they darted and swam beneath the water. She had been fascinated watching the eggs form, then the tiny tadpoles as they grew until finally they could leave the water as adults.

A shadow formed over her head and Rhea turned in fear, then shock as the form of Rowan stood before her. "They said you were dead."

Rowan smiled sadly and gestured to the woods. "Considering this place is not the real reflection of your current world, that is probably true. I only remember riding to Steinbrekka and seeing the Gormellyn. What happened after I stepped next to the pool-" he shrugged.

"Oh." Rhea looked down at her fingers as her eyes felt the pressure of tears once again.

He moved quickly and embraced her, and Rhea put her arms around his sturdy chest and buried her face into his loose shirt, taking in a deep breath as his scent soothed and comforted her. "If it is any consolation, I certainly do not want to be dead. Let us just forget about that part and sit here by the stream awhile and talk. I have missed you this past week. I've missed you ever since we came back from Kylassame. If I had a second chance there would be no more doubts, no more talk of a bleak future. I would take you to Kylassame and we would live in peace, far from the horrors of the court."

They sat by the stream and Rhea laid her head on his shoulder. His arm came around her waist and she sighed as her soul slid into a deep contentment. "Let's just stay here forever, Rowan. Can we do that? I don't want to go back there. I just want to spend my life here with you." She closed her eyes and smelled the pine scent of the air.

The sound of a gong rang through the woods and Rhea's eyes burst open to see the dust of the arena in front of her. The King's fist was twisted angrily into the fabric of her back and the women beside her looked amazed and frightened. The crowd was hushed and milled nervously around their seats while hesitation and anxiety flowed around the arena like the grasses in the stream.

Rhea looked down in amazement as one by one the intended victims of the game turned toward her and bowed their heads in respect. None of the women, children, or men had been touched and had been spared from as much as a scratch on their persons. The guards stood in a group on the far side of the arena with weapons sheathed and brows pursed in confusion.

King Verikhan stood and hastily dismissed the crowds. He pointed to Nyssa and then to Rhea and his eyes shone with barely contained rage. "Daughter, you will bring this woman to my chamber. Immediately. There will be no side adventures and no attempts at escape. You are both well aware of whose lives are at stake if you decide to take such a course."

They nodded then, lips tight and faces pale as the man stalked back towards the room.

Nyssa turned to Rhea and gave her a quick hug. "Come on, we had better get moving and talk while we walk. He does not make empty threats." They quickly moved down the hallway and crossed the courtyard. "How did you do that? That was incredible."

"How did I do what? What happened with the games, Nyssa? After the King made me stand I just shut my eyes and blocked out everything that was happening. I was in the woods with Rowan…" her voice trailed off as she remembered the woods and how it felt so real, down to the warmth of his body against her own.

"Nothing happened. The guards advanced and then just…stopped. It was as if all desire for them to cause harm had fled from their bodies and they were unable to perform. They just formed a little group, sheathed their weapons and left the villagers alone. Rhea, it has been an entire day, look."

Rhea looked up at the sun as it began to dip down to the horizon. "An entire day…but it seemed like it had been only minutes in the dream. I don't understand this, Nyssa."

"I do not understand either. Be careful tonight. He is going to be angry and will be even less inclined to make this a gentle experience for you. Just… survive it and we will keep trying to figure out how to change things permanently around here. Keep faith that we will save you in the end."

Chapter Thirty-Eight

The Court

"Stupid, meddling woman!" The force of the King's hand sent Rhea sprawling into the corner of a sturdy wardrobe. "I do not know what game you are pulling, but all of this will stop immediately or punishment will be swift and severe for you and your servants."

Rhea stood slowly, one long heel having snapped during the fall. She used the thick wood as a support and lifted her head to the man. "I am playing no games, my Lord, nor do I have any knowledge of what happened. I attended the game as you asked and sat there as instructed. I had nothing to do with the outcome."

His massive body moved swiftly as an angry bear and pressed Rhea against the smooth wood. "Nothing to do with the outcome? We have never had a game with results such as this, or the one that caused our people to turn traitor, until you entered this realm." His breathing quickened at his proximity to the woman. "This is not natural. You are not natural. This must be stopped for the safety of the realm."

"I had nothing to do with those games and anyone you ask will inform you of that fact. I stand by that and my assurance of my innocence in those matters."

The King grabbed Rhea's shoulders roughly in his large hands and swung her body towards the bed, smiling as the woman's foot hit a low trunk, broke the heel of the second shoe and sent her sprawling. "You can proclaim all you want, but here I am King. Here I make decisions and those decisions are final." He walked over to where she lay askew on the floor and dragged her to a standing position with a hand in her hair.

Rhea smiled as the King emitted a loud curse after grabbing one of the sharpened hair pins. "I am well aware of that, my Lord. I think everyone here is aware of that."

He responded by viciously yanking the pin out of Rhea's hair, pleased at the cry of pain, then flung it across the room to clatter against the door. "I can see now that I have afforded you far too much freedom in this court, my little poppet. Rest assured that after tonight that will no longer be the case." His hand grabbed the back of Rhea's neck and squeezed the fragile bones until tears sprang to her eyes.

"You may have the fear of your subjects, but you will never have respect." Rhea clamped her eyes shut as the pain from her constricting neck muscles and spine threw stars across her vision.

The man laughed then and shoved Rhea onto the bed as he walked to lock the door. "And this matters to me? As long as I have obedience I care not how it is attained."

Rhea quickly rolled off of the bed, putting the large piece of furniture between her and the enraged man. "If you want an heir so badly, you can't kill me. You know what the Gormellyn said."

He turned, hand on the door lock and faced her with a grin, "Ah, but that is the best part. You hardly need to be conscious to be bedded and I will find my pleasure in it one way or another."

Then a sudden crash from the hallway rang out as two bodies spilled into the room, the first toppling the King onto the ground and the second rushing for Rhea. She backed against the wall in fear before realizing that the man in front of her was Matt.

"We've got to hurry, come on. I don't know how long he will stay down." Matt grabbed her hand and pulled her toward the door to the room.

Rhea looked back at the form of the still healing Savin as he rolled in combat with the larger form of the King. "But Savin, he's not well."

Matt pushed her out of the door and into the hallway. "He's well enough to know what he's gotten into. Come on, Nyssa has a horse ready for you and we need to move now."

Her broken heels now functioned as well-attached sandals and Rhea ran through the stone hallways in near silence, grabbing Matt at intervals to pull him into rooms as various guards loyal to the King passed by. Five long minutes later they emerged from the winding hallways of the castle and stopped just short of the heavily cloaked Nyssa standing with Kataolya.

Nyssa gave the fastenings of the saddle one last tug before Brokkan hastily helped Rhea to mount. "Ride as fast as you can to Steinbrekka. Do not stop, do not look back. The horse knows the way so give her the lead. Stay there until we come to you."

Rhea nodded and took a second to look at the castle before fleeing into the darkness.

~ * ~ * ~

Kataolya skidded to a nervous stop at the edge of the clearing at the sight of the Ellyn massing around the waterhole. Rhea hopped off and gave the horse a quick pat of assurance before turning her loose and running into the throng of tiny, agitated bodies. They milled around her ankles, coarse fur brushed against the sides of her feet and she felt the occasional small slice from a claw as a creature scurried to get out of way too hastily.

She ran for the ledge, thin fingers forcing her tired body up the small stone ladder until she could climb onto the ledge above. Blind hope had her press her hands against the wall in a desperate search for the cave of the Aos Si, but only solid stone was found at her finger tips. Rhea heard a bugle of fear from her horse and turned to see her newest nightmare as he rode through the mass of now furious creatures that bit and slashed at the intruder.

Sharp stone bit into the delicate soles of Rhea's feet as she scrambled up the steep incline to the summit of the rock. She reached the top of the summit and glanced around, momentarily fearful of the surging, angry creatures on the ledge below. Strands of hair blew across her face and she grabbed a hairpin in her hand as she turned to face the path to the top.

"You did not think you could get away quite that easily did you, my pet?" The man stepped onto the ledge, his face red with anger and crisscrossed with thin lacerations from the battle with Savin. "I should think you could do better than sending a half-crippled traitor to aid in your escape."

"I'm surprised you would follow me here. After the words of the Gormellyn, I would think you would be wise enough to stay away from this place." Rhea's gown whipped around her legs as the wind picked up and swirled around her. Her breath came hard and fast from the headlong ride and the hasty climb to the summit while her heart beat a frantic rhythm against her ribs.

The King moved forward slowly, progress slowed by wind that pushed against his broad body and sucked the air from his lungs. His bare chest heaved with the effort of the motion as he yanked a knife from his elaborately carved belt. Steel blue eyes glittered in the moonlight as they focused on the woman in front of him.

For every step forward Rhea took one back until she found herself directly below the bright moon. Below her feet the stone shimmered with a thin layer of ice and she saw the frost growing from beneath her feet and flowing across the stone. Bright, colorful stars swirled in the sky above and were reflected in the ice mirror below, and Rhea afforded herself the span of one breath to marvel that her gown seemed to swirl in rhythm with the celestial beings. The embroidered animals of the gown seemed to warm against her skin and dance with a life of their own as the woman picked up her chin and eyes flashed in defiance.

"I am the Lady Rhea Aralia, the chosen Lady of Steinbrekka. I have walked along pathways of which you could only dream and have allies beyond your wildest imagination. I belong here with the creatures of this place, and you, the man they call Verikhan, are very much an intruder on this land and an imposter. You are not welcome on this land and you are not invited to remain on this rock." Rhea took a deep breath as a steady heat filled her body, and saw the hesitation in the man's face as the ice spread to his feet and caused his footing to become unsteady.

Rhea looked behind the looming man as the Ellyn began to scale the butte and work their way between the man and the woman, a seething, angry mass of fangs and claws. Suddenly the King's hands flew to his ears as the keening cry of the Aos Si filled the air.

Rhea smiled as the women materialized in front of her and gave a bow of respect. The three women paused their cries to say, "Welcome home, sister," and then resumed the high pitch wail that disturbed the King so greatly. The song fell upon Rhea's ears as a gentle cry, a sad lament of heartache and loneliness that spoke of the life lived at Steinbrekka.

A soft mew behind her shoulder caused Rhea to take her eyes from the weakening King and she squatted down to get closer to the small gray cat sitting on the ice. "You aren't just a little gray cat are you?"

The cat shook her head, blinked once, then closed her eyes and quickly morphed into the shape of the elderly gray woman of Steinbrekka. "Hello, my dear. You may want to turn away now. The creatures of this world are unhappy with the intruder in their midst, and the Malakhor comes to take his due."

She glanced over her shoulder to see the large white cat and his equally daunting black twin slowly circling the King, hands still clutched to his ears and eyes tightly closed against the increasing light of the moon. A snarl, then Rhea spun around to face away as the cats pounced onto their prey and the Ellyn chattered in excitement.

The crawling mass made short work of the body of the once King. Each tiny fang took a piece of clothing and slowly dragged the heavy man down from the butte and into the dark woods beyond the stone. Rhea's leg muscled tensed, then melted and she sat down quickly on the ice, the quick end to a desperate night taking away her courage and resolve. She pulled her knees to her chest and wrapped her arms around them, then let her head droop onto her arm as she took deep clean breaths to settle her heaving stomach.

"Hello, my dear Lady. I thank you for bringing us our opportunity for retribution." The deep voice caused Rhea to look up at the figure of the Gormellyn as he sat calmly at the perimeter of the ice and curled his tail around his sharply clawed feet.

"I just wanted to escape from him. I didn't know what would happen. I just came here because, I guess, because I felt safer here than anywhere else. I just got on Kataolya and we ran, and she came here." Her chest shuddered and she drew a shaky breath.

"The mare of the Lady Queen is a wise and a good companion for our new Lady. The creatures of Steinbrekka will not harm you, for you are well loved." The creature came close and looked into Rhea's face. "You do not look well, my dear. What troubles you?"

Rhea began to laugh as quiet chuckles of disbelief gave way to hysteria. "What troubles me? I was kidnapped, but I learned to adapt to that. Then I learned about whole towns of people who have been starved and left to die. Then I found out that the person I was in love with, wait, did I mention I fell in love? Well, the person I fell in love with was actually the blood-born heir of the realm that was ruled by a tyrant, but had been treated like a slave his whole life. Then my best friend was ripped to shreds in front of my eyes, which resulted in him coming back to me, which resulted in Rowan coming here and getting killed-" She paused and angry fingers dashed at the tears that fell down her cheeks. "I don't think I could even begin to identify what troubles me at this particular moment. There is just too much."

The Gormellyn lifted a small claw to scratch under his chin. "Well, then perhaps I should ask what the creatures of Steinbrekka could do to make some of your trouble be lessened in quantity or depth." Claws scratched across the ice and stone as the Ellyn returned to the rock and milled behind their leader. Gentle eyes passed on Rhea as the creatures chattered among themselves and began to groom one another.

"How could you make my troubles less?" Rhea's eyebrows furrowed and she stared at a loose thread on her gown. "I want to feel safe again. I want to be able to sleep every night in a warm bed. I want to know that when I wake up there will be no crisis, no death, and no immediate sense of impending doom." The stone ladybug pressed against her chest and she suppressed a sob with a shuddered breath. "I want Rowan back in my arms and for him to be safe."

Suddenly the sky erupted with a multitude of swirling stars as every imaginable color exploded into dance in the black above and reflected their wild pathways across the stone surfaces. The wind rose so abruptly that Rhea was pushed to her feet, and her dress whipped against her fatigued legs while her hair swirled through the sky. The air turned frigidly hostile and as the ice spread and thickened under her feet, the thick chill caused the woman to react in violent shivers.

"You asked me what I wanted and I gave you an honest answer! Next time don't ask if you are going to get angry!" Rhea felt hot frustration flood through her body and chase the cold away from her skin. Her eyes glazed over as the last bit of sorrow and grief left her body and she became consumed with wrath. "You were the one who brought him here, who told him that he needed to be here. Why didn't you just kill him in the castle if that was your intent? What games are you playing with us?"

Small red eyes looked calmly at the woman and the Gormellyn slowly blinked. "I never said why he needed to be here. I am vengeance, and retribution, and punish those who pretend to be anything other than their true selves. Rowan was a Prince who pretended to be a guard, deceitful and false. He would let his sister take the throne without a fuss, and continue living in the world as nothing more than a common man. What purpose would his existence serve with you gone and another worthy person on the throne?" A thin red tongue ran across sharp fangs as he cocked his head to the side. "Do you not agree with my assessment of his character?"

Rhea pushed the long strands of hair from in front of her face and raised her voice to be heard within the maelstrom. "I most certainly do not agree. He was acting to serve and protect the less fortunate of the realm. He took care of his own and led those who needed a leader. He is loved in this world and needed, even if he were to never formally take the throne. He was a man who simply went through his life being an honorable man. He did what his mother would have wanted him to do when he protected those who needed protecting even without the status to back him up and with the knowledge that it may see his death. Rowan certainly did not deserve your vengeance and he did not deserve to die!"

The black creature merely chuckled and slid in a carefree movement across the ice. "Such anger, such passion. It flows from your spirit like water from a stream. Tell me, Lady, why do you care so much, when you will just be leaving this world in a few days and this will only be a distant memory?"

"Whoever said I was leaving? It wasn't until recently that I even knew it was an option. I have decided nothing and am sick of others telling me what I am going to do!" Rhea ran a hand through her hair as the wind began to die down around her, startled as she stared at auburn strands mixed in with blonde.

Ayewok cleared her throat delicately and then placed a kind hand on Rhea's shoulder. "You will leave us, my dear, that much is known. Without Rowan, there is no point in you staying after all. The enchantment of the physical body was meant to last only as long as you needed to remain in the realm, and was triggered to fade away so you could return back to your life." Gentle eyes stared into Rhea's. "Take your Matt back to your world and be happy, Rhea. Go back with our blessing and tell our story to your grandchildren."

Rhea felt her heart skip a beat and she clenched her fists tightly to her sides, feeling the small embroidered creatures in the now tattered gown. "No. You asked me what I wanted, and I told you what it was. You placed no terms or limits on the question, and I know that your power enables you to do many things beyond the scope of a mortal creature. Bring him back and let me make my own decision regarding where I shall stay in the world."

"It will not be easy. In fact, none can bring a person back from the dead, even a being as powerful as me." The Gormellyn tilted his head to the side and gazed up at the already exhausted woman. "I suppose then that it is a good thing he was not killed, but merely suspended in life. It would have been a grievous error indeed. You may try to bring him back to your side. He is not so far away after all." He turned and scampered down the narrow path to the ledge and Rhea followed on shaky legs.

"What do you mean, I may try to bring him back? Aren't you going to bring him back? You said he wasn't dead, but Nyssa saw the scene. Why won't you tell me anything! I am sick of people playing games with me!" Her feet skidded on loose pebbles and she grabbed onto a protruding rock to slow her descent to the ledge. Her words caught in her throat as the stone scraped a layer of skin from her palms and her muscles clenched in protest of their violent treatment.

Then she looked down, and saw Rowan's bare body suspended in the pool below, trapped beneath a layer of thick ice.

She screamed then, full of fury, and her desperate love for the man fueled her swift and unsteady decent down the path. Rhea hit the path and slowed just enough to drop to her knees, then use her bruised and bloodied hands to grip the edge of the cliff ledge and before dropping onto the ground below. She felt the muscles twist in her ankle as she collapsed onto the rock floor and cursed under her breath, then saw Rowan's arm move under the water, and quickly dragged her body over to the pool. The ice was too thick to break under her weight, and Rhea wasted precious seconds as she banged her fist upon the thick mass, leaving small handprints in blood. Rowan's green eyes cried the need for air below the ice and his fist hammered against the solid ceiling.

Sharpness pricked her hip, and she looked down to see the small hairpin from earlier had fallen in the windstorm and become stuck in the fabric of her belt, sinking into her flesh. She yanked it out in one clean motion and began to pick at the ice below her as one would carve a pumpkin, quelling her panic and deliberately placing each stab to form a circle above Rowan's head.

Rowan pushed up on the ice as the pin fell the final time and the circle gave way, pushing up and sliding across the ice to rest at the feet of the Malakhor. She saw the man's head surface and felt relief as he drew in a deep breath of precious air. Then the ice under Rhea shattered and she felt nothing but surrender as the cold water rushed into her lungs and the world went dark.

Chapter Thirty-Nine

The Court

Nyssa walked into the large kitchen and smiled at the figure huddled by the fire. "You are allowed to use the fireplace in the formal room now, yet still I find you in the kitchen. Your friends are worried that you are pulling away from everyone, Rowan. We love you, come let us help you through this transition."

Rowan turned around and gave his sister a small smile, then lifted the small mug from the table beside him. "Everyone knows the best fire is the kitchen fire. Besides, here I can get food and hot drink without having to move more than a few feet." Green eyes shimmered as he stared into the fire. "Besides, I am not good company right now. May never be good company again. Being around people hurts too much."

His sister picked the fallen blanket from the floor and repositioned it around his shoulders. "You are a co-reagent now, Rowan. You could just snap your fingers and people would bring you food and drink without you having to move. Besides, we are used to you being sullen and moody."

He shrugged and continued to stare into the orange fire. It had been a week since Rhea had freed him from the ice, but still he felt the chill deep in his bones and could not seem to get enough of the fire's warmth. His heart, he was convinced, would remain locked in ice for eternity. "I think I spent too long being the one doing the bringing, Nyssa. I am thinking it might be better for me to just go to Kylassame and leave you here to run things." He worked up a smile for her. "Well, you and Sebast, I should say."

She blushed deeply and stole half of the biscuit he was eating in response. "We are still working on that. It is a slow process to convince the people he did not cause all of our problems and it will not be fixed in a week." A sly smile spread across her face. "Besides, what will you do in Kylassame? Finally take up Amanda on her offer of courtship? The woman has only been trying to woo you her entire adult life."

Rowan closed his eyes and dropped his face into the palm of his hands. "Stop, Nyssa. Do not even suggest... It is too soon to even joke like that."

An unsteady voice filled with amusement trickled through the kitchen. "I should hope so. I'm not even dead or gone yet and you are pushing him into the arms of another woman."

His head shot up and Rowan stood too quickly, the blood rushing from his head forcing him to lean on the table for support and abandon his attempt to run across the room. "Rhea, you are alive! You are here, healed." He glared at his sister. "You knew she was healed and did not tell me!"

Nyssa shrugged and helped Rhea walk over to the fire and gently sat her down next to the man. "You still owed me for the Sebast incident. According to my tally this makes us even."

Rhea curled up under the blanket, the heat of the fire and the man beside her soaking through her muscles and relaxing away the chill that still held her. "Besides, I've only been okay for like, five hours or something. It's not like Nyssa has been keeping this from you for days."

He wrapped his arms around her and pulled the woman closer to his body, reassured of her presence with every rise and fall of her chest. "I thought I lost you. After resigning myself to losing you to other people for so long, I thought I finally lost you completely. We can start looking at the future now, assuming you still want a future with me."

She took in a deep but shaky breath and stared at Rowan's chest, unable to meet his eyes. "We need to talk about that, Rowan. Ayewok says that if we are to open the portal it has to be done tomorrow. I know that Matt wants to go back, no matter what the consequences are or what is happening in the other world."

"And what is it that you want, Rhea?" His voice came out as a barely audible whisper as he pressed his lips to her hair and dreaded the answer.

Rhea leaned her forehead against the soft fabric of his shirt. "I don't know. I wish I had more time to decide, to figure out what to do. I want you. I want to stay with you, to watch the realm recover and prosper and be here. To love you and have your children and watch them grow. I also want to see my family and let them know that I'm okay. I miss them and it would crush me that they would go their entire life thinking I had died when I'm alive and well and happy." She looked up at him and began to cry at the look of helplessness and sadness reflected from his eyes. "I want a future with you, Rowan, but I can't desert my family either. I don't know how to make them both work without hurting someone. Please tell me you understand."

Rowan gently wiped away the tears, "I understand, Rhea, truly I do. It does not make my heart ache any less, but I do understand. Did Ayewok say what was needed to create the link?"

She shook her head. "No. She just said that you hold the key and that it would be revealed at sunrise." A shudder snaked up her spine. "Rowan, I need to think. I'm sorry but I think I need to be alone for a little while to think about what to do."

"I understand. Can I at least escort you to your room?" He asked quietly.

"I would like that very much."

He stood slowly, then held out an arm for additional support as he gently took her hand and pulled her to her feet. Rhea turned toward Nyssa and gave her a brave smile. "I will see you in the morning, Nyssa. Thank you for everything."

They walked down the hallways in silence, her small hand clasped in his larger one. Several times lips would part as if to say something and then close again, and the stone walls around them seemed to bear down heavier with each step toward Rhea's room. After far too short a time they arrived, and Rowan reached down to caress an auburn lock of hair that fell on Rhea's face before opening the door.

"I want you to know that I will love you, no matter what you decide to do when the sun rises. And if you go back and find a way to return, there will always be a home for you in this realm if you only ask for one. You have changed everything in this realm for the better, and for that we owe a debt so great we could never repay it. The people, the land, the very constellations have changed and grown to become more than we could have imagined, and all thanks to you." He bent down and kissed her softly on the lips, then sank back into the shadows of the hallway as she softly closed the door behind her.

Chapter Forty

The Court

Hazy morning light filtered through the windows of her bedroom as the sun rose the next morning, casting the room in an orange glow. Rhea pulled the soft blanket over her head in a futile effort to keep it from reaching her eyes and forcing her to awaken for the day. She had stayed up long into the night, only to fall into an exhausted sleep as the night guard changed in the early hours of morning. Her mind was still in turmoil, and she had come no closer to the decision which would change her life forever.

A low thump accompanied the feeling of weight on the bed as Ayewok, as a cat, jumped onto the bed and stared at the still sleeping figure. Lianna walked in then and gently pulled the covers back from Rhea's face.

"Staying in bed will not make the sun rise any slower, Rhea."

Rhea rolled over and buried her face, swollen and pink from tears, in the silk pillow beside her. "It used to work when I was little and didn't want to go to school."

A gentle hand stroked the smoothed, braided hair for a moment before Lianna stood up and went to open one of the trunks on the floor. "Cassie sent over some clothes from Kylassame for you. She said you would feel more comfortable in these if you decide to go back. She said it would attract far too much attention if you arrived in a royal gown. I suppose it best if you fit the part of that society again."

Rhea stood up slowly at the sight of the faded blue jeans and fitted purple shirt. She changed into the clothes slowly, the feel of the fabric strange and rough on her skin after so many months wearing nothing but silk and finely woven cotton dresses.

Lianna looked at her and blinked rapidly to clear back the tears. "I forget that you are not from here, but that is hard to do when you wear those clothes." She stepped forward and embraced the other woman. "Walk lightly, Rhea, and choose with your heart. We will never forget you and will always love you."

The two women left the room and walked down the long hallway to the courtyard as the gray cat padded along behind their feet. They moved slowly to accommodate Rhea's still-fragile condition, and she stopped on many occasions to lean against the wall and struggle to take in a deep breath to continue on the way. The woman leaned her forehead against the cool marble wall and worked to get her emotions in check. Every step felt like goodbye, and she was not ready for that yet. She still had not made up her mind about what choice she would make and she was running out of time.

They stepped out into the dawn light and saw several horses saddled where people had gathered in the courtyard. Rowan walked over and gave a small bow of greeting, then escorted Rhea over to the black mare and helped her onto the broad back. Lianna mounted the small gray mare and moved beside Rhea, offering silent companionship. Rowan picked up Ayewok, gently lifting her onto his saddle before swinging onto his gelding and leading the party out of the courtyard.

As they passed through stands of pine, Matt urged his horse forward until he rode evenly with Rhea on the wide path. His blue eyes shone with excitement and his skin was flushed with joy as he babbled on about the things he would do once he crossed into their old world.

"The first thing I'm doing is taking a shower, a real one, with running water and soap out of a bottle. Then I'm going to order a pizza and eat it while I'm watching TV, and maybe play on my laptop at the same time. Then I'm going to the mall and buy some new clothes. Then I'm going to buy a ton of music and sit and listen to it in my car. Oh, and then you and I are going to see a movie in a movie theater and buy a giant buttered popcorn and eat ourselves sick."

Rhea smiled weakly at his enthusiasm and reached down to scratch Kataolya's neck as the horse pulled at the reins. "We'll see. Time doesn't always work the same, Matt. You may go back and it's a thousand years in the future and just as strange as this world."

Clear aqua eyes looked over into her hazel ones. "Well, at least it would be closer to what is regular. Besides Rhea, I can't stay here. The more I hear about what I've done to the people here, the sicker it makes me, and I don't think I could ever get them to start looking at me differently. I'll take my chances with going through the magic portal thingy."

His face softened and he reached over to give her arm a comforting squeeze. "You need to come back too, Rhea. You don't belong here, not really. This will always be the place where you were kidnapped, and beaten, and had countless injuries done. You need to come back with me where you can be safe. Your family would be worried and you need to go back and let them start living their lives again instead of looking for you."

Rhea leaned her head back to stare at the clear sky above. *Why is it such a beautiful day when I feel like my heart is being ripped from my chest?* "I know that, Matt, that I owe it to my family to go back." She smiled as Faulks flew over the party and dipped his wings, sunlight gleaming off the white undersides of his feathers and making beautiful flashes of light in the sky. "It's just hard, is all. I've made a life for myself here too, and the bad parts are gone, with only the good parts of it remaining."

The look of incredulity on his face caused her smile to fade, "Rhea, you can't honestly be thinking about staying here! You've been her for what, eight months? You are going to throw away twenty-five years of your life for a place you discovered over the last eight months? A place where you never wanted to be in the first place? You would just put aside all of that history, and your family, and all of your friends because you might be happy here? That is sheer insanity."

The woman looked ahead of the line and gave Rowan a wave of reassurance as he began to move his horse back, alarmed at the increased volume of the conversation. "Matt, you are assuming that I was constantly happy in my old life. It doesn't work that way. Even then I had good days and I had bad days, and there were some nights when I wished with all of my heart that I could escape the regular world and find some place magical and better."

"So escape to Montana or California or something! Go to a place where you can escape the regular world but still have a telephone and be able to call your mom every once in a while. It's selfish to stay here, and dangerous. What happens if I leave and the portal closes and you don't like it here and you don't get a second chance? You'll just spend the rest of your life here being miserable! You aren't from here, Rhea. You don't fit in here."

"I know, Matt! I know. I've thought of these things but I don't have any answers yet. Now be quiet so I can think for the remaining minutes of our ride." Rhea pulled the hood of her cloak over her head, effectively shutting out further conversation.

She put the hood down again when Kataolya stepped into a large clearing among the trees, circular and covered with a spongy moss. Rhea watched as Rowan dismounted from his horse, and then gently placed Ayewok in the center of the mossy bed. A swirl of color and light followed and once again the gray woman stood in front of Rhea, hand beckoning.

Rhea swung off her mount carefully and rested her body for a minute against the mare's broad shoulder. She could hear the ticking of time in her head as each second counted down to when she would have to make that final decision. Her feet hesitated as they glided over the thick green carpet of growth and she stopped in front of the man and the woman, her skin growing clammy and damp with anxiety.

Ayewok looked upon the woman with kind eyes before beckoning for Matt to join them, as well. He dismounted quickly and practically skipped into the center of the clearing, his entire demeanor exuding joy and relief. The woman turned to Rowan and placed a soft hand on his arm.

"Rowan de Nespa, co-reagent of Kaldalangra, I am going to have to ask for the watch you have tucked into your pocket."

The man paled, took a deep breath and then reached into his jacket to remove the turquoise inset watch that Rhea had been wearing the day she had been captured. He looked at Rhea with sorrow and regret.

"I am sorry, Rhea. At first I just put it in my pocket because it was not like anything I had seen before, and I thought the people at Kylassame would like it, could duplicate it. Then I realized I loved you, and thought, selfishly, that I could keep at least a little part of you with me when I could not have you."

She stared at the watch, the steady movement of the second hand hypnotizing her and slowly clearing her head. "It's alright, Rowan." She pulled the stone ladybug from its safe place around her neck. "If you cannot keep a part of me, then it is only fair that I return this to you as well." Her feet moved toward the man with surety, and she embraced him after tying the thin cord that held the pendant around his neck.

Ayewok gently took the watch from Rowan and placed it in a small bowl of water that had appeared in the center of the clearing. "Alright, my children, it is time for these two to be going on their way. Stand back a bit now."

The three stepped back, Rhea sliding her hand into Rowan's comfortable grip as Ayewok began to speak words of enchantment. The air around them felt thick and wet, as if they had walked through a giant cloud in the middle of the summer. The bowl in front of them began to shimmer then, the water turning a brilliant green and then flowing out of the bowl, covering the moss that quietly lay within the few feet of the vessel. The water began to flow upward, a glowing and moving turquoise column that surrounded the bowl and stopped at the tree canopy. The viewers began to see shapes moving within the curtain then, men and women who appeared to be walking down a road, dressed in blue jeans and wearing clothes in similar style to those worn by Rhea and Matt.

Matt turned to Ayewok. "Is it possible to tell when we will be returning?"

The old woman turned her yellow eyes to the man and cocked her head to the side. "Would that affect whether you went or stayed young man?"

He shook his head. "I'm going no matter what. Whether it was back in the times of the caveman or five thousand years in the future, I'm going back. Anything is better than here."

Only Rhea noticed the tightening of the lips and eyes that signaled the wise woman's displeasure at the answer. Ayewok gestured to the water column and spoke. "I have examined the watch and believe that it is March the third of the year two thousand and nine, give or take a few days."

Rhea's brow furrowed as she stared at the people walking inside the column of water, seemingly oblivious to their observers. "But that's only a month after I disappeared. Nothing would have changed in that world for me. Well, I would have missed a few weeks of classes but a month...my parents may not have even known that I was gone."

Matt took a step toward the column before turning to hold out a hand to Rhea. "See, Rhea? It's a sign that you need to go back. Your life would not have changed at all really. Your apartment will be a little messier, and your landlord would just now be contacting people to see where you were since rent would have been late. Everything would be back to the way it was before you were kidnapped!"

Ayewok walked over to Rhea then. "It is as he says, my dear. Now, time is beginning to run out. The portal will close soon and if you have not passed through, you will have to stay here forever." The wise woman embraced her then, and whispered, "You have been good for us. Live your life to the fullest and be happy, my child. We will not forget you." She broke the embrace and stepped back, one boney finger wiping away the tear that fell from an amber eye.

Rhea nodded and turned to kiss Rowan fiercely, then stepped forward and embraced Matt. "You go on through; I just need a moment alone with Rowan. You can start to come up with a story of where we've been all of this time."

He smiled and kissed her on the cheek, then stepped through the wall of water without hesitation. For a moment it felt as if he had stepped off the edge of the earth, and then felt a sensation of floating. His feet lightly touched the cement of a sidewalk and he looked around, delighted to see he was standing in front of Rhea's apartment building. He turned around and was surprised to see a slight shimmer in the air, as if a mirage had appeared to be rising from the heat of the road in front of him.

Matt watched as Rhea and Rowan had a short conversation, gesturing wildly and with many glances toward the portal. He gave an impatient sigh as she kissed Rowan goodbye, and he began to plan their first week back in the regular world. They were both long due for a shower, and then maybe they would just rent a movie and spend the night in her apartment. Sure, she would miss Rowan, but he was confident that he could quickly get her to forget all about him and the strange world they had just come from.

He frowned in confusion as Rowan smiled and carefully slid a necklace over Rhea's head. She turned toward the column and took one step forward, then calmly stood looking through the water. Matt gestured for her to hurry up, for the curtain in front of him began to dance and sway as the solid wall began to evaporate into thin air.

Rowan stepped forward and slid an arm around her waist, and Rhea leaned into his body with a smile that shone like sunlight. She raised a hand in farewell as the air cleared and the sound of cars filled his ears.

326

He heard a crinkle in the pocket of his jeans and looked down in curiosity; sure there had been no paper in it before he crossed through the portal.

Matt,

I don't expect you to understand, and I'm sorry for any hurt this causes, but I'm not coming back. Maybe I'm throwing away 25 years of living, and I know that this will hurt my family and friends, but I'm still not coming back. I belong here now. My heart and my soul beat in time with the land of this realm, and the people who walk upon the back of this earth have filled a deep void in my soul.

It is true that I have experienced much hardship and pain during my stay in Kaldalangra, but that has been mixed with joy and love, as well. When I think of the future in my old world, I can see nothing but emptiness, a constant void that needs to be filled by stories of fantasy worlds and hopeful wishes. There I would continue to work day in and day out just to pay my bills and would constantly wonder why I felt that there was always something missing in my life.

Here, I see nothing but potential and hope in my future. I am sorry if this hurts you, but when I look into my future I see Rowan, and children, and a wonderful adventure. The people of Asimina, Albadarl, and Kylassame have given me a purpose in life other than simply making ends meet and dragging my butt out of bed each morning just to see what happens.

The world in which we lived was not always a happy one for me. Every day I had to deal with people looking down on me for my faith, for my belief in nature spirits, because I looked a certain way or acted in a certain manner that was different than what was "regular". I hid this from the people I love for so long, but I would rather take my chances with new hardships popping up here, than the ones I knew would be waiting for me for my entire life if I crossed back over.

Please give everyone my love and tell them that I am happy and confident in my decision. I have also included letters for my parents, a

327

few friends, and my landlord. I have all my trust that you will see the letters safely into their hands so that they may know the choice I made, and be happy for me. You have always been a wonderful friend, and I wish you all the happiness in the world.

Love for always,

Rhea Aralia

The Lady of Steinbrekka

Novels by Kristi Strong

Land of Kaldalangra series

The Lady of Steinbrekka

Heart of Kylassame

Soul of Asimina

Standalone Novels

Finding Keepers

Author Biography

Fixing broken computers, wrangling a very spirited little toddler, and creating a world with mysterious people are all parts of the average day for Kristi Strong. A graduate of James Madison University, she uses her degree in anthropology and fascination of cultures to draw inspiration for her fantasy novels.

Connect with Kristi

StrongNovels.Blogspot.com

StrongNovels@live.com

Facebook.com/StrongNovels

Twitter.com/StrongNovels

www.ingramcontent.com/pod-product-compliance
Lightning Source LLC
Chambersburg PA
CBHW030415180626
46812CB00005B/2017